THREE SECONDS

THREE SECONDS

Anders Roslund & Börge Hellström

Translated from the Swedish by Kari Dickson

SILVEROAK

New York / London

Roz

For Vanja,

who made our books better

SILVEROAK
New York / London

An Imprint of Sterling Publishing Co., Inc. (New York)
and Quercus Publishing Plc (London)
387 Park Avenue South
New York, NY 10016

SILVEROAK BOOKS is a trademark of Sterling Publishing Co., Inc.

ISBN 978-1-4027-8592-4 (hardcover)
ISBN 978-1-4027-8878-9 (paperback)
ISBN 978-1-4027-8593-1 (ebook)

Library of Congress Cataloging-in-Publication Data Available

Distributed in Canada by Sterling Publishing
c/o Canadian Manda Group, 165 Dufferin Street
Toronto, Ontario, Canada M6K 3H6

For information about custom editions, special sales, and premium and corporate
purchases, please contact Sterling Special Sales at 800-805-5489 or
specialsales@sterlingpublishing.com.

Manufactured in the United States of America

2 4 6 8 10 9 7 5 3 1

www.sterlingpublishing.com

Cast of Characters

Piet Hoffmann, criminal and infiltrator, employed by the Swedish Police Service

Ewert Grens, Detective Superintendent, Stockholm City Police

Erik Wilson, handler for Piet Hoffmann and Detective Superintendent, Stockholm City Police

Zofia Hoffmann, Piet Hoffmann's wife

Lars Ågestam, the public prosecutor

Sven Sundkvist, Stockholm City Police, Ewert Grens's closest colleague

Mariana Hermansson, Stockholm City Police, also a member of Ewert Grens's team

The state secretary for the Ministry of Justice

The national police commissioner

Fredrik Göransson, Chief Superintendent, Stockholm City Police

Rasmus Hoffmann, five-year-old son of Piet Hoffmann

Hugo Hoffmann, three-year-old son of Piet Hoffmann

Lennart Oscarsson, chief warden, Aspsås Prison

Martin Jacobson, principal officer, Aspsås Prison

Sterner, military sniper

Nils Krantz, forensic technician, Stockholm City Police

Ludvig Errfors, forensic pathologist

Zbigniew Boruc, Deputy CEO, Wojtek Security International—Polish Mafia

Grzegorz Krzynówek, the Roof, Wojtek Security International—Polish Mafia

PART ONE

sunday

AN HOUR TO MIDNIGHT.

It was late spring, but darker than he thought it would be. Probably because of the water down below, almost black, a membrane covering what seemed to be bottomless.

He didn't like boats, or perhaps it was the sea he couldn't fathom. He always shivered when the wind blew as it did now and Świnoujście slowly disappeared. He would stand with his hands gripped tightly around the handrail until the houses were no longer houses, just small squares that disintegrated into the darkness that grew around him.

He was twenty-nine years old and frightened.

He heard people moving around behind him, on their way somewhere, too; just one night and a few hours' sleep, then they would wake in another country.

He leaned forward and closed his eyes. Each journey seemed to be worse than the last, his mind and heart as aware of the risk as his body; shaking hands, sweating brow, and burning cheeks, despite the fact that he was actually freezing in the cutting, bitter wind. Two days. In two days he'd be standing here again, on his way back, and he would already have forgotten that he'd sworn never to do it again.

He let go of the railing and opened the door that swapped the cold for warmth and led onto one of the main staircases where unknown faces moved toward their cabins.

He didn't want to sleep, he couldn't sleep—not yet.

There wasn't much of a bar. M/S *Wawel* was one of the biggest ferries between northern Poland and southern Sweden, but all the same; tables with crumbs on them, and chairs with such flimsy backs that it was obvious you weren't supposed to sit there for long.

He was still sweating. Staring straight ahead, his hands chased the sandwich around the plate and lunged for the glass of beer, trying not to let his fear show. A couple of swigs of beer, some cheese—he still felt sick and hoped that the new tastes would overwhelm the others: the big, fatty piece

5

of pork he'd been forced to eat until his stomach was soft and ready, then the yellow stuff concealed in brown rubber. They counted each time he swallowed, two hundred times, until the rubber balls had shredded his throat.

"*Czy podać panu coś jeszcze?*"

The young waitress looked at him. He shook his head, not tonight, nothing more.

His burning cheeks were now numb. He looked at the pale face in the mirror beside the till as he nudged the untouched sandwich and full glass of beer as far down the bar as he could. He pointed at them until the waitress understood and moved them to the dirty dishes shelf.

"*Postawić ci piwo?*" A man his own age, slightly drunk, the kind who just wants to talk to someone, doesn't matter who, to avoid being alone. He kept staring straight ahead at the white face in the mirror, didn't even turn around. It was hard to know for sure who was asking and why. Someone sitting nearby pretending to be drunk, who offered him a drink, might also be someone who knew the reason for his journey. He put twenty euros down on the silver plate with the bill and left the deserted room with its empty tables and meaningless music.

He wanted to scream with thirst and his tongue searched for some saliva to ease the dryness. He didn't dare drink anything, too frightened of being sick, of not being able to keep down everything that he'd swallowed.

He had to do it, keep it all down, or else—he knew the way things worked—he was a dead man.

HE LISTENED TO THE BIRDS, AS HE OFTEN DID IN THE LATE AFTERNOON when the warm air that came from somewhere in the Atlantic retreated reluctantly in advance of another cool spring evening. It was the time of day he liked best, when he had finished what he had to do and was anything but tired and so had a good few hours before he would have to lie down on the narrow hotel bed and try to sleep in the room that was still only filled with loneliness.

Erik Wilson felt the chill brush his face, and for a brief moment closed his eyes against the strong floodlights that drenched everything in a glare that was too white. He tilted his head back and peered warily up at the great knots of sharp barbed wire that made the high fence even higher, and had to fight the bizarre feeling that they were toppling toward him.

From a few hundred meters away, the sound of a group of people moving across the vast floodlit area of hard asphalt.

A line of men dressed in black, six across, with a seventh behind.

An equally black vehicle shadowed them.

Wilson followed each step with interest.

Transport of a protected object. Transport across an open space.

Suddenly another sound cut through. Gunfire. Someone firing rapid single shots at the people on foot. Erik Wilson stood completely still and watched as the two people in black closest to the protected person threw themselves over said person and pushed them to the ground, and the four others turned toward the line of fire.

They did the same as Wilson, identified the weapon by sound.

A Kalashnikov.

From an alleyway between two low buildings about forty, maybe fifty meters away.

The birds that had been singing a moment ago were silent; even the warm wind that would soon become cool, was still.

Erik Wilson could see every movement through the fence, hear every arrested silence. The men in black returned the fire and the vehicle

7

accelerated sharply, then stopped right by the protected person in the line of fire that continued at regular intervals from the low buildings. A couple of seconds later, no more, the protected body had been bundled into the backseat of the vehicle through an open door and disappeared into the dark.

"Good."

The voice came from above.

"That's us done for this evening."

The loudspeakers were positioned just below the huge floodlights. The president had survived this evening, once again. Wilson stretched, listened. The birds had returned. A strange place. It was the third time he had visited the Federal Law Enforcement Training Center, or the FLETC, as it was called. It was as far south in the state of Georgia as it was possible to go; a military base owned by the American state, a training ground for American police organizations—the DEA, ATF, U.S. Marshals, Border Patrol, and the people who had just saved the nation once more: the Secret Service. He was sure of it as he studied the floodlit asphalt: it was their vehicle, their people and they often practiced here at this time of day.

He carried on walking along the fence, which was the boundary to another reality. It was easy to breathe—he'd always liked the weather here, so much lighter, so much warmer than the run-up to a Stockholm summer, which never came.

It looked like any other hotel. He walked through the lobby toward the expensive, tired restaurant, but then changed his mind and carried on over to the elevators. He made his way up to the eleventh floor which for some days or weeks or months was the shared home of all course participants.

His room was too warm and stuffy. He opened the window that looked out over the vast practice ground, peered into the blinding light for a while, then turned on the TV and flicked through the channels that were all showing the same program. It would stay on until he went to bed, the only thing that made a hotel room feel alive.

He was restless.

The tension in his body spread from his stomach to his legs to his feet, forcing him up off the bed. He stretched and walked over to the desk and the five mobile phones that lay there neatly in a row on the shiny surface, only centimeters apart. Five identical handsets between the lamp with the slightly overlarge lampshade and the dark leather blotting pad.

He lifted them up one by one and read the display screen. The first four: no calls, no messages.

The fifth—he saw it before he even picked it up.

Eight missed calls.

All from the same number.

That was how he'd set it up. Only calls from one number to this phone. And only calls to one number from this phone.

Two unregistered, pay-as-you-go cards that only phoned each other, should anyone decide to investigate, should anyone find their phones. No names, just two phones that received and made calls to and from two unknown users, somewhere, who couldn't be traced.

He looked at the other four that were still on the desk. All with the same setup: they all were used to call one unknown number and they were all called from one unknown number.

Eight missed calls.

Erik Wilson gripped the phone that was Paula's.

He calculated in his head. It was past midnight in Sweden. He rang the number.

Paula's voice.

"*We have to meet. At number five. In exactly one hour.*"

Number five.

Vulcanusgatan 15 and Sankt Eriksplan 17.

"We can't."

"*We have to.*"

"Can't do it. I'm abroad."

Deep breath. Very close. And yet hundreds of miles away.

"*Then we've got a bastard of a problem, Erik. We've got a major delivery coming in twelve hours.*"

"Abort."

"*Too late. Fifteen Polish mules on their way in.*"

Erik Wilson sat down on the edge of the bed, in the same place as before, where the bedspread was crumpled.

A major deal.

Paula had penetrated deep into the organization, deeper than he'd ever heard of before.

"Get out. Now."

"*You know it's not that easy. You know that I've got to do it. Or I'll get two bullets to the head.*"

"I repeat, get out. You won't get any backup from me. Listen to me, get out, for Christ's sake!"

The silence when someone hangs up mid-conversation is always deeply unnerving. Wilson had never liked that electronic void. Someone else deciding that the call was over.

He went over to the window again, searching in the bright light that seemed to make the practice ground shrink, nearly drown in white.

The voice had been strained, almost frightened.

Erik Wilson still had the mobile phone in his hand. He looked at it, at the silence.

Paula was going to go it alone.

monday

HE HAD STOPPED THE CAR HALFWAY ACROSS THE BRIDGE TO LIDINGÖ. The sun had finally broken through the blackness a few minutes after three, pushing and bullying and chasing off the dark, which wouldn't dare return now until late in the evening. Ewert Grens rolled down the window and looked out at the water, breathing in the chill air as the sun rose into dawn and the cursed night retreated and left him in peace.

He drove on to the other side and across the sleeping island to a house that was idyllically perched on a cliff with a view of the boats that passed by below. He stopped in the empty parking lot, removed his radio from the charger, and attached a microphone to his lapel. He had always left it in the car when he came to visit her—no call was more important than their time together—but now, there was no conversation to interrupt.

Ewert Grens had driven to the nursing home once a week for twenty-nine years and had not stopped since, even though someone else lived in her room now. He walked over to what had once been her window, where she used to sit watching the world outside, and where he sat beside her, trying to understand what she was looking for.

The only person he had ever trusted.

He missed her so much. The damned emptiness clung to him, he ran through the night and it gave chase, he couldn't get rid of it, he screamed at it, but it just carried on and on . . . he breathed it in, he had no idea how to fill such emptiness.

"Superintendent Grens."

Her voice came from the glass door that normally stood open when the weather was fine and all the wheelchairs were in place around the table on the terrace. Susann, the medical student who was now, according to the name badge on her white coat, already a junior doctor. She had once accompanied him and Anni on the boat trip around the archipelago and had warned him against hoping *too much*.

"Hello."

"You here again."

"Yes."

He hadn't seen her for a long time, since Anni was alive.

"Why do you do it?"

He glanced up at the empty window.

"What are you talking about?"

"Why do you do this to yourself?"

The room was dark. Whoever lived there now was still asleep.

"I don't understand."

"I've seen you out here twelve Tuesdays in a row now."

"Is there a law against it?"

"Same day, same time as before."

Ewert Grens didn't answer.

"When she was alive."

Susann took a step down.

"You're not doing yourself any favors."

Her voice got louder.

"Living with grief is one thing. But you can't regulate it. You're not living *with* grief, you're living *for* it. You're holding on to it, hiding behind it. Don't you understand, Superintendent Grens? What you're frightened of has already happened."

He looked at the dark window, the sun reflecting an older man who didn't know what to say.

"You have to let go. You have to move on. Without the routine."

"I miss her so much."

Susann went back up the steps, grabbed the handle of the terrace door and was about to shut it when she stopped halfway, and shouted: "I never want to see you here again."

IT WAS A BEAUTIFUL FLAT ON THE FOURTH FLOOR OF VÄSTMANNAGATAN 79. Three spacious rooms in an old building, high-ceilinged, polished wooden floors, and full of light, with windows that faced out over Vanadisvägen as well.

Piet Hoffmann was in the kitchen. He opened the fridge and took out yet another carton of milk.

He looked at the man crouching on the floor with his face over a red plastic bowl. Some little shit from Warsaw: petty thief, junkie, spots, bad teeth, clothes he'd been wearing for too long. He kicked him in the side with the hard toe of his shoe and the evil-smelling prick toppled over and finally threw up. White milk and small bits of brown rubber on his trousers and the shiny kitchen floor, some kind of marble.

He had to drink more. *Napij się kurwa.* And he had to throw up more.

Piet Hoffmann kicked him again, but not so hard this time. The brown rubber around each capsule was to protect his stomach from the ten grams of amphetamine and he didn't want to risk even a single gram ending up somewhere it shouldn't. The fetid man at his feet was one of fifteen prepped mules who in the course of the night and morning had carried in two thousand grams each from Świnoujście, onboard M/S *Wawel*, then by train from Ystad, without knowing about the fourteen others who had also entered the country and were now being emptied at various places in Stockholm.

For a long time he had tried to talk calmly—he preferred it—but now he screamed *pij do cholery* as he kicked the little shit, he had to damn well drink more from the bloody milk carton and he was going to fucking *pij do cholery* throw up enough capsules for the buyer to check and quality-assure the product.

The thin man was crying.

He had bits of puke on his trousers and shirt and his pimply face was as white as the floor he was lying on.

Piet Hoffmann didn't kick him anymore. He had counted the dark

15

objects swimming around in the milk and he didn't need any more for the moment. He fished up the brown rubber: twenty almost-round balls. He pulled on some kitchen gloves and rinsed them under the tap, then picked off the rubber until he had twenty small capsules which he put on a porcelain plate that he had taken from the kitchen cupboard.

"There's more milk. And there's more pizza. You stay here. Eat, drink, and throw up. We want the rest."

The sitting room was warm, stuffy. The three men at the rectangular dark oak table were all sweating—too many clothes and too much adrenaline. He opened the door to the balcony and stood there for a moment while a cool breeze swept out all the bad air.

Piet Hoffmann spoke in Polish. The two men who had to understand what he was saying preferred it.

"He's still got eighteen hundred grams to go. Take care of it. And pay him when he's done. Four percent."

They were very similar, in their forties, dark suits that were expensive but looked cheap, shaved heads; when he stood close to them he could see an obvious halo of day-old brown hair. Eyes that were devoid of joy, and neither man smiled very often. In fact, he'd never seen either of them laugh. They did what he said, disappeared into the kitchen to empty the mule who was lying there, throwing up. It was Hoffmann's shipment and none of them wanted to explain to Warsaw that a delivery had gone all wrong.

He turned to the third man at the table and spoke in Swedish for the first time. "Here are twenty capsules. Two hundred grams. That's enough for you to check it."

He was looking at someone who was tall, blond, in shape, and about the same age as he was, around thirty-five. Someone wearing black jeans, a white T-shirt, and lots of silver around his fingers, wrists, and neck. Someone who'd served four years at Tidaholm for attempted murder, and twenty-seven months in Mariefred for two counts of assault. Everything fit. And yet there was something he couldn't put his finger on, like the buyer was wearing a costume, or was acting and not doing it well enough.

Piet Hoffmann watched him as he pulled a razor blade from the pocket of his black denim jacket and cut one of the capsules down the middle, then leaned forward over the porcelain plate to smell the contents.

That feeling again. It was still there.

Maybe the guy sitting there, who was going to buy the lot, was just strung out. Or nervous. Or maybe that was precisely what had made Piet call Erik in the middle of the night, whatever it was that wasn't right, this intense feeling that he hadn't been able to express properly on the phone.

It smelled of flowers, tulips.

Hoffmann was sitting two chairs away but could still smell it clearly.

The buyer had chopped up the yellowish, hard mass into something that resembled powder, scooped some up on the razorblade, and put it in an empty glass. He drew twenty milliliters of water into a syringe and then squirted it into the glass and onto the powder which dissolved into a clear but viscous fluid. He nodded, satisfied. It had dissolved quickly. It had turned into a clear fluid. It was amphetamine and it was as strong as the seller had promised.

"Tidaholm. Four years. That's right, isn't it?"

It had all looked professional, but it still didn't feel right.

Piet Hoffmann pulled the plate of capsules over in front of him, waiting for an answer.

"Ninety-seven to two thousand. Only in for three. Got out early for good behavior."

"Which section?" Hoffmann studied the buyer's face.

No twitching, no blinking, no other sign of nerves.

He spoke Swedish with a slight accent, maybe a neighboring country. Piet guessed Danish, possibly Norwegian. The buyer stood up suddenly, an irritated hand slightly too close to Piet's face. Everything still looked good, but it was too late. You noticed that sort of thing. He should have got pissed off much earlier, swiped that hand in front of his face right at the start: *Don't you trust me, you bastard.*

"You've seen the judgment already, haven't you?"

Now it was as if he was *playing* irritated.

"I repeat, *which section?*"

"C. Ninety-seven to ninety-nine."

"C. Where?"

He was already too late.

"What the fuck are you getting at?"

"*Where?*"

"Just C, the sections don't *have* numbers at Tidaholm."

He smiled.

Piet Hoffmann smiled back.

"Who else was there?"

"That'll fucking do, okay?"

The buyer was talking in a loud voice, so he would sound even more irritated, even more insulted.

Hoffmann could hear something else.

Something that sounded like uncertainty.

"Do you want to get on with business or not? I was under the impression that you'd asked me here because you wanted to sell me something."

"*Who else was there?*"

"Skåne. Mio. Josef Libanon. Virtanen. The Count. How many names do you want?"

"Who else?"

The buyer was still standing up, and he took a step toward Hoffmann. "I'm going to stop this right now."

He stood very close, the silver on his wrist and fingers flashing as he held his hand up in front of Piet Hoffmann's face.

"No more. That's enough. It's up to you whether we carry on with this or not."

"Josef Libanon was deported for life and then disappeared when he landed in Beirut three and a half months ago. Virtanen has been put away in a maximum security psychiatric unit for the past few years, unreachable and dribbling due to chronic psychosis. Mio is buried—"

The two men in expensive suits with shaved heads had heard the raised voices and opened the kitchen door.

Hoffmann waved his arm at them to indicate that they should stay put.

"Mio is buried in a sandpit near Ålstäket in Värmdö, two holes in the back of his head."

There were now three people speaking a foreign language in the room.

Piet Hoffmann caught the buyer looking around, looking for a way out.

"Josef Libanon, Virtanen, Mio. I'll carry on: Skåne, totally pickled. He won't remember whether he did time in Tidaholm or Kumla, or even Hall for that matter. And as for the Count . . . the wardens in Härnösand remand cut him down from where he was hanging with one of the sheets around his neck. Your five names. You chose them well. As none of them can confirm that you did time there."

One of the men in dark suits, the one called Mariusz, stepped forward with a gun in his hand, a black Polish-made Radom, which looked new as he held it to the buyer's head. Piet Hoffmann *utspokój się do diabła* shouted at Mariusz; he shouted *utspokój się do diabła* several times, Mariusz had better *utspokój się do diabła* take it easy, no fucking guns to anyone's temple.

Thumb on the decocking lever, Mariusz pulled it back, laughed, and lowered the gun. Hoffmann carried on talking in Swedish.

"Do you know who Frank Stein is?"

Hoffmann studied the buyer. His eyes should be irritated, insulted, even furious by now.

They were stressed and frightened and the silver-clad arm was trying to hide it.

"You know that I do."

"Good. Who is he?"

"C. Tidaholm. A sixth name. Satisfied?"

Piet Hoffmann picked his mobile phone up from the table.

"Then maybe you'd like to speak to him? Since you did time together?"

He held the telephone out in front of him, photographed the eyes that were watching him and then dialed a number that he'd learned by heart. They stared at each other in silence as he sent the picture and then dialed the number again.

The two men in suits, Mariusz and Jerzy, were agitated. *Z drugiej strony.* Mariusz was going to move, he should be on the other side, to the right of the buyer. *Bliżej głowy.* He should get even closer, keep the gun up, hold it to his right temple.

"I apologize. My friends from Warsaw are a bit edgy."

Someone answered.

Piet Hoffmann spoke to whoever it was briefly, then showed the buyer the telephone display.

A picture of a man with long dark hair in a ponytail and a face that no longer looked as young as it was.

"Here. Frank Stein."

Hoffmann held his anxious eyes until he looked away.

"And you . . . you still claim that you know each other?"

He closed the mobile phone and put it down on the table.

"My two friends here don't speak Swedish. So I'm saying this to you, and you alone."

A quick glance over at the two men who had moved even closer and were still discussing which side they should stand on to aim the muzzle of the gun at the buyer's head.

"You and I have a problem. You're not who you say you are. I'll give you two minutes to explain to me who you actually are."

"I don't understand what you're talking about."

"Really? Don't talk crap. It's too late for that. Just tell me who the hell you are. And do it now. Because unlike my friends here, I think that bodies only cause problems and they're no bloody good at paying up."

They paused. Waiting for each other. Waiting for someone to speak louder than the monotonous smacking sound coming from the dry mouth of the man holding his Radom against the thin skin of the buyer's temple.

"You've worked hard to come up with a credible background and you know that it crumbled just now when you underestimated who you were dealing with. This organization is built around officers from the Polish intelligence service and I can check out what the fuck I like about you. I could ask where you went to school, and you might answer what you've been told, but it would only take one phone call for me to find out whether it's true. I could ask what your mother's name is, if your dog has been vaccinated, what color your new coffee machine is. One single phone call and I'll know if it's true. I just did, made one phone call. And Frank Stein didn't know you. You never did time together at Tidaholm, because you were never there. Your sentence was faked so you could come here and pretend to buy freshly produced amphetamine. *So I repeat*, who are you? Explain. And then maybe, just maybe, I can persuade these two not to shoot."

Mariusz was holding the handgrip of the gun hard. The smacking noises were more and more frequent, louder. He hadn't understood what Hoffmann and the buyer were saying, but he knew that something was about to go down. He screamed in Polish, "*What the fuck are you talking about? Who the fuck is he?*" then cocked his gun.

"Okay."

The buyer felt the wall of immediate aggression, tense and unpredictable.

"I'm the police."

Mariusz and Jerzy didn't understand the language.

But a word like *police* doesn't need to be translated.

They started shouting again, mainly Jerzy, he roared that Mariusz should damn well pull the trigger, while Piet Hoffmann raised both his arms and moved a step closer.

"Back off!"

"He's the police!"

"I'm going to shoot!"

"Not now!"

Piet Hoffmann lurched toward them, but he wouldn't make it in time, and the man with the metal pressed against his head knew. He was shaking, his face contorted.

"I'm a police officer, for fuck's sake, get him off me!"

Jerzy lowered his voice and was *bliżej* almost calm when he instructed Mariusz to stand closer and to *z drugiej strony* swap sides again—it was better to shoot him through the other temple after all.

HE WAS STILL LYING IN BED. IT WAS ONE OF THOSE MORNINGS WHEN YOUR body doesn't want to wake up and the world feels a long way off.

Erik Wilson breathed in the humidity.

The south Georgia morning air that slipped in through the open window was still cool, but it would soon get warmer, even warmer than yesterday. He tried to follow the fan blades that played on the ceiling above his head, but gave up when he got tears in his eyes. He'd only slept for an hour at a time. They had talked together four times through the night and Paula had sounded more and more tense each time, a voice with an unfamiliar edge, stressed and desperate, on the verge of fleeing.

He had heard familiar sounds from the great FLETC training grounds for a while now, so it must be past seven o'clock, early afternoon in Sweden—they would be done soon.

He propped himself up, a pillow behind his back. From his bed he could look out through the window at the day that had long since dawned. The hard asphalt yard where the Secret Service had protected and saved a president yesterday was empty, but the silence after a pretend gunshot still reverberated. A few hundred meters away, in the next practice ground, a number of bright-eyed Border Patrol officers in military-like uniforms were running toward a white-and-green helicopter that had landed near them. Erik Wilson counted eight men clambering on board, who then disappeared into the sky.

He got out of bed and had a cold shower, which nearly helped. The night became clearer, his dialogue with fear.

I want you to get out.

You know that I can't.

You risk ten to fourteen years.

If I don't complete this, Erik, if I back out now, if I don't give a damn good explanation . . . I risk more than that. My life.

In each conversation and in many different ways, Erik Wilson had tried to explain that the delivery and sale could not be completed without his backing. He got nowhere, not with a buyer and the seller and mules already in place in Stockholm.

It was too late to call it off.

He had time for a quick breakfast: blueberry pancakes, bacon, that light white bread. A cup of coffee and *The New York Times*. He always sat at the same table in a quiet corner of the dining room as he preferred to keep the morning to himself.

He'd never had anyone like Paula before, someone who was so sharp, alert, cool; he was working with five people at the moment and Paula was better than all the others put together, too good to be a criminal.

Another cup of black coffee, then he had to rush back to the room: he was late.

Outside the open window, the green-and-white helicopter whirred high above the ground and three Border Patrol uniforms were hanging from a cable below, about a meter apart, as they shimmied down into pretend dangerous territory near the Mexican border. Yet another practice, always a practice here. Erik Wilson had been at the military base on the east coast of the United States for a week now; two weeks left of this training session for European policemen on informers, infiltration, and witness protection programs.

He closed the window as the cleaners didn't like them being open—something about the new air-conditioning in the officers' accommodation, that it would stop working if everyone aired their rooms whenever they pleased. He changed his shirt, looking at the tall and fairish middle-aged man in the mirror who should by now have been making his way toward a day indoors in a classroom with his fellow students and policemen from four American states.

He stood still. Three minutes past eight. They should be done now.

Paula's mobile phone was the extreme right of the five on the desk and just like all the others only had one number stored.

Erik Wilson didn't even have time to ask.

"It's a total fucking mess."

SVEN SUNDKVIST HAD NEVER LEARNED TO LIKE THE LONG, DARK, AND, AT times, damp corridors of the homicide unit. He had worked with Stockholm City Police all his adult life, and from his office at one end of the unit, not far from the pigeonholes and vending machines, had investigated every category of crime in the penal code. This morning, as he made his way through the dark and damp, he stopped suddenly as he passed the open door to his boss's office.

"Ewert?"

A large, rather bulky man was crawling along one of the walls.

Sven knocked gingerly on the doorframe.

"Ewert?"

Ewert Grens didn't hear him. He continued to crawl in front of a couple of large brown cardboard boxes and Sven repressed that sinking feeling. He had once before seen the obstreperous detective superintendent sit on another floor in the police headquarters. Eighteen months ago. Grens had sat on the floor in the basement with a pile of papers from an old case in his lap and slowly repeated two sentences over and over. *She's dead. I killed her.* A twenty-seven-year-old preliminary investigation into an assault on a constable, a young policewoman who had been seriously injured and would never again be able to live outside a nursing home. When he read the report later, Sven Sundkvist had come across her name in several places. Anni Grens. He had had no idea that they were married.

"Ewert, what on earth are you doing?"

He was packing something into the large brown cardboard boxes. That much was plain to see. But not what. Sven Sundkvist knocked again. The room was completely silent, and yet Ewert Grens still didn't hear him.

It had been a difficult period.

Like all others who grieve, Ewert's first reaction had been denial—*it hasn't happened*—and then anger—*why have they done this to me?* But he hadn't moved on to the next phase, he just carried on being angry, his way of dealing with most things. Ewert's grieving process had probably not started until very recently, a few weeks ago—he was no longer as irascible, but more reserved, more pensive, he talked less and presumably thought more.

Sven went into the room. Ewert heard him, but didn't turn around, sighing loudly instead as he often did when he was irritated. Something was bothering him. It wasn't Sven, something had been bothering him since he had gone to the nursing home, which usually gave him peace. Susann, the medical student who had been there for so long and looked after Anni so well and who had now become a junior doctor, her comments, her disgust, *you can't regulate your grief*, well it was bloody easy enough for a little girl to run around Lidingö spreading her twenty-five-year-old wisdom, *what you're frightened of has already happened*. What the hell did she know about loneliness?

He had driven away from the nursing home faster than he'd intended, straight to the police headquarters, and, without knowing why, gone down to the stores to get three cardboard boxes and carried them to the office that he'd had for as long as he could remember. He had stood for a while in front of the shelf behind his desk and the only things that meant anything to him: the cassettes of Siw Malmkvist songs that he had recorded and mixed himself, the early record sleeves from the sixties that still had strong colors, the photograph of Siwan that he had taken one evening in Kristianstads Folkets Park; everything that belonged to a time when all was good.

He had started to pack it all away, wrapped in newspaper, and then stacked one box on top of the next.

"She doesn't exist anymore."

Ewert Grens sat on the floor and stared at the brown cardboard.

"Do you hear me, Sven? She will never sing in this room again."

Denial, anger, grief.

Sven Sundkvist was standing directly behind his boss, looking down at his balding pate and seeing images from all the times he had waited while Ewert slowly rocked back and forth alone in his room in the dismal light— early mornings and late evenings and Siw Malmkvist's voice, standing dancing with someone who wasn't there, holding her tight in his arms. Sven realized that he would miss the irritating music, the lyrics that had been forced on him until he knew them by heart, an intrinsic part of all the years he had worked with Ewert Grens.

He would miss the picture.

He should laugh, really, because finally they were gone.

Ewert had gone through his adult life with a crutch under each arm. Anni. Siw Malmkvist. And now, finally, he was going to walk alone. Which was presumably why he was crawling around on the floor.

Sven sat down on the tired sofa and watched him lift up the last box and put it on top of the two others in a corner of the room, then laboriously and carefully tape it up. Ewert Grens was sweating and determined. He pushed the boxes until they were exactly where he wanted them and Sven wanted to ask how he felt, but didn't, it would be wrong, mostly out of consideration to himself, because the very fact that Ewert was doing what he was doing was answer enough in itself. He was moving on, though not yet aware of it himself.

"What have you done?"

She hadn't knocked.

She had walked straight into the room and stopped abruptly in the absence of music, in front of the gaping hole on the shelf behind the desk.

"Ewert? What have you done?"

Mariana Hermansson looked at Sven who first nodded at the gap on the shelf and then at the pile of three cardboard boxes. Never before had she been to his room without hearing music, the now removed Siw Malmkvist. She didn't recognize it without her voice.

"Ewert . . ."

"You want something?"

"I want to know what you've done."

"She no longer exists."

Hermansson went over to the empty shelf, ran a finger along the dusty lines left by the cassettes, the cassette player, speakers, and a black-and-white photo of the singer that had stood there all these years.

She wiped off a dust ball, hid it in her hand.

"*She* doesn't exist?"

"No."

"Who?"

"Her."

"Who? Anni? Or Siw Malmkvist?"

Ewert finally turned around and looked at her.

"Did you want something, Hermansson?"

He was still sitting on the floor, leaning against the boxes and wall. He had been grieving for nearly a year and a half now, lurching between a breakdown and madness. It had been an awful time, and she had told him to go to hell more than once and just as many times apologized afterward. On a couple of occasions she had almost given up, resigned and walked away from this difficult man's bitterness that seemed to have no end. She had gradually come to believe that one day he would capitulate, go to pieces completely, lie down and never get up again. But his face now, in the midst of all the suffering, had something purposeful about it, a determination that had not been there before.

Some cardboard boxes, a gaping hole on a bookshelf, things like that could spark unexpected relief.

"Yes, I did want something. We've just had a call-out. Västmannagatan 79."

He was listening, she knew that, he was listening to her in that intense way that she had nearly forgotten.

"An execution."

PIET HOFFMANN LOOKED OUT OF ONE OF THE BEAUTIFUL APARTMENT'S BIG windows. It was a different flat in a different part of the center of Stockholm, but they were similar, three carefully renovated rooms, high ceilings and light-colored walls. Only there was no prospective buyer lying on the wooden floor here, with a gaping hole in one temple and two in the other.

Down on the wide pavement, groups of well-dressed people were making their way, full of anticipation, into a matinee performance at the large theater; breathless and slightly hammy actors going in and out of doors onto the stage, proclaiming their lines.

Sometimes he longed for that kind of life, just everyday, normal people doing normal things together.

He left the dressed-up, excited people and the window with a view of both Vasagatan and Kungsbron, and crossed the largest room in the flat, his room, his office with its antique desk and two locked gun cabinets and an open fire that was very effective. He heard the last mule spewing up in the kitchen—she had been at it for a long time now. She wasn't used to it: it took a couple of trips before you were. Jerzy and Mariusz were standing by the sink with yellow rubber gloves on, picking out the bits of brown rubber that the young woman threw up, along with the milk and something else, in the two buckets on the floor in front of her. She was the fifteenth and final mule. They had emptied the first one in Västmannagatan, and had been forced to empty the rest here. Piet Hoffmann didn't like it. This flat was his protection, his cover, he didn't want it to be linked with either drugs or Poles. But they didn't have time. Everything had gone wrong. A person had been shot through the head. He studied Mariusz; the man with the shaved head and expensive suit had killed someone only a couple of hours ago, but showed nothing. Maybe he couldn't, maybe he was being professional. Hoffmann wasn't frightened of him, and he wasn't frightened of Jerzy, but he respected the fact that they had no limits; if he had made them nervous, suspicious of his loyalty, the shot that had been fired could just as easily have been aimed at him.

Anger chased frustration chased dread and he struggled to stand still with all the turmoil inside him.

He had been there and he hadn't been able to prevent it.

To prevent it would have meant death for him.

So another person had died instead.

The young woman in front of him was done. He didn't know her, they had never met. He knew that she was called Irina and she came from Gdansk, that she was twenty-two and a student and was prepared to take a risk that was far greater than she imagined and that was enough. She was a perfect mule. Just the sort they were looking for. Of course there were others, junkies from the suburbs of larger cities who flocked in their thousands, willing to use their bodies as containers for less than she was paid, but they had learned not to use drug addicts as they were unreliable and often seemed to throw up by themselves long before they reached their destination.

Inside, the anger and frustration and dread, more emotions, more thoughts.

There hadn't been any operation. But there had been a delivery over which he had no control.

There hadn't been any results. The Poles should have been back in Warsaw by now, his tool for mapping and identifying another partner.

There hadn't been any deal. They had shipped in fifteen mules unnecessarily, ten experienced ones who they supplied with two hundred capsules each and five new ones who took one hundred and fifty capsules each, in total more than twenty-seven kilos of freshly produced amphetamine which, once it had been cut for sale, would come to eighty-one kilos with a street value of 150 kronor per gram.

But without any backup, there was no operation, no result, not even a deal.

It was an unchecked delivery that had ended in murder.

Piet Hoffmann gave the young, wan woman called Irina a brief nod. The money had been in his trouser pocket since the morning, counted and rolled up in bundles. He pulled out the last bundle and flicked through the banknotes so she could see it was all there. She was one of the new ones and didn't yet have the capacity that the organization expected. She had only delivered fifteen hundred grams on her first trip, which would be three times as much when cut to its sellable form, worth a total of 675,000 kronor.

"Your four percent. Twenty-seven thousand kronor. But I've rounded it up to three thousand euros. And if you dare to swallow more next time, you'll earn more. Your stomach stretches a little each time."

She was pretty. Even when her face was pale and her hairline sweaty. Even when she had been on her knees in a three-room flat in Sweden, puking up her guts for a couple of hours.

"And my tickets."

Piet Hoffmann nodded to Jerzy, who took out two tickets from the inner pocket of his dark jacket. One for the train from Stockholm to Ystad and one for the ferry from Ystad to Świnoujście. He held them out to her, and she was just about to take them when he pulled back his hand and smiled. He waited a bit then held them out again, and just when she was about to take them, he pulled back his hand, again.

"For fuck's sake, she's earned them!"

Hoffmann snatched the tickets from him and gave them to her.

"We'll be in touch. When we need your help again."

The anger, the frustration, the dread.

They were finally alone in the flat that functioned as an office for one of Stockholm's security firms.

"This was my operation."

Piet Hoffmann took a step closer to the man who had shot and killed a person that morning.

"*I* am the one who speaks the language and *I* am the one who gives the orders in this country."

It was more than anger. It was rage. He had contained it since the shooting. First they had to take care of the mules, empty them, secure the delivery. Now he could release it.

"If anyone is going to shoot, it's on my order *and only my* order."

He wasn't sure where it was coming from, why it was so intense. Whether it was disappointment that a business partner had not materialized. Whether it was frustration because a person who probably had the same brief as he did had been killed without reason.

"And the gun, where the fuck is it?"

Mariusz pointed at his chest, to the inner pocket of his jacket.

"You murdered someone. You can get life for that. And you're so fucking stupid that you've still got the gun in your pocket?"

Rage and something else tearing at him. *You should have been reporting back to Poland.* He blocked out the feeling that might equally be fear, took a step toward the man who was smiling, pointing at his inner pocket, and stopped when they were face to face. *Play your role.* That was all that mattered, power and respect, taking and never letting go. *Play your role or die.*

"He was a policeman."

"And how the fuck d'you know that?"

"He said so."

"And since when did you speak Swedish?"

Piet Hoffmann took measured breaths. He realized that he was irritated and tired as he walked over to the round kitchen table and the metal bowl that contained 2,749 regurgitated and cleaned capsules: a good twenty-seven kilos of pure amphetamine.

"He said police. I heard it. You heard it."

Hoffmann didn't turn around when he replied.

"You were at the same meeting as me in Warsaw. You know the rules. Until we're done here, it's *me*, and *only me*, who decides."

HE HAD BEEN UNCOMFORTABLE DURING THE SHORT JOURNEY FROM Kronoberg to Vasastan. Or rather, he'd been sitting on something. When Hermansson swung into Västmannagatan and pulled up outside number 79, he lifted his heavy body a touch while he felt around on the seat with his hand. Two cassettes. Siw mixes. He held the hard plastic cases in his hand and looked at the music that should have been packed away, and then at the passenger seat and glove compartment. There were two more cassettes in there. He bent down and pushed them as far under the seat as possible. He was as scared of being near them as he was of forgetting to take them with him, the last four remnants of another life that would remain packed away in a cardboard box sealed with tape.

Ewert Grens preferred sitting here in the back.

He no longer had any music to play and he had no desire to listen to or answer the frequent calls on the radio. And anyway, Hermansson drove considerably better than both Sven and he did in the busy city traffic.

There wasn't much room on the street; three police cars and forensics' dark-blue Volkswagen bus double-parked alongside a tight row of residents' cars. Mariana Hermansson slowed down, drove up onto the pavement, and stopped in front of the main door, which was guarded by two uniformed policemen. They were both young and pale and the one closest rushed over to the unknown men and a woman in a red car. Hermansson knew what he wanted and at precisely the same moment that he tapped on the window, she rolled it down and held up her police ID.

"We're investigators. All three of us."

She smiled at him. Not only did he look young, he was probably considerably younger than she was. She guessed he was in his first weeks of service, as there weren't many who didn't recognize Ewert Grens.

"Was it you who took the call?"

"Yes."

"Who raised the alarm?"

"Anonymous, according to the CCC."

"You mentioned an execution?"

"We said it *looked* like an execution. You'll understand when you get there."

Up on the fourth floor, the door farthest away from the elevator was open. Another uniformed colleague was standing watch. He was older, had been in the force longer; he recognized Sundkvist and gave him a nod. Two steps later Hermansson had her ID ready and was just about to show it, and she wondered if she would ever stay anywhere long enough to be recognized by more than her immediate colleagues—she didn't think so, she wasn't the sort who stayed.

They put on their white coats and transparent shoe covers and went in. Ewert had insisted on waiting for the elevator that was slow down and slow up, so he'd be there soon.

A long hallway, a bedroom with nothing in it but a narrow bed, a kitchen with nice cupboards painted in a shade of green, and a study with an abandoned desk and empty shelves.

And one more room.

They looked at each other, and went in.

The sitting room really only had one piece of furniture. A large, rectangular oak dining table with six matching chairs. Four of them were by the table, the fifth had been pushed back at an angle, as if the person sitting there had gotten up suddenly. The sixth was lying on the floor. The heavy chair had for some reason fallen and they went over to establish why.

The dark patch on the carpet was the first thing they saw.

A large, brownish stain with uneven edges. They guessed about forty, maybe fifty centimeters in diameter.

Then they saw the head.

It was in the middle of the stain, on top of it, as if it were floating. The man looked relatively young—it was hard to tell as his face was mangled, but his body was strong, and his clothes were not the sort that older men often wear: black boots, black jeans, a white T-shirt, lots of silver around his neck, wrists, and fingers.

Sven Sundkvist tried to concentrate on the gun in his right hand.

If he only looked at it for long enough, if he blanked everything else out, he might avoid the ugliness of death that he would never understand.

It was shiny and black, nine-millimeter caliber and a make that he didn't often see at crime scenes: Radom, a Polish weapon. He bent down closer to it, thereby distancing himself from the life that had spilled out onto the expensive carpet and left a large dark stain. It seemed that the ejector was stuck in the discharge position and he could clearly see the bullet casing in the chamber. He studied the barrel, the butt, the grip safety, looking for something to fix his eyes on, anything but death.

Nils Krantz was standing farther away, flanked by two younger colleagues. Three forensic technicians who together would scour every nook and cranny in the room. One of them had a video camera in his hand and was filming something on the white wallpaper. Sven took a step away from the head, and looked at what the camera was focused on: a small discolored patch of something, something harmless and sufficiently far away from the lifeless eyes.

"The victim has *one* entrance wound from *one* shot to the head."

Nils Krantz had sneaked up behind his filming colleague and was now close to Sven Sundkvist's ear.

"But *two* exit wounds."

Sven turned away from the wallpaper and discoloring and looked askance at the older forensic scientist.

"The entrance wound is larger than both exit wounds because of the contact gas pressure."

Sven heard what Krantz was saying, but he didn't understand and chose not to ask. He didn't need to know and instead followed the finger that was pointing at the discoloring on the wallpaper.

"By the way, what we're just filming and what you're looking at right now comes from the victim, brain tissue."

Sven Sundkvist took a deep breath. He had wanted to avoid death and had therefore chosen to focus on the discoloring on the wallpaper, but he had only found more death, as real as it ever could be. He lowered his eyes and heard Ewert come in to the room.

"Sven?"

"Yes?"

"Perhaps you should go down and talk to our colleagues who took the call? And maybe some neighbors? The people who aren't *here*."

Sven looked at his boss with gratitude, hurried away from the dark stains on the carpet and discoloring on the wallpaper, while Ewert Grens hunkered down to get closer to the dead body.

THE BALANCE OF POWER HAD BEEN REDISTRIBUTED AND RESTORED. BUT IT would happen again. And he had to win every time.

Carry on acting. Or die.

He stood between Mariusz and Jerzy at Hoffmann Security's round kitchen table, emptying 2,750 capsules of amphetamine. The latest delivery from the factory in Siedlce. Their white medical-gloved fingers first picked off the brown rubber that was there to protect the mule's stomach in case of any leaks, then cut open the capsule with a knife and poured the powder into large glass bowls where it was mixed with grape sugar. One part amphetamine from eastern Poland to two parts grape sugar from the supermarket on the corner. Twenty-seven kilos of pure drugs transformed into eighty-one kilos that could be sold on the street.

Piet Hoffmann put a metal tin on some kitchen scales and filled it with exactly one thousand grams of cut amphetamine. A piece of tin foil was placed carefully over the powder and then something that resembled a sugar lump was put on the foil. He held a match to the methaldehyde pellet and when the white square started to burn, he closed the lid of the tin. The flames would then die when the oxygen ran out and one kilo of amphetamine would be vacuum-packed.

He repeated this operation, one tin at a time, eighty-one times.

"Benzine?"

Jerzy opened the bottle of petroleum ether, splashed some of the colorless fluid on the tin lids and sides and then rubbed the metal surfaces with cotton wool. He lit another match and a bluish flame flared that he then smothered with a rag after ten seconds.

All the fingerprints had now been removed.

THE BLOODSTAINS WERE SMALLEST ON THE HALL CARPET, SLIGHTLY BIGGER on the wall at the other end of the spacious sitting room, even bigger by the table, and largest by the overturned chair. They also got darker and deeper the closer to the body they were, and the most visible was the large patch on the carpet in which the lifeless head was floating.

Ewert Grens was sitting so close that if the body on the floor had started to whisper he would hear it. This death didn't feel like anything, it didn't even have a name.

"The entrance wound, Ewert, here."

Nils Krantz had crept around on all fours, filmed and photographed. He was one of the few experts Grens actually trusted and had proved often enough that he wasn't the kind of person who would take shortcuts just so he could get home an hour earlier to watch TV.

"Someone held the gun hard to his head. The gas pressure between the muzzle and the temple must have been enormous. You can see for yourself. Half the side's been blown off."

The skin on his face was already gray, his eyes empty, his mouth a straight line that would never talk again.

"I don't understand. One entrance wound. But two exit wounds?"

Krantz held his hand near the hole that was as large as a tennis ball in the middle of the right side of the head.

"I've only seen this a couple of times in thirty-odd years. But it happens. And the autopsy will confirm it—that it's only one shot. I'm sure of it."

He tugged at the sleeve of Grens's white overalls, his voice eager.

"One shot to the temple. The bullet was jacketed, half lead and half titanium, and it split when it hit one of the skull bones."

Krantz got up and stretched his arm in the air. It was an old flat and the ceiling was about three meters high. A few hairline cracks, but otherwise in good shape, except for where the forensic technician was pointing: a deep gash in the whitewash.

"We took half the bullet down from there."

Small pieces of plaster had fallen where careful fingers had dug out the hard metal.

Some way off, there was a considerably larger tear in some soft wood.

"And that is from the other half. The kitchen door was obviously closed."

"I don't know, Nils."

Ewert Grens was still sitting by the head that had too many holes.

"The call-out said execution. But having looked . . . it could just as easily be suicide."

"Someone has tried to make it look like that."

"What do you mean?"

Krantz slid his foot closer to the hand that was holding a gun.

"That looks staged. I think that someone shot him and *then* put the gun in his hand."

He disappeared out into the hall and came back immediately with a black case in his hand.

"But I'll check it. I'll do a GSR test on the hand. Then we'll know."

Ewert started to calculate, looked over at Hermansson; she was doing the same.

One hour and forty-five minutes since the alarm was raised, they still had plenty of time. The body hadn't yet started to attract enough foreign particles to make a residue test worthless.

Krantz opened his case and looked for a round tube of fingerprint-lifting tape. He pressed the tape against the victim's hand several times, in particular the area between the index finger and thumb. Then he went out into the kitchen, to the microscope that had been set up on the worktop, put the fingerprint-lifting tape on the glass plate, and studied it through the ocular.

A few seconds passed.

"No gunshot residue."

"As you thought."

"So the hand that was holding the gun didn't fire it."

He turned around.

"This is murder, Ewert."

HE PUT HIS LEFT HAND TO HIS RIGHT SHOULDER AND PULLED AT THE leather strap until the pressure on his shoulders was released and he could hold the holster with one hand. He opened it and pulled out a Radom with a nine-millimeter caliber. He did a recoil operation, put the last bullet in the magazine, so that fourteen were in place.

Piet Hoffmann stood still for a while, his breathing so loud he could hear himself.

He was alone in the room and the flat that looked out over Vasagatan and Kungsbron. The last mule had taken the train south a couple of hours ago, and Mariusz and Jerzy had just started their car and headed off in the same direction.

A long day, but it was still only the afternoon and he had to stay awake for hours yet.

The gun cabinets stood on the floor behind the desk. Two identical cabinets, a couple of meters high, about a meter wide, a smaller shelf on top and two rifles on a considerably larger shelf below. He put the gun on the top shelf in the first cabinet, and the full magazine in the same place in the second.

He walked through the rooms that had functioned as offices for Hoffmann Security AB for two years now. One of Wojtek Security International's many branches. He had visited most of them several times, and the ones farthest north in Helsinki, Copenhagen, and Oslo more often.

The fireplace with its dark tiles and white frame was beautiful, the sort that he knew Zofia wanted at home. He fished up a handful of small dry twigs from the bottom of the wood basket and lit them, then waited until the larger, thicker logs that he placed on top started to burn before taking his clothes off. The jacket, trousers, shirt, underpants, and socks were all eaten by the yellow flames. Next, a pile of Jerzy's and Mariusz's clothes. The flames were red and intense now, and he stood naked in front of the fire, enjoying the warmth until they died down sufficiently for him to close the bathroom door and shower away this awful day.

A person had had half his head blown off.

A person who probably had the same job as he had, but had a less solid background.

He turned on the shower and the hot water pummelled his skin, testing his pain threshold, but he knew if he persevered, his body would eventually go numb and be filled with a strange calm.

He'd been doing this for too long; he sometimes forgot who he was and it frightened him when his life as someone else encroached on his life as a husband and father, and day-to-day reality in a house in a neighborhood where people cut their grass and weeded their flowerbeds.

Hugo and Rasmus.

He had promised to pick them up just after four. He turned off the water and took a clean towel from the shelf by the mirror. It was nearly half past four. He hurried back into the office, checked that the fire had died down, opened the wardrobe and picked out a white shirt, a gray jacket, and worn jeans.

You have sixty seconds to leave and lock the flat.

He jumped and realized that he would never get used to the electronic voice that spoke to him from the coded lock on the front door, as soon as he had punched in the correct six digits.

The alarm will be activated in fifty seconds.

He should contact Warsaw immediately, he should have done it already, but had waited on purpose, he wanted to know that the delivery was secure first.

The alarm will be activated in forty seconds.

He locked the front door of Hoffmann Security AB and closed the wrought-iron gate. A security firm. That was how the organization worked. That was how all branches of the Eastern European mafia worked. Piet Hoffmann remembered his visit to St. Petersburg a year ago, a city with eight hundred security firms, established by ex-KGB men and intelligence agents, different fronts for the same business.

He was halfway down the stairs when one of his two phones rang.

The mobile phone that only one person knew about.

"Wait a minute."

He had parked the car just down Vasagatan. He opened the door and got in, then carried on the conversation without the risk of being overheard.

"Yes?"

"You need my help."

"I needed it yesterday."

"I've booked a return flight and will be back in Stockholm tomorrow. Meet you at number five at eleven. And I think you should make a trip yourself, before then. For the sake of your credibility."

THE GAPING HOLES IN THE DEAD MAN'S HEAD SEEMED EVEN LARGER FROM a distance.

Ewert Grens had followed Nils Krantz into the kitchen, but turned around again after a while to look at the man who was lying by an overturned chair and had *one* entrance wound in his right temple and *two* exit wounds in his left. He had been investigating murders for as long as the man on the floor had been alive and had learned one truth—each death is unique, with its own story, its own sequence of events, its own consequences. Every time he was faced with something he had not seen before, and he knew even before he looked into the empty eyes that they were looking in a direction that he couldn't follow.

He wondered where this particular death had ended, what these eyes had seen and were looking toward.

"Do you want to know or not?"

Krantz had been squatting on the kitchen floor for a bit too long.

"Otherwise I've got plenty else to be getting on with."

His hand was close to a crack in the marble floor. Ewert Grens nodded, *I'm listening.*

"That spot there, can you see it?"

Grens looked at something that was whitish with uneven edges.

"Bits of stomach lining. And it's definitely no more than twelve hours old. There are several similar spots in this area."

The forensic scientist drew a circle with his hand in the air around himself.

"All with the same content. Food remains and bile. But also something far more interesting. Bits of rubber."

When Grens looked closer, he could see the white spots with uneven edges in at least three places.

"The rubber is partly corroded, probably by stomach acids."

Krantz looked up.

"And traces of rubber in vomit, we know what that means."

Ewert Grens gave a loud sigh.

Rubber meant human containers. Human containers meant drugs. A dead man in connection with a delivery meant a drugs-related murder. And a drugs-related murder always meant investigation and lots of hours, lots of resources.

"A mule, a swallower who's delivered the goods right here in the kitchen."

He turned toward the sitting room.

"And him? What do we know about him?"

"Nothing."

"Nothing?"

"Not yet. You have to have something to do, Grens."

Ewert Grens went back into the sitting room and over to the man who no longer existed, watched as two men took hold of the dead man's arms and legs, as they lifted him and put him into a black body bag, as they pulled up the zipper and put the body bag on a metal stretcher that they only just managed to push down the narrow hall.

HE LEFT VASAGATAN AND THEN GOT CAUGHT IN A TRAFFIC JAM BY SLUSSEN. It was nearly five o'clock and he should have been at the kindergarten an hour ago.

Piet Hoffmann sat in the car and desperately tried to fend off the stress and heat and irritation caused by the afternoon traffic, which he could do nothing about. Three lanes at a standstill as far down the tunnel as he could see. To combat this battle with the city, he often thought about the soft skin on Zofia's face when he stroked it, or Hugo's eyes when he managed to ride his bike on his own, or Rasmus's hair, splashed with carrot soup and orange juice, standing out in every direction. It didn't work. *Who did you do time with?* Images of the people he was thinking about merged every time into images of a deal in a flat in Västmannagatan that had ended in another man's death. *Skåne. Mio. Josef Libanon. Virtanen. The Count. How many names do you want?* Another infiltrator with the same mission as he had. *Who else?* But the other infiltrator who sat facing him just didn't act as well. *Who else?* He, if anyone, should know what a faked background looked like, how it was put together, and which questions were needed to make it collapse. They had both been working for the police in their respective ways and ended up in the same place. He didn't have any choice, otherwise they might both have died, and one was in fact enough, one who wasn't him.

He had seen people die before. It wasn't that. It was part of his daily life and his credibility required it; he had learned to shrug off dead people who weren't close to him. But he had been in charge of this operation. A murder, he risked life imprisonment.

Erik had phoned from the airport outside Jacksonville. Nine years as a secret civil servant on the unofficial payroll of the Swedish police had taught Piet Hoffmann that he was valuable. The authorities had magicked away offenses in both a private and professional capacity before, so Erik Wilson should be able to make this one vanish too. The police were good at that, a few secret intelligence reports on the right bosses' desks was usually enough.

The temperature had risen in the stationary car and Piet Hoffmann dried away the sweat from his shirt collar just as the blasted line started to move. He fixed his eyes on a number plate that was edging slowly forward a few meters ahead and forced his mind back to images of Hugo and Rasmus and his real life, and twenty minutes later got out of the car in the visitors' parking lot at Hagtornsgården, in the midst of all the flats in Enskededalen.

By the front door he suddenly stopped with his hand in the air, a few centimeters from the handle. He listened to the voices of the noisy, boisterous children who were playing and smiled, lingering awhile in the best moment of the day. He went to open the door, but stopped again; something tight across his shoulders. He quickly felt under his jacket, heaved a sigh of relief—he *had* remembered to take off his holster.

He opened the door. It smelled of baking, a late snack for some of the children who were sitting around a table in the lunchroom. The noise was coming from farther in, the big playroom. He sat down on a low stool in the entrance, near the tiny shoes and colorful jackets on pegs marked with the children's names and hand-drawn elephants.

He nodded at one of the young women, a new member of staff.

"Hi."

"Are you Hugo and Rasmus's dad?"

"How did you guess? I haven't—"

"Not many left."

She disappeared behind some shelves filled with well-used jigsaw puzzles and square wooden building blocks and reappeared almost immediately with two boys aged three and five who made his heart laugh.

"Hello, Daddy."

"Hello-lello, Daddy."

"Hello-lello-lello, Daddy."

"Hello-lello-lello—"

"Hello, you two. You both win. We haven't got time for anymore hellos today. Maybe tomorrow. Then there will be more time. Okay?"

He reached out for the red jacket and pulled it on to Rasmus's outstretched arms, then sat him on his lap to take his indoor shoes off the feet that wouldn't keep still, and put on his outdoor shoes. He leaned forward and glanced at his own shoes. Shit. He'd forgotten to put them in the fire. The black shininess might be a film of death, with traces of skin and blood and brain tissue—he had to burn them as soon as he got home.

He checked the child car seat that was strapped onto the passenger seat, facing backward. It felt as secure as it should and Rasmus was already picking at the pattern on the fabric as was his wont. Hugo's seat was more like a hard square that made him sit a bit higher and he fastened the seat belt tight before giving his soft cheek a quick kiss.

"Daddy's just going to make a quick phone call. Will you be quiet for a while? I promise to be finished before we drive under Nynäsvägen."

Capsules with amphetamine, child car seats secured, shoes shiny with the remains of death.

Right now he didn't want to see that they were different parts of the same working day.

He closed his phone the moment the car passed the busy main road. He had managed to make two quick calls, the first to a travel agent to book a ticket on the 6:55 p.m. SAS flight to Warsaw, and the second to Henryk, his contact at the head office, to book a meeting there three hours later.

"I did it! I finished on this side of the road. Now I'm only going to talk to you."

"Were you talking to work?"

"Yes, the office."

Three years old. And he could already distinguish between the two languages and what Daddy used them for. He stroked Rasmus's hair and felt Hugo leaning forward to say something behind him.

"I can speak Polish too. *Jeden, dwa, trzy, cztery, pięć, sześć, siedem—*"

He stopped, and then carried on in a slightly darker voice: "—eight, nine, ten."

"Very good. You know lots of numbers."

"I want to know more."

"*Osiem, dziewięć, dziewięć.*"

"*Osiem, dziewięć . . . dziewięć?*"

"Now you know them."

"Now I know."

They drove past the Enskede flower shop and Piet Hoffmann stopped, reversed and got out.

"Wait here. I'll be back in a moment."

A couple of hundred meters farther on, a small red plastic fire engine was standing in front of the garage and he just managed to avoid it, but only by scraping the right-hand side of the car against the fence. He released the seat belts and child car seats and watched his children's feet run over the moss green grass. They both threw themselves down onto the ground and crawled through the low hedge into the neighbor's garden, where there were three children and two dogs. Piet Hoffmann laughed and felt a warmth in his belly and throat. Their energy and joy—sometimes things were just so simple.

He held the flowers in one hand as he opened the door to the house that they had left in such a rush—it had been one of those mornings when everything took a little bit longer. He would tidy away the breakfast dishes that were still on the table, and pick up the trail of clothes that spread through every room downstairs, but first he had to go down into the cellar and the boiler room.

It was May and the timer on the boiler would be turned off for a long time yet, so he started it manually by pressing the red button, then he opened the door and listened to it cranking into action and starting to burn. He bent down, undid his shoes and dropped them into the flames.

The three red roses would go on the middle of the kitchen table in the vase that he liked so much, the one they'd bought at the Kosta Boda glassworks one summer. Plates for Zofia, Hugo, and Rasmus in the places where they had sat every day since they left the flat the same summer. Half a kilo of defrosted ground beef from the top shelf in the fridge which he browned in the frying pan, salt and pepper, cream, and two tins of chopped tomatoes. It was starting to smell good. He dipped a finger in the sauce, which tasted good too. A half-full pan of water and a bit of olive oil so that the pasta wouldn't boil over.

He went upstairs to the bedroom. The bed was still unmade and he buried his face in the pillow that smelled of her. His overnight bag was in the wardrobe, already packed: two passports; wallet with euros, zloty, and U.S. dollars; a shirt, socks, underwear, and a toilet bag. He picked it up and carried it down into the hall. The water had started to boil, half a bag of dry spaghetti into the bubbling water. He looked at the clock. Half past five. He didn't have much time, but he would make it.

It was still warm outside, the last of the sun would soon disappear behind the roof of the neighboring house. Piet Hoffmann went over to the hedge that would have to be pruned properly this summer. He saw two children he recognized on the other side and called to them that food was ready. He heard a taxi approaching down the narrow road. It pulled up and parked in the driveway by the garage. The red plastic fire engine survived once again.

"Hi."

"Hi."

They hugged each other, like they always did and every time he thought he would never let go.

"I can't eat with you. I have to go to Warsaw this evening. An emergency meeting. But I'll be home again tomorrow night. Okay?"

She shrugged.

"No, not really. I was looking forward to having the evening together. But okay."

"I've made supper. It's on the table. I've told the boys food is ready so they're on their way. Or at least, they should be."

He kissed her quickly on the lips.

"One more. You know."

One more. Always an even number. His hand on her cheek, two more kisses.

"Now it's three. So one more."

He kissed her again. They smiled at each other. He picked up his bag and walked over to the car, looked back at the hedge and the hole at the bottom in the middle where the children would appear.

No sign of them. He wasn't surprised.

He smiled again and started the engine.

EWERT GRENS LOOKED AT THE MAT THAT DISAPPEARED UNDER THE passenger seat and Sven Sundkvist. He had pushed the two cassettes in there. Two more were lurking in the glove compartment. He would take them with him sometime, pack them away, forget them.

The two young but slightly less pale uniformed police were still standing on the pavement between the hood of the car and the entrance to Västmannagatan 79. Hermansson had started to reverse when one of them came over and knocked on the window, and Sven rolled it down.

"What do you think?"

Ewert Grens leaned forward from the backseat.

"You were right. It was an execution."

It was late afternoon at Kronoberg, and finding a parking place on Bergsgatan wasn't easy. Hermansson drove around the tired police headquarters three times before parking on Kungsholmsgatan, by the entrance to Normalm Police and the County Criminal Police, despite protests from Ewert Grens. Grens nodded vaguely at the security guard and walked in through the entrance he hadn't used for years; he had long since learned to appreciate routine and had stuck to his rigidly in order not to fall apart. One corridor and a narrow staircase and then they came out into the County Communication Center, the heart of the vast building. In a room the size of a small football field, a police officer or a staff employee sat at every second computer, watching the three small screens in front of them and the considerably larger ones that covered the walls from floor to ceiling, ready to deal with the four hundred or so emergency calls that came in every day.

Holding a cup of coffee each, they sat down next to a woman in her fifties, one of the civvies, and the sort of woman who put her hand on the arm of the person she was talking to.

"At what time?"

"Twelve thirty-seven, and a minute or so earlier."

The woman who still had her hand on Ewert's arm typed in 12:36:00, and then the silence that felt like eternity, as is often the case when several people sit together listening to nothing.

Twelve thirty-six twenty.

An automatic voice, the same one that was used in the rest of the police world, followed by the voice of a real woman who was crying as she reported a domestic at an address in Mariatorget.

Twenty thirty-seven ten.

A child screaming about a dad who'd fallen down the stairs and there was alotalotalot of blood coming from his cheek and hair.

Twelve thirty-seven fifty.

A scraping sound.

Obviously somewhere indoors. Possibly a mobile phone.

Unknown number on the screen.

"Pay-as-you-go card."

The female operator had removed her hand from Ewert Grens, so he didn't answer in order to avoid anymore physical contact. It was years since anyone had touched him and he didn't know how to relax anymore.

"Emergency services."

The scraping sound again. Then a buzzing interference. And a man's voice that was tense, stressed, but he spoke in a whisper that was trying to sound calm.

"A dead man. Västmannagatan 79."

Swedish. No accent. He said something more, but the buzzing sound made it difficult to hear the last sentence.

"I want to listen to it again."

The operator slid the cursor back along the time code that stretched across one of the computer screens like a black worm.

"A dead man. Västmannagatan 79. Fourth floor."

That was it. The buzzing disappeared and the call was cut. The monotone electronic voice said *twelve thirty-eight thirty* and a distressed old man reported a robbery in a newsagent on Karlavägen. Ewert Grens thanked her for her help.

They walked together through the endless corridors of the police headquarters to the homicide unit. Sven Sundkvist slowed down to talk to his boss who limped more with each passing year, but refused to use a walking stick.

"The flat, Ewert. According to the owner, it was rented out a couple of years back to a Pole. I've asked Jens Klövje at Interpol to find him."

"A mule. A body. A Pole."

Ewert Grens stopped by the stairs that would take them up two stories. He looked at his colleagues.

"So, drugs, violence, Eastern Europe."

They looked at him, but he didn't say any more and they didn't ask. They went their separate ways at the coffee machine, and with a cup in each hand he managed to open the door to his office. Out of habit he went to the bookshelf behind his desk, lifted his arm and then suddenly stopped. It was empty. Straight lines of dust, ugly squares of varying sizes: the cassette player had stood there, and all his cassettes, and there, two identical squares, the speakers.

Ewert Grens ran his fingers through the traces of a lifetime.

The music he had packed away that belonged to another era would never again play in this room. He felt like he'd been tricked, tried to get used to a silence that had never existed here before.

He didn't like it. It was so damn loud.

He sat down on the chair. *A mule, a body, a Pole.* He had just seen a man with three big holes in his head. *So, drugs, violence, Eastern Europe.* He had worked for thirty-five years in the city police force and seen crime rise steadily, get worse. *In other words, organized crime.* Not surprising that he sometimes chose to live in the past. *That's to say, mafia.* When he started out as a young policeman who had thought he could make a difference, the mafia had been something far away in southern Italy, in American cities. Today, executions like the one he had just seen, the brutality, it was all so dirty—colleagues in every district could only stand by and watch while money was laundered from all kinds of organized crime: drugs, gun running, trafficking. Every year, new players made a violent debut in police investigations, and in recent months he had been introduced to the Mexican and Egyptian mafias. This was another he had not come across before, the Polish mafia, but it had the same ingredients: drugs, money, death. They investigated a bit here and a bit there, but would never catch up; every day the police risked their lives and sanity and every day they lost a little more control.

Ewert Grens sat at his desk for a long time, looking at the brown cardboard boxes.

He missed the sound.

Of Siwan. Of Anni.

Of a time when everything was far simpler.

THE ARRIVALS HALL AT FRÉDÉRIC CHOPIN AIRPORT IN WARSAW WAS ALWAYS overcrowded. The number of departures and arrivals had increased steadily in line with the airport's expansion and he had lost his luggage twice in the past year in a chaos of bewildered travelers and large forklift trucks that drove too fast and too close.

Piet Hoffmann walked past the luggage carousel with his small overnight bag already in hand and went out into a city that was larger than Stockholm, which he had left two hours earlier. The dark leather in the taxi smelled of cigarettes and for a moment, as he looked out at the city that had changed beyond recognition, he was a child again, with his mom and dad on either side on the narrow backseat, on their way to visit Granny. He called Henryk at Wojtek and confirmed that the plane had landed and he would meet them at the time and place agreed. He was just about to hang up when Henryk told him that two other people would be there. Zbigniew Boruc and Grzegorz Krzynówek. Deputy CEO and the Roof. Piet Hoffmann had visited Wojtek International's head office for meetings with Henryk every month for the past three years. Hoffmann had gradually won his trust and Henryk had been a helping hand from behind as Piet worked his way up the organization. Henryk was one of the many people who trusted him and who, without knowing it, was trusting a lie. The deputy CEO, however, Hoffmann had met only once before. He was a military man, and one of the many former secret police who had started and run the mother company from a forbidding building in the center of Warsaw. An army major with a straight back who still moved in the manner of an intelligence officer despite the applied veneer of a businessman—they were careful to call themselves that: businessmen. A meeting with the deputy CEO and the Roof, he didn't get it. He leaned back in the smoked leather car seat and felt something in his chest that might be fear.

The taxi sped through the light evening traffic, past the big parks, and as they approached the part of town called Mokotów, elegant embassies appeared behind the dirty window. He tapped the driver on the shoulder and asked him to stop, he still had two phone calls to make.

"It'll cost you more."

"Just stop, please."

"It'll be twenty zloty more. The price you got was without stops."

"Just stop the car, for Christ's sake!"

He had leaned forward and was talking straight into the driver's ear, his unshaven cheek looking shiny and soft as the car pulled off Jana Sobieskiego and parked between a newspaper stand and a pedestrian crossing on al. Wincentego Witosa. Piet Hoffmann stood in the evening chill and listened to Zofia's tired voice explaining that Hugo and Rasmus had both fallen asleep with their pillows beside her on the sofa and that they had to get up early tomorrow, one of the nursery's many outings to the Nacka reserve, something to do with a wood and spring theme.

"Piet?"

"Yes?"

"Thank you for the flowers."

"I love you."

He loved her so much. One night away, that was all he could bear. It was never like that before—before Zofia he hadn't felt the loneliness strangling him in unattractive hotel rooms, that it was pointless to breathe without having someone to love.

He didn't want to hang up and stood for a long time with the phone in his hand, looking at one of Mokotów's expensive houses and praying that her voice wouldn't vanish. Which it did. He switched mobile phones and made another call. It would soon be five in the afternoon on the East Coast of the USA.

"Paula's meeting them in half an hour."

"Good. But it doesn't *feel* good."

"I'm in control."

"There's a risk that they'll demand that someone takes responsibility for the fiasco in Västmannagatan."

"It wasn't a fiasco."

"A person died!"

"That's not relevant here. What's important is that the delivery is safe. We can tough out the consequences of the shooting in a matter of minutes."

"That's what you say."

"You'll get a full report when I see you."

"Eleven hundred hours at number five."

He waved in irritation when the taxi driver hooted his horn. A couple of minutes more in the dark loneliness and cool air. He was sitting between Mom and Dad again, traveling from Stockholm and Sweden to a town called Bortoszyce, only a few miles from the Soviet border, in an area that is now called Kaliningrad. They had never called it that. They refused. For Mom and Dad it was always Königsberg; Kaliningrad was the invention of madmen. He had caught the contempt in their voices, but as a child had never been able to understand why his parents had left the place they always yearned for.

The hooting driver swore loudly as they pulled out of al. Wincentego Witosa and drove past well-manicured green areas and big business properties. Not many people around in this part of town. There seldom are in places where the price per square meter is adapted to supply and demand.

They had emigrated at the end of the sixties. He had often asked his father why but never got an answer, so he had nagged his mother and been given a few scraps about a boat, and that she was pregnant, and about some nights in the dark on the high sea when she was convinced they would die, and that they had gone ashore somewhere near a place called Simrishamn in Sweden.

Right onto ul. Ludwika Idzikowskiego, quarter of an hour to go.

In the past few years he had visited this country, which belonged to him, so many times. He could have been born here, grown up here and then he would have been very different, like the people in Bortoszyce who had tried to keep in touch for so long after his mother and father died, and who had eventually given up when he gave nothing back. Why had he done that? He didn't know. Nor did he know why he never got in touch when he was nearby, why he had never gone to visit.

"Sixty zloty. Forty for the journey and twenty for that bloody stop that we hadn't agreed on."

Hoffmann left a hundred-zloty note on the seat and got out of the car.

A big, dark, old building in the middle of Mokotów—as old as a building could be in Warsaw, which had been totally destroyed seventy years ago. Henryk was waiting for him on the steps outside. They shook hands but didn't say much; neither of them knew how to do small talk.

The meeting room was at the end of a corridor on the tenth floor. Far too light and far too warm. The deputy CEO and a man in his sixties, who he assumed was the Roof, were waiting at the end of the oblong table. Piet Hoffmann accepted their unnecessarily firm handshakes and then went to sit down on the chair that had already been pulled out. There was a bottle of water on the table in front of it.

He didn't shy away from their piercing eyes. If he had done that, chosen to retreat, it would be over already.

Zbigniew Boruc and Grzegorz Krzynówek.

He still didn't know if they were sitting there because he was going to die. Or because he had just penetrated farther.

"Mr. Krzynówek will just sit and listen. I assume that you haven't met before?"

Hoffmann nodded to the elegant suit.

"We haven't met, but I know who you are."

He smiled at the man whom he had seen over the years in Polish newspapers and on Polish television, a businessman whose name he had also heard whispered in the long corridors at Wojtek, which had emerged from precisely the same chaos as every other new organization in an Eastern European state; a wall had suddenly fallen and economic and criminal interests merged in a grab and scramble for capital. Organizations that were established by the military and police and that all had the same hierarchical structure, with the Roof on top. Grzegorz Krzynówek was Wojtek's Roof and he was perfect. A champion with a central position, extremely robust financially and unassailable in a society that required laws, a guarantee that combined finance and criminality, a facade for capital and violence.

"The delivery?"

The deputy CEO had studied him long enough.

"Yes."

"I assume that it's safe."

"It's safe."

"We'll check it."

"It will still be safe."

"Let's continue then."

That was all. That was yesterday.

Piet Hoffmann wasn't going to die this evening.

He wanted to laugh—as the tension vanished something else bubbled up and longed to escape, but there was more to come. No threats, no danger, but more ritual that required continued dignity.

"I don't appreciate the condition you left our flat in."

First he made sure that the delivery was safe. Then he asked about the dead man. The deputy CEO's voice was calmer, friendlier now that he was talking about something that wasn't as important.

"I don't want my people here to have to explain to the Polish police, on the request of the Swedish police, why and how they rent flats in central Stockholm."

Piet Hoffmann knew that he had to answer this question too. But he took his time, looked over at Krzynówek. *Delivery. I don't appreciate the condition you left our flat in.* The respected businessman knew exactly what they were talking about. But words are strange like that. If they're not used officially, they don't exist. No one here in this room would mention twenty-seven kilos of amphetamine and a killing. Not so long as a person who officially didn't know anything about it was sitting in their midst.

"If the agreement that I, and only *I*, have the authority to lead an operation in Sweden had been respected, this would never have happened."

"I'd like you to explain."

"If your people had followed your instructions instead of using their own initiative, the situation would never have arisen."

Operation. Own initiative. The situation.

Hoffmann looked at the Roof again.

These words. We're using them for your sake.

But why are you here? Why are you sitting next to me listening to all this that means everything and nothing?

I'm not frightened anymore.

But I don't understand.

"I assume that this will not be repeated."

He didn't answer. The deputy CEO would have the last word. That was the way things worked and Piet Hoffmann knew what to do, how to play the game, otherwise, he also knew, the end was nigh. The instant he became Paula, he no longer existed—he would end up like the buyer ten hours ago, in a car on his way to a Warsaw backstreet with two Poles and a cocked gun to his head.

He knew his role, his lines, his history, he wasn't going to die. Dying was for other people.

The Roof moved, not much, but gave a definite nod to the deputy CEO.

He looked satisfied. Hoffmann was approved.

The deputy CEO had hoped for that and counted on it. He got up, almost smiling. "We have plans to expand in the closed market. We've already invested and taken market shares in your neighboring Nordic countries. Now we're going to do the same in your country. In Sweden."

Piet Hoffmann looked at the Roof in silence, then at the deputy CEO.

The closed market.

The prisons.

THE HARSH LIGHT FROM THE ANGLEPOISE LAMPS WAS REFLECTED IN BOTH metal spoons. Nils Krantz lifted up one of them and filled it with a light blue powder and water before asking Ewert Grens to pull back the green sheet that covered the person on the table in the middle of the room.

A naked man's body.

Pale complexion, well built, and not particularly old.

A face with no skin, a skull on top of an otherwise complete body.

A strange sight. The bones had been cleaned so the observer could get as close as possible, the skin that was in the way of a clear answer had been scrubbed off.

"Alginate. We use it. It works. There are more expensive brands, but we don't waste them on autopsies."

The forensic scientist separated the lower jaw from the upper jaw and pushed the metal spoon with the light blue fluid against the teeth in the upper jaw and held it there until it hardened.

"Photographs, fingerprints, DNA, dental imprints. I'm pleased with that."

He took a couple of steps back into the sterile room and nodded to Ludvig Errfors, the forensic pathologist.

"Entrance wound."

Errfors pointed to the bare skull bone on the right temple.

"The bullet went in through the *os temporale* and then lost speed just here."

He drew a line in the air with his finger from the large hole in the temple to the middle of the skull.

"*Mandible.* The jaw bone. The trajectory shows clearly that the jacket of the bullet hit this hard bone and split into two smaller bullets with two exit wounds on the left side of the head. One through the mandible and one through the *os frontale.*"

Grens looked at Krantz. The forensic scientist had been right from the start, there on the floor in the flat.

"And this, Ewert, I want you to have a look at this, in particular."

Ludvig Errfors was holding the dead man's right arm, a peculiar sensation when the muscles don't react, the fact that something that was so recently alive can become so rubbery.

"You see that? The visible marks around the wrist. Someone held his hand post mortem."

Grens looked at Nils Krantz again who gave a satisfied nod. He had been right about that too. Someone had moved the arm after he'd died. Someone had tried to make it *look* like suicide.

Ewert Grens left the brightly lit table in the middle of the room and opened one of the windows out in the corridor. It was dark outside, and the late evening was deepening into night.

"No name. No history. I want more. I want to get closer to him."

He looked at Krantz, then at Errfors. He waited. Until the pathologist cleared his throat.

There was always more.

"I've looked at a couple of the fillings in his teeth. Take this one here, in the middle of the lower jaw. About eight, maybe ten years old. Most probably Swedish. I can deduce that from the way the work has been done, the quality, a plastic material that is noticeably different to the ones that the greater part of Europe import from Taiwan. I had a body here last week, a Czech who had a root filling in his lower jaw, cement in all the canals, which was . . . well, far from what we would see as acceptable here."

The pathologist moved his hands from the skinless face to the torso. "He's had his appendix removed. See the scar here. A good cosmetic job. That, and the way in which the large intestine has been sewn up—both indicate that the operation was done in a Swedish hospital."

A muffled sound and the feeling that the ground was moving. Just before midnight, and a truck had driven through the secured area, passing close to the window of the Solna institute of forensic medicine.

Ludvig Errfors caught the question in Grens's eyes.

"Nothing to worry about. They unload a short distance away. No idea what, but it's the same every evening."

The pathologist moved away from the table; it was important that Ewert Grens came closer.

"The fillings, the appendix and what I would call a Northern European appearance. Ewert, he's Swedish."

Grens studied the face that was a death mask of white, washed bone.

We found traces of bile, amphetamine and rubber.
But they didn't come from you.
We've confirmed a drug deal with the Polish mafia.
But you're Swedish.
You weren't a mule. You weren't the seller.
You were the buyer.
"Any traces of drugs?"
"No."
"Are you sure?"
"No syringe marks, nothing in the blood, nothing in the urine."
You were the buyer, but didn't use drugs yourself.
He turned to Krantz.
"The alarm call?"
"What about it?"
"Have you managed to analyze it yet?"
Nils Krantz nodded. "I've just come back from Västmannagatan. I've got a theory. I went back to check it out. That sound you can hear just before the person who raised the alarm is about to finish with *fourth floor*? Right at the end of the brief call?" He watched Grens, he remembered. "Well, I had a hunch that it was the compressor in the fridge in the kitchen. Same frequency. Same interval."
Ewert Grens's hand brushed the dead man's leg.
"So the call was made from the kitchen?"
"Yes."
"And the voice? Did it sound Swedish to you?"
"No accent whatsoever. Mälardal dialect."
"Then we have two Swedes. In a flat at the same time that the Polish mafia was concluding a drug deal, which ended in assassination. One of them is lying here. The other one raised the alarm."
His hand moved toward the dead man's leg again, as if he hoped that it would somehow move.
"What were you doing there? What were you *both* doing there?"

HE HAD BEEN SO SCARED. BUT HE WASN'T GOING TO DIE. HE HAD MET THE
Roof for the first time and it hadn't meant death, so that meant he was
further in. He didn't know how or where, only that Paula was getting closer
to the breakthrough he had risked his life for every day, every minute for
the past three years.

Piet Hoffmann sat beside the empty chair in the far-too-brightly-lit
meeting room. Grzegorz Krzynówek had just left with his elegant suit and
clean appearance and words that pretended to be something other than
organized crime and money, and violence to get more money.

The deputy CEO no longer had tight lips when he spoke, nor strained
to keep his back straight. He opened a bottle of Żubrówka and mixed it
with apple juice: there was an intimacy and confidentiality associated with
drinking vodka with the boss, so Hoffmann smiled at the piece of grass in
the bottle which wasn't particularly good, as that was polite and the
custom, and at the former intelligence officer in front of him who had so
meticulously transgressed his class and even swapped the ugly glasses from
the kitchen table for two expensive, hand-blown tumblers, which his
enormous hands were not quite sure how to hold.

"Na zdrowie."

They looked each other in the eye and emptied their glasses, and the
deputy CEO poured another.

"To the closed market."

He drank up and filled the glasses a third time.

"We're speaking plain language now."

"I prefer it."

A third glass was emptied.

"The Swedish market. It's time for it. Now."

Hoffmann found it hard to sit still. Wojtek already controlled the Norwegian
market. The Danish market. The Finnish. He was starting to understand what
this was all about. Why the boss had been sitting there. Why he himself was
holding a glass of something that tasted like bison grass and apple juice.

He had been heading here for so long.

"There are about five thousand people in prison in Sweden. And nearly eighty percent of them are big-time consumers of amphetamines, heroin, and alcohol, aren't they?"

"Yes."

"Which was also the case ten years ago?"

"Yep, back then too."

Twelve bloody awful months in Österåker prison.

"One gram of amphetamine costs one hundred and fifty kronor on the street. In the prisons it's three times as much. A gram of heroin costs a thousand kronor on the street. On the inside, three times as much."

Zbigniew Boruc had had this conversation before. With other colleagues in other operations in other countries. It was always about the same thing. Being able to calculate.

"Four thousand locked up drug addicts—the amphetamine freaks who take two grams a day, the heroin addicts who use one gram a day. Just one day's business, Hoffmann . . . between eight and nine million kronor."

Paula had been born nine years ago. He had lived with death every day since then. But this, this moment, made it all worthwhile. All the damn lies. The manipulation. This was where he was headed. And now he had arrived.

"An unprecedented operation. Initially, though, big money has to be invested before we can even start, before we get anything back."

The deputy CEO looked at the empty chair between them.

Wojtek had the power to invest, to wait as long as it took for the closed market to be theirs. Wojtek had a financial guarantee, the Eastern European mafia's variant of the consigliere, but with more capital and more power.

"Yes. It's an unprecedented operation. But possible. And you are going to lead it."

EWERT GRENS OPENED THE WINDOW. HE NORMALLY DID AROUND midnight to listen to the clock on Kungsholms Church and then another one that he had never managed to locate, he only knew that it was farther away and couldn't be heard on nights when the wind swallowed any fragile sound. He had been pacing around his office with a strange sensation in his body, the first evening and night in the police headquarters without Siwan's voice anywhere in the dark. He had got so used to falling asleep to the past, and at this time of night had always listened to one of the cassettes he had recorded and mixed himself.

There was nothing here now that even remotely resembled peace.

He had never been bothered by all the night sounds that played outside his window before, and already he loathed the cars on Bergsgatan that accelerated as they approached the steep incline on Hantverkargatan. He closed the window and sat down with the sudden silence and the fax that he had just received from Klövje, from the Swedish section at Interpol. He read the interview, which he was reliably informed had been requested by the Swedish police, with a Polish citizen who had been the registered tenant of the flat in Västmannagatan 79 for the past two years. A man with a name that Ewert Grens didn't recognize and couldn't pronounce, forty-five years old, born in Gdansk, registered in the electoral roll for Warsaw. A man who had never been convicted or even suspected of any crime and who, according to the Polish policeman who had questioned him, had, without any doubt, been in Warsaw at the time when the incident in Stockholm took place.

You're involved in some way.

Ewert Grens held the printout in his hand.

The door was locked when we got there.

He got up and went out into the dark corridor.

There were no signs of a break-in and no signs of violence. Two cups from the coffee machine. *Someone had used a key to get in and out.* A cheese sandwich wrapped in plastic and a banana-flavored yogurt from the vending machine. *Someone who is linked to you.*

He stood there in the silence and dark, emptied one cup of coffee and ate half the yogurt, but left the sandwich in the bin. It was too dry, even for him.

He felt safe here.

The big, ugly police headquarters where colleagues were swallowed up or hidden away, the only place where he could bear to be, really—he always knew what to do here, he belonged; he could even sleep on the sofa if he wanted to and avoid the long nights on a balcony with a view of Sveavägen and a capital that never stopped.

Ewert Grens went back to the only room in the homicide unit where the lights were still on, to the boxes of packed-away music, which he gave a light kick. He hadn't even gone to the funeral. He had paid for it, but hadn't taken part, and he kicked the boxes again, harder this time. He wished he had been there, maybe then she would be gone, truly gone.

Klövje's fax was still lying on the desk. A Polish citizen who could in no way be linked to a dead body. Grens swore, marched across the room and kicked one of the boxes for the third time, his shoe leaving a small hole in the side. He hadn't gotten anywhere. He didn't know anything except that a couple of Swedes had been in the flat while the Polish mafia were completing a drug deal, and that one of them was now dead and the other had raised a whispered alarm from near a fridge in the kitchen—a Swedish voice with no accent, Krantz was certain of that.

You were there and raised the alarm while someone was being murdered.

Ewert Grens stood by the cardboard boxes, but didn't kick them again.

You are either the murderer or a witness.

He sat down, leaned back against the boxes, covering the recent hole.

A murderer doesn't shoot someone, make it look like suicide, and then ring and raise the alarm.

It felt good to sit with his back to the forbidden music, he was probably just going to stay there on the hard floor through the night, until morning.

You're a witness.

HE HAD BEEN SITTING BY THE WINDOW FOR TWO HOURS, WATCHING THE specks of light that were so tiny when they were far away and then slowly grew as they sank through the dark toward the runway at Frédéric Chopin. Piet Hoffmann had lain down fully clothed on the hard hotel bed just before midnight, and tried to sleep, but had soon given up—the day that had started with someone being killed in front of him and ended with the responsibility of taking over the drug market in Swedish prisons continued to live inside him; it whispered and screamed until he couldn't be bothered to block his ears and wait for sleep.

It was blowing hard outside the window. Hotel Okęcie was just eight hundred meters from the airport and the wind often swept over the open ground, creating spots of light that were prettiest when the branches on the trees refused to stay still. He liked to sit here, for one night at a time, looking out over this last piece of Poland, where he always observed but never took part, even though he should feel at home here—he had cousins and aunts and an uncle here. He looked like them and talked like them but was forever someone who didn't belong.

He was nobody.

He lied to Zofia and she held him tight. He lied to Hugo and Rasmus and they hugged their daddy. He lied to Erik. He lied to Henryk. He had just lied to Zbigniew Boruc and drank another Żubrówka with him.

He had been lying for so long that he'd forgotten what the truth looked and felt like, who he was.

The specks of light had now become a huge plane that had just landed; it swerved in the strong crosswinds and the small wheels bounced out of control a couple of times on the asphalt before sinking down and rolling the plane toward some steps by the newer part of the arrivals hall.

He leaned forward to the window and rested his forehead on the cool glass.

The day that wouldn't end, that whispered and screamed.

A person had stopped breathing in front of him. He had realized too late. They had the same role, were part of the same game, but on different sides. A person who perhaps had children, a wife, who had maybe also lived a lie for so long that he didn't know who he was anymore.

My name is Paula. What was yours?

He sat on the windowsill, looking out into the dark, as he cried.

It was the middle of the night in a hotel room a few kilometers from central Warsaw. He had a real person's death on his hands and he cried until he could cry no more and sleep took him, and he fell headlong into something that was black and couldn't be lied to.

tuesday

EWERT GRENS HAD WOKEN WHEN THE FIRST LIGHT FORCED ITS WAY through the thin curtains and started to irritate his eyes. He was sitting on the floor with his back against the three stacked cardboard boxes, but he then lay down on the hard linoleum to avoid the dawn light and slept for another couple of hours. It wasn't a bad place to sleep; his back barely ached and he had been able to keep his stiff leg stretched almost straight the whole night, which he never got room for on the soft corduroy sofa.

No more nights there.

Suddenly he was wide awake, rolled over onto his belly and used his arms to lever up his bulky frame. From the tin on his desk he grabbed a blue marker, which released a strong odor as he wrote on each side of the brown cardboard boxes.

PI Malmkvist.

Ewert Grens looked at the taped-up boxes and laughed out loud. He had been able to sleep with the packed music and felt more rested than he had done for a long time.

A couple of dance steps, no singing, no music, just unaccompanied steps.

He tried to lift the box on top, but it was far too heavy, so he pushed it out of the room and down the long corridor to the elevator. Three floors down, to the cellar, to the property store. He wrote a reference number on the top of the box with the marker again—*19361231.* Then he went down another corridor, even darker than the last, and pushed and sweated on to the door that opened into confiscated property.

"Einarsson."

A young lad, civilian staff, was standing behind the long wooden counter that felt so old. Every time Grens came here he was reminded of a grocer's shop he often went to as a boy on his way home from school, a shop near Odenplan which had long since disappeared and was now yet another café for teenagers who drank milky coffee and compared mobile phones.

"Can I help you?"

"I want Einarsson to look after this."

"Yes, but I—"

"Einarsson."

The young man snorted loudly, but said nothing. He left the counter and went to get a man of Ewert's age, with a black apron tied tightly around his rotund body.

"Ewert."

"Tor."

One of the policemen who had been really good and then after years of working together, had suddenly sat down one morning and explained that he couldn't face all the crap anymore, let alone investigate it. They had talked a lot about it at the time and Ewert had understood that that was how things could be when you had something to live for, when you yearned for days without pointless deaths. Einarsson had sat there and did not get up until his superiors had opened the door to the basement and the confiscated goods that were indeed a part of ongoing investigations, but which seldom stayed with you all evening.

"I've got some boxes I want you to look after."

The older man behind the counter took the things and read the square letters in blue marker.

"PI Malmkvist. What the hell is that?"

"Preliminary investigation Malmkvist."

"I realize that. But I've never heard of the case."

"Closed investigation."

"But then it shouldn't—"

"I want you to keep them here. In a safe place."

"Ewert, I—"

Einarsson was silent, studied Grens for a long time, then the box. He smiled. Preliminary investigation Malmkvist. Reference number 19361231. He gave another even broader smile.

"Jesus, that's her birthday, isn't it?"

Grens nodded. "A closed investigation."

"Are you sure about that?"

"I'll be down with another two boxes."

"In that case . . . investigations like this are best stored here. If the stuff is unique, I mean. Better than some unsafe attic or damp cellar."

Ewert Grens hadn't realized how tense he was until, to his surprise, he felt his shoulders, arms, and legs slowly relax. He hadn't been sure that Einarsson would understand.

"I need a chain of custody record. So, if you could just fill these in now. Then I can find a safe place."

Einarsson handed him two blank forms and a pen.

"In the meantime, I'll mark clearly that it's classified information. Because it is, isn't it?"

Grens nodded again.

"Good. Then it can only be opened by authorized persons."

The policeman, who had once been a detective himself and who now wore a black apron and worked behind a counter in the basement, slapped a red sticker over the flaps of the box, a seal that could not be broken by anyone other than the man who could identify himself as DS Ewert Grens.

Ewert was full of gratitude as he watched his colleague struggle over to the shelves with the cardboard box in his arms.

Someone who didn't need an explanation.

He left the form on the counter and turned to leave when he heard Einarsson singing one of Siw Malmkvist's songs somewhere between the rows of seized property.

The tears I cried for you could fill an ocean

The Swedish version of "Everybody's Somebody's Fool." Ewert Grens stopped and shouted in the direction of the cramped storage space.

"Not now."

But you don't care how many tears I cry

"Einarsson!" Ewert bellowed, and Einarsson popped his head around some shelves in surprise.

"Not now, Einarsson. You're disturbing my grief."

He felt lighter when he left—the basement was almost attractive and he shook his head at the elevator and decided instead to take the stairs three floors up. He was about halfway when the mobile phone in the inner pocket of his jacket began to chime.

"Yes?"

"Are you heading the investigation into the murder in Västmannagatan 79?"

Ewert Grens was out of breath. He didn't often take the stairs.

"Who's asking?"

"Says who?"

The voice was Danish, but easy to understand, probably from somewhere near Copenhagen, the part of Denmark that Grens had worked with most over the years.

"Was it you or me who phoned?"

"Apologies. Jacob Andersen, crime operations unit Copenhagen, or what you call homicide."

"And what do you want?"

"To know whether you are leading the investigation into the murder in Västmannagatan 79."

"Who said it was a murder?"

"I did. And it's just possible that I know who the victim is."

Grens stopped on the last step, tried to catch his breath while he waited for the voice that had presented itself as a Danish policeman to continue.

"Do you want me to call you back?"

"Put the phone down."

Grens hurried to his room, found the file he was looking for in the third drawer of his desk. He leafed through it for a moment or two and then left it open in front of him as he dialed the switchboard of Copenhagen police and asked for Jacob Andersen from the crime operations unit.

"Andersen." It was the same voice.

"Put the phone down."

He called the switchboard again and asked to be transferred to Jacob Andersen's mobile phone.

"Andersen."

The same voice.

"Open the window."

"What?"

"If you want the question answered, then open the window."

He heard the voice put the phone down on the desk and fiddle for a while with a rusty window hook.

"Okay?"

"What can you see?"

"Hambrogade."

"Anything else?"

"The water if I lean out far enough."

"Half of Copenhagen can see water."

"Langebro."

Grens had looked out of the window from the crime operations unit several times. He knew that it was the water by Langebro that was sparkling in the sun.

"Where does Moelby sit?"

"My boss?"

"Yes."

"In the room opposite. He's not here right now. Otherwise—"

"And Christensen?"

"There is no bloody Christensen here."

"Good. Good, Andersen. Now we can continue."

Grens waited; it was the Danish voice that had phoned him, so it was the one that should continue. He went over to his own window. Not much water to be seen in the dreary courtyard of the police headquarters.

"I have reason to believe that the dead person worked for us. I'd like to see a photograph, if possible. Could you fax one to me?"

Ewert Grens reached for a folder that was lying on his desk, checked that Krantz's pictures were still there, the ones that had been taken in the flat, when the face still had skin.

"You'll get a photo in five minutes. I'll wait for the call when you've had a look."

Erik Wilson enjoyed walking in the center of Stockholm.

Mad people, suits, beautiful women, pushers, strollers, running clothes, dogs, bikes, and the odd person who wasn't going anywhere. Half past ten, mid-morning in the city. He had passed them all on the recently repaired pavement in the short distance from the police headquarters to Sankt Eriksplan. It was cooler here, easier to breathe; it had already been too warm in southern Georgia, and in a few weeks it would be unbearable. He had left Newark Liberty International in the afternoon, just after five local time, and landed at Arlanda eight hours later, early in the morning. He must have slept a bit on the plane, fallen asleep despite the two old ladies in the seats in front who chatted incessantly, and the man in the seat beside him who coughed loudly every five minutes. As the taxi approached the city and the police headquarters at Kronoberg, he asked the driver to stop first at Västmannagatan 79, the address he had been given by Paula. Wilson showed his ID to the security guard at the door of the fourth-floor flat, with blue-and-white tape crisscrossed over the doorway and a sign that said it was a secured crime scene, and then walked on his own through the abandoned rooms that not even a day earlier had witnessed a man being killed. He started by the large, dark patch on the carpet under the table in the sitting room. A life had seeped away just here. An overturned chair was lying by the edge of the patch, the stain of death. He peered at a hole in the ceiling and another hole in the closed kitchen door, obvious damage from the split bullet. Then he stood for a while by the pins and flags that marked the discoloring on the sitting room wall, and which was interesting in terms of the angle and force of the shot. That was what he had come for, to analyze the blood splashes. That was what he needed for the next meeting, that and Paula's version. Erik Wilson concentrated on the funnel-shaped area that the guys from forensics had marked out with two pieces of string, one end of which had no flags and no blood and no brain tissue. He studied and memorized it until he was certain of exactly where the two people who were important to him had been at the moment the shot was fired: where the person who fired had stood and where the person who *hadn't* fired must have been standing.

There was a pleasant breeze blowing on Sankt Eriksbron as he looked out over the boats, trains, cars—that was what he liked so much about walking, being able to pause for a while, to look.

He had heard Paula's version of events and the tension last night on his mobile phone, and now that he had had the opportunity to study the flat in peace and quiet, it looked like what he said was true. He knew that Paula was capable and that if the choice had been between life and death, Paula had both the strength and the ability to kill. It could easily have been he who fired the shot, but Wilson was now certain that that was not the case. Paula had sounded more and more harassed and frightened with every phone call. After nine years working together as handler and infiltrator the close contact had developed into trust, and Erik Wilson had learned to hear when he was telling the truth.

He stopped in front of the door to Sankt Eriksplan 17, brittle glass in an old wooden frame, so close to the heavy traffic of the main road. He looked around. A face passed by but didn't notice. He checked again, then went in.

He had left the marks and splashes of blood in Västmannagatan, then taken the waiting taxi to Kronoberg and finally to an office in the homicide unit. According to the Duty Management System, a detective had already been assigned to the case. Ewert Grens, assisted by Sven Sundkvist and Mariana Hermansson. Grens and Wilson had worked together in the same unit for a number of years, but he didn't really know the strange detective superintendent. He had tried to make contact for a long time, without any response whatsoever, and had then just given up, decided that he did not need an old man in his life who had once been the best, but now just listened to Siw Malmkvist and was bitter. Erik Wilson stayed in front of the computer. He switched from the DMS to the Crime Reporting system and searched for Västmannagatan 79, and found three hits in the past ten years. He called up the most recent entry, dealing in stolen goods, one ton of refined copper that was sold by a man with a Finnish name in one of the flats on the ground floor.

Erik Wilson closed the door to Sankt Eriksplan 17 and paused in the silence, away from the traffic frenzy. The stairwell was dark and when he was unsuccessful in his third attempt to turn on the lights he decided to take the small elevator up to the fifth floor, getting out into a construction site. The flat was being totally renovated, so the tenants had been moved out. He stood on the brown paper and listened to nothing until he was certain that he was alone, then opened the locked door with STENBERG written on the letter box, went into the two rooms and kitchen and checked over the furniture that was protected by transparent plastic sheeting. This was how he operated. A couple of the biggest private landlords in the city gave him the keys and work schedules for flats that were empty and being renovated. This was number five. Wilson had used it for just under a month; he'd met several different infiltrators here. He would keep it until the renovation was finished and the tenants had moved back in.

He pulled back the plastic from the kitchen window, opened it, and looked out over the communal gardens at the back, with carefully raked gravel paths and some new outdoor furniture over by the two swings and short slide. Paula would be there in a minute. He'd come out of the back door of the house opposite that had an entrance at Vulcanusgatan 15. Always in an empty flat, always with a communal garden at the back that could be accessed from another address.

Erik Wilson closed the window and taped the plastic back against the glass, just as the door below opened and Paula hurried along the gravel path.

Ewert Grens impatiently clutched the folder that contained Nils Krantz's photographs of a dead man. Ten minutes earlier, he had sent one of them to a fax machine in the crime operations unit in Copenhagen, a photograph of a head that had been washed, but still had skin, before the autopsy. There were three other pictures in the folder and he studied them while he waited. One taken from the front, one from the left side, one from the right. A considerable amount of his working day was taken up looking at pictures of death and he had learned that it was often difficult to distinguish whether someone was asleep or actually dead. This time it was fairly obvious as there were three great holes in the head. If he hadn't been to the scene or been handed a photograph by someone from forensics or received it by fax from a colleague somewhere else, he usually started by looking for the shiny steel stand that the head always rests on, and if he found it, it was a photograph from an autopsy. He looked at the pictures again and wondered what he would look like, what a person studying the photo of his head on a steel stand would think.

"Grens."

The phone finally rang and he put the folder down on the desk.

"Jacob Andersen, Copenhagen."

"Well?"

"The photograph you faxed."

"Yes?"

"It's probably him."

"Who?"

"One of my informers."

"*Who?*"

"I can't say. Not yet. Not before I'm absolutely certain. I don't want to disclose an informer unnecessarily. You know how it works."

Ewert Grens knew how it worked and didn't like it. The need to protect the identity of covert human intelligence sources—CHIS—had increased as they had become more numerous, and sometimes was more important than the need for the police to provide each other with correct information. Nowadays, when each and every policeman could call themselves a handler and had the right to make their own CHIS contacts, the secrecy was more often a hindrance than a help.

"What do you need?"

"Everything you've got."

"Dental impressions. Fingerprints. We're waiting for the DNA."

"Send it."

"I'll do that straightaway. And I assume that you'll call again in a few minutes."

The head on the steel stand.

Grens stroked his finger over the smooth photographic paper.

An infiltrator. From Copenhagen. One of two people who spoke Swedish in a flat when a Polish mafia execution took place.

Who was the other one?

Piet Hoffmann walked down the gravel path through the dull communal garden. A quick glance up at the fifth floor of the building opposite, where he caught a glimpse of Wilson's head in a window that happened not to be protected by plastic. He had left Frédéric Chopin on the first plane just after eight, the Polish carrier LOT. He had spent the night with his forehead pressed against a cold windowpane, but he wasn't particularly tired. Anxiety and adrenaline from a day that had included a person being killed and an important meeting in Warsaw jostled in his breast; he was definitely heading somewhere and had no idea how to stop. He had called home and Rasmus had picked up the phone and didn't want to let go of the receiver because he had so much to tell; it hadn't been easy to follow it all, something about a cartoon and a monster that was green and horrible. Piet Hoffmann swallowed and shook, as you do when you miss someone more than you were physically prepared for—he would see them this evening and he would hold all three of them tight until they asked him to let go. He got to the fence and opened the gate, and moved from the garden of Vulcanusgatan 15 to that of Sankt Eriksplan 17, and then in through the back door to the stairs that remained dark, even though he flicked the switch for the lights several times. Five flights of steep stairs, never an elevator with the risk of getting stuck, each step covered with brown paper that made it difficult to move without making a noise. He checked the bells and names on the letter boxes. The door with STENBERG on it opened from inside at eleven hundred hours precisely.

Erik Wilson had taken the plastic off two chairs and the table in the kitchen and was now uncovering the gas range and a cupboard under the sink. He hunted around until he found a pan and a jar of something that looked like instant coffee.

"The Stenbergs' treat. Whoever they are."

They sat down.

"How's Zofia?"

"I don't know."

"You don't know?"

"We haven't seen much of each other in the past couple of days. But her voice—we spoke for quite a long time on the phone last night and again this morning—and I can hear it, she knows that I'm lying, that I'm lying more than usual."

"Take care of her. You know what I mean?"

"You know damn well that I take good care of her."

"Good, that's good, Piet. Nothing you do is worth more than her and the kids. I just want you to remember that."

He didn't like the instant coffee much, there was a stale aftertaste, reminiscent of the coffee in the more expensive restaurants in Warsaw.

"He should never have said he was the police."

"Was he?"

"I don't know. I don't think so. I think he was like me. And that he was bloody frightened."

Wilson nodded. He probably had been frightened. And in a panic had flung out the words that he thought would protect him. But had had the opposite effect.

"I heard him scream *I'm the police*, a gun being cocked and then a shot."

Hoffmann put his cup down—the instant coffee was undrinkable, no matter how hard he tried.

"It's been a while since I saw someone die close at hand. That silence when they stop breathing and you hold on to the last breath until it ebbs away."

Erik Wilson was looking at someone who had been touched by death and lived with the responsibility for it; the rather lean man in front of him who could be hard as nails when he needed to be was someone else right now. It was three years since they had taken the first steps to infiltrate Wojtek Security International. The national crime operations division had identified the company as a flourishing branch of the Eastern European mafia that was already established in Norway and Denmark. The CHIS controller at City Police had forwarded the intelligence report to Wilson and reminded him of Paula's background, that Polish was his other mother tongue and that he was in ASPEN, the criminal intelligence database, and had a criminal record that was solid enough to withstand any checks and probing.

They were there now.

Paula had courage, authority, and criminal credibility, and had reached the top of the organization—he had communicated directly with the deputy CEO and the Roof in Warsaw, behind the facade of what was supposed to be a Polish security firm.

"I heard him cock the gun but wasn't quick enough."

Erik Wilson looked at his infiltrator and friend, at the face that switched between Piet and Paula.

"I tried to calm them down, but could only go so far . . . Erik, I had no choice, you see that, don't you? I have a role to play and I have to do it bloody well, otherwise . . . otherwise I'm a dead man too."

It was always unexpected; his face had become completely Paula now.

"It was him who didn't play his role well enough. Something wasn't right. You have to be a criminal to play a criminal."

Erik Wilson didn't need convincing, he knew the score, that Paula risked death every day as a consequence, that people like him, squealers, were hated by their own. But still, without really knowing why, he wanted to test Piet's innocence before doing everything he could to ensure that he got criminal immunity.

"The shot . . ."

"What about it?"

"What angle?"

"I know what you're after, Erik. I'm covered."

"What angle?"

Piet Hoffmann knew that Wilson had to ask his questions, that was just the way it was.

"Right temple. Left angle. Held to the head."

"Where were you?"

"Directly opposite the dead man."

Erik Wilson cast his mind back to the flat he had recently visited, to the patch on the floor and the flags on the wall, to a cone-shaped corridor where there was no blood or brain tissue.

"Your clothes?"

"Nothing."

So far, the right answers.

There was no blood in the corner opposite the dead man.

The person who had fired the shot would have been sprayed with blood.

"Do you still have them? The clothes?"

"No. I burned them. To be on the safe side."

Hoffmann knew what Erik was looking for. Proof.

"But I took the killer's clothes. I offered to burn them and I saved the shirt. In case it was needed."

Always on your own. Trust no one but yourself.

That was how Piet Hoffmann lived, that was how he survived.

"I guessed as much."

"And the gun. I've got that too."

Wilson smiled.

"And the alarm?"

"That was me."

Correct answer again.

Wilson had *twelve* passed through the County Communication Center *thirty-seven* when he left Kronoberg and had checked *fifty* the recording.

"I listened to it. You were in a state. You had reason to be. But we'll sort this out. I'll start working on it as soon as we've said good-bye, in a while."

Ewert Grens was tired of waiting. It was twenty minutes since their last conversation. How long did it take to verify a dead man's dental impressions and fingerprints? Jacob Andersen from Copenhagen had talked about an informer. Grens sighed. The national police authority's future vision: private individuals as covert human intelligence, much cheaper than detectives, and the police could get rid of an informer if necessary, burn them without any responsibility or militant unions. A future that was not his—he would have retired by then—when police work would be interchangeable with criminals who ratted on their own.

Twenty-four minutes. He phoned up himself.

"Andersen."

"You're taking your bloody time."

"Ah, it's you, Ewert Grens."

"Well?"

"It's him."

"You sure?"

"The fingerprints were enough."

"Who?"

"We called him Carsten. One of my best infiltrators."

"Not the damn code name."

"You know how it works, as his handler, I can't—"

"I'm leading a murder investigation. I'm not interested in your hush-hush secrecy. I want a name, a personal identity number, an address."

"You won't get it."

"Civil status. Shoe size. Sexual orientation. Underpants size. I want to know what he was doing at the murder scene. Who he was working for. Everything."

"You won't get it. He was one of several infiltrators involved in this operation. So you can't get any information whatsoever."

Ewert Grens slammed the receiver down on the desk before shouting into it: "So . . . let's see . . . first of all, the Danish police are operating on Swedish territory without informing the Swedish police! And when the shit hits the fan and the operation ends in a murder, the Danish police still don't give the Swedish police any information, even though they are trying to solve the murder. Andersen, how does that sound?"

The telephone receiver slammed down onto the desk again, harder this time. He wasn't shouting anymore, it was more like a hiss.

"I know that you've got a job to do, Andersen, and that's why you're behaving the way you are. But I have too. And if I haven't solved this in . . . say twenty-four hours, then we're going to have a meeting, no matter what you think, and you and I are going to exchange information until there is nothing left to tell."

Piet Hoffmann felt lighter.

He had answered the deputy CEO's questions about the incident at Västmannagatan correctly and so avoided a trip to the edge of town and two bullets in the head. And he had just answered Erik's questions correctly, the only person who could confirm his true mission and who was now working to avert a trial and sentence.

The meeting with the Roof in Warsaw, their financial guarantee for the work involved in taking over the closed market in Sweden, this was what they had been waiting for.

"Four thousand captive, big-time consumers. Prices three times higher than outside the walls. Eight, maybe nine million kronor per day. If everyone pays, that is."

Hoffmann pulled a piece of plastic off the kitchen table.

"But that's not the plan."

Erik Wilson listened and leaned back. This moment made it all worth it.

Three hellish years constructing a person and role that was dangerous enough to penetrate an organization that they otherwise couldn't get near. Paula's information was worth the work of forty detectives—he knew more about this mob than the Swedish police.

"The plan is to control the outside as well."

This moment was what motivated him to put up with the exposure, the constant threat.

"There are people who can pay for their drugs from their cell, who have plenty of money."

The moment when an organization was about to expand, take power, become something else.

"And there are others who can't pay, but we keep selling to them and they keep consuming and when they've served their sentence, they're released with a couple of T-shirts, three hundred kronor and a ticket home. Wojtek's boys. That's how we'll recruit new criminals on the outside. When they've done their time they'll be given the choice between working to pay off their debt or two bullets."

The moment when the Swedish police could make their move, squash the criminal expansion, the moment that would never come again.

"Do you understand, Erik? This country has fifty-six prisons. And more are being built. Wojtek will control every single one. But also an army of indebted serious criminals on the outside."

The Eastern European mafia's three areas of operation.

Arms. Prostitution. Drugs.

Wilson sat at what would soon once more be a plastic-covered kitchen table with a view out to the communal gardens. Criminal organizations were in control and the police could only stand by and watch. Now Wojtek was about to make their final move. First the prisons, then the streets. But this time there was a massive difference. This time the police had their own man at the top. The police knew where, how, and exactly when it would be possible to sweep in and launch a counterattack.

Erik Wilson watched Paula open the gate, close it, and disappear into the house on the other side of the garden.

It was time to call another meeting.

At the government offices.

They had to have guarantees that he wouldn't be held responsible for the murder in Västmannagatan 79, so they could continue their infiltration work, even from inside prison.

THERE WERE STILL TWO CARDBOARD BOXES IN ONE CORNER OF THE ROOM. Soon he would push them down the corridor, down to Einarsson and the protection of a classified stamp and safe storage in the property store.

She had been all on her own.

He hadn't really understood that at the time, it had been all about him, about his own fear and how lonely *he* had been.

He hadn't even gone. When she was being buried, he had lain, clean-shaven, in a black suit, on the corduroy sofa in his office and stared at the ceiling.

Ewert Grens turned around—he couldn't bear to look at the boxes that were so strongly associated with her; he was ashamed.

He had tried to forget about Västmannagatan 79 for a while—he was getting nowhere and his desk was full of ongoing investigations that were getting older and harder to solve by the hour. He looked through the preliminary investigation files and put them to the side, one after the other. *Attempted extortion* and pimply youths from the Södra Station area who had threatened shop owners in Ringens Centrum. *Car theft* and an unmarked police car that had been found stripped of its computer and communication equipment in a tunnel under the Sankt Eriksbron. *Violation of a woman's integrity* and a former husband who had repeatedly breached his restraining order and gone to his former wife's domicile on Sibyllegatan. Uninteresting and soulless, but nonetheless, such investigations were his daily fare and he would sort them out later. He was good at that, after all, at reality. But not right now. A dead man was lying in the way.

"Come in."

Someone had knocked on the door. Even a knock echoed in a room with no music.

"Do you have a moment?"

Grens looked up at the doorway and someone he didn't particularly like. He didn't know why, there was no real reason, but sometimes that's just the way it is, something that you can't put your finger on, that bothers you all the same.

"No, I don't have time."

Thick blond hair, slim, bright-eyed, eloquent, intellectual, presumably attractive, still quite young.

Erik Wilson was everything that Ewert Grens was not.

"Not even for a simple question?"

Grens sighed.

"There's no such thing as a simple question."

Erik Wilson smiled and came in. Grens was about to protest, but stopped himself. Wilson was one of the few who had never complained about the loud music in their shared corridor. Perhaps he had the right to pop into the silence.

"Västmannagatan 79. The shooting. If I've understood correctly . . . you're the one investigating?"

"That's what you say."

Erik Wilson looked the curmudgeonly detective superintendent in the eye. The day before he'd had a look on the computer at the CR system and was convinced that he had found a good enough excuse to hide his real purpose.

"Just a thought. Was it on the ground floor?"

A Finnish name, stolen goods, a ton of refined copper.

"No."

According to the entry in the register, a case that was no longer open, and a sentence that would already have come into force.

"A year ago. Same address. I investigated a Finnish man who was dealing in serious amounts of stolen refined copper."

A minor crime that Grens had not investigated, so presumably he lacked the same knowledge that Wilson did.

"And?"

"Same address. Was just curious. Is there any connection?"

"No."

"Are you sure about that?"

"I'm sure about that. This involves some Poles. And a dead Danish infiltrator."

Erik Wilson had the information he wanted.

Grens was investigating.

Grens already had dangerous information.

And Grens would continue to dig and delve. The older man was glowing in the way that he sometimes did, when he was at his best.

"Infiltrator?"

"You . . . I don't think you've got anything to do with this."

"Well, you've certainly whetted my curiosity."

"Close the door when you leave."

Wilson didn't protest, he didn't need anymore. He was already out in the corridor when Grens's voice cut through the dust.

"The door!"

Two steps back, Wilson shut the door and walked to the neighboring one.

Chief Superintendent Göransson.

"Erik?"

"Do you have a moment?"

"Sit down."

Erik Wilson sat down in front of the man who was his boss and who was Grens's boss and who was also the CHIS controller in the city police district.

"You've got a problem."

Wilson looked at Göransson. The room was big, the desk was big. Perhaps that was why he always looked so small.

"Have I?"

"I've just been to see Ewert Grens. He's investigating the killing at Västmannagatan. The problem is that I'm not investigating, and I know considerably more about what happened than the appointed investigator does right now."

"I don't understand why that should be a problem."

"Paula."

"Right?"

"Do you remember him?"

"I remember him."

Wilson knew that he wouldn't need to explain much more.

"He was there."

The automatic voice.

Twelve thirty-seven fifty.

Scraping sounds. Obviously somewhere indoors. The voice was tense, whispered, with no accent.

A dead man. Västmannagatan 79. Fourth floor.

"One more time."

Nils Krantz pressed play on the CD player and carefully adjusted the speakers. By this point they both recognized the humming of a fridge that made it difficult to hear the last two words.

"One more time."

Ewert Grens listened to the only link they had to a man who had witnessed a murder and then decided to vanish.

"Again."

The forensic scientist shook his head.

"I've got a lot to do, Ewert. But I can burn a CD for you so you can listen to it as much and as often as you like."

Krantz burned the sound file of the alarm call that was received by the County Communication Center a matter of minutes after the man had been shot onto another disc.

"What do I do with it?"

"You don't have a CD player?"

"I think Ågestam gave me a machine once, after we'd had a small confrontation about a father who shot and killed his daughter's murderer. But I've never used it. Why should I?"

"Here, borrow this one. And give it back when you're done."

"One more time?"

Krantz shook his head again.

"Ewert?"

"Yes?"

"You don't know how to use it?"

"No."

"Put on the headphones. And press play. You'll manage."

Grens sat at the far end of the forensics department. He pressed a few random buttons and gingerly pulled at a rather long cord, and then jumped when the alarm voice was suddenly there again, in the headphones.

It was all he knew about the person he was looking for.

"One more thing."

Nils Krantz gestured to his ears. Ewert had to take the headphones off.

"We've scoured Västmannagatan 79. All the rooms. And we've found nothing that can be linked to the investigation."

"Look again."

"I'll have you know that we're not sloppy. If we didn't find anything the first time, we won't find it the second time. You know that, Ewert."

Ewert Grens did know that. But he also knew that there was nothing else, that right now he had gotten absolutely nowhere with the investigation. He hurried through the vast building with the CD player in his hand, toward the exit to Kungsholmsgatan. A few minutes later, he waved down a passing patrol car from the pavement, opened the door, got into the backseat and asked the astonished policeman to drive him to Västmannagatan 79 and to wait for him there.

He made his way up to the fourth floor, stopping briefly in front of the door with a name plate with the Finnish name that Wilson had tried to push him to discuss this morning, then continued on to the flat that was still being guarded by contracted security men in green uniforms. He looked at the big bloodstain and the markers on the walls, but this time it was the kitchen that interested him and a spot near the fridge where Krantz was one hundred percent certain that the man had been standing when he called and raised the alarm. *You sound calm despite the fact that you're frightened.* He put the headphones on and pressed the two buttons that had worked the last time. *You are precise, systematic, purposeful.* The voice again. *You can cut yourself off and carry on functioning, despite the fact that you're in the midst of chaos.* Grens walked between the sink and the worktop, listening to someone who had been in exactly the same place and had whispered a message about a dead man while the people on the other side of the door stood next to the body that was still bleeding heavily. *You're involved in the murder but chose to raise the alarm and then disappear.*

"This thing is damn marvelous."

He had rung Nils Krantz as he walked down the stairs.

"What are you talking about?"

"The machine that you lent me. Jesus, I can listen to it when I want, as many times as I want."

"That's good, Ewert. Great. Speak to you again soon."

The car was double-parked outside the front door, waiting, the policeman ready behind the wheel, with his safety belt still on.

Grens clambered into the backseat.

"Arlanda."

"Excuse me?"

"I want to go to Arlanda."

"This is not a taxi, you know. I knock off in quarter of an hour."

"Then I think you should stick on the blue light. It's quicker."

Ewert Grens leaned back in the seat when the car approached Norrtull and the northbound E4. *Who are you?* He had the headphones on, so he would be able to listen to it several times before they stopped outside Terminal 5. *What were you doing there?* He was on his way to see someone who knew more about at least one of the people who had been in the flat when a lead and titanium bullet had penetrated one man's head, and he would not return until he knew more himself. *Where are you now?*

He held the plastic bag in his hand, swinging slowly back and forth between the steering wheel and the door.

Piet Hoffmann had left number five at half past eleven that morning, an empty flat that could be accessed from two addresses. He had felt stressed, the shooting at Västmannagatan, the breakthrough with Wojtek, trust or potential death sentence, stay or run. When he closed the gate to the communal gardens, his phone had rung. Someone from the nursery who mentioned fever and two little boys with burning cheeks lying on a sofa, who needed to be picked up so they could go home. He had gone straight to Hagtornsgården in Enskededalen, collected the two hot, sleepy children, and then headed toward the house in Enskede.

He looked at the plastic bag, at the shirt that was in it, gray and white checks that were now covered in blood and tissue from a person.

He had put the boys to bed, where they had each fallen asleep clutching an unread comic. He had phoned Zofia, promised to stay at home with them, and she had kissed the receiver twice—always an even number.

He looked out of the car window at a clock above a shop door. Six more minutes. He turned around. They sat there silently, with shiny eyes and floppy bodies. Rasmus was almost flat out on the backseat.

He had wandered around in the watchful house, every now and then giving a sleeping, feverish cheek a worried caress, and had realized that he didn't have any choice. There was a bottle of Calpol, children's pain reliever, in the door of the fridge and after much protest that it tasted horrible and they would rather be ill, both had eventually swallowed a double dose, served to them in a dessert spoon. He had carried them out to the car, driven the short distance to Slussen and Södermalm, and parked a couple of hundred meters from the entrance on Hökens Gata.

Rasmus was now actually lying on the backseat. Hugo was half on top of him. Their flaming cheeks were slightly less red for a while as the Calpol worked its magic.

Piet Hoffmann felt something in his chest that was possibly shame.

I'm so sorry. You shouldn't be here.

Right from the start, when he had been recruited, he had promised himself that he would never put anyone he loved in danger. This was the only time. It would never happen again. It had almost happened once before, a few years ago, when there had been an unexpected knock on the door and Zofia had asked the two visitors in for coffee. She had been charming and pleased and had no idea of who she was serving: the deputy CEO and the number four. They were just checking out in more detail someone who was on his way up. Hoffmann had explained to her later that they were two of his clients and she believed him, as she always did.

Two more minutes.

He leaned over to the back and kissed their surprisingly cool foreheads, said that he had to leave them on their own for a very short while, that they had to promise to sit still like big boys.

He locked the car door and went in through the entrance to Hökens Gata 1.

Erik had gone in through the door to Götgatan 15 twenty minutes earlier and was watching him now from a window on the second floor, as he always did when Paula crossed the communal gardens.

Meeting place number four at fourteen hundred hours.

An empty flat, a beautiful central flat that was being renovated for the next few months, one of six meeting places. Two flights up, the door with LINDSTRÖM on the letter box. He nodded at Erik and handed him the plastic bag that had been lying in one of the locked gun cabinets and contained a shirt with bloodstains and gunshot residue, the one that Mariusz had been wearing twenty-four hours earlier, then he hurried back down to the children.

The steps from the SAS plane down to the runway at Copenhagen Airport were made of aluminum and too shallow to take one step at a time yet too high when he tried to take two. Ewert Grens looked at his fellow passengers, who were having the same problem. Ungainly movements down toward a small bus that was waiting to drive them to the terminal building.

Grens waited by the last step for a white car with blue stripes and the word POLICE written on it, with a young uniformed man behind the wheel, similar to the Swedish officer who had dropped him off near the departures hall at Arlanda just under an hour ago. The young man hurried out, opened the door to the backseat and saluted the Swedish detective superintendent. A salute. It had been a while. Just as he had done for his bosses in the seventies. No one seemed to do that anymore, now that he was a boss, which he was happy about. Found all that submissive waving hard to stomach.

There was already someone else in the back.

A man in his forties in civilian clothes, similar to Sven, the sort of policeman who looks nice.

"Jacob Andersen."

Grens smiled.

"You said that your office looked out over Langebro."

"Welcome to Copenhagen."

After driving four hundred meters, the car stopped by a door that was roughly in the middle of the terminal building. They went into the airport police station. Ewert Grens had been there several times before, so he made his way to the meeting room at the back, where there was coffee and Danish pastries on the table.

They picked you up by car. Booked a meeting room in the local station. Served you coffee and cake.

Grens looked at his Danish colleagues who were sorting out plastic cups and sugar.

It felt good, as if the strange standoffishness, the silent opposition to working together had evaporated.

Jacob Andersen wiped his fingers on his trousers after eating a sticky pastry and then put an 8 × 10 photograph down in the middle of the table. A color copy, enlarged several times. Grens studied the picture. A man somewhere between thirty and forty, crew cut, fair, coarse features.

"Carsten."

In the autopsy room, Ludvig Errfors had described a man of northern European appearance with internal surgical and dental work that would indicate that he had probably grown up in Sweden.

"We have a different system here. Male code names for male informers, female code names for female informers. Why make it more confusing than necessary?"

I saw you on the floor; you had three gaping holes in your head.

"Carsten. Or Jens Christian Toft."

I saw you later on Errfors's autopsy table, your face stripped of skin.

"Danish citizen, but born and raised in Sweden. Convicted of aggravated assault, perjury, and extortion and had served two years in D Block at Vestre Prison in Copenhagen when he was recruited by us. In much the same way that you do. Sometimes we even recruit them when they're on remand."

I recognize you, it's you, even in that picture from the autopsy when you were being washed, you looked the same.

"We trained him, gave him a background. He was paid by Copenhagen Police as an infiltrator to initiate deals with as many of the big players in organized crime as possible. Hells Angels, Bandidos, the Russians, Yugoslavians, Mexicans . . . whichever gang you like. This was the third time that he had initiated a deal with the Polish group, Wojtek."

"Wojtek?"

"Wojtek Security International. Security guards, bodyguards, CIT. Officially. Just like in all the other Eastern European states. A facade for organized crime."

"Polish mafia. Now it has a name. Wojtek."

"But it was the first time he was dealing with them in Sweden. Without backup. We wanted to avoid an operation on Swedish territory. So it was what we call an uncontrolled purchase."

Ewert Grens apologized. He had the photo of the dead man in one hand and his mobile phone in the other as he left the room and went out into the departures hall, dodging the bags that were hurrying toward a new queue.

"Sven?"

"Yes?"

"Where are you?"

"In my office."

"Get in front of the computer and do a multisearch for Jens Christian Toft in all the databases. Born in 1965."

He bent down and picked up a bag that had fallen off a smiling, sunburned old lady's cart. She thanked him and he smiled back as he listened to Sven Sundkvist pull out his chair, and then the irritating note that sounds like a tune every time you turn on the computer.

"Ready?"

"No."

"I haven't got much time."

"Ewert, I'm logging on. It takes a bit of time. There's not a lot I can do to change that."

"You can open it faster."

A couple of minutes of clacking on the keyboard, Grens walking restlessly between the travelers and the check-in desks, waiting for Sven's voice.

"No hits."

"Not anywhere?"

"No criminal record, not in the driver's license register, he's not a Swedish citizen, his fingerprints haven't been recorded, he's not in the criminal intelligence database."

Grens walked slowly around the bustling departures hall twice.

But he had a name. He now knew who had been lying in a dark patch on the sitting room floor.

It meant nothing.

He wasn't interested in the dead man. A lifeless identity was only meaningful if it helped him to get closer to the perpetrator. It was his job to check the name, but it wasn't to be found in any Swedish register, so it didn't make the slightest difference.

"I want you to listen to this."

Ewert Grens was once again sitting in the room with the oversize Danish pastries and miniature cups in Kastrup police station.

"Not yet."

"It's not much. But it's all I've got."

A voice whispering seven words to the emergency services was still his closest link to the murderer.

"Not yet, Grens. Before we carry on, I want to make sure that you are absolutely clear about the terms of this meeting."

Jacob Andersen took the CD player and headphones but put them down on the table.

"You didn't get any information earlier on the phone because I wanted to know who I was talking to. And whether I could trust you. Because if it becomes known that Carsten was working for us, there's a risk that other infiltrators—who he had recommended and backed for Wojtek—might also die. So what we talk about here doesn't go beyond these walls. Okay?"

"I don't like all this cloak-and-dagger stuff surrounding informers and their operations. It interferes with other investigations."

"Okay?"

"Okay."

Andersen put on the headphones and listened.

"Someone raising the alarm from the flat."

"I realize that."

"His voice?" Ewert Grens pointed at the photograph on the table.

"No."

"Have you heard it before?"

"I'd need to hear more to be able to give you a definite answer."

"That's all we've got."

Jacob Andersen listened again.

"No. I don't recognize the voice."

Carsten, who was called Jens Christian Toft, was dead in the picture but it felt almost like he was looking at him, and Grens didn't like it. He pulled the photo toward him and flipped it over.

"I'm not interested in him. I'm interested in who shot him. I want to know who else was in the flat."

"I have no idea."

"You must've damn well known who he was going to meet for one of *your* operations!"

Jacob Andersen didn't like people who raised their voices unnecessarily.

"Next time you talk to me like that, this meeting is over."

"But if it was you who—"

"Understood?"

"Yes."

The Danish detective superintendent continued.

"The only thing I know is that Carsten was going to meet representatives from Wojtek and a Swedish contact. But I don't have any names."

"A Swedish contact?"

"Yes."

"Are you sure about that?"

"That's the information I have."

Two Swedish voices in a flat where the Polish mafia was tying up a deal. One was dead. The other raised the alarm.

"It was you."

Andersen looked at Grens, taken aback.

"Excuse me?"

"The Swedish contact."

"What are you talking about?"

"I'm saying that I'm going to find the bastard."

The house was only a couple of hundred meters from the heavy traffic on Nynäsvägen, which thundered through any thoughts. But you only had to drive down a couple of little back streets, past the school and a small park, to discover another world. He opened the car door and listened. You couldn't even hear the hum of the heavy trucks that were trying to overtake one another.

She was standing in the driveway, waiting in front of the garage when he swung in.

So beautiful, with her slippers still on and not enough clothes.

"Where have you been? Where have the children been?"

Zofia opened the back door and stroked Rasmus on the cheek, lifted him up in her arms.

"Two clients, I'd forgotten about them."

"Clients?"

"A security guard who had to have a bulletproof vest and a shop that needed its alarm system adjusted. I had no choice. And they didn't have to sit in the backseat for long."

She felt both their brows.

"They're not too warm."

"Good."

"Maybe they're getting better."

"I hope so."

I kiss her on the cheek and she smells of Zofia, as I cobble together a lie.

It's so simple. And I'm good at it.

But I can't bear to tell yet another one, not to her, not to the kids, not anymore.

The wooden steps creaked as the two parents carried their feverish children indoors and up to bed, their small bodies under white duvets. He stood there for a while looking at them. They were already asleep, snoring and snuffling as people do when they're fighting lurking bacteria. He tried to remember what life was like before these two boys whom he loved more than anything in the world, empty days when he had only himself to think of. He remembered it well, but felt nothing, he had never been able to comprehend how what had once been so important, so strong and so absolute, was suddenly meaningless as soon as someone small had come along, looked at him, and called him Daddy.

He walked from one room to the other and kissed them each on the forehead. They were starting to get hot again, the fever burning on his lips. He went back down to the kitchen and sat on a chair behind Zofia and watched her back as she washed the dishes, which would then be put away in a cupboard in his home, her home, *their* home. He trusted her. That was what it was, he felt a trust that he had never dared dream of. He trusted her and she trusted him.

And she trusted him.

He had just lied to her. He seldom thought about it, it was habit. He always considered the plausibility of a lie before he was even conscious that he was going to lie. This time the lie had been reluctant. He sat behind her and it still felt unreasonable, demanding, hard to bear.

She turned around, smiled, stroked his chin with a wet hand.

The hand that he so often yearned for.

But now it just felt uncomfortable.

Two clients, I'd forgotten about them. And they didn't have to sit in the backseat for long.

What if she hadn't trusted him? *I don't believe you.* What if she hadn't accepted his lie? *I want to know what you've really been up to.*

He would have fallen. He would have collapsed. His strength, his life, his drive, he had built it all up around her trust.

Ten years earlier.

He's locked up in Österåker prison, just north of Stockholm.

His neighbors, his mates for twelve months—they all have their own way of living with the shame. They have carefully constructed their defense, their lies.

The man opposite, in cell 4, a junkie who stole to pay for his habit, who burgled fifteen houses a night in some suburbs, and his damned insistence that *I never hurt children, I always shut the door to their room, I never steal anything from them*; his mantra and defense to help him bear the shame, a homemade set of morals that made him seem a little better than he was, to himself at least, that kept self-loathing at bay.

Piet knew, just like everyone else knew, that the man in cell 4 had pissed on that morality long ago. He stole whatever he could sell, from the children's rooms as well, because the need for drugs was stronger than his self-respect.

And the man farther down in cell 8, who had been sentenced for assault so many times, who had devised another life lie, his own morals with another mantra, to keep himself afloat: *I never hit women, only men, I would never hit a woman.*

Piet knew, just like everyone else knew, that the man in cell 8 had separated word from deed long ago. He hit women too, he hit anyone who crossed his path.

Made-up morals.

Piet had scorned them, just as he had always held those who lied to themselves in contempt.

He looked at her. The soft hand had been uncomfortable.

He only had himself to blame. He had trampled all over his own morals, the very reason he was still someone he liked: *my family, I will never use my family for lies, I will definitely never force Zofia and the boys to get caught up in my lies.*

And now he'd done it, just like the man in cell 4 and the man in cell 8 and all the others he had despised.

He had lied to himself.

There was nothing left of him that he could like.

Zofia turned off the water—she was done. She wiped around the sink and then sat down on his knee. He held her, kissed her on the cheek, twice like she always wanted, he burrowed his nose in the dip between her neck and shoulder, staying where the skin was softest.

Erik Wilson opened an empty document on the computer that he only used after a meeting with an infiltrator.

```
M pulls a gun
(Polish 9mm Radom)
from shoulder holster.
M cocks the gun and holds it to
the buyer's head.
```

He tried to remember and write down Paula's account from their meeting at number five.

To protect him. To protect himself.

But more than anything, to have a reason for paying out police reward money, should anyone ask why and when. Without an intelligence report and the pot for rewarding information from the general public, Paula would not be paid for his work or be able to remain anonymous and off the official payroll, nor would any of his colleagues.

```
P orders M to calm down.
M lowers the gun, takes a step
back, his weapon half-cocked.
```

When the confidential intelligence report left his desk and was taken to the commissioner of the county criminal police, via Chief Superintendent Göransson, Wilson would delete it from the computer hard disk, activate the code lock and turn off the machine, which was not connected to the Internet for security reasons.

```
Suddenly the buyer shouts
"I'm the police."
```

Erik Wilson wrote it, Göransson checked it and the county commissioner unit kept it.

If anyone else read it, if anyone else knew . . . the infiltrator's life was at risk. If the wrong people found out about Paula's identity and operations, it would be as good as a death sentence.

```
M again aims the gun
at the buyer's head.
```

The Swedish police would not strike this time. They would not arrest anyone, or seize anything. The Västmannagatan 79 operation had had one single purpose: to strengthen Paula's position in Wojtek, a drug deal as part of Wojtek's day-to-day business.

```
P tries to intervene and
the buyer screams "police."
```

```
M holds the gun harder to
the buyer's head and pulls the trigger.
```

Every infiltrator had an as yet unspoken death sentence as his or her constant companion.

Erik Wilson read the last lines of the secret report several times.

It might have been Paula.

```
The buyer falls to the floor, at a right angle to
the chair.
```

It might *not* have been Paula.

The person or persons who had worked on the Danish informer's background had done a lousy job. Erik Wilson had constructed Paula himself. Step by step, database by database.

He knew that he was good at it.

And he knew that Piet Hoffmann was good at surviving.

Ewert Grens waited in one of Copenhagen airport's beer-smelling bars drinking Danish mineral water from a brown paper cup.

All these people on their way somewhere armed with Toblerone and chocolate liqueur in sealed plastic bags. He had never been able to understand why people worked for eleven months of the year to save enough money to then go away in the twelfth.

He sighed.

He hadn't gotten any further with the investigation. He didn't know much more now than he had when he left Stockholm a few hours ago.

He knew that the dead man was a Danish informer. That he was called Jens Christian Toft. That he worked for the Danish police and had initiated a deal with a criminal organization.

Nothing about the murderer.

Nothing about who had raised the alarm.

He knew that there had been a Swedish contact person in the flat with Polish representatives from a branch of the Eastern European mafia that went by the name of Wojtek.

That was it.

No faces, no names.

"Nils?"

Grens had managed to get hold of Nils Krantz in one of the forensics offices.

"Yes?"

"I want you to extend the search area."

"Now?"

"Now."

"By how much?"

"As much as you need. Every garden, stairwell and trash can in the block."

"Where are you? There's a lot of noise in the background."

"In a bar. Danes trying to drown their fear of flying."

"And what are you doing in—?"

"Nils?"

"Yes?"

"If there's anything there that can help us, find it."

He drank what was left of the warm mineral water, grabbed a handful of peanuts from the bowl on the bar, and walked toward the gate and the line of people who were waiting to board the plane.

The secret report from Västmannagatan 79 comprised five closely written letter-size sheets which were stuffed into a plastic sleeve that was too small. Chief Superintendent Göransson had already read it four times within an hour when he took off his glasses and looked up at Erik Wilson.

"Who?"

Wilson had watched the face that was often confused, almost bashful, despite its owner's powerful position.

With every reading of the report it became redder, more tense.

Now it was about to explode.

"Who is the dead man?"

"An infiltrator, possibly."

"Infiltrator?"

"*Another* infiltrator. We think he was working for our colleagues in Denmark. He didn't know Paula. And Paula didn't know him."

The head of homicide was holding five thin sheets of paper that felt heavier than all the department's preliminary investigations put together. He put them down on the desk beside another version of the same murder at the same time at the same address. A report that had been given to him by Ågestam, the public prosecutor, on the progress that Grens, Sundkvist, and Hermansson were making with the official investigation.

"I want a guarantee that any part Paula may have played in the murder in Västmannagatan stays here. In this report."

Göransson looked at the two piles of paper in front of him. Wilson's secret report about what had *actually* happened. And Grens's ongoing investigation that contained and would continue to contain only as much as the two policemen here in this room allowed it to contain.

"Erik, that's not the way it works."

"If Grens finds out— It's just not possible. Paula is close to a breakthrough. For the first time we can actually break a mafia branch before it's fully established. We've never managed that before. Göransson, you know just as well as I do, this town is not run by us anymore, it's run by them."

"I won't give any guarantees for a high-risk source."

Erik Wilson slammed the desk hard. He had never done that with his boss before.

"You know that's not true. You've had reports about his work for the last nine years. You know that he has *never* failed."

"He is and will always be a criminal."

"That's one of the prerequisites for a good infiltrator!"

"Accomplice to murder. If he's not a high-risk source, then what is he?"

Wilson punched the desk again.

He reached for the plastic sleeve, forced the five sheets into it, then gripped it firmly.

"Fredrik, listen to me. Without Paula, this opportunity is lost. And we won't get it again. What we lose now, we'll lose forever; we only need to look at the prisons in Finland, Norway, and Denmark. How long can we just stand by and watch?"

Göransson held up his hand. He needed to think. He had listened to what Wilson had to say, and he wanted to understand the full implications.

"You want the same solution as for Maria?"

"I want Paula to continue. For at least two more months. We'll need him for that long."

The head of homicide had decided.

"I'm going to call a meeting. At Rosenbad."

When Erik Wilson left Chief Superintendent Göransson's office, he walked slowly down the corridor, hovering outside Ewert Grens's open door, but the office was empty. The detective superintendent who would never close his investigation was not there.

wednesday

A WALL OF PEOPLE.

He had forgotten that at eight in the morning, it stretched from the metro platform through the corridors up onto Vasagatan.

The car was still standing in the driveway, alongside a red plastic fire engine, in case the children's fever got worse, in case Zofia had to drive to the doctor or the drugstore. Piet Hoffmann yawned as he zigzagged through the commuters who were moving too slowly, still sleepy. He had gotten out of bed every hour through the night as their temperatures rose. The first time was just after midnight when he had opened all the windows in both boys' rooms, folded the blankets back from their hot bodies and then alternated between the two bedsides until they went back to sleep. The last time was around five, when he forced a dose of Calpol into them. They needed to rest, sleep, to get better again. Two whispering parents in dressing gowns had agreed at dawn how to divide up the day, as they always did when one of them was ill or the nursery had a planning day. He would work in the morning, then come home, they would have lunch together, then Zofia would go to work in the afternoon.

Vasagatan wasn't exactly beautiful, a sad and soulless stretch of asphalt, but it was still where many visitors, having just gotten off the train or out of the airport bus or taxi, emerged into the Stockholm of water and islands that the shiny tourist brochures had promised them. Piet Hoffmann was late and didn't pay much attention to what was beautiful or ugly as he approached the Sheraton hotel and the table nearest the bar at the far end of the elegant lobby.

They had met thirty-six hours earlier in a spacious, dark building on ul. Ludwika Idzikowskiego in Mokotów in central Warsaw. Henryk Bak and Zbigniew Boruc. His contact and the deputy CEO.

He greeted them, firm handshakes from men who were careful to demonstrate that they gave firm handshakes.

The visit was the head office's way of showing they were serious.

This was where it all started. This was a priority operation. Delivery times and dates to the prison would be managed directly by Warsaw.

They let go of each other's hand and the deputy CEO sat down again by the half-empty glass of orange juice on the table. Henryk started to walk beside Hoffmann toward the exit, but then slowed down and carried on half a step behind him, as if he were unsure of the way or just wanted to have control. Vasagatan was just as soulless from this angle. They passed the entrance to the metro and then crossed the road between the passing cars and followed the pavement on the other side to a doorway, where a security firm had offices on the first floor.

They didn't talk to each other, just as they hadn't spoken on their way to meet the Roof one and a half days earlier in Warsaw. They were silent as they climbed the stairs to the door of Hoffmann Security AB, and then carried on to the second, third, fourth, and fifth floors, and right on up to the single metal door into the loft.

Piet Hoffmann opened it and they went into the dark. There was a black switch somewhere on the wall. He felt around and eventually found it after having fumbled considerably lower down than he could remember it being. They locked the door from the inside and were careful to leave the key in the lock, so that no one else could get in. The storeroom with number 26 on the door was empty, except for four summer tires that were lying on top of each other in the far corner. He picked up the top one and pulled out the hammer and chisel that were inside the rim, then went back out into the narrow passage with the dim lighting and followed the large, shiny aluminum pipe that was suspended a few centimeters above their heads to where it met the wall and disappeared into a fan heater. He placed the tip of the chisel against the edge of the steel band that joined the pipe and the heater and then hit it hard with the hammer until the band moved and he could take out eighty-one whitish metal tins from the temporary opening.

Henryk waited until the tins were lined up on the loft floor and then picked out three: the tin farthest to the left, one from the middle, and the second to last on the right.

"You can keep the others."

Hoffmann put the remaining seventy-eight tins back in the hiding place in the fan heater while Henryk peeled off the protecting foil from the three that were left and the loft filled with a scent of tulips that was so strong it was almost unbearable.

A yellow, solid lump at the bottom of each tin.

Manufactured amphetamine cut with two parts grape sugar.

Henryk opened his black briefcase and set up some simple scales beside a stand with test tubes, a scalpel, and a pipette. One thousand eighty-seven grams. A kilo of amphetamine plus the weight of the tin. He nodded to Hoffmann: it was exact.

Henryk used the scalpel to scrape at one of the lumps until a piece no bigger than would fit in the first test tube loosened. He put the pipette into the second test tube, which contained phenylacetone and paraffin, sucked up the fluid and then released it over the loose bit of amphetamine, and shook the test tube a couple of times. He waited for a minute or two, then held the test tube up to the window: a clear bluish fluid equaled strong amphetamine, a dark cloudy fluid meant the opposite.

"Three or four times?"

"Three."

"Looks good."

Henryk sealed the tin with the foil and closed the lid, repeated the same procedure with the two others, looked again at the bluish clear fluid and, satisfied, asked his Swedish colleague to put them back in the heater, then hammer the band back in place until they heard the clicking noise that told them that the ventilation pipe was whole again.

The door to the loft was locked properly from the outside. Six flights of stairs down to the asphalt of Vasagatan. They walked in silence.

The deputy CEO was still sitting at the same table, a new half glass of orange juice in front of him.

Hoffmann waited by the long reception desk while Henryk sat down next to Wojtek's number two.

Clear bluish fluid.

Eighty-one kilos of cut amphetamine.

The deputy CEO turned around and nodded. Piet Hoffmann felt something relax in the pit of his stomach as he walked across the expensive hotel lobby.

"All those bloody bits. They just get stuck to your teeth."

The deputy CEO pointed to his half-empty glass of juice and ordered two more. The waitress was young and smiled at them, just as she smiled at all the guests who gave her a hundred-kronor tip and might well order again.

"I will be leading the operation on the outside. You're leading inside, from Kumla, Hall, or Aspsås. Maximum-security Swedish prisons."

"I need a coffee."

A double espresso. The young waitress smiled again.

"It was a long night."

He looked at the deputy CEO, who paused.

It could be a demonstration of power. Maybe it was.

"Nights sometimes are. Long."

The deputy CEO smiled. He wasn't looking for respect. He was looking for a strength he could trust.

"Right now we've got four people in Aspsås, and three in both Hall and Kumla. In different sections, but they're able to communicate. I want you to be arrested within the week for a crime that is serious enough to merit a sentence in one of them."

"Two months. Then I'm done."

"You'll be given all the time you need."

"I don't want more. But I do want a guarantee. That you'll get me out at exactly that point."

"Don't worry."

"A guarantee."

"We'll get you out."

"How?"

"We'll look after your family when you're inside. And when you're done, we'll look after you. New life, new identity, money to start over again."

The lobby of the Sheraton was still empty.

Those who had come to the capital on business wouldn't check in until the evening. Those who had come in search of museums and monuments were already out and about with a fast-talking guide and new Nike trainers.

He had finished his coffee. He motioned to the waitress, another double espresso and one of those little mint wafers.

"Three kilos."

The deputy CEO put his glass of juice down next to the others.

He was listening.

"I'll be caught with three kilos. I'll be questioned and plead guilty. I'll explain that I'm working on my own, so I get a short remand as charges can be brought immediately. I'll be given a substantial sentence by the city court—three kilos of amphetamine is a priority crime in Swedish courts, and I'll say that I accept the sentence, so I won't have to wait until it enters into force. If everything goes smoothly, I should be behind bars in the right institution within two weeks."

Piet Hoffmann was sitting in a hotel lobby in the center of Stockholm, but was in fact looking around the small cell in Österåker prison from ten years ago.

Hideous days when voices screamed *urine test* and grown men lined up to stand in the mirrored room where gimlet eyes inspected their penises and urine. Horrendous nights with spot inspections, standing barely awake in your underpants outside the cell door while a gang of screws stripped, smashed, and emptied everything and when they were done, just walked away from the chaos.

He would deal with it this time. He was there for reasons greater than the humiliation.

"When you're in place, there'll be two stages to the operation. In exactly the same way that we took one prison after the other in Norway from Oslo prison, or in Finland from Riihimäki, which was the first."

The deputy CEO leaned forward.

"You'll knock out any competition that's already there. Then we'll deliver our products through our own channels. To begin with, the remaining seventy-eight kilos that Henryk just approved: you'll use that to dump prices. Everyone inside has to learn that we are the dealers. Amphetamine for fifty kronor a gram instead of three hundred. Until we've got it all. Then we'll raise it. Fuck, maybe we'll do more than that. *Keep buying.* We'll bump it up to five hundred, why not six hundred per gram. *Or stop injecting.*"

Piet Hoffmann was back in the cramped cell in Österåker. Where drugs ruled. Where those who *owned* the drugs ruled. Amphetamine. Heroin. Even bread and rotten apples left for three weeks in a bucket of water in a cleaning cupboard—the minute they changed into twelve percent moonshine, it was the owner of the cleaning bucket who ruled.

"I need three days to knock out the competition. During that time I don't want to have any contact and it's my responsibility to take in enough gear."

"Three days."

"From day four, I want one kilo of amphetamine to be delivered once a week through Wojtek's channels. It's my job to see that it's used. I don't want anyone hiding or storing anything, nothing that resembles competition."

Hotel lobbies are strange places.

No one belongs there. No one has any intention of staying there.

The two tables closest to them, which had been empty until now, were suddenly transformed into two groups of Japanese tourists who sat down to wait patiently for the rooms they had booked, which weren't ready yet.

The deputy CEO lowered his voice.

"How will you get it in?"

"That's my responsibility."

"I want to know how you're going to do it."

"The same way that I did at Österåker ten years ago. The same way that I've done it several times since in other prisons."

"How?"

"With all due respect, you know that I'm capable, that I'll take responsibility for it, and that should be enough."

"Hoffmann, *how?*"

Piet Hoffmann smiled—it felt unnatural—for the first time since last night.

"Tulips and poetry."

THE DOOR WASN'T PROPERLY SHUT.

He distinctly heard footsteps out in the corridor, and they were hurrying toward him.

He didn't want any visitors right now. He wasn't going to share this with anyone.

Erik Wilson got up from his chair and checked the door handle. It *was* already closed. He had imagined it, the steps scraping on the floor, getting louder and louder, were not there. He was more anxious, more stressed than he realized.

Two meetings in a matter of hours.

The longer one at number five with Paula's version of the murder in Västmannagatan and his report from the meeting in Warsaw, and the considerably shorter one at number four when a plastic bag containing a bloody shirt changed hands.

Wilson looked over at the locked cupboard by the wall on the other side of the room.

It was in there. A murderer's battledress.

It wouldn't stay there much longer.

The steps out in the corridor had disappeared, as had the ones in his head. He looked at the computer screen.

```
Name Piet Hoffmann
Personal ID number 721018-0010
Number of hits 75
```

His most important tool over the past nine years for developing the best infiltrator he'd ever heard of.

ASPEN, the criminal intelligence database.

He had started as soon as Piet was released from Österåker, his first day of freedom and first day as a newly recruited infiltrator. Erik Wilson had himself met him at the gate, driven him the fifty kilometers to Stockholm in his own car and when he had dropped him off, he carried on straight to the police headquarters and recorded the first observation of 721018-0010 in ASPEN, intelligence that from that moment would be available to every police officer who logged on to find out more about Piet Hoffmann. A concise, but accurate account of how, on his release, the suspect was met at the gates of Österåker by a car and two previous convicts and known criminals with confirmed links to the Yugoslavian mafia.

Over the years he had successively made him more dangerous *observed near the property that was raided in connection with suspected arms dealing* and more violent *observed fifteen minutes before the murder in Östling in the company of the suspect, Marković* and more ruthless. Wilson had varied his formulations and the degree of misinformation, and with each new observation had added to the myth of Piet Hoffmann's potency until, according to a database on a computer, he was one of the most dangerous criminals in Sweden.

He listened again. More footsteps out in the corridor. The sound got clearer, louder, until they passed his door and slowly disappeared again.

He tilted the screen up.

KNOWN.

In two weeks' time, Piet would be given a long prison sentence and then take over enough power to control the drug supply, the kind of force that was treated with respect inside.

DANGEROUS.

Which was why Erik Wilson now wrote this in capital letters.

ARMED.

The next colleague to check Piet Hoffmann in the database would now be presented with a special page and a special code that was only used for a handful of criminals.

KNOWN DANGEROUS ARMED

Any patrol with access to this truth, which was their own intelligence after all, would know him to be extremely dangerous and confront him as such, and this reputation would then accompany him in the secure transport that would transfer him from custody to prison.

HE HELD THE MOBILE PHONE TO HIS EAR. ACCORDING TO THE AUTOMATIC voice that spoke every ten seconds, it was exactly half past twelve when the dark door with HOLM on the letter box opened from inside and Piet Hoffmann walked into a plastic-sheeted flat on the second floor. The parquet floor was uneven and creaked, probably due to water damage.

Number two.

Högalidsgatan 38 and Heleneborgsgatan 9.

Erik Wilson had made some instant coffee, as he usually did, and as normal, Hoffmann did not drink it. A soft sofa in what must have been the TV room, transparent plastic sheeting to protect the fabric during the two-month renovation that rustled when they moved and after a while clung to the film of sweat on his back.

"We'll use this."

Piet Hoffmann knew that they didn't have much time.

He could see it in Erik's eyes, for the first time, as they darted around the room, restless and unfocused. The man who had been his contact for nine years and who had never laughed or cried was stressed, and therefore doing what stressed people often do, trying to hide it, thus making it all the more obvious.

Hoffmann opened a small tin that once had been manufactured and sold for storing tea leaves, but which now contained the yellow, cohesive substance smelling strongly of tulips.

"Blossom."

Erik Wilson carefully scraped off a piece with the plastic knife that Hoffmann gave him, put it to his tongue, felt it burning, and knew he would get a blister there.

"Bloody strong. Two parts grape sugar?"

"Yep."

"How much?"

"Three kilos."

"Enough for a fast-track trial and a long sentence in a high-security prison."

Piet Hoffmann pressed down the lid and put the tin back in his inner pocket. The other eighty-one kilos were still in the fan heater in the loft of the turn-of-the-century building on Vasagatan. He would later describe to Wilson where and how to find it. But not yet. It still had to be cut one more time, his own share, which he sometimes did, sold it on.

"I'm going to need three days to knock out all other business. Wojtek will get the reports they need to continue. *Then* we'll do what we set out to do. Eliminate."

Erik Wilson should have felt calmer, happier, curious. His best infiltrator was on his way to prison, exactly where both the Swedish police and Wojtek had planned for him to be, and he would start and end a mafia branch expansion. He wasn't used to the stress and he saw that Piet had clocked it.

"I'm trying to solve Västmannagatan in the usual way. A report to the head of homicide and the secret locker. But . . . it's not enough this time. *Murder, Piet!* We'll have to take it higher than police headquarters. We have to go to Rosenbad. And you're going to come too."

"You know that's not possible."

"You don't have any choice."

"Erik, for fuck's sake, I can't just stroll in through the main entrance of the Government Offices, together with the police and politicians!"

"I'll collect you from 2B."

Piet Hoffmann sat on the sofa that was protected with plastic sheeting that was sticking to his back and slowly shook his head.

"If anyone sees me . . . I'm dead."

"In the same way that you'll be dead the minute anyone in prison discovers who you are. Only, you'll be banged up then. You need the authorities. To get out. To survive."

He left the instant coffee in the second-floor flat and instead drank a dark roast coffee with warm milk in a café on the corner of Pålsundsgatan, and tried to concentrate on the sound of Italian crooners and a table of giggling girls who had swapped their school lunches for a plate of cinnamon buns, and two people at a table at the back who were trying to look like poets and talking too loudly about writing, but only succeeded in being an imitation of others who talked too loud.

Erik was right. *Always on your own.* He had no choice. *Trust no one but yourself.*

He put down his empty coffee cup and walked over Västerbron accompanied by a cautious sun, paused quietly for a while by the railings, twenty-seven meters above the water, and wondered how it would feel to jump, the seconds that were all and nothing before your body slammed into the transparent surface. He phoned home and spoke to Zofia from the middle of Norr Mälarstrand and, yet another lie, told her that her work was just as important as his but that he couldn't come home and hold the fort until later on tonight. He heard her raise her voice and then put the phone down when he couldn't bear to lie anymore.

The asphalt became harder the closer to the heart of the city he came.

When he walked into a multistory garage opposite an expensive department store, the pavement on Regeringsgatan was empty despite the fact it was only early afternoon. He climbed the narrow stairs up to the first floor, moved between the parked cars in section B until he spotted the black minivan with darkened windows in the far corner by the concrete wall. He went over and tried the handle on one of the back doors. It was unlocked. He opened the door to the backseat of the abandoned car, then looked at his watch. He would have to wait ten more minutes.

Zofia had not stopped talking when he put the phone down. She had continued to talk to him in his head as he walked along the water at Norr Mälarstrand and past the ugly buildings at Tegelbacken, and was there beside him with her frustration on the seat in the empty car. She wasn't to know that he was the sort who lied.

He shivered.

It was always cold in these sterile garages, but this particular chill came from within, a chill that neither clothes nor movement could change. There is nothing that chills like self-contempt.

The door to the driver's seat opened.

He checked his watch. Ten minutes exactly.

Erik usually waited somewhere on the floor above, where you could see every car in Section B if you bent down, and anyone who might be too close. He didn't turn around when he got in, said nothing, just started the minivan and drove the short distance from Hamngatan to Mynttorget, and in through the gate to the small stone yard and the building where the MPs had their offices. They got out and were no sooner through the door than a security guard came to meet them and asked them to follow him down two flights of stairs and along a corridor under the Riksdag building that came out in Rosenbad; it only took a few minutes to walk along the corridor between the two centers of political power in Sweden, and it was the only way to get into the Government Offices without being seen.

He checked the door, only a few meters from the main security office by the official entrance to Rosenbad. He held the door handle until he was certain that it was locked.

It was hard to move.

The sink merged into the toilet seat and the whitewashed walls pressed against him.

The thin oblong digital recorder was in his trouser pocket, with the cigar case and plastic tube from the drugstore. He pushed in a button on the front, it flashed green. The battery was fully charged. He held it in front of his mouth and whispered: *Government Offices, Tuesday the tenth of May* and was careful not to turn it off as he slipped it into the cigar case which he would cover in lubricant until it glistened.

Paper towels around the base of the toilet. The microphone wire slipped through the small hole in the top of the cigar case.

He had done this many times before; fifty grams of amphetamine or a digital recorder, a prison or the Government Offices, the only way to safely transport something that you didn't want to be found.

He undid his trousers and sat down, the cigar case between his thumb and forefinger. He leaned forward and pushed it slowly up his anus, short thrusts until he felt it slip in a few centimeters, only then to slide out again and land on the paper towels.

Another attempt.

He pushed again, short thrusts, centimeter by centimeter, until it disappeared.

The microphone cord was long enough for him to pull it from his anus, along his crotch to his groin, where he fixed it to his skin with a small piece of tape.

The security guard behind the glass window was wearing a gray-and-red uniform, an older man with almost-white hair and a shy smile. Piet Hoffmann stared at him for a bit too long, then looked away when he realized it.

He reminded him of his father. He would have looked just like that.

"Your colleague has already gone in."

"Toilet, had to go."

"Sometimes you just have to. State secretary for the Ministry of Justice, is that right?"

Piet Hoffmann nodded and wrote his name in the visitors' book just under Erik Wilson, while the white-haired man checked his ID.

"Hoffmann, is that German?"

"From Königsberg. Kaliningrad. But a long time ago. My parents."

"What do you speak then? Russian?"

"When you're born in Sweden, you speak Swedish."

He smiled at the man who for a moment could have been his father. "And a fair bit of Polish."

He had spotted the camera as soon as they had arrived, right at the top of the glass box; he looked straight at it as he passed, stopped for a couple of seconds, his visit registered yet again.

It took seven minutes to walk behind a third security guard from the entrance and along a corridor on the second floor. It came over him so suddenly. He wasn't prepared. The fear. He was standing in the elevator when it hit him, felled him, made him shake. He had never felt fear like it before, fear that spilled over into panic, and then angst, and when he still couldn't breathe, death.

He was frightened of a man lying on the floor with three gaping wounds in his head and a breakthrough in a conference room in Warsaw and nights in a small cell and a death sentence that would become even more critical inside those walls, and Zofia's cold voice and the children's feverish skin and of no longer being able to tell the difference between the truth and lies.

He sat down on the floor of the elevator, exhausted, and avoided the guard's eyes until his legs stopped shaking so much and he dared to walk gingerly to the door that was standing half open at the end of a rather nice corridor.

One more time.

Piet Hoffmann stopped a couple of meters from the door, emptied himself as he always did of all thoughts, all feelings, pushed them aside and kicked them down and then he had put on his armor—that thick, horrible layer, his goddamn shield, he was good at it, at not letting himself feel anything—one more time, one more bloody time.

He knocked on the door frame and waited until the feet that he heard scraping the floor stood in front of him. A policeman in civvies. He recognized him. They had met on two occasions. Erik's boss; the one called Göransson.

"Do you have anything that should be left out here?"

Piet Hoffmann emptied his inner pocket and trouser pockets of two mobile phones, a stiletto, folding scissors and put it all in an empty glass fruit bowl on the table opposite the door.

"Hold out your arms and spread your legs."

Hoffmann nodded and turned his back to the man who was tall and thin with an ingratiating smile.

"Apologies. You know that we have to do this."

The long, slim fingers felt over his clothes, against his neck, back, chest. When they pressed against his backside and balls, they touched the thin microphone cord twice without feeling anything. It slipped down a bit and Piet Hoffmann held his breath until it got stuck, about halfway down his thigh. It felt like it was going to stay there.

Big windows with deep white sills and a view over the still waters of Norrström and Riddarfjärden. The room smelled of fresh coffee and detergent and there were six chairs around the meeting table. He was last, only two places left, he moved toward one of them. They studied him without a word. He passed behind their backs and made sure to feel the fabric of his trousers with a casual hand: the microphone was still there, but facing in the wrong direction. He adjusted it as he pulled out a chair and sat down.

He recognized all four people, but had met only two of them before, Göransson and Erik.

The state secretary was sitting closest to him and she pointed to a document in front of her, then got up and held out her hand.

"The document— I've read it. I assumed . . . I assumed that it concerned a . . . woman?"

She had a firm handshake. She was like the others, the ones who press too hard and think that it's the same as power.

"Paula."

Piet Hoffmann kept hold of her hand.

"That's my name, in here."

The uncomfortable silence dragged out and while he waited for someone to start speaking, he looked down at the papers that the state secretary had referred to.

He recognized Erik's way of expressing himself.

Västmannagatan 79. The secret report.

A copy of the same document lay in front of each of them. They were already part of the chain of events.

"This is the first time that Paula and I have met like this."

Erik Wilson was careful to look everyone straight in the eye when he spoke.

"With other people. In a room that we haven't secured. Where we don't have control."

He held up the report, the detailed description of a murder witnessed by one of the people at a meeting table in the Government Offices.

"An unprecedented meeting. And I hope that we will leave having made an unprecedented decision."

Ewert Grens had been lying on the office floor when Sven Sundkvist had knocked on his door a couple of minutes earlier and walked in. Sven hadn't said anything, hadn't asked any questions. He just sat down on the corduroy sofa and waited, like he always did.

"It's better here."

"Here?"

"On the floor. The sofa is starting to get too soft."

He had slept there for a second night. His stiff leg didn't ache at all and he had more or less gotten used to the cars accelerating all the way up the steep slope on Hantverkargatan.

"I want to report on Västmannagatan."

"Anything new?"

"Not much."

Ewert Grens lay on the floor and peered at the ceiling. There were some large cracks near the lamp, which he had never paid attention to before. Whether they were new or whether the music had always just been in the way.

He sighed.

He had investigated murders all his adult life. Västmannagatan 79, a feeling somewhere in his chest—there was something that didn't fit. They had identified the body, the flat owner, even the remains of amphetamine and bile from the mule. They had bloodstains and the angle from which the gun was fired. They had a witness with a Swedish voice who chose to raise the alarm and a Polish security firm that meant the Eastern European mafia.

They had as good as bloody nothing.

They were no closer to a solution than they had been in Copenhagen Airport the evening before.

"There are fifteen flats in that block. I've interviewed everyone who was there at the time of the murder. Three of them have observations that might be of interest. On the ground floor— Are you listening, Ewert?"

"Carry on."

"On the ground floor there's a Finn who can give a pretty good description of two men he'd never seen before, as he has the best possible observation point—everyone who goes in or out passes his door. Pale, shaved heads, dark clothes, forties. Only through the peephole and only for a few seconds, but you can actually see and hear more than I thought from there and he also mentioned a Slavic language, so it all fits."

"Polish."

"In terms of the tenant, that would seem likely."

"Mules, bodies, Poles. Drugs, violence, Eastern Europe."

Sven Sundkvist looked down at the older man on the floor. He just lay there and couldn't care less what anyone else thought, with a confidence that Sven could never achieve, as he was the sort who, no matter how much he had tried to change it over the years, wanted to be liked and therefore tended to be amenable and not make a fuss.

"There's a young woman who lives on the fourth floor, a couple of doors down from the crime scene, and an old man up on the fifth floor above. Both of them were at home at the time of the murder and said that they heard what they describe as a clear bang."

"A bang?"

"Neither of them was willing to say more than that. They don't know anything about weapons and couldn't say whether it was a gunshot. But they are both certain that what they called a *bang* was loud and a sound that was not a normal part of the building."

"That's all?"

"That's all."

The ringing from the phone on the desk was sharp and irritating, and did not let up, despite the fact that Sven remained sitting on the sofa and Ewert stayed on the floor.

"Should I answer?"

"I can't understand why they don't give up."

"Should I answer it, Ewert?"

"It's on my desk."

He got up patiently and lumbered toward the loud ringing.

"Yes?"

"You sound out of breath."

"I was lying on the floor."

"I want you to come down here."

Grens and Sundkvist didn't say anything, they just left the room and went down the corridor, waited impatiently for an elevator that took forever to go down. Nils Krantz was at the door to the forensics department and showed them into a narrow room.

"You asked me to extend the search area. I did. All the stairwells between numbers seventy and ninety. And in the trash store of Västmannagatan 73, in a paper recycling container, we found this."

Krantz was holding a plastic bag. Ewert Grens leaned closer and put on his reading glasses a few moments later. Something in fabric, gray-and-white checks, partially covered in blood, a shirt perhaps, or maybe a jacket.

"Very interesting. This could be our breakthrough."

The forensic scientist opened the plastic bag and put the fabric on something that looked like a serving tray, and with a bent finger pointed at the obvious stains.

"Bloodstains and gunshot residue that take us back to the flat in Västmannagatan 79, as it's the victim's blood and gunpowder from the same charge that we found in the flat."

"Which doesn't get us anywhere. Which doesn't give us a damn shit more than we already knew."

Krantz pointed at the gray-and-white piece of clothing.

"It's a shirt. It's got the victim's blood on it. But there's more. We've identified another blood group. I'm certain that it belongs to the person who fired. Ewert, this is the shirt that the murderer was wearing."

A courtroom. That's what it felt like. A room that smelled of power. A document that described a violent incident lying on an important table. Göransson was the prosecutor who checked the facts and asked the questions; the state secretary was the judge who listened and made the decisions; Wilson, to his right, was the defense who claimed self-defense and asked for leniency. Piet Hoffmann wanted to get up and walk away, but was forced to stay calm. After all, he was the accused.

"I didn't have any choice. My life was in danger."

"You always have a choice."

"I tried to calm them down. But I could only go so far. I'm supposed to be a criminal, through and through. Otherwise I'm dead."

"I don't understand."

It was a bizarre feeling. He was sitting one floor away from the Swedish prime minister in the building that ruled Sweden. Outside, down on the pavement in the real world, people were walking back from lunch with a warm low-alcohol beer and a cup of coffee because they'd chosen to pay five kronor more, while he was here, with those in power, trying to explain why the authorities should not investigate a murder.

"I'm their number one in Sweden. The people who were in the flat have been trained by the Polish intelligence service and know how to sniff out anything that doesn't feel right."

"We're talking about murder. And you, Hoffmann, or Paula, or whatever I should call you, could have prevented it."

"The first time they put the gun to the buyer's head, I managed to stop them shooting. But the next time, he had just exposed himself, he was the enemy, a snitch, dead . . . *I didn't have a bloody choice.*"

"And as you didn't have a choice, neither do we, and so should we just pretend that the whole thing never happened?"

All four of them looked at him, each with the report in front of them on the table. Wilson, Göransson, and the state secretary. The fourth person had remained silent. Hoffmann couldn't understand why.

"Yes, if you want to break this new mafia branch before it gets established. If you want to do that, then you don't have any choice."

This courtroom was like all the others, just as cold, no real people. He had been in this situation five times before, the accused, in front of people he did not respect but who would decide whether he should be part of society or live in a few square meters behind a secure door. A couple of suspended sentences, a couple of acquittals due to lack of evidence, and just one prison sentence, and a year from hell in Österåker.

That time he had not been successful in defending his case. He would not do it again.

Nils Krantz leaned nearer the computer screen as he pointed to the image of small red peaks that all pointed upward over different numbers.

"The top row, if you look here, is from Copenhagen police. The DNA profile of a Danish citizen called Jens Christian Toft. The man who was killed in Västmannagatan 79. The bottom row is from the National Laboratory of Forensic Science, an analyzis of all the bloodstains on the shirt over there that we found in the trash at Västmannagatan 73 that are at least two by two millimeters. You see, identical rows. Every single STR marker—that's the red peaks—is exactly the same length."

Ewert Grens listened to him, but still only saw a very uniform pattern.

"I'm not interested in him, Nils. But I am interested in the murderer."

Krantz considered a sarcastic retort or irritated comment. But he did neither, chose to ignore Grens instead, as it often felt better.

"But I also asked them specifically to give the same priority to analyzing even smaller spots of blood. Too small to stand up as evidence in court. But big enough to establish any marked difference."

He showed the next image.

A similar pattern, red peaks, but with larger distances and different numbers.

"These are from another person."

"Who?"

"I don't know."

"You've got the profile."

"But no hits."

"Don't be so damn difficult, Nils."

"I've matched and compared them with everything I've got access to. I'm certain it's the murderer's blood. But I'm equally certain that this DNA won't be found in any Swedish database."

He looked at the detective superintendent.

"Ewert, the murderer is probably not Swedish. The course of action, the Radom gun, no DNA matches. You'll have to start looking farther afield, in other places."

It looked like it would be a lovely evening. The sun was already dipping like a ripe orange at the point where the sky melted into Riddarfjärden, the only thing you could see from the large window of the state secretary's office. Piet Hoffmann looked into the light that made the sad, expensive birch meeting table look even sadder. He longed to be out of here, for Zofia's soft body, for Hugo's laugh, Rasmus's eyes when he said *Daddy*.

"Before we continue the meeting—"

He wasn't there. He was as far away from it all as he could be in a room that contained power and the people who could decide whether he should be put even further away.

Erik Wilson, the defense lawyer in this trial, cleared his throat.

"Before we continue the meeting, I want a guarantee that Paula will not be charged for anything that might have happened in Västmanna-gatan 79."

The state secretary had one of those faces that showed no emotion.

"I understood that that was what you wanted."

"You've dealt with similar cases before."

"But if I am to grant criminal immunity, I also have to understand why."

The microphone was still in place, halfway down his thigh.

But it was about to slip again, he could feel the tape was gradually becoming unstuck. The next time he got up, he was sure that it would not stay where it was.

"I'd be more than happy to explain why."

Wilson gripped the report firmly in one hand.

"We could have smashed the Mexican mafia in an expansion phase nine months ago. We could have eliminated the Egyptian mafia in an expansion phase five months ago. If we'd had the mandate for our infiltrators to respond in full. But it didn't happen. We stood by and watched as two more players happily helped themselves. *Now* we have another opportunity. This time, with the Poles."

Piet Hoffmann tried to sit still and with one hand under the table attempted to untangle the wire and the pieces of tape that had started to stick together.

Small movements with searching fingers.

"Paula will continue to infiltrate. He will be in the right place at the point when Wojtek takes over all drug dealing in Swedish prisons. He is the one who will supply Warsaw with reports about deliveries and sales and at the same time supply us with information about how and when to launch an attack and smash them."

He'd got it. A microphone the size of a pinhead under the material of his trousers. He fixed it again, trying to pull it up, back toward his groin, as it sat better there and it was easier to point in the direction of whoever was talking.

He stopped abruptly.

Göransson, who was sitting directly opposite him, suddenly started to stare, his gaze unflinching.

"High-security Swedish prisons. And Wojtek are going to concentrate on two categories of prisoner. First of all, *the millionaires*, the ones who have earned their money through organized crime and are inside for a long time, and who will transfer their ill-gotten gains gram by gram, day by day, to a property on ul. Ludwika Idzikowskiego. And then *the lackeys*, the ones who have no money and who leave prison with substantial debts and in order to survive, pay off these debts by selling large quantities of drugs or committing violent crimes, debts that Wojtek can link to a dangerous criminal network."

He let go of the microphone and placed both his hands on the table, where they were visible.

Göransson was still looking directly at him and it was as hard to breathe as it was to swallow, each second an hour, until he looked away.

"I can't say it any more clearly than that. It's you who decides. Let Paula continue or stand by and watch once again."

The state secretary looked at each of them, and then out of the window at the sun, which was so beautiful. Maybe she also longed to be out.

"Could I ask you to leave the room?"

Piet Hoffmann shrugged and started to walk toward the door, but stopped suddenly. The microphone. It had come unstuck and slithered down between his right leg and the material of his trousers.

"It will only take a couple of minutes. Then you can come back in."

He said nothing. But he held up his middle finger as he left the room. He heard a tired sigh behind him. They had observed it, were irritated, kept their eyes averted. That was what he had intended, he wanted to avoid any questions about what was being dragged behind his foot as he shut the door.

The state secretary's face still gave nothing away.

"You mentioned nine months. Five months. The Mexican and Egyptian mafia. I said no because the criminals you use as infiltrators can only be deemed to be high risk."

"Paula is not a *high-risk* source. He is Wojtek's ticket to expansion. The whole operation is built around him."

"I will never give criminal immunity to someone who neither you nor I trust."

"*I do* trust him."

"Then perhaps you can explain to me why Chief Superintendent Göransson body-searched him out there not long ago."

Erik Wilson looked at his boss and then at the woman with the blank face.

"*I* am Paula's handler, *I* am the one who works with him every day. I trust him and Wojtek is already here! We've never managed to position an infiltrator so centrally in an expanding organization before. With Paula, we can cut them down with one fell swoop. If he's given immunity with regard to Västmannagatan. If he is allowed to operate fully from the inside."

The state secretary went over to the window and the golden sun, and a view of the capital that was going about its afternoon business without any idea of the decisions that governed it. Then she turned and looked at the fourth participant in the meeting who had not yet said anything.

"What do you think?"

She had opened her door for Detective Superintendent Wilson and Chief Superintendent Göransson. But it was in decisions like this that she turned to the top man in the police authority and asked him to sit down at the table with her and listen.

"The criminal elite, multimillionaires, major criminals as Wojtek's financiers. The criminal grass roots, those indebted, the petty thieves, as Wojtek's slaves."

The national police commissioner had a sharp, nasal voice.

"I don't want that to happen. You don't want that to happen. Paula doesn't have time for Västmannagatan."

Piet Hoffmann had a couple of minutes.

He checked the CCTV close to the elevators, and positioned himself right underneath to be certain that he was in a blind spot. He made sure that he was on his own and then undid his trousers and soon got hold of the thin microphone wire and pulled it up to his crotch and positioned it on his groin.

The tape had dislodged.

Göransson's hands had disturbed it when he searched him.

A few more minutes.

He pulled a thread loose from one of the inner seams, and with clumsy fingers tied the wire to the fabric and angled the microphone toward the zipper of his trousers, then pulled down his sweater as far as he could over the waistband.

It was not the best solution. But it was the only one he had time for.

"You can come in again now."

The door midway down the corridor was open. The state secretary waved to him and he tried to walk as naturally as he could, with short steps.

They had decided. At least, that's what it felt like.

"One more question."

The state secretary looked first at Göransson, then at Wilson.

"Just over twenty-four hours ago, a preliminary investigation was opened. I'm guessing it's being led by the city police. I want to know how you'll, er, deal with that."

Erik Wilson had been waiting for her question.

"You've read the report that I sent to the head of homicide."

He pointed at the copies of the document that were still lying in front of each one of them on the table.

"And this is the report that the investigators, Grens, Sundkvist, Hermansson, and Krantz, have written. What they know, what they've seen. Compare it with the contents of my report, with the actual events and background as to why Paula was taking part in the operation in the flat."

She leafed quickly through the pages.

"A real report. And one that shows how much our colleagues know."

She didn't like it. As she read, the dead face came alive for the first time, the mouth, the eyes, as if it was warding off the contempt and a decision that she thought she would never have to consider.

"And now? What's happened since this was written?"

Wilson smiled, the first smile for a long time in a room that was being suffocated by its own solemnity.

"Now? If I've understood rightly, the investigators have just found a shirt in a plastic bag in a garbage bin near the scene of the crime."

He looked at Hoffmann, still with a smile on his face.

"A shirt covered in blood and gunshot residue. But . . . blood that's not recorded in any Swedish database. My guess is that it may be a red herring, one that will get them nowhere but that will take time and effort to investigate."

The shirt was gray-and-white checks and had stains that now, after twenty-four hours, were more brown than red. Ewert Grens picked at it in irritation with a glove.

"The murderer's shirt. The murderer's blood. But yet we're getting nowhere."

Nils Krantz was still sitting in front of the image of red peaks above various numbers.

"No identity. But maybe a place."

"I don't understand."

The cramped room was just as damp and dark as all the other rooms in forensics. Sven looked at the two men beside him. They were the same age, balding, not particularly jolly, tired but thorough, and, perhaps the greatest similarity, they had lived for their work until they became their work.

The younger generation that was just starting out was not likely to ever be the same. Grens and Krantz were the sort of men who no longer had a natural place.

"The smaller flecks of blood, the ones that belong to the murderer, don't come from anyone in our databases. But a person with no name has to live somewhere and always takes something with them when they move around. I usually look for traces of persistent and organic pollutants that are stored in the body, difficult to break down, that have a long life and don't dissolve easily—sometimes they point the investigation in the direction of a specific geographic place."

Krantz even moved like Grens. Sven, who had never noticed it before, looked around to see if there was a sofa, suddenly convinced that the forensic scientist also stayed in his office sometimes when the light had faded and his own flat meant loneliness.

"But not this time. There's nothing in the blood that can link your murderer to a specific place, country or even continent."

"Damn it, Nils, you just said—"

"But there's something else on the shirt."

He unfolded the shirt on the workbench with great care.

"In several places. But here in particular, at the bottom of the right arm. Flower fragments."

Grens leaned forward in an attempt to see something that could not be seen.

"It's Blossom. Polish Yellow."

They were finding it more and more often in raids. The smell of tulips. Chemical amphetamine from factories that used flower fertilizer instead of acetone.

"Are you sure?"

"Yes. The ingredients, smell and even the yellow color, like saffron, a sulphate that gives off color in running water."

"Poland. Again."

"And, I know exactly where it comes from."

Krantz folded the shirt with small movements, just as carefully as he had unfolded it.

"I've analyzed amphetamine with exactly this composition in connection with two other investigations in less than a month. We now know that it is manufactured in an amphetamine factory just outside Siedlce, a town about a hundred kilometers east of Warsaw."

The strong sunlight had become uncomfortably warm and made his jacket itch on his neck and his shoes feel too tight.

It was fifteen minutes since the state secretary had left the room for a brief meeting in an even bigger room, and a decision that would mean all or nothing. Piet Hoffmann had a dry mouth and swallowed what should have been saliva, but now was anxiety and fear.

Strange.

A small-time dealer who had served a sentence in a locked cell in Österåker prison. A family man with a wife and two young boys whom he had come to love more than anything else in the world.

He was someone else now.

A man of thirty-five, sitting on the edge of a desk in a building that was the symbol of power, the state secretary's phone in his agitated hand.

"Hi."

"When are you coming back?"

"Later on this evening. This meeting seems to be going on forever. And I can't leave. How are they?"

"Do you care?"

Her voice upset him. It was cold, hollow.

"Hugo and Rasmus, how are they?"

She didn't answer. She stood there in front of him—he knew every expression, every gesture, her slim hand massaging her forehead, her feet fidgeting in oversize slippers. Any minute now she would decide whether or not she could bear to carry on being angry.

"They're a bit better. An hour ago their temperature was one-oh-one point three."

"I love you."

He put the phone down, looked at the people around the table and then at the clock. Nineteen minutes had passed. Damn saliva, there wasn't any, no matter how much he tried to swallow. He stretched and had started to walk toward his empty chair over at the far end of the table when the door opened.

She was back, with a tall, well-built man, half a step behind her.

"This is Pål Larsen, the director general."

She had made her decision.

"He's going to help us. With what happens next."

Piet Hoffmann heard what she was saying, and should perhaps have laughed or clapped his hands. *He's going to help us. With what happens next.* She had made up her mind to overlook his presence which, legally, was tantamount to accomplice to murder. She was taking a risk. And deemed that it was one worth taking. He knew of at least two other occasions where she had granted a secret pardon to infiltrators who had been given a prison sentence. But he was fairly certain that she had never before chosen to overlook what she knew about an unsolved crime—solutions normally stopped at the level of the police.

"I want to know what this is about."

The director general of the Swedish Prison and Probation Service made it quite clear that he had no intention of sitting down.

"You are going to—now, how did we put it—*help* us position someone."

"And who are you?"

"Erik Wilson, City Police."

"And you think that I should help you with a placement?"

"Pål?"

The state secretary smiled at the director general.

"Me. You're going to help me."

The well-built man in a tight suit said nothing, but his body language betrayed his frustration.

"Your task is to position Paula—the man sitting next to me here—in Aspsås prison to serve a sentence he will be given once he has been arrested for the possession of three kilos of amphetamine."

"Three kilos? That'll be a long sentence. Then he'll have to go to a holding prison first, Kumla, before being transferred."

"Not this time."

"Yes, he—"

"Pål?"

The state secretary had a voice that was soft but could give surprisingly harsh instructions.

"Deal with it."

Wilson weathered the embarrassing silence.

"When Paula arrives at Aspsås, his work duties will already be fixed. He'll start as the new cleaner in the administration block and workshop."

"Prison management usually only grants cleaning duties as a reward."

"Then reward him."

"And who the hell is Paula? He must have a name? Do you? Because you can talk for yourself, can't you?"

The director general of the Prison and Probation Service was used to giving orders and being obeyed, not being given them and having to obey.

"You'll get my name and personal details. So that you can put me in the right prison, give me the right work and make sure that at lockup time exactly two days after I've arrived, there will be an extensive spot check of every cell in the prison."

"What the hell—"

"With dogs. That's important."

"With dogs? And what happens when we find what you've planted? To the fellow prisoner who you've wasted your drugs on? No chance. I don't buy it. It means putting my staff at risk and as a result, someone being charged for a crime they didn't commit. I just won't buy it."

The state secretary stepped closer to Larsen, put her hand on the arm of his jacket and looked straight at him while she spoke in a soft voice.

"Pål, just sort it out. I appointed you. And that means that you decide what happens in the Prison and Probation Service. You decide what you and I agree that you should decide. And when you leave, could you please shut the door behind you."

There was a bit of a draft from an open window farther down the corridor.

Perhaps that was why the door slammed so loudly.

"Paula will continue to infiltrate the organization from the inside. We have to make him more dangerous."

Erik Wilson waited until the noise from the door subsided.

"He will have committed some serious crimes. He'll be given a long sentence. He'll only be able to operate freely from his cell if he gets respect.

And when the other prisoners check his criminal record, and you can be sure that they will, on the first day in fact, they will find all the answers we want them to."

"How?"

A hint of a frown on the state secretary's blank face.

"How will he get that background?"

"I normally use one of my civilian contacts. Someone who works in the national courts administration, a civil servant who files information directly in the criminal records database. An original document from there . . . well, it's never been questioned yet by anyone in a prison corridor."

He had expected more questions. About how often he tampered with the national court administration databases. How many people were walking around with false convictions.

He didn't get any.

They were sitting at a meeting table where elastic solutions were not unusual and the names and titles of key people who adjusted flows or shortened waiting times for court cases were not required.

"In thirty-eight hours, a wanted person will be arrested and questioned."

He looked at Hoffmann.

"He will plead guilty, state that he acted alone, and a couple of weeks later will agree with a city court judgment and a long sentence that is to be served in Aspsås, one of the country's three high-security prisons."

The room was still irritatingly bright and wiltingly warm.

They all stood up. They were done.

Piet Hoffmann wanted to hammer down the door and run out of the building and not stop until he was holding Zofia's body tight in his arms. But not yet. He wanted it to be formulated as clearly as possible so that there could only be one interpretation.

Always on your own.

"Before I leave, I'd like you to summarize exactly what you are guaranteeing me."

He had expected to be dismissed. But she realized that he needed to hear it.

"I'll deal with it."

Piet Hoffmann stepped closer and felt the loose cord slapping against the fabric of his trousers. He leaned slightly to the right, so that it would be directly in front of her; it was important that he caught absolutely everything.

"How?"

"I guarantee that you won't be charged for anything that happened at Västmannagatan 79. I guarantee that we will do our best to help you complete your operation in prison. And . . . that we will look after you when the work is done. I know that you will then have a death threat and be branded throughout the criminal world. We will give you a new life, a new identity, and money to start over again abroad."

She gave him a vague smile. At least, that's what it looked like when the bright light caught her face.

"I guarantee you this in my capacity as a state secretary of the Ministry of Justice."

Wojtek or the Government Offices. It didn't really matter. Same choice of words, same promises. Two sides of the law with the same exit route.

It was good. But not good enough.

Trust no one but yourself.

"I still want to know how."

"We've already done this three times before."

A glance over at the national police commissioner. He nodded to her.

"Officially, you will be pardoned. On humanitarian grounds. That doesn't need to be explained in any more detail. Medical or humanitarian grounds are sufficient for a decision that the Ministry of Justice will then stamp as confidential."

Piet Hoffmann stood in front of her in silence for a few seconds.

He was pleased. He was close enough.

She had said what he wanted to hear and clearly enough for it to be heard again.

They walked side by side down the underground corridor that linked the government offices with the parliament building and stopped by an elevator that took them to Gamla Stan and Mynttorget 2. They should have been in a hurry, there wasn't much time left, but it was as if they were both trying to understand where they were actually going.

"You're an outlaw now."

Erik Wilson stopped.

"From now on, you're dangerous to both sides. Wojtek, who will kill you the instant you're exposed as an infiltrator. And for the people who were around the table with us just now too. You now know things that no one in that room will admit. They'll sacrifice you the moment you're a threat, they'll burn you in the same way that the authorities have burned other informers when it's a matter of protecting power. You're Wojtek's main man. You're our main man. But if anything happens, Piet, you're on your own."

Piet Hoffmann knew what fear felt like and he would fight it off, as he always did, but he needed just a little more time, he wanted to stay in the dark under the streets of Stockholm; if he did that they wouldn't get into the elevator and then into the parked car that was waiting in the courtyard and he wouldn't need to fight anymore.

"Piet?"

"Yes?"

"You have to be in control, at all times. If everything goes wrong . . . the authorities won't look after you, they'll burn you."

He started to walk.

He had exactly thirty-eight hours left.

PART TWO

THE BLACK MINIVAN STOPPED IN A DARK CONCRETE CORNER OF THE MULTI-story garage.

Second floor, section A.

"Thirty-eight hours."

"See you."

"Outlawed. Don't you forget it."

Piet Hoffmann put his hand on Erik Wilson's shoulder and then got out of the backseat and breathed in the air that tasted of carbon dioxide. The narrow stairs led down to Regeringsgatan and the capital that was always in a rush.

Tulips. Church. SwissMiniGun. Ten kilos. Library. Wind meter. Letters. Transmitters. Nitroglycerine. Safety deposit box. CD. Poetry. Grave.

Thirty-seven hours and fifty-five minutes left.

He started to walk along the pavement, passing close to people who looked at him without seeing him, strangers who lacked smiles. He longed for a particular house in a quiet street a few kilometers south of the city, the only place where he wasn't hounded and nothing demanded that he survive. He should call her again. Tulips and nitroglycerine and wind meter, he knew that he was capable and that he could do it in time, but Zofia, he still had no idea what to do about her. If danger and risk were involved, it was enough to be in control, then he could steer the outcome, but with Zofia he was never in control at all, he wasn't able to influence her reactions and feelings, no matter how he tried, he had no way of approaching her on his own terms.

He loved her so much.

Now he was doing the same as everyone else, hurrying along the city streets without a smile on his face: Mäster Samuelsgatan, Klara Norra Kyrkogata, Olof Palmes gata, and into a flower shop called Rose Garden on the corner of Vasagatan, which fronted onto Norra Bantorget. Two customers before him. He relaxed, lost himself in the red and yellow and blue flowers that all had names on small, square signs that he read and promptly forgot.

"Tulips?"

The young woman also had a name on a square badge that he had read several times and forgotten.

"Maybe I should vary it a bit?"

"Tulips always work well. In bud? From the cold room?"

"As usual."

One of the few flower shops in Stockholm that had tulips in May, perhaps because there was one customer of about thirty-five, who regularly came in and bought large bunches if they had been stored at max five degrees and still hadn't come out.

"Three bunches? One red, and two yellow?"

"Yes."

"Twenty-five stems in each bunch? And the plain white cards?"

"Please."

Rustling tissue paper around each bunch. *With thanks for a successful partnership, Aspsås Business Association* on the card in each of the yellow bunches, and *I love you* on the one for the red bunch.

He paid and walked a couple of hundred meters down Vasagatan to a door with a plaque that said Hoffmann Security AB, first floor. He opened the door, turned off the alarm, and walked straight across the kitchen to the sink where he had emptied fourteen mules of between fifteen hundred and two thousand grams of amphetamine each, the day before.

There was a vase in one of the kitchen cupboards. He found it in the one above the extractor fan and filled the heavy crystal glass with water and the bunch of twenty-five red tulips. The other two bunches, fifty light-green stems with as yet unopened, yellow buds, lay lined up across the worktop.

He turned the oven on to what he guessed was about 125 degrees. It was hard to distinguish exactly where one line changed to two on the old dial.

The fridge went down from 45 to 35 degrees, and just to be sure, he put a thermometer on the top shelf, as the gauge that was incorporated inside the plastic door was too crude and in any case, difficult to read.

Piet Hoffmann left the kitchen and the flat with an IKEA bag in his hand, went up the stairs two at a time to the loft and the shiny aluminum pipe, and knocked off the steel band in the way that he had when Henryk had been with him in the morning. Eleven tins, one at a time, from the fan heater into the bag. Then he locked up again and went down with eleven kilos of cut amphetamine in his arms.

I need three days to knock out the competition.

He checked the oven. It was warm, 125 degrees. He opened the fridge, checked the thermometer on the top shelf, 40 degrees, like in the flower shop, but he had to get the temperature down to 35.

I want to know how you're going to do it.

First tin out of the IKEA bag. One thousand grams of amphetamine. More than enough for fifty tulips.

With tulips and poetry.

He had cleaned the sink meticulously, but he still found some remains from yesterday that had gotten stuck to the edges of the metal plughole. The unplanned shooting and mules who, in a panic, had to be emptied in the one place they must never be linked to. He turned on the tap and let the hot water run while he picked off the last bits of vomit and milk and brown rubber.

The fireproof gloves were in one of the drawers with the cutlery. He laid a tulip on each one and put them into the oven, with the round buds nearest to the door. He loved the moment when it happened. Spring and life encapsulated on the end of a green stem. The buds suddenly woke up in the warmth of the oven and revealed their true color for the first time.

He took them out when they were just a couple of centimeters open, he had to be careful not to wait too long, to lose himself in the beauty, color, and life.

He put them down on the worktop and took out the box of condoms—no ribs and no lubricant and definitely no scent—and carefully poked half a condom down into each bud, then filled it with amphetamine, one tip of a knife at a time. Three grams in the small buds, four in the slightly larger ones, pressed it down hard to get as much as possible in. Then he popped the two amphetamine-filled tulips on a serving dish in the humming freezer between the sink and the range.

They had to lie there in −65 degrees for ten minutes. Until the buds had closed again, gone back to sleep and hidden their glory. Only then would he move them from the freezer to a fridge regulated to 35 degrees and a long rest that would delay them flowering.

The next time they opened it would be at room temperature on a prison warden's desk.

When he wanted them to.

Piet Hoffmann stood in his large office looking out of the window at the people and cars on Kungsbron and Vasagatan, as was his wont. He had filled fifty tulips with a total of 185 grams of 30 percent amphetamine, without even thinking about the fact that the whitish-yellow powder had stolen years of his life and there had been a time when every waking hour was used to steal enough to get more for the next day. The rehab center, the fear, the prison sentence, the drug had been all-consuming and everything else meaningless until the morning she was suddenly standing in front of him. He had never injected since. She had forced him to hold on to her hand hard, as only people who trust each other can.

The cigar case was lying on the desk. The digital recorder beside it.

The document— I've read it. I assumed . . . I assumed that it concerned a . . . woman?

A recorder small enough to be transported in your anus.

Now it was voices on the computer.

That's my name, in here.

He copied the whole recording onto two separate CDs and put one in a brown and one in a white 8 × 10 envelope. He took down four passports from the top shelf in the gun cabinet, put three of them in the brown envelope and the fourth in the white envelope. Finally, he got out two small transmitters and two earpieces and put one in each envelope.

"It's me."

He had dialed the only number stored on the mobile phone.

"Hello."

"Västmannagatan. Your colleague's name, I've forgotten it. The guy who's investigating."

"Why?"

"Erik, I've only got thirty-five hours left."

"Grens."

"His whole name."

"Ewert Grens."

"Who is he?"

"I don't like the sound of this. What are you up to?"

"For Christ's sake, Erik. Who?"

"One of the older ones."

"Good?"

"Yes, he's good. And that makes me uneasy."

"What do you mean?"

"He's . . . he's the sort who doesn't give up."

Piet Hoffmann wrote the name on the front of the brown envelope in big, clear letters, then the address underneath in smaller letters. He checked the contents. A CD, three passports, one earpiece.

The sort who doesn't give up.

Erik Wilson enjoyed the last of the sun as it sank slowly into Lake Vättern. A moment of peace after Piet's strange phone call about Ewert Grens a short while ago, and before a meeting that would make an infiltrator even more dangerous. He had sensed the change hour by hour in recent days, how Piet retreated more and more. The last conversation he had had was with someone who could only be called Paula. He knew that it was necessary and even what he preached, but it still shocked him every time someone he liked became someone else.

He had walked the short distance from Jönköping station to the Swedish Court Administration offices on several occasions in recent years, and if he cut down along Järnvägsgatan and Västra Storgatan, he could be at the heavy entrance door in just five minutes.

He was there to manipulate the system.

And he was good at it, at recruiting people, regardless of whether it was someone serving a sentence who could be used to infiltrate other criminal networks or a civil servant who could be used to add or delete a line or two here and there in a database. He was good at making them feel important, getting them to believe that they were helping society, as well as themselves, good at smiling when necessary and laughing when necessary and ingratiating himself with the infiltrator and informer so that they liked him more than he would ever like them.

"Hi."

"Thank you so much for staying late."

She smiled, a woman in her fifties whom he had recruited several years ago in connection with a case in Göta Court of Appeal. They had met in the courtroom every day for a week, and over dinner one evening had agreed that her position gave her authority to make changes in the databases that might be of assistance to the Swedish police in their ongoing work to map organized crime.

They walked up the steps of the imposing court building together and she waved over to the security guard *I've got a visitor*, then they continued to Administration on the first floor. She sat down at her computer and he pulled over a chair from the neighboring empty desk and waited while she typed in her user name and password, and swiped a small plastic card along the top of her keyboard.

"Who?"

Her authorization card on a lanyard around her neck; she fiddled with it nervously.

"721018-0010."

He leaned his arm on the back of her chair. He knew she liked it.

"Piet Hoffmann?"

"Yes."

"Stockrosvägen 21, 122 32 Enskede."

He looked at the screen and the first page of the Swedish National Police Board's records for Piet Hoffmann.

```
1.SERIOUS FIREARMS OFFENSES 08-06-1998
CHAPTER 9, PART 1, SECTION 2 THE FIREARMS ACT

2.UNLAWFUL DISPOSAL 04-05-1998
CHAPTER 10, PART 4, SPC

3.UNLAWFUL DRIVING 02-05-1998
PART 3, SECTION 2 RTOA (1951:649)

IMPRISONMENT ONE (1) YEAR SIX (6) MONTHS

04-07-1998 SENTENCE COMMENCED
01-07-1999 RELEASED ON PAROLE
Remaining term of imprisonment six months
```

"I just want to make a couple of adjustments."

He might have touched her back as he leaned toward the screen. Never more than that, the illusion of togetherness. They both knew what it was about, but she let herself be fooled because she needed something that resembled human contact, and he pretended because he needed someone to work for him. They used each other in the same way that a police handler and informer did, a silent agreement that was never defined, but that was a prerequisite for wanting to meet in the first place.

"Adjustments?"

"I want you . . . to add just a few things."

He changed position, leaned back, his hand near her back again.

"Where?"

"The first page. The Österåker bit."

"Sentenced to one year and six months."

"Change it to five years."

She didn't ask why. She never did. She trusted him, trusted that the detective superintendent from the crime operations unit in Stockholm was sitting close to her in the best interests of society and crime prevention. Light fingers dancing on the keyboard as the line with ONE (1) YEAR SIX (6) MONTHS became FIVE (5) YEARS.

"Thank you."

"Is that all?"

"Next line. Convicted of serious firearms offenses. That's not enough. I want you to add a couple more offenses. Attempted murder. Aggravated assault on an officer."

Only one computer on, only one desk lamp on in the large room on the first floor of the National Courts Administration. Wilson was aware of the risk that the woman who had stayed late was taking; while her colleagues had left long ago and were now lounging around on sofas in living rooms watching TV, she weighed the feeling of being important against the risk of prosecution and gross document forgery.

"Now he's got a longer sentence and more *ratio decidendi*. Anything else?"

She printed off the relevant page of 721018-0010's criminal record and gave it to the man who was sitting so close and made her feel alive. She waited while he read and after a while seemed to lean in even closer.

"That's fine. For today."

Erik Wilson held two pieces of paper that made the difference between respect and suspicion. Within the first hour of being inside Aspsås Prison walls, Piet Hoffmann would have to prove his convictions to insistent fellow prisoners and doing five years for ATTEMPTED MURDER AND AGGRAVATED ASSAULT ON AN OFFICER was the same as getting the security classification: powerful and capable of killing, if necessary.

Paula would be seen as what he was pretending to be from the very minute he entered his cell.

Erik Wilson stroked the smiling woman on the arm, gave her a fleeting kiss on the cheek, and she was still smiling as he rushed away to get the late train back to Stockholm.

The house looked smaller as the dark started to gnaw at the corners.

The facade was leached of color, the chimney and new tiled roof sank lower over the upstairs windows.

Piet Hoffmann stood between the two apple trees in the garden and tried to see into the kitchen and sitting room. It was half past ten, it was late, but she was usually still up at this time, somewhere to be seen behind the white or blue curtains.

He should have phoned.

The meeting at Rosenbad had finished just after five and then spilled over into the three bunches of tulips from the flower shop and the CD copies of a recording made in a room at the Government Offices and two letters addressed to two people who would never receive them and then up into the dark loft again and eleven tins with eleven kilos of amphetamine in a bag and buds that two by two were first put in the oven, then the freezer before being put in the fridge and suddenly the evening had disappeared without him having called.

Thirty-three hours left.

He opened the front door that was locked. No TV humming in the sitting room, no light over the round table in the kitchen, no radio from the study and the slow P1 talk shows that she liked so much. He had come home to a hostile house, to reactions that he couldn't control and that scared him.

Piet Hoffmann swallowed the feeling of being so totally fucking alone.

He had actually always been lonely, never had many friends as he dropped them one by one because he didn't understand the point, didn't have many relatives as he lost touch with those who hadn't dropped him first. But this was a different loneliness, one that he hadn't chosen himself.

He turned the light on in the kitchen. The table was empty, no blobs of jam and crumbs from *just one more cookie*, it had been wiped in circles until everything had been cleaned off. If he leaned forward he could even see the stripes from a J-cloth on the shiny pine surface. They had sat there eating supper, just a few hours ago. And she had made sure that they finished their meals. He had not been there and wouldn't be part of it later either.

The vase was in the cupboard over the sink.

Twenty-five red tulips, he straightened the card, *I love you*, they would stand in the middle of the table where the card was visible.

He tried to put his feet down as quietly as possible on the stairs, but every tread creaked in warning and the ears that were listening would know he was near. He was frightened, not of the anger he would confront any minute now, but of the consequences.

She wasn't there.

He stood in the doorway and looked into an empty room. The bedspread was still on the bed and hadn't been touched. He continued on to Hugo's room and coughs from a throat that was only five years old and swollen. She wasn't there either.

One more room. He ran.

She was lying on the short, narrow bed snuggled close to their youngest son. Under the blanket, curled up. But she wasn't asleep, her breathing wasn't that regular.

"How are they?"

She didn't look at him.

"Have they still got a temperature?"

She didn't answer.

"I'm so sorry, I couldn't get away. I should have called, I know, I know that I should have."

Her silence. It was worse than everything else. He preferred open conflict.

"I'll look after them tomorrow. The whole day. You know that."

That damn silence.

"I love you."

The stairs didn't creak as much when he went down. His jacket was hanging on the coat rack in the hall. He locked the front door behind him.

Thirty-two hours and thirty minutes left. He wouldn't sleep. Not tonight. Not tomorrow night. He would have plenty of time to do that later, locked up in five square meters for two weeks on remand, on a bunk with no TV and no newspapers and no visitors, he could lie down then and close out all this shit.

Piet Hoffmann sat in the car while the rest of the street went to sleep. He often did this, counted slowly to sixty and felt his body relaxing limb by limb.

Tomorrow.

He'd tell her everything tomorrow.

The windows in the neighboring houses that shared his suburban life went black one by one. The blue light of a TV still shone upstairs at the Samuelssons' and the Sundells'; a light that changed from yellow to red in the Nymans' cellar window, where he knew one of their teenage sons had a room. Otherwise, night had fallen. One last look at the house and the garden he could touch if he wound down the window and stuck out his hand, he was sure of it, which were now blanketed in silence and blackness, not even the small lights in the sitting room were on.

He would tell her everything tomorrow.

The car crept along the small streets as he made two phone calls; the first about a meeting at midnight at number two, the second about another meeting later at Danviksberget.

He wasn't in a rush anymore. An hour to hang around. He drove toward the city, to Södermalm and the area around Hornstull, where he had lived for so many years when it was still a rundown part of town that the city suits sneered at if they happened to stray there. He parked down by the waterfront on Bergsunds Strand, by the beautiful old wooden bathhouse that some crazy people had fought so hard to pull down a few years back and was now a hidden gem in this hip area, where women could swim on Mondays and men on Fridays. It was warm, even though night was at hand, so he took off his jacket and walked along the asphalt, with his eyes on the luminous water that reflected the headlamps of the occasional car that crept down past the flats looking for a place to park.

A rather hard park bench for ten minutes, a slow beer at Gamla Uret where the bartender, whom Hoffmann knew from late nights in another life, had a very loud laugh, a couple of articles in a forgotten evening paper, oily fingers from the bowl of peanuts at the far end of the bar.

He had frittered away the hour.

He started to walk toward Högalidsgatan 38 and Heleneborgsgatan 9, and a flat on the second floor with an uneven parquet floor.

Erik Wilson was sitting on a plastic-covered sofa when the man who now could only be Paula opened the front door and crossed the water-damaged hall floor.

"It's not too late. To pull out. You know that."

He looked at him with something that resembled warmth, which he shouldn't do but that was the way it was. An infiltrator should be an instrument, something that he and the police authorities could use for as long as it was productive or simply abandon if things got too risky.

"You're never going to be particularly well paid. You'll never get any official thanks."

With Piet, though, or Paula, it was different. He had become something more. A friend.

"You've got Zofia. And the boys. I've no idea what that feels like, but . . . I think about it sometimes, long for it. And if I had . . . there's no bloody way that I'd risk it for someone who wouldn't even say thanks."

Wilson was very aware that right here, right now, he was doing something that he shouldn't. Giving a unique infiltrator an argument for backing out when the authorities needed him most.

"This time you're taking a risk that is far bigger than before. I said it yesterday in the tunnel on the way over from Rosenbad. *Piet, look at me when I'm talking.* I'll say it again. *Look at me!* The moment you've completed our mission, you'll be on Wojtek's hit list. Are you sure you understand what that means, really means?"

Nine years as an infiltrator. Piet Hoffmann looked at the plastic-covered furniture and chose a green, or possibly brown, armchair. No. He wasn't sure anymore that he did understand what it entailed or why they were in fact sitting here facing each other in a secret meeting place while his wife and children slept in a silent house. Sometimes it's just like that. Sometimes something starts and then carries on and days become months and years without you being able to reflect on it. But he remembered clearly why he said yes, and what they had said about a sentence that could instead be served with regular leave and then when he was released, a life where his criminal activity could be simplified, as long as he worked for the police they would turn a blind eye to his own criminal record, hide it away and make sure that the criminal operations unit and public prosecutor didn't bother him. It had all seemed so bloody simple. He hadn't even considered the lies, the danger of being exposed as a snitch, the lack of appreciation and protection. He didn't have a family then. He existed only for himself, and then barely.

"I'm going to finish this."

"No one will blame you if you pull out."

He'd started, and then continued. He'd learned to live for the kicks, for the adrenaline that forced his heart to explode in his chest, for the pride of knowing that he was better at this than anyone else, he who had never been best at anything.

"I'm not going to pull out."

He was addicted. He didn't know what life was like without the adrenaline, the pride.

"Well, we've talked about it openly then."

He was one of those people who had never managed to finish anything.

He was going to do it this time.

"I really appreciate you asking, Erik. I realize that it's not really your job. *But, yes, we have talked openly about this.*"

Erik Wilson had asked the question. And got the answer he wanted to have.

"In case anything should happen."

He changed his position on the uncomfortable plastic-covered sofa.

"If you're about to be exposed, you can't escape very far in a prison, but you can demand to be put in isolation."

Wilson looked at Paula, Piet.

"You might be given a death sentence. But you're not going to die. When you've asked to be put in isolation, once you have that protection, contact us and wait for a week. That's the time we'll need to get the papers sorted for someone to come and get you out."

He opened the black briefcase that was standing by his feet and put two folders on the coffee table between them. A new section from the Swedish National Police Board's criminal records and an equally new interrogation transcript which was now included in the documentation of a ten-year-old preliminary investigation.

INTERROGATING OFFICER JAN ZANDER (IO): A nine millimeter Radom.

PIET HOFFMANN (PH): Right.

IO: When you were arrested. Recently fired. Two bullets were missing from the magazine.

PH: If you say so.

Piet Hoffmann read through the amended documents in silence.

"Five years."

"Yes."

"Attempted murder? Aggravated assault on an officer?"

"Yes."

IO: Two shots. Several witnesses confirm it.

PH: (silence)

IO: Several witnesses in the block of flats on Kaptensgatan in Söderhamn whose windows face the lawn where you fired two shots at Constable Dahl.

PH: Söderhamn? There, I've never been there.

Erik Wilson had worked with each little piece in detail so that, all together, it would add up to a credible and tenable background.

"Does it— Do you think it'll work?"

Any change to a judgment in a criminal record always required a new hearing for the investigation that had once taken place, and new entries in the Prison and Probation Service files from the prison where the sentence was served, according to the changes.

"It works."

"According to the judgment and preliminary investigation records, you hit a police officer in the face three times with a loaded Radom pistol and didn't stop until he fell unconscious to the ground."

IO: You tried to kill a police officer on duty. One of my colleagues. I want to know why the hell you did that?

PH: Is that a question?

IO: I want to know why!

PH: I never shot at a policeman in Söderhamn. Because I never went to Söderhamn. But if I had been there and if I had shot at your colleague it would have been because I don't particularly like the police.

"You then turned the gun, cocked it, and fired two shots. One hit him in the thigh. The other in the left upper arm."

Wilson leaned back against the plastic.

"No one who looks at your background and has access to parts of your criminal record or the preliminary investigation will be in any doubt. I also added a note farther down about handcuffs. You were in handcuffs the whole time you were being questioned. For security reasons."

"That's good."

Piet Hoffmann folded together the two pieces of paper.

"Give me a couple of minutes. I just want to go through them once more. Then I'll know it."

He held the court judgment that had never been pronounced and the hearing that had never taken place, but still were his most important tools for carrying out his role in the prison corridors.

Thirty-one hours left.

thursday

THE BELLS IN BOTH TOWERS OF HÖGLID CHURCH STRUCK THE HOUR AFTER midnight as he left Erik Wilson and number two via the communal gardens and an entrance on Heleneborgsgatan. It was still unusually warm outside, whether it was the spring turning to summer or the kind of warmth that comes from inside when the body is tense. Piet Hoffmann took off his jacket and walked toward Bergsunds Strand and his car that was parked close enough to the water's edge for the headlights to illuminate the dark water when he started the engine. He drove from west to east Södermalm and the night, which should have been thronging with people who had longed for the warmth all winter and now didn't want to go home, was empty, the noisy town had fallen to rest. He accelerated after Slussen, along Stadsgårdskajen, then braked and turned off just before Danvikstull bridge and the municipal boundary with Nacka. Down Tegelviksgatan and then left into Alsnögatan to the barrier that blocked the only road up to Danviksberget.

He got out into the dark and jangled his keys until he found the piece of metal that was about half the size of a normal key; he'd carried it with him for a while now; they'd met fairly frequently in recent years. He opened and closed the barrier and drove slowly along the winding road up the hill to the outdoor café at the top that had been serving cinnamon buns with a view of the capital for decades now.

He stopped the car in a deserted lot and listened to the surf by the cliffs where the sea flowed into Saltsjön. A few hours earlier, customers would have sat here, holding hands while they talked or yearned or just drank their café lattes in the kind of silence that is shared. A forgotten coffee cup on a bench, a couple of plastic trays with crumpled napkins on another. He sat down by the building with its closed wooden shutters and a table chained to a lump of gray concrete. Piet Hoffmann looked out over the city where he had lived for the greater part of his life, but he still felt like a stranger, someone who was just visiting for a while and would soon move on, wherever it was he was actually going.

He heard footsteps.

Somewhere in the blackness behind him.

At first faint and far away, feet against a hard surface, then closer and clearer, gravel that loudly proclaimed how much the person walking on it was trying not to be heard.

"Piet."

"Lorentz."

A dark, solid man of his own age.

They embraced each other as usual.

"How much?"

The dark, solid man sat down in front of him, elbows heavy on the table which dipped slightly. They had known each other for exactly ten years. One of the few people he trusted.

"Ten kilos."

They had done time together at Österåker. Same unit, neighboring cells. Two men who became close in a way that they would never have done if they'd met anywhere else but there, cooped up and without much choice, they had become best friends, without realizing it at the time.

"Strength?"

"Thirty?"

"Factory?"

"Siedlce."

"Blossom. That's good. It's what they want. And I don't need to bullshit about the quality. But personally, I can't stand the smell."

Lorentz was the only name he would never give to Erik. He liked him. He needed him. Lorentz sold on what Piet had cut, to earn some money for himself.

"But thirty percent . . . too strong for Plattan and Centralen. No one there should have anything stronger than fifteen, otherwise there's just trouble. This— I'll sell it in the clubs, the kids want it strong and have the money to pay."

Erik had realized that there was someone whose name he was not going to get. And why. So Piet could continue to earn money from his own business and Erik and his colleagues turned a blind eye and sometimes even facilitated it, in exchange for continued infiltration.

"Ten kilos of thirty percent gear is a fuck of a lot. I'll take it, obviously. Like I always do when you ask. But—and now I'm talking to you as a friend, Piet—are you sure that you've got everything under control if anyone starts to ask questions?"

They looked at each other. The supposed question could be interpreted as something else. Distrust. Provocation. It wasn't. Lorentz meant exactly what he said and Piet knew that he was asking because he was concerned. Before, what he'd done was to cut a little more of the supplies that he got from somewhere to sell on somewhere else, for his own purposes. But this time he needed big money and for other reasons, so some of the vacuum-packed tins of uncut gear had been moved from the fan heater shaft to an IKEA bag only a few hours after Henryk's visit.

"I've got everything under control. And if I ever have to use the money from this lot one day, it'll be because it's too late to answer those questions."

Lorentz didn't ask any more.

He had come to understand that everyone had their reasons and made their choices and if they didn't want to talk about it, it was pointless trying.

"I'll deduct fifty thousand for the explosives. You gave me such goddamn short notice, Piet, that it cost more than usual."

One hundred kronor per gram. A million kronor for ten kilos.

Nine hundred fifty thousand in cash, the rest in explosives.

"You've got everything?"

"Pentyl."

"Not good enough."

"And nitroglycerine. High detonation velocity. Packed in plastic pockets."

"That's what I want."

"You'll get the detonator and fuse thrown in."

"If you insist."

"It's going to be a big fucking bang."

"Good."

"You're a law unto yourself, Piet."

The two cars were parked in the dark with open trunks when a blue IKEA bag with ten one-kilo tins of thirty percent amphetamine and a brown briefcase with 950,000 kronor in notes and two highly explosive packages swapped places. Now he had to move fast. He drove back down the narrow winding road from Danviksberget, opened the barrier with the key and carried on toward Enskede and the house that he constantly longed for.

It was too late by the time he realized he had driven over it. It was so dark in the driveway and the red plastic fire engine was impossible to see. Piet Hoffmann rolled forward about half a meter, and then got down on his hands and knees and felt around by the right front wheel until he found Rasmus's favorite car. It wasn't in the best condition, but if he used a red felt pen on the door to make it look like enamel and bent the white ladder that was supposed to be fixed to the middle of the roof back in shape, then maybe it could be returned to service in the sandpit or the floor upstairs within a few days.

They were in there, asleep. The other plastic fire engines. Under the beds, sometimes even in the beds of the two boys he was going to hug so hard in a few hours' time.

He opened the trunk and then the brown briefcase that was right at the back behind the spare wheel and hesitated before taking out two small packages and leaving the 950,000 kronor in notes untouched.

Slowly through the shadows in the garden.

He didn't turn on any lights until he was in the kitchen and had shut the door; he didn't want to wake Zofia with any irritating, unnecessary light, nor did he want to be caught out by naked feet on their way to the toilet or the fridge. He sat down at the table that had been wiped so well, the marks from the cloth still showing. In a few hours, they would eat breakfast here together, sticky, messy, and noisy.

The packages were lying in the middle of the table. He hadn't checked them, he never did. When they were from Lorentz, that was enough. He opened the first one, which looked like a thin pencil case, and took out a long cord. At least, that was what it seemed to be, like eighteen meters of thin, coiled cord. But for anyone who knew anything about explosives, it was something completely different. A pentyl fuse and the difference between life and death. He unwound it, felt it, then cut it in the middle and put back the two nine-meter lengths. The other package was square, a plastic sleeve with twenty-four small pockets, a bit like the ones that his dad had had in the green album where he kept his coins from the time he had called Königsberg his home, used coins that were of no particular value. Once, when his body was screaming for another fix, Piet had tried to sell them and had realized that the brown bits of metal that he had never been interested in were very worn and of no value to collectors other than his father, who saw a value that was connected to his memories from times gone by. He gingerly touched each little pocket, the transparent fluid inside, a total of four centiliters of nitroglycerine divided into twenty-four flat plastic pockets.

Someone let out a whimper.

Piet Hoffmann opened the door.

The same whimper again, then silence.

He started to go up the stairs. Rasmus was having a nightmare, but this time it disappeared without need for comfort.

So he went down instead, to the cellar and his personal gun cabinet that stood in one of the storerooms. He opened it and there they were, several on one shelf. He took one of them and went upstairs again.

The world's smallest revolver, SwissMiniGun, no bigger than a car key.

He had bought them direct from the factory in La Chaux-de-Fonds last spring, six-millimeter bullets in the miniature revolver's cylinder, each one powerful enough to kill. He rested the weapon on his palm and weighed it as he swung his arm backward and forward across the table—only a few grams were needed to end a life.

He closed the kitchen door for a second time and started to saw both ends of the trigger guard with a hacksaw blade—the metal band that ran around and protected the trigger was too small, he couldn't get his index finger in and he was removing it so he could squeeze the trigger and shoot—a couple of minutes was all that was needed for it to fall to the floor.

He then held the tiny gun with only two fingers, raised it and aimed at the dishwasher, pretending to fire.

A deadly weapon no longer than a toothpick, but still too big.

So he was going to divide it up into even smaller components with the minute screwdriver that reminded him of his granny in Kaliningrad, where she kept it in a drawer under her sewing machine that stood in the bedroom and seemed like a huge bit of furniture to a seven-year-old. First, with great care, he undid the screw on one side of the wooden butt, put it down on the white surface of the worktop so that he could see it—he mustn't lose it. The next screw was on the other side of the butt and closer to the hammer. Then with the point of the screwdriver against the pin in the middle of the revolver, he tapped it lightly a couple of times until it fell out and the toothpick-size gun broke up into six separate parts: the two butt sides, the revolver frame with the barrel and cylinder pivot and trigger, the cylinder with six bullets, the barrel protector, and a part of the frame that didn't have a name. He put each piece in a plastic bag and carried them out with eighteen meters of pentyl fuse and four centilitres of thinly packaged nitroglycerine, all of which was then placed on top of 950,000 kronor in a brown bag behind the spare tire in the trunk of the car.

Piet Hoffmann had sat on one of the kitchen chairs and watched the light force back the night. He had been waiting for her for hours, and now he heard her heavy tread on the wooden stairs, foot flat down on the surface in the way that she always did when she hadn't had enough sleep. He often listened to people's steps—they clearly reflected what was going on inside and it was always easier to work out how someone was feeling by closing his eyes when he or she approached.

"Good morning."

She hadn't seen him and she jumped when he spoke.

"Hi."

The coffee was already made, so he poured in just the amount of milk she liked in the morning. He carried the cup over to the beautiful and tousled and sleepy woman in a dressing gown, and she took it. Such tired eyes, she had been furious for half the night and then slept in a bed with a feverish child for the other half.

"You haven't slept at all."

She wasn't irritated, her voice didn't sound it, she was just tired.

"Just worked out that way."

He put some bread, butter, and cheese on the table.

"Their temperatures?"

"They've gone down. For the moment. A few more days at home, maybe just two."

More footsteps, much lighter, feet that were bright from the moment they left the bed and touched the floor. Hugo was oldest but still woke up first. Piet went over to him, picked him up, and kissed and squeezed his soft cheeks.

"You're prickly."

"I haven't shaved yet."

"You're more prickly than normal."

Bowls, spoons, glasses. They all sat down, Rasmus's chair still empty, but they would leave him to sleep as long as he needed to.

"I'll take them today."

She had expected him to say that. But it was hard. Because it wasn't true.

"The whole day."

The set table. Not so long ago, nitroglycerine had lain there beside some pentyl fuse and a loaded gun. Now it was laden with porridge and yogurt and crispbread. The cornflakes crunched noisily and some orange juice was spilled on the floor. They ate their breakfast as they usually did until Hugo banged his spoon down on the table.

"Why are you angry with each other?"

Piet exchanged glances with Zofia.

"We're not angry."

He had turned to his oldest son as he spoke and instantly realized that this five-year-old was not going to be satisfied with a platitude and therefore decided to hold his challenging eyes.

"Why are you lying? I can tell. You *are* angry."

Piet and Zofia looked at each other again and then she decided to answer.

"We *were* angry. But we're not anymore."

Piet Hoffmann looked at his son with gratitude and felt his shoulders dropping. He had been so tense, longing to hear those words, but he hadn't dared ask the question himself.

"Good. No one's angry. Then I want more bread and more cornflakes."

His five-year-old hands poured more cereal on what was already in his bowl and put some cheese on another slice of bread which then lay next to the first one that hadn't even been started yet. His parents chose not to say anything. This morning he was allowed to do as he pleased. He was wiser than they were right now.

He sat on the wooden step by the front door. She had just left. And he still hadn't said what he needed to say, it just hadn't worked out that way. Tonight. Tonight he would tell her. About everything.

He'd given Hugo and Rasmus a dose of Calpol as soon as her back had disappeared down the narrow path between the Samuelssons' and Sundells' houses. Then half a dose more. Thirty minutes later their temperatures had dropped and they were dressed and ready for nursery.

He had twenty-one and a half hours left.

*

Piet Hoffmann had ordered Sweden's most common car, a silver Volvo. It wasn't ready, neither cleaned nor checked. He didn't have time to spare, so instead chose a red Volkswagen Golf, Sweden's second-most common car.

Someone who doesn't want to be seen or remembered should stand out as little as possible.

He parked near the churchyard and fifteen hundred meters away from the enormous concrete wall. A long and open decline all the way down, meadows of grass that were green but not that tall yet. That was where he was going. Aspsås prison, one of the country's three high-security prisons. He was going to be arrested, held on remand, prosecuted, sentenced, and locked into a cell within the next ten, maybe twelve, or max fourteen days.

He got out of the car and squinted into the sun and wind.

It was going to be a beautiful day, but looking at a prison wall, all he could think of was hatred.

Twelve fucking months inside another all-encompassing concrete wall, the only emotion that was left.

He had for a long time thought it was simply the rebellion of a young person against everything that restricted or hemmed him in. It wasn't. He was no longer particularly young, but the feeling was just as potent when he looked at the wall. Hatred of the routines, the tyranny, the isolation, the locked doors, the attitudes, the work with square blocks of wood in the workshops, the suspicion, the secure transport, urine tests, body searches. Hatred of the screws, the pigs, uniforms, rules, whatever represented society, that bloody hatred that he'd shared with the others, the only thing they had in common, that and the drugs and the loneliness. That hatred had forced them to talk to each other, even to strive for something, rather strive for something that was driven by hatred than nothing at all.

This time he would be locked up because he wanted to be—no time to feel anything at all, he was there to complete something and then leave.

He stood by the rental car in the morning sun and light wind. In the distance, at one end of the high wall, he could see identical redbrick bungalows and a small town built up around the big prison. Those who didn't work as prison guards in the corridors worked in the construction company that repaired the floor in Block C, or the catering company that supplied the ready portions to the dining hall, or the electricians who adjusted the lighting in the yard. The people who lived in freedom on one side of the wall in Aspsås were completely dependent on those who were locked up on the other side.

I guarantee that you won't be charged for anything that happened at Västmannagatan 79.

The digital recorder was still in his trouser pocket. He had listened to her voice several times in the past few hours, his right leg and the microphone had been close to her and her words were clear and easy to understand.

I guarantee that we will do our best to help you complete your operation in prison.

He opened the gate. The path had been raked recently, his every step erasing the traces of a careful church warden. He looked at the graves that were well tended, simple headstones with small squares of grass, as if the people in the bungalows carried on living in the same way after death, with just enough distance between them not to interfere but close enough never to be alone, not too much and not too big, just a clearly marked separate space.

The churchyard was surrounded by a stone wall and trees that had been planted long ago and still stood at regular intervals, with enough space to allow for growth but still give the impression of a protective screen. Hoffmann went closer, sycamore maples with leaves that had just sprung and that moved in the breeze, which meant that the wind strength was between two and five meters a second. He looked at the small branches, they were moving too, between seven and ten meters a second. He tilted back his head, trying to see if the bigger branches were moving, some way to go before it was fifteen meters per second.

The heavy wooden door was open, and he entered a church that was too large: the white ceiling up high, the altar way back, it felt so big that the whole town of Aspsås could fit in the hard pews and there would still be space. One of those buildings from a time when power was measured in size.

The nave was empty except for the warden who was moving some wooden chairs from just by the christening font, silent apart from a scraping sound up in a gallery near the organ.

He went in and put a twenty-kronor note in one of the collection boxes on the table by the entrance, then nodded at the warden who had heard some movement and turned around. He went back out into the vestibule, waited until he was certain that he wasn't being watched before opening the gray door to the right.

He slipped in as quickly as he could.

The staircase was steep, with treads from a time when people were shorter. The door at the top swung open with a little pressure from a crowbar in the gap around the doorframe. The simple aluminum ladder leaned against a narrow hatch in the roof, the entrance to the church tower.

He stopped.

A sound made its way up. Muffled notes from the organ.

He smiled, the scraping that he had heard earlier in the nave from the gallery had been a cantor preparing the day's psalms.

The aluminum ladder swayed unsteadily when he pulled a pipe wrench from his bag and grabbed the hook of the padlock on the hatch. One firm thrust and it sprang open. He opened the hatch, climbed into the tower, and ducked down under the enormous cast-iron bell.

One more door.

He opened it and went out onto the balcony with a view that was so stunning that he was forced to stand still and follow the sky down to the woods and the two lakes and what looked like a rugged mountain in the far distance. With his hands on the rail, he inspected the balcony, which was not large—there was enough space to lie down. It was windier up here. The same wind that amused itself with leaves and small branches at ground level moved more freely here and the balcony shook when it was caught by a gust that tried to pull it along. He looked at the wall and the barbed wire and the buildings with bars on the windows. Aspsås prison was just as big and just as ugly from here and the view was uninterrupted, nothing in the way: it was possible to see every inmate in the heavily guarded prison yard, every pointless metal fence, every locked door in the concrete.

And . . . that we will look after you when the work is done. I know that you will then have a death threat on you, branded throughout the criminal world. We will give you a new life, a new identity, and money to start over again abroad.

The recorder was in his hand and her voice just as clear, despite the monotonous moan of wind.

I guarantee you this in my capacity as a state secretary of the Ministry of Justice.

If he succeeded.

If he carried out his work behind those walls down there exactly as they had planned, he would have a death sentence on him, he would have to get out, away.

He put down his shoulder bag and from the front pocket took out a thin black cable and two transmitters, both silver and about the size of a small coin, attached one transmitter to each end of the cable, which was about half a meter long, and fixed it to the outside of the railing with Blu-Tack, facing the prison, where it would be invisible to anyone standing on the church tower balcony.

He squatted down and with a knife cut off a couple of centimeters of the black protective covering on the cable to expose the metal wires so he could splice it to another piece of cable which he then also attached to the outside of the railing. He lay down, his body close to the railing, and wired that cable to what looked like a small piece of black glass.

Always alone.

He stuck his head out through the railings to check that the two cables, two transmitters, and solar cell were properly attached to the outside.

Trust only yourself.

The next time someone stood out here and spoke, he or she would do so without knowing that every word, every sentence could be heard by someone who had been sentenced to serve time down there, inside the walls of Aspsås prison.

He paused to look at the view again.

Two extremes, so close, so far apart.

If he stood on the church tower's windy balcony with his head cocked, he could see the glittering water and treetops and endless blue sky.

If he bent his head even farther, he met a separate world with a separate reality, nine square concrete buildings that from a distance looked like a collection of identical Lego pieces, where the most dangerous individuals in the country were crammed together and locked up with days that were totally predictable.

Piet Hoffmann knew that he would be given the job of cleaner in Block B, one of the conditions from the meeting at the Government Offices and one of the tasks that the general director of the Swedish Prison and Probation Service had been ordered to sort out. He concentrated therefore on the Lego piece that stood roughly in the middle of the world that was framed by a seven-meter-high wall and with binoculars studied, section by section, the building that he did not know yet but which in a couple of weeks' time would be his day-to-day reality. He picked out a window on the second floor, the workshop, the largest workplace for inmates at Aspsås who chose not to study. A window that was positioned near the roof, with reinforced glass and closely spaced metal bars, but with the binoculars he could still see several of the people in there working on the machines, faces and eyes that stopped every now and then to look out and yearn—so dangerous when all you could do was count the days and pass the time.

A closed system with no escape.
If I'm exposed. If I'm burned. If I'm alone.
He would no longer have any choice.
He would die.

He lay down on the balcony, crawled over to the railing holding an imaginary gun with both hands, and aimed at the window he had just decided on, on the second floor of Block B. He studied the trees by the churchyard wall—the wind had increased and the bigger branches were moving now.
Wind strength twelve meters per second. Adjust eight degrees to the right.
He aimed his imaginary gun at a head that was moving around inside the workshop window. He opened his bag and took out a rangefinder, aimed it at the same window.
He had already estimated the distance to be around fifteen hundred meters.
He checked the display, a hint of a smile.
It was exactly fifteen hundred and three meters from the balcony of the church tower to the reinforced window.
Distance fifteen hundred and three meters. Clear view. Three seconds from firing to impact.
His hands gripped the nonexistent gun hard.

It was five to ten when he walked back past the graves and protecting sycamore trees, down the neatly raked gravel path to the car that was parked outside the gate. He was on schedule—he had managed to sort out what he had to at the church and would be the first customer in Aspsås library when it opened.

A separate building on the square, tucked between the bank and the supermarket, a librarian in her fifties who was as friendly as she looked.

"Can I help you?"

"In a moment. I just want to check some titles."

A children's corner with cushions and small chairs and Pippi Longstocking books stacked in equal piles, three plain tables for anyone who wanted to study or just read for a while in peace, a sofa with headphones for listening to music and computers for surfing the Internet. It was a nice little library, quiet with a prevailing atmosphere of meaningful time in contrast to the prison wall that dominated the view through each window, signaling trouble and detention.

He sat down at one of the screens by the lending desk and searched in the library catalogue. He needed the titles of six books and looked for ones that presumably had not been borrowed for a long time.

"Here."

The friendly librarian looked at his handwritten list.

Byron *Don Juan*
Homer *The Odyssey*
Johansson *Nineteenth Century Stockholm*
Bergman *The Marionettes*
Bellman *My Life Writings*
Atlantis Collection of World Literature *The French Landscape*

"Poetry . . . and titles which . . . no, I don't think we'll find any of them up here."

"I thought as much."

"It will take a while to get them up."

"I need them now."

"Well, I'm on my own here and . . . they're in storage. That's what we do with books that are not borrowed very often."

"I would really appreciate it if it was at all possible to get them now. I don't have that much time."

She gave a sigh, a little one, like someone who has been asked to do something that is a problem, but also actually a joy.

"Well, you're the only one here at the moment. And I'm sure there won't be many more in until just before lunch. I'll go down to the basement if you could just keep an eye on things for me here."

"Thank you so much. Only hardback copies, please."

"I'm sorry?"

"Not paperback or those flimsy bindings."

"Paper bindings? They're cheaper for us to buy. And the content is the same."

"Hardbacks, please. It's the way I read. Or rather, where I read."

Piet Hoffmann sat down on the librarian's chair by the lending desk and waited. He had been here before and borrowed books that weren't popular and were therefore kept in storage in the basement as he had in several other libraries in the small communities close to the country's high-security prisons. He had borrowed books from Kumla public library, whose customers included the inmates of Kumla prison, and Södertälje public library, which had had customers from Hall prison for many years. And when prisoners inside the walls that were only a few hundred meters from the library ordered their books, they were always collected from here, Aspsås library, and what's more, if they were titles from storage, the borrower could be certain to get precisely the book he had ordered.

She was out of breath when she opened the heavy door up from the basement.

"Steep stairs."

She smiled.

"I guess I should perhaps jog a bit more."

Six books on the lending desk.

"Are these okay?"

Hardbacks. Big. Heavy.

"Tulips and poetry."

"Excuse me?"

"Perfect, just as I like them."

The square was windy, relatively sunny, nearly empty. An old lady with a walker labored over the cobbles, a man of roughly the same age with plastic bags on the handlebars of his bike was rummaging in a garbage can with both hands, looking for empty bottles. Piet Hoffmann drove slowly out of the small town, which he would return to in ten days' time, in handcuffs and a secure police van.

"I still want to know how."

"We've already done this three times before."

A closed system with no escape.

An exposed infiltrator, a snitch, as hated in prison corridors as perverts, pedophiles, or rapists, always at the bottom of the hierarchy that ruled in European prisons, which gave murderers and major drug dealers their status and power.

"Officially, you will be pardoned. On humanitarian grounds. That doesn't need to be explained in any more detail. Medical or humanitarian grounds are sufficient for a decision that the Ministry of Justice will then stamp as confidential."

If anything happened. Her promise was all that he had. That, and the things he had prepared himself.

He looked at the clock on the dashboard. Eighteen hours to go.

A few miles out of Stockholm, driving slightly too fast through sleepy suburbs, one of his two mobile phones rang. An irritated woman's voice, one of the nursery teachers from Hagtornsgården.

Both boys had a temperature.

He drove toward Enskededalen, it was his turn today and the Calpol had stopped working.

A wise woman, a couple of years younger than he was, Hugo and Rasmus had always been safe with her.

"I don't understand it."

The same woman who had phoned him only a couple of days ago about two sick little boys. Now she was sitting in front of him in the office, frowning at him while two warm children waited on a bench out in the playroom.

"That you . . . both of you . . . it's just not like you, after all these years, you, if anyone, just wouldn't play that stupid Calpol trick. I just don't understand."

"I'm not quite sure what you're—"

He had started to defend himself as he always did when someone accused him of something. But then stopped. This was not an interrogation, the nursery teacher was not the police, and he was not suspected of a crime.

"We have rules here. You know them. You both know them. Rules that say when a child is welcome and when he or she is not. This is a workplace, a workplace for adults, and for your children and other people's children."

He was ashamed and didn't answer.

"And what's more— Piet, it isn't good for the children. It's not good for

Hugo or Rasmus. You can see for yourself how they look. Being here when their little bodies are overheated . . . it could have other, more serious consequences. Do you understand that?"

When a person crosses a boundary he promised never to cross.

Who is he then?

"I understand and it will never happen again."

They flopped on his shoulders as he carried them out to the car. They were hot and he kissed their foreheads.

One more time. Just one more time.

He explained to them what they had to do. They had to get better. He gave them each a dose of Calpol.

"I don't want it."

"Just one more time."

"It's yucky."

"I know. This is the last time. I promise."

He kissed them on the forehead again and started to drive in a direction that Hugo realized was not home.

"Where are we going?"

"To Daddy's office. We'll just be there for a little while. Then we're done. Then we can go home."

A couple of minutes' drive up the main road into the city via Skanstull and Söderleden; he switched lanes in the tunnel under Södermalm and drove toward Hornsgatan and the road down to Mariatorget. He parked outside the video shop that was squeezed between the supermarket and bowling alley, rushed in, keeping his eyes on the backseat of the car through the window, and picked out three videos: twelve episodes of *Winnie the Pooh*. The children knew all the lines by heart already, but it was one of the few he could cope with. The sound wasn't as hysterical as most others: adults as cartoon characters shouting in falsettos, pretending to be children.

The next time he stopped was right outside the door on Vasagatan. Hugo and Rasmus were still just as hot and tired and he wanted them to walk as little as possible. They had been with him to Hoffmann Security AB before, several times in fact, curious as children always are about where Mommy and Daddy work, but never when he was actually working—for them it was just a place where Daddy went while he waited for his children to finish playing at nursery.

Half a liter of vanilla ice cream, two big glasses of Coke and twelve episodes of waddling *Winnie the Pooh*. He set them up in the spacious office in front of the TV screen with their backs to the desk and explained that he had to go up to the loft for a few minutes, but they didn't hear him, they were busy watching something about Rabbit and Eeyore and a wooden cart that they wanted Pooh to sit in. Piet Hoffmann got three tins out of the fan heater, carried them down and put them on the floor, cleared his desk so he would have space to work.

Six books that belonged to Aspsås library that were seldom asked for and therefore had a note stuck on the front page, STORAGE, in blue print.

A plastic bag with a disassembled miniature revolver.

Some pentyl fuse that had been cut into two nine-meter lengths.

A plastic sleeve with four centilitres of nitroglycerine divided up into twenty-four pockets.

A tin of thirty percent amphetamine.

He took a tube of glue from the drawer of the desk, a packet of razorblades, and a packet of Rizla papers, thin with a sticky edge, generally used by people who like rolling their own cigarettes.

Tulips.

And poetry.

He opened the first book. Lord Byron's *Don Juan*. It was perfect. Five hundred forty-six pages. Hardback. Eighteen centimeters long, twelve wide.

He knew it would work. Over the past ten years, he had prepared a couple of hundred novels, poetry, and essay collections to hold ten to fifteen grams of amphetamine, and been successful each time. Now, for the first time, he would borrow the modified books himself and empty them in a cell in Aspsås prison.

I need three days to knock out the competition. During that time I don't want to have any contact and it's my responsibility to take in enough gear.

He opened the front cover and with a razorblade cut through the hinge until it loosened and the spine of five hundred forty-six pages of *Don Juan* was revealed, then he tidied up the loose ends with the blade. He flicked through to page 90, held all the pages together and with a strong hand ripped them off and put them down on the desk. Then he flicked to page 390 and ripped off the next thick pile.

It was these pages, from 91 to 390, he was going to work with.

With a pencil he drew a rectangle that was fifteen centimeters long and one centimeter wide in the left-hand margin of page 91. Then, with the razor blade, he cut along the lines, deeper and deeper, millimeter by millimeter until he had cut through the whole pile, three hundred pages. His hand worked the razor blade well and even the slightest unevenness and loose strip was shaved off. He lifted the middle section of the book, which now had a new hole that was fifteen centimeters long, one centimeter wide and three centimeters deep, back into place and glued it together. He felt the edges with his fingertips, there was still some unevenness, so he lined the walls with Rizla papers. If he was going to fill it with amphetamine, it was important that the surfaces were even, and there was space for fifteen grams in this book, as it was particularly thick.

The first ninety pages were still intact and he put them back where they should be, over the hole, glued them to the spine and the loose front board and then pressed Lord Byron's classic hard against the desk with both hands until he was certain that every page was glued in place.

"What are you doing, Daddy?"

Hugo's face peered at him from behind his elbow, close to the recently prepared book.

"Nothing. Just reading a bit. Why don't you watch the show?"

"It's finished."

He stroked Hugo's cheek and got up; there were two more films, Winnie the Pooh had to eat more honey and get more scoldings from Rabbit before he was finished with everything.

Piet Hoffmann prepared *The Odyssey*, *My Life's Writings*, and *French Landscape* in the same way. In two weeks' time, an inmate serving time at Aspsås prison who was interested in literature would be able to borrow as many as four books, containing a total of forty-two grams of amphetamine.

Two books left.

With a new razorblade, he cut a rectangular hole in the left-hand margin of *Nineteenth Century Stockholm* and *The Marionettes*. In the first, he put the pieces of what a reader, who knew how, might be able to reassemble into a miniature revolver; the hardest piece was the cylinder loaded with six bullets, which was wider than he thought, but he managed to press it down carefully into the cavity by taking off some of the Rizla papers. A gun with the power to kill if the bullet hit its target. He had seen one for the first time six months ago in Świnoujście, when a wired mule had tried to throw up 2,500 grams of heroin in the toilet at the ferry terminal, before even boarding the boat. Mariusz had opened the door to see the mule lying on the floor with a plastic bag to his mouth and he hadn't said a word, just moved in sufficiently close and aimed the short barrel at one of his eyes and killed him with one bullet. In the second hole, in the last book, he put a detonator the size of a large nail and a receiver the size of a penny—the kind that you put in your ear to receive and listen to sounds from two transmitters that are attached with Blu-Tack to the railings on a church tower balcony.

Two nine-meter pieces of pentyl fuse and a plastic envelope with twenty-four centilitres of nitroglycerine were still left on the desk. He took a furtive glance over at two small backs that were watching a cartoon about a fat bear. They laughed suddenly, a jar of honey had gotten stuck on Pooh's head. Hoffmann went out into the kitchen, opened another tub of ice cream, and put it down on the table between them, stroked Rasmus on the cheek.

It was going to be hardest to hide the pentyl fuse and plastic sleeve with nitroglycerine without anything showing.

He chose the largest book, *Nineteenth Century Stockholm*, twenty-two centimeters long and fifteen centimeters wide. He cut open the front and back of the library cover and pulled out the porous paperlike filling and replaced it with the explosive and fuse, glued it up again, tidied the edges and then leafed through all six books to make sure that the hinges were properly glued and it wasn't possible to see any of the rectangular holes.

"What's that?"

Hugo's face popped up over the top of the desk again. The second video had finished.

"Nothing."

"What *is* that, Daddy?"

He pointed at the shiny metal tin full of thirty percent amphetamine.

"That? Oh . . . just grape sugar."

Hugo stood there, he was in no hurry.

"Don't you want to watch the rest? There's another video."

"I will in a minute. There's two letters there, Daddy. Who are they to?"

Inquisitive eyes had spotted the two envelopes that were lying high up in the open gun cabinet.

"I'm not going to send them."

"But they've got names on them."

"I'll finish them later."

"What do they say?"

"Shall I put the video on now?"

"That's Mommy's name. On the white one. It looks like it. And the one on the brown one starts with an E, I can see that too."

"Ewert. His name's Ewert. But I don't think he'll get it."

The ninth part of *Winnie the Pooh* was about Piglet's birthday and an outing with Christopher Robin. Hugo sat down beside Rasmus again and Piet Hoffmann checked the contents of the brown envelope—a CD of the recording, three passports, and a transmitter—stamped it and put it in his brown leather bag along with the six prepared books from Aspsås library. Then, to the white envelope which Hugo had noticed had Zofia's name on it—a CD, the fourth passport, and a letter with instructions—he now added 950,000 kronor, in notes, and put the envelope in his brown leather bag along with the rest.

Fifteen hours left.

He stopped *Winnie the Pooh*, helped the two children who were starting to heat up again put their shoes on, then went into the kitchen and the fridge and put fifty tulips with green buds into a cool box and carried this and the leather bag and two boys downstairs to the car that was parked right outside the front door, with a parking ticket tucked under the windshield wiper.

He looked at the two red faces in the backseat.

Two more stops.

Then he would put them to bed, with clean sheets, and sit there and watch them until Zofia came home.

They lay in the car while he went into the Handelsbanken branch on Kungsträdgårdsgatan, and down into the basement and a room full of rows of safe deposit boxes. He opened the empty box with one of his two keys and put in one brown envelope and one white envelope, locked it and emerged from the building a couple of minutes later, got in the car and drove to Hökens Gata on Södermalm.

He looked at them again—he was so ashamed.

He had overstepped the boundary. The two boys whom he loved more than anything in the backseat, and amphetamine and nitroglycerine in the trunk.

He swallowed, they weren't going to see him crying, he didn't want them to.

He parked as close to the entrance to Hökens Gata 1 as he dared. Number four, fifteen hundred hours. Erik had already gone in from the other door.

"I don't want to walk anymore."

"I know. Just here, then we'll go home. I promise."

"My legs hurt. Daddy, they really, really hurt."

Rasmus had sat down on the first step. His hand was warm when Piet took it, he lifted him up on one arm, with the cool box and leather bag in the other hand. Hugo would have to walk up the stairs himself, like you sometimes do when you're the oldest.

Three floors up, the door with LINDSTRÖM on the letter box opened from the inside at exactly the same time that his watch alarm started to bleep.

"Hugo. Rasmus. This is Uncle Erik."

Small hands were held out and shaken, he felt Erik Wilson's withering look: *What the hell are they doing here?*

They went into the plastic-wrapped sitting room of the flat that was being renovated, and despite being tired, they looked curiously around at all the strange furniture.

"Why is there plastic everywhere?"

"There's work being done."

"What do you mean, work?"

"They're making the flat new and they don't want things to get dirty."

He left them in the rustling sofa and went into the kitchen, and another piercing look. He cocked his head.

"I didn't have a choice."

Wilson didn't say anything—it was as if he'd lost track when he saw two children in a world that dealt in life and death.

"Have you spoken to Zofia?"

"No."

"You have to speak to her."

He didn't answer.

"Piet, you can make all the excuses in the world. You know that you have to. Jesus Christ, you have to fucking talk to her, man!"

Her reactions, the ones he couldn't control.

"This evening. When the boys have gone to bed. I'll talk to her then."

"You can still back out."

"You know I'm going to finish this."

Erik Wilson nodded and looked at the blue cool box that Piet lifted onto the table.

"Tulips. Fifty. They'll be yellow."

Wilson stared at the green stems and green buds that were lying among the white, square ice packs.

"I'll put them in the fridge. It should be about 35 degrees. I want you to look after them. And the same day that I go in through the gate of Aspsås prison, I want you to send them to the address I give you."

Wilson put his hand into the cool box and flipped over one of the white cards with the bouquet.

"With thanks for a successful partnership, Aspsås Business Association."

"Correct."

"And where should they be sent?"

"Aspsås prison. The chief warden."

Erik Wilson didn't ask anymore questions. It was better not to know.

"How much longer do we have to wait?"

Hugo had grown bored of sliding his fingers over the plastic and making it rustle.

"Just a little while. Go back in to Rasmus. I'll be there in a minute."

Wilson waited until the small feet had disappeared into the gloom of the hall.

"You'll be arrested tomorrow, Piet. After that, we'll have no contact whatsoever. You won't communicate with me or anyone else from the city police. Until you're ready and you tell us that you want out. It's too dangerous. If anyone suspects that you're working for us . . . you're dead."

Erik Wilson walked down the corridor in Homicide. He was uneasy and slowed down outside Ewert Grens's office, as he had done every time he went past in recent days, curious eyes peering into the empty office and the music that was no longer there. He wondered what the detective superintendent who was investigating the murder in Västmannagatan was up to, what he knew, how long it would take before he started asking the questions that no one could answer.

Wilson sighed, it didn't feel right, those children, they were so young. It was his job to encourage infiltrators to take big risks to get the information that the police depended on, but he wasn't sure that Piet had fully understood what he had to lose. They had gotten too close, he genuinely cared about him.

If anything happens, abort.

If anyone discovers who you are, you have a new mission.

To survive.

Wilson closed the door to his office and turned on his computer, which was not connected to the Internet for security reasons. He had explained to Piet, while the two boys pulled at their dad's arms, that he would go back to FLETC and southern Georgia in the meantime, to finish what he had been forced to interrupt a couple of days ago. He was not convinced that the man in front of him had actually been listening; he had said yes and he had nodded, but he was already on his way home to his last night of freedom for a long time. The computer screen was filled with an empty document and Erik Wilson started to write an intelligence report for the county commissioner, via Chief Superintendent Göransson, which would then be deleted from his own hard disk: a background report for the arrest of a wanted and violent criminal with three kilos of Polish amphetamine in his car trunk, a report that would not be delivered until tomorrow, as it had not happened yet.

He had waited on his own by the kitchen table for two hours.

A beer, a sandwich, a crossword, but he hadn't drunk, eaten, or written anything.

Hugo and Rasmus had gone to sleep upstairs a long time ago. They had had pancakes with strawberry jam and too much whipped cream first and then he had put them to bed and opened their windows and watched them fall asleep after only a few minutes.

He heard them now, the steps that he knew so well.

Through the garden, up the front steps and then the creak as the door opened and he felt a tightening in the pit of his stomach.

"Hi."

She was so beautiful.

"Hi."

"Are they asleep?"

"Have been for a couple of hours."

"And how's the temperature?"

"It'll be gone tomorrow."

She gave him a light kiss on the cheek and smiled, she didn't notice that the world was about to fall to pieces.

Another kiss, on the other side, twice, as always.

She didn't notice that the damn floor was heaving.

"We have to talk."

"Now?"

"Now."

A slight sigh.

"Can't it wait?"

"No."

"Tomorrow? I'm so tired."

"By then it'll be too late."

She went upstairs to change, soft trousers and the thick sweater with too-long sleeves. She was all he had ever wanted and she looked at him in silence as she curled up in the corner of the sofa and waited for him to start talking. He had thought of making food with a strong scent of either India or Thailand, opening a bottle of expensive red wine and then starting to tell her, gently, after a while. But he had realized that what was false and had to be explained became even falser when it was disguised by enjoyment and intimacy. He leaned forward, hugged her—she smelled good, she smelled of Zofia.

"I love you. I love Hugo. I love Rasmus. I love this house. I love knowing that there's someone who calls me *my husband* and someone else who calls me *Daddy*. I didn't know it was possible. I've gotten used to it, I'm completely dependent on it now."

She pulled herself into a ball even more and withdrew farther into the corner of the sofa. She could tell that he'd been rehearsing what he had to say.

"I want you to listen to me, Zofia. But most of all, I want you to sit there and not leave until I have finished."

He always knew more about every situation than those he would later share it with. If he was more prepared, he would have more control and someone who has control is always the one who decides.

Not now.

Her feelings, her reactions, they scared him.

"Then— Zofia, you can do what you like. Listen to me and then do what you want."

He sat opposite her and in a quiet voice, started to tell a story about a prison sentence ten years ago, about a policeman who had recruited him as an infiltrator and about continued criminal activity and the police who turned a blind eye, about a Polish mafia organization called Wojtek, about secret meetings in flats that were being renovated, that she had dropped off her husband and collected him from a shell company that he had called Hoffmann Security AB, about a fabricated criminal record and suspect database and prison records that described him as extremely violent and classified him as psychopathic, that the illusion that was one of Sweden's most dangerous men would be arrested tomorrow morning at six thirty in a pool hall in central Stockholm, about the expected trial and outcome, a sentence with years in prison, a life behind high walls that would start in about ten days and continue for two months, about having to look his wife and children in the eye each day and know that their trust and confidence were built on a lie.

friday

THEY HAD LAIN BESIDE EACH OTHER IN BED AND TRIED VERY HARD TO avoid touching.

She had been completely still.

Now and then he had stopped breathing, scared that he might not hear what she didn't say.

He sat on the edge of the bed, knew that she was awake, that she was lying there looking at his false back. He had continued to talk as they shared a cheap bottle of wine and when he was done, she just got up, disappeared into the bedroom and turned off the light. She hadn't spoken, screamed, only silence.

Piet Hoffmann got dressed, suddenly in a hurry to get away—it wasn't possible to stay with the nothingness. He turned around and they looked at each other without saying anything until he gave her a key to a safe deposit box in the Handelsbanken branch on Kungsträdgårdsgatan. If she still wanted to share a life together she should go there if he contacted her and said that everything had kicked off. She should open the safe deposit box and she would find one brown and one white envelope and she should do exactly what the handwritten letter instructed her to do. He wasn't sure if she had listened, her eyes had been distant, and he fled to the two small heads that were sleeping on two small pillows and he breathed in the smell of them and stroked them on the cheek and then left the house in the residential area that was still fast asleep.

Two and a half more hours. His face in the rearview mirror. A dark chin with salt-and-pepper stubble that was even more obvious on his cheeks—he had been a much younger man the last time he had stopped shaving. It itched a little, it always did to begin with, and then the straggled hair. He tugged at it, not much better really, it was actually too thin to grow.

He would be arrested soon, transported in a police van to Kronoberg remand prison, be issued with baggy prison clothes.

He drove through the dawn, his final trip to a small town to the north of Stockholm with a church and a library that he had visited less than twenty-four hours ago. The weak light and confused wind were his only companions in the square at Aspsås; not even the magpies and pigeons and the bum who usually slept on one of the benches were there. Piet Hoffmann opened the returns box to the right of the library entrance and dropped in six books that were not borrowed often enough to merit being visible on the shelves. He then continued on to the church that took up so much space with its white facade, into the churchyard that was blanketed in a soft mist, and looked up at the church tower that had a view over one of the country's high-security prisons. He picked the locks of the solid wooden door and the considerably smaller door just inside and went up the uneven steps and an aluminum ladder to a closed hatch just under a cast-iron bell that must weigh several hundred kilos.

Nine square concrete buildings inside substantial walls, which looked more like Lego blocks in their own world than ever before.

He looked toward the window he had chosen and aimed at it with an imagined gun, then took a silver receiver from his pocket—an earpiece identical to the one that was now hidden in a cavity in the left-hand margin of *The Marionettes*. He leaned over the railing, for a moment feeling like he might fall to the ground, and he held on to the iron railing with one hand while he checked that the two transmitters, a black cable, and a solar cell were still properly fixed where they should be. He put the receiver in his ear and one finger on a transmitter and ran it lightly back and forth—a crackling and snapping in his ear told him it was working fine.

He went down again, to the graves that lay side by side, but not too close, to the mist that blotted out death.

A merchant and his wife. A senior pilot and his wife. A mason and his wife. Men who had died as titles and professions and women who had died as the wives of their betitled husbands.

He stopped in front of a stone that was gray and relatively small and the resting place of a captain. Piet Hoffmann saw his father, the way he imagined him at least, the simple boat that had gone out from the border area between Kaliningrad and Poland and disappeared with its fishing nets over the Danzig Bay and Baltic Sea for weeks on end, his mother who later stood there and watched the slow progress into shore and then ran down to the harbor and his father's embrace. That wasn't how it had been. His mother had often talked about the empty nights and the long wait, but never about running feet and open arms. That was the picture he had painted for himself when he, as a child, had asked curious questions about their lives in another time, and it was the image he chose to keep.

A grave that hadn't been looked after for years. Moss crept over the corners of the stone and the small bed was overgrown with weeds. That was the one he was going to use. *Captain Stein Vidar Olsson and wife. Born 3 March 1888. Died 18 May 1958.* He had lived to be seventy. Now he was not even a gravestone that people came to visit. Piet Hoffmann held his mobile phone in his hand, his contact with Erik that would be cut in less than two hours. He turned it off, wrapped it in plastic wrap, put it in a plastic bag, got down on his knees and started to dig up the earth with his hands at the bottom right of the headstone, until he had a sufficiently large hole. He looked around, no other dawn visitors in the churchyard, dropped the telephone into the ground and covered it with earth and then hurried back to the car.

Aspsås church was still veiled in morning mist. The next time he would see it would be from the window of a cell in a square concrete building.

He'd managed it. He'd finished all his preparations. Soon he would be entirely on his own.

Trust only yourself.

He missed her already. He had told her and she hadn't said a word, somehow like being unfaithful—he would never touch another woman, but that was how it felt.

A lie that was never ending. He, if anyone, knew all about it. It just changed shape and content, adapted to the next reality and demanded a new lie so that the old one could die. In the past ten years he had lied so much to Zofia and Hugo and Rasmus and all the others that when this was all over, he would have forever moved the boundary between lies and truth; that was how it was, he could never be entirely sure where the lie ended and the truth began, he didn't know any longer who he was.

He made a sudden decision. He slowed down for a few kilometers and let it sink in that this really was the last time. He had had a feeling all year and now it had caught up with him, now he could feel it again and interpret it. That was how he worked. At first something vague that tugged at him somewhere in his body, then a period of restlessness when he tried to understand what it meant, then insight, a sudden, powerful understanding that had been so close for so long. He would sit out this sentence at Aspsås and he would finish his work there, and after that, never again. He had done his service for the Swedish police, for little thanks other than Erik's friendship and ten thousand kronor a month from their reward money, so that he didn't officially exist. He was going to live another life later, when he knew what a true life really looked like.

Half past five. Stockholm was starting to wake up. There were only a few cars on the road, the odd person rushing to catch a train or bus. He parked on Norrtullsgatan opposite the primary school and opened the door to a café that opened early and served porridge and stewed apples and a cheese sandwich and an egg and black coffee on a red plastic tray for thirty-nine kronor. He saw Erik as soon as he walked in, a face over by the newspaper stand that disappeared behind *Dagens Nyheter* in order to avoid eye contact. Piet Hoffmann ordered his breakfast and chose a corner on the other side of the room as far away from him as he could get. There were six other customers: two young men from a construction site in high-viz jackets and four considerably older men dressed in suits, with their hair combed for the only fixed point in the day. Breakfast cafés often looked like this, men who didn't have anyone and fled the loneliness of eating alone—women seldom did that, maybe they coped with loneliness better than men, maybe they were more ashamed and didn't want to make it public.

The coffee was strong and the porridge was a bit lumpy, but it would be the last meal for a while where he could decide what he wanted, how he wanted it and where he wanted it. He had avoided the breakfasts at Österåker, too early in the day to eat with people whose only common reference point was the need for drugs, the sort he'd been afraid of, but had met with aggression, scorn, distance, anything that didn't resemble weakness, in order to survive.

Erik Wilson walked past his table on his way out, nearly bumped into it. Hoffmann waited exactly five minutes and then followed, a couple of minutes' walk to Vanadisvägen. He opened the door of a silvery-gray Volvo and sat down in the passenger seat.

"You came in the red Golf, the one that's parked by the school?"

"Yes."

"From the OK gas station at Slussen, like normal?"

"Yep."

"I'll take it back this evening. You might find it hard to deliver it yourself."

They pulled out of Vanadisvägen, drove slowly along Sankt Eriksgatan, and didn't say anything between the first two sets of red lights on Drottningholmsvägen.

"Have you got everything sorted?"

"Sorted."

"And Zofia?"

Piet Hoffmann didn't answer. Wilson stopped the car by a bus stop on Fridhemsplan, made it clear that he wasn't going any farther.

"And Zofia?"

"She knows."

They sat there at the start of the morning rush, with groups of people or long lines on the move now, rather than just the odd person.

"I made you even more dangerous in ASPEN yesterday. The patrol that arrests you will be full of preconceived ideas and adrenaline. It'll be violent, Piet. You can't be armed, because then it might get really nasty. But no one, no one who sees it, no one who hears about it or reads about it will even suspect who you're actually working for. And by the way, there's a warrant out for your arrest."

Piet Hoffmann started.

"A warrant? Since when?"

"A few hours ago."

The place still smelled of cigarette smoke. Or perhaps he just imagined it. There had always been a funk above the green felt. Piet Hoffmann leaned down toward it and sniffed, and he caught it again, the smell of smoke that was indelibly linked to the blue chalk on your fingertips and ashtrays on the corner of every pool table . . . he could even hear the coarse, sneering laughter when someone missed and a hard ball misfired. He downed half the cup of black coffee from the 7-Eleven on Fleminggatan in one gulp and looked at the clock. It was time. He checked again that the knife that he usually kept in his back pocket really wasn't there and then walked over to the window that looked out over Sankt Eriksgatan. He stood still, pretending to talk to someone on his mobile phone until he was sure that the man and the woman in the front of the patrol car had seen him.

They had been tipped off by an anonymous untraceable phone call that a serious, wanted criminal was going to be in Biljardpalatset this morning.

And then there he was in the window.

They had his name, and when they pressed enter again on the car computer keypad, they also got his life.

KNOWN DANGEROUS ARMED

They were both young and new and had never come across this particular code in the criminal intelligence database that was only used for a handful of criminals.

```
Name Piet Hoffmann
ID number 721018-0010
Number of hits 75
```

They skimmed down quickly, got the clear picture that this person was extremely dangerous *observed fifteen minutes before the murder in Östling in the company of the suspect, Marković* and familiar with weapons *observed near the property that was raided in connection with suspected arms dealing* and had previously threatened and fired at and wounded policemen and was likely to be armed.

"Command, this is car 9027. Over."

"This is command. Over."

"We require backup for immediate arrest."

He heard the sirens closing in between the city buildings and guessed that the sound and blue flashing lights would be turned off somewhere on Fleminggatan.

Two dark blue police vans stopped outside fifteen seconds later.

He was prepared.

"This is car 9027. Over."

"Describe the suspect."

"Piet Hoffmann. Very violent on previous arrests."

"Last observation?"

"The entrance of Biljardpalatset. Sankt Eriksgatan 52."

"Appearance?"

"Gray hooded top. Jeans. Fair hair. Unshaven. About one meter eighty tall."

"Anything else?"

"Likely to be armed."

He didn't try to run away.

When the doors *police* were flung open at both ends of the deserted pool hall and several uniformed police ran in with *on the floor* drawn guns, Piet Hoffmann turned calmly round from the pool table, careful to keep both hands visible all the time. He *fucking well get down on the floor* didn't lie down voluntarily but fell to the ground after two powerful strikes to his head and one more when bleeding he *fucking pigs* held his middle finger up in the air and then he couldn't remember much more than a pair of handcuffs locking around his wrists, a kick in the ribs and the acute pain in his neck when it all stopped.

ERIK WILSON HAD BEEN SITTING IN THE CAR OPPOSITE THE ENTRANCE TO the Kronoberg garage when two dark blue police vans had passed and sped off in the direction of Sankt Eriksgatan. He had waited until they turned off their sirens and then he had driven up to the barrier by the attendant's office, shown his ID, and rolled slowly toward the automatic door to the Police Authority's garage under Kronobergsparken. He had parked in a steel cage in front of the elevator up to the remand prison and from the driver's seat observed the steady stream of police vehicles going in or out.

He had been waiting for half an hour when he rolled down both his windows so he could hear better, his whole body tense. He had tried to shake off the discomfort and dread but hadn't been particularly successful. He breathed in the damp gas-perfumed air and listened to a car stopping on the other side of the garage and someone getting out, then another, followed by sleepy footsteps in the opposite direction.

Then he saw the large bay doors being pulled to one side.

It had taken thirty-five minutes for eight specially trained policemen to locate and arrest one of the country's most documented and dangerous people.

The dark blue van came in and he watched it approach the final couple of hundred meters before driving into the steel cage and parking about a car's length away.

If anything happens, abort your mission and ask for voluntary isolation. To survive.

Two uniformed colleagues got out first. Then a man with a swollen face, gray hooded top, jeans and handcuffs.

The police, who had been instructed to arrest a wanted and presumably armed dangerous criminal, had confronted him in the only way they knew how.

With violence.

"Hey, I don't like fucking faggot police touching me."

Erik Wilson saw Piet Hoffmann suddenly turn toward the policeman standing nearest to him and spit in his face. The uniformed officer didn't say anything, show anything, and Piet spat again. A quick glance at his colleagues, who just happened to look away, then the policeman stepped forward and kneed Piet Hoffmann in the balls.

Only a criminal.

He groaned in pain, and again after a kick to the stomach, then got up and with his hands locked behind his back was being escorted by four uniformed policemen to the elevator and the remand prison, when Erik Wilson heard him say loudly to the face he had just spat at:

"Watch it, you prick. I'll get you. Sooner or later, we'll meet again. Sooner or later I'll put two bullets in you just like I did with that prick in Söderhamn."

Only a criminal can play a criminal.

PART THREE

monday

THEY WERE STANDING SO CLOSE TO HIM.

Two of them behind him who would rub right up against his back if he took a step back in the confined space, two more in front, staring in his eyes, ears, nose, their every breath warm moisture on the skin of his face.

They had been warned.

All the wardens in Stockholm's Kronoberg remand prison had read the documents about one of Sweden's most dangerous criminals, and they had all heard the story that ten days ago, when he had just been arrested in the pool hall by Sankt Eriksgatan, he spat in the face of one of their colleagues as they walked through the parking lot and then threatened him with two bullets the next time they met.

This time he was being transported elsewhere. The small elevator down to the metal cage in the garage under Kronobergsparken and then the transport bus to Aspsås prison. There were four of them, two more than usual, and the prisoner was in handcuffs and leg irons. They had even considered a waist restraint, but decided against it.

He was the kind who hated everything and used what little intelligence he had to cause trouble; they had seen a few over the years, serious criminals with a one-way ticket to an early grave. The wardens kept a constant eye on the prisoner and each other; it was in the short distance from the elevator to the waiting bus that he had spat the last time, only to get an almighty knee in the balls in return when three of them happened to look the other way at the same time.

They were waiting, prepared, he was going to make a move soon, they knew it.

He was silent as they escorted him to the bus. He was silent as he got on. He was silent as he sat down on one of the backseats. The prisoner who hated everything and needed extra guards was silent as they drove through the underground garage toward the exit and security desk by Drottningholmsvägen. Then it started.

"Where the fuck you going?"

As he was being shoved onto the bus, the prisoner whose name was Hoffmann had noticed another guy already sitting there in equally baggy clothes with the Prison and Probation Service logo on his chest. He had stared at him, waited until he caught his eye.

"Österåker."

One of the other prisons to the north of Stockholm. The transport bus from the remand often took several prisoners to various prisons where they would serve their sentences.

"And what the fuck you in for?"

The prisoner whose name was Hoffmann got no answer.

"One more time. What the fuck you in for?"

"Assault."

"What you get?"

"Ten months."

The wardens looked at each other. This wasn't good.

"Ten months, eh? Guessed as much. You look like one of them. Little shits who beat up their women don't get much more than that."

Hoffmann had lowered his voice to a growl and tried to move closer as the bus passed through the security barrier and headed north along Sankt Eriksgatan.

"What d'you mean?"

The prisoner who was going to Österåker had noticed the change in Hoffmann's tone and his aggression, and tried without realizing to back away.

"That you're the kind of guy who only hits women. The kind that the rest of us have a problem with."

"How the fuck . . . how the fuck d'you know that?"

Piet Hoffmann smiled to himself. He'd guessed right. And he knew that the guards were listening—that was what he wanted, them to listen and then to talk about the dangerous prisoner with threatening behavior who needed extra cover.

"You can always tell a cowardly little prick who deserves to die."

They were listening and Piet Hoffmann was sure that they'd already realized what his next move would be. They had all seen it before. It was always dangerous and a risk to transport pedophiles and wife beaters with other prisoners. He looked at the seat in front, his voice calm.

"You've got five minutes. But only five minutes, mind."

They both turned around and the guard in the passenger seat was about to answer when Hoffmann interrupted.

"Five minutes to chuck this bastard out. Otherwise . . . things could get messy in here."

They'd tell the other guards later.

Word would spread, to people inside as well.

It was all about building respect.

The guard in the passenger seat sighed loudly before making a call on the radio, saying that a car had to be sent immediately to the prison transport bus that was waiting by Norrtull as there was a prisoner who needed to be picked up and taken to Österåker in a separate vehicle.

Piet Hoffmann had never been inside the walls of Aspsås prison before. He had mapped out all the buildings from the church tower and had studied the bars in front of every window, and while on remand, with Erik's help, he had learned about the prisoners and staff in all the corridors of Block G, but when both iron gates opened and the bus headed toward the central security, it was the first time that he had actually been inside one of the country's highest-security prisons. It was hard to move with the tight, heavy leg irons on, each step was too short and the sharp metal cut into his skin. Two guards right behind him and two just as close in front when they pointed to the door to the left of the normal visitors' door, the one that went straight into registration and more guards from security. They undid the restraints and he could move his arms and legs freely while he was naked and bent over double, with a rubber-gloved hand checking up his ass and another pulling at his hair like a comb and a third feeling around in his armpits.

He'd been issued new clothes that hung off him and were just as ugly as the others, and was then escorted to a sterile waiting room where he sat on a wooden chair and didn't say a word.

Ten days had passed.

For twenty-three hours of the day he had lain on a bunk behind a metal door with a peephole in from the corridor. Five square meters and no visitors, no newspapers, no TV, no radio. Time to break you and make you compliant.

He had gotten used to having someone there. He had forgotten how much loneliness reinforced your longing.

He missed her so much.

He wondered what she was doing right now, what she had on, how she smelled, if her steps were long and relaxed, or short and irritated.

Zofia might not be there for him anymore.

He had told her the truth and she would do with it what she wanted and he was so scared that in a couple of months he would no longer have anyone to miss, he would be nothing.

He had been staring at the white walls of the waiting room for four hours when two guards from the day shift opened the door and explained that a cell in G2 Left would be his home at the start of the long sentence. One in front and one behind as they started to walk through a wide passage under the prison yard, a few hundred meters of concrete floor and concrete walls, a locked internal door with a security camera and another passage and then steep stairs up to Block G.

He had left behind the days cooped up in remand at Kronoberg and the fast-track trial, where he did exactly what he told Henryk and the deputy CEO he would do.

He had admitted to possession of three kilos of amphetamine in the trunk of a rented car.

He had got the prosecutor to confirm that he was acting alone and was solely responsible for the crime.

He had declared himself satisfied with the judgment and had signed the document and thereby avoided any unnecessary wait for it to enter into force.

The following day, here he was walking through one of the passages in Aspsås prison on his way to a cell.

"I'd like to have six books."

The warden in front of him stopped.

"Excuse me?"

"I'd like to borrow—"

"I heard what you said. I was just hoping that I'd heard wrong. You've only been here a few hours, you're not even in your unit yet, and you start talking about books."

"You know it's my right."

"We'll talk about that later."

"I need them. It's important to me. Without books I won't survive this."

"Later."

✂

You don't understand.

I'm not here to serve some shitty sentence.

I'm here to knock out all the drug dealers in your leaky prison in a matter of days and then take over myself.

Then I'll carry on working, analyzing, putting together the pieces until I know everything I need to know, and with that knowledge I will destroy the Polish organization's operations, in the name of the Swedish police.

I don't think you've understood that.

The unit was completely deserted when he arrived, sandwiched between two young and quite nervous guards.

Ten years had passed and it was a completely different prison, but it could well have been the same unit as back then: he was back on the corridor with eight cells on each side, the well-equipped kitchen, the TV corner with card games and thoroughly thumbed newspapers, the table tennis table at the far end of the small storeroom with a broken bat hanging in the middle of the tattered net, the pool table with the dirty green baize and every ball safely locked away . . . even the smell was the same: sweat, dust, fear, and adrenaline and perhaps a hint of moonshine.

"Name?"

"Hoffmann."

The principal prison officer was as short as he was round and he nodded at the two guards from inside his glass box, indicating that from here on he would take charge.

"Haven't we met before?"

"Don't think so."

He had small eyes that seemed to pierce everything he looked at and it was hard to imagine that there was actually a person in there.

"From your papers, I understand that you . . . Hoffmann, was it? . . . are someone who is familiar with the way things work in a place like this."

Piet Hoffmann nodded silently at the principal officer. He wasn't there to tell some fat fucking inspector that he deserved a thrashing.

"Yes. I know very well how it works."

The unit would be empty for another three hours, until they came back from the workshop or the library and classroom. He had time for a guided tour with the unit's principal officer to learn how and where he should piss and why lock-in time was seven thirty and not seven thirty-five, and still have plenty of time to sit down in his own cell and come to terms with the fact that from now on this was his home.

Piet Hoffmann positioned himself in the TV corner a few minutes before the others were due back. He had seen photos of all the other fifteen prisoners in the unit and knew their backgrounds, and if he sat here he could see every single one as they came in, but more important, he himself would be seen, it would be obvious that there was someone new in Cell 4, someone who wasn't scared, someone who didn't hide and wait for the right moment to sneak out and show his papers for approval, someone who had already sat down in someone else's favorite chair and taken someone's marked cards and started to play solitaire on someone's table without even asking if he could.

He was looking for two faces in particular.

A heavy, almost square pale face with small eyes that were set too close together. A thinner, longer face with a nose that had been broken in several places and not healed well and a chin and a cheek that had been sewn up by a hand that wasn't a doctor's.

Stefan Lygás and Karol Tomasz Penderecki.

Two of the four members of Wojtek who were serving long sentences at Aspsås, his helpers in knocking out the competition and taking over the drug market, and his executioners the moment he was exposed as Paula.

The first questions were asked at supper. Two of the older men, thick gold around bull necks, one on either side of him with their warm plates and sharp elbows. Stefan and Karol Tomasz got up to stop them but he waved to them, they should hold off, he would let the two men ask the same questions that he had on the prison bus a few hours ago; it was all about the same thing really, respect based on the shared hate of perverts.

"We want to see your papers."

"That's what you say."

"Have you got a problem with that?"

Stefan and Karol Tomasz had already done the bulk of the work. They had been talking about the fact that Piet was coming for the past few days, what he had been taken in for, who he'd worked with, his status with one of the Eastern European mafias. They had managed to get in copies of 721018-0010 from the National Police Board criminal records, the criminal intelligence database, prison records, and his most recent judgment, via Stefan's lawyer.

"No, but I've got a problem with people sitting too close."

"Your papers, for fuck's sake!"

He would ask them into his cell and he would show them his papers and then he wouldn't have to answer any more questions. The new prisoner in Cell 4 wasn't a sex offender or a wife beater, but in fact had precisely the background he claimed to have; he would probably even get a few smiles and a cautious slap on the shoulder—prisoners who had shot at policemen and were convicted of attempted murder and aggravated assault of an officer were the kind who didn't need to fight for their status.

"You'll get my judgment, if you just shut it now and let me finish my food."

They played stud poker later with toothpicks that cost a thousand kronor each and he sat in the place that he'd taken from someone who no longer dared to take it back and he boasted about the fucking pig in Söderhamn who had begged for his life when he aimed at his forehead and he smoked rollies for the first time in years and he talked about a woman he was going to fuck senseless on his first supervised leave and they laughed loudly and he leaned back and looked around at the room and the corridor that was full of people who had longed to get away for so long that they no longer knew where.

tuesday

HE HAD DRIVEN SLOWLY THROUGH THE STOCKHOLM DARK WHICH NOW had turned to light—one of those nights again, long hours of turmoil and restlessness. He hadn't been there for more than two weeks, but at around half past three he had found himself in the middle of the Lidingö bridge once again, looking at the sky and water, *I never want to see you here again*, he had been on his way to the nursing home that he was no longer allowed to visit and the window where she no longer sat, *what you are frightened of has already happened*, when he suddenly turned around, drove back toward the houses and people, the capital that was so big and yet so small, where he had lived and worked all his life.

Ewert Grens got out of the car.

He had never been here before. He hadn't even known he was on his way here.

He had thought about it so many times and planned and started to drive, but never made it. Now, here he was standing by the southern entrance that was called Gate 1 and his legs felt rubbery like they would both collapse and there was pressure in his chest from his stomach or maybe his heart.

He started to walk but then stopped after a few steps.

He couldn't do it, his legs lacked the strength and whatever it was that was pressing inside came in regular thumps.

It was a gentle dawn and the sun shone so beautifully on the graves and grass and trees, but he wasn't going to go on. Not this morning. He would turn back to the car and drive into the city again as North Cemetery disappeared into the distance in his rearview mirror.

Maybe next time.

Maybe then he'd find out where her stone was, and maybe then he would go all the way there.

Next time.

The corridor at Homicide was deserted and dark. He helped himself to a forgotten, rather dry slice of bread from the basket on the table in the staff room and pressed two cups of coffee out of the machine and then continued down to the office that would never sing again. He ate and drank his simple breakfast and lifted up the thin file for an ongoing investigation that was at a standstill. They had managed to identify the victim within the first couple of days as an informant for the Danish police, had secured traces of drug mules and amphetamines and confirmed that there had been at least one other Swedish-speaking person in the flat at the time of the murder, the voice that had raised the alarm that he had now listened to so often it had become a part of him.

They had discovered a Polish mafia branch called Wojtek, assumed to have a head office in Warsaw, and then they hit a wall.

Ewert Grens chewed the dry, hard bread and drank up the coffee that was left in the plastic cup. He didn't often give up. He wasn't the sort to do that. But this wall was so long and high and no matter how much he had pushed and shoved and shouted in the past two weeks, he had not managed to get around it or beyond it.

He had followed up the bloodstains on the shirt that was found in a garage and had come to a dead end in a register with no matches.

Then he had gone to Poland with Sven to follow up the yellow stains that Krantz had found on the same item of clothing and had ended up in the remains of an amphetamine factory in a town called Siedlce. For a couple of days they had worked closely with some of the three thousand policemen assigned to a special police force to combat organized crime, and had encountered a sense of helplessness, a hunt that never gave results, a nation with five hundred criminal groups that fought every day for a slice of the domestic Polish capital cake, eighty-five even larger criminal groups with international connections, police who frequently took part in armed battles, and a nation that raked in more than five hundred billion kronor every year from the production of synthetic drugs.

Ewert Grens remembered the smell of tulips.

The amphetamine factory that was connected to the stains on the murderer's shirt had been in the basement of a block of flats in the middle of a rundown and dirty neighborhood a couple of kilometers west of the center—uniform buildings once built in their thousands as a temporary solution to an acute housing problem. Ewert Grens and Sven Sundkvist had sat in the car and watched a raid that had ended in a shoot-out and the death of a young policeman. The six people who were in some of the rooms in the basement had then not said a peep to either the Polish or Swedish interrogating officers, and had remained silent, just sneering or staring at the floor, as they knew, of course, that anyone who opened their mouth would not live for long.

Grens swore out loud in the empty room, opened the window and shouted something at someone in civvies who happened to be walking along the asphalt path across the courtyard of Kronoberg, then wrenched open the door and limped up and down the long corridor until his back and forehead were wet with sweat, then sat down on his chair to catch his racing breath.

He had never felt like this before.

He was used to anger, almost addicted to it. He always looked for conflict, hid himself away in it.

It wasn't that.

This feeling, like it was there, the truth, as if the answer was staring at him, laughing at him, a peculiar feeling of being so close without being able to see.

Ewert Grens took the file in his hand and went to lie down with his legs outstretched on the floor behind the corduroy sofa. He started to leaf through the papers starting with the voice informing the police about a dead man in Västmannagatan, through the following two weeks working at full capacity with access to all technical resources, to his trips to Copenhagen and Siedlce.

He swore again, maybe shouted at someone again.

They hadn't gotten anywhere.

He was going to lie on the floor until he understood whose voice he had listened to so many times, what it was he didn't understand and couldn't quite get hold of, why the feeling that the truth was close at hand, laughing at him, was so intense.

HE HEARD THE KEYS JANGLING.

Two guards unlocking and opening the cells at the far end, the ones with a view over the large gravel pitch, Cell 8 and opposite, Cell 16.

He braced himself, prepared himself for the twenty minutes each day that could mean death.

It had been a godawful night.

Despite having been awake for days, he had lain there, waiting for sleep that never came. They were there with him, Zofia and Hugo and Rasmus, they had stood outside the window and sat on the edge of his bed, lain down beside him and he had been forced to drive them away. They no longer existed; inside he had to stop feeling, he had a mission that he had chosen to complete and that left no room for dreaming—he had to suppress, forget. Anyone who dreamed in prison soon went under.

They were getting closer. The keys jangled again, Cell 7 and Cell 15 were opened and he heard a faint *morning* and someone else reply *go to hell.*

He had eventually gotten up—when Zofia had disappeared and the dark outside was densest he had held the dread at bay with chin-ups and sit-ups and jumping on and off the bed with both his feet held together. There wasn't much space and he had hit the wall a couple of times, but it was good to sweat and to feel his heart beating in his rib cage.

His work had already begun.

In a matter of hours on that first afternoon he had earned himself the respect in the unit that he needed to continue. He now knew who was in charge of supplies and dealing, in which units and in which cells. One of them was here, the Greek in Cell 2; the other two were on separate floors in Block H. Piet Hoffmann would get in the first grams soon, the ones he was responsible for and that he would use to blow out the competition.

The guards were even closer, opened Cell 6 and Cell 14. Only a couple of minutes more.

The time after the cells were opened, between seven and seven twenty, was crucial. If he survived that, he would survive the rest of the day.

He had prepared himself in the way that he would prepare himself every morning. In order to survive, he had to assume that in the course of the evening or night, someone had found out about his other name, that there was a Paula who worked for the authorities, a snitch who was there to break the organization. He was safe as long as the cell was locked, a closed door would hold off an attack, but the first twenty minutes once the cell had been opened, after the first *good morning*, were the difference between life and death; a well-planned attack would always be carried out when the guards had disappeared into their room for a cup of coffee and a break—twenty minutes with no staff in the unit and the time when several of the many murders in prison had been carried out in recent years.

"Good morning."

The guard had opened the door and looked in. Piet Hoffmann was sitting on the bed and stared at him without replying—it wasn't how he felt, it was just something he said because the rules said he should.

The idiot guard didn't give in, he would stand there and wait until he got an answer, confirmation that the prisoner was alive and that everything was as it should be.

"Good morning. Now fucking leave me in peace."

The guard nodded and carried on, two cells at a time. This was when Hoffmann had to act. When the last door was opened it was too late.

A sock around the handle, he pulled the door—that normally couldn't be locked or closed completely from the inside—toward him, jamming it by forcing the fabric of the sock between the door and door frame.

One second.

He put the simple wooden chair that normally stood by the wardrobe just inside the threshold, careful to make sure that it blocked the greater part of the doorway.

One second.

The pillow and blanket and trousers were made to look like a body under the covers, the blue arm of his training jacket a continuation of the body. It wouldn't fool anyone. But it was an illusion that would be given a fast double take.

Half a second.

Both the guards disappeared down the corridor. All the cells were unlocked and open now and Piet Hoffmann positioned himself to the left of the door, with his back to the wall. They could come at any moment. If they had found out, if he had been exposed, death would strike immediately.

He looked at the sock around the handle, the chair in front of the door, the pillows under the blanket.

Two and a half seconds.

His protection, his time to hit back.

He was breathing heavily

He would stand like this, waiting, for twenty minutes.

It was his first morning in Aspsås prison.

THERE WAS SOMEONE STANDING IN FRONT OF HIM. TWO THIN SUIT LEGS that had said something and were now waiting for an answer. He didn't reply.

"Grens? What are you doing?"

Ewert Grens had fallen asleep on the floor behind the brown corduroy sofa with an investigation file on his stomach.

"What about our meeting? It was you who wanted it this early. I assume that you've been here all night?"

His back ached a bit. The floor had been harder this time.

"That's none of your business."

He rolled over and heaved himself up, using the arms of the sofa for support, and the world spun ever so slightly.

"How are you?"

"That's none of your business either."

Lars Ågestam sat down on the sofa and waited while Ewert Grens went over to his desk. There was no love lost between them. In fact, they couldn't stand each other. The young prosecutor and older detective superintendent came from different worlds and neither had any inclination to visit the other anymore. Ågestam had tried at first, he had chatted and listened and watched until he realized it was pointless, Grens had decided to hate him and nothing would change that.

"Västmannagatan 79. You wanted a report."

Lars Ågestam nodded.

"I get the distinct feeling that you're getting nowhere."

They weren't getting anywhere. But he wouldn't admit it. Not yet.

Ewert Grens fully intended to keep hold of his resources, which Ågestam had the power to remove.

"We're working on several theories."

"Such as?"

"I'm not prepared to say anything yet."

"I can't imagine what you've got. If you did have something, you'd give it to me and then tell me to shove off. I don't think you've got anything at all. I think it's time to scale down the case."

"Scale down?"

Lars Ågestam waved his skinny arm at the desk and the piles of ongoing investigations.

"You're not getting anywhere. The investigation is at a standstill. You know as well as I do, Grens, that it's unreasonable to tie up so many resources when an investigator is having no success."

"I never give up on a murder."

They looked at each other. They came from different worlds.

"So, what have you got then?"

"You never scale down murder cases, Ågestam. You solve them."

"You know—"

"And that is what I have done for thirty-five years. Since you were running around peeing in your diaper."

The prosecutor wasn't listening anymore. You just needed to decide that you weren't going to hear anything and then you didn't. It was a long time now since Ewert Grens had been able to hurt him.

"I read through the conclusions of the preliminary investigation. But it was . . . quick. You mentioned a number of names on the periphery of the investigation that haven't been fully probed. Do that. Investigate every name on the periphery and close it. You've got three days. Then we'll meet again. And if you haven't got anything more by then, you can make as much fuss as you like, I will scale down the case."

Ewert Grens watched the determined suit-back leave his office and would no doubt have shouted after it if the other voice hadn't already been there, the one that had been in his head every hour for two weeks now, that was once again whispering and wheedling its way in, persistently repeating the short sentences, driving him mad.

"A dead man. Västmannagatan 79. Fourth floor."

He had three days.

Who are you?

Where are you?

He had stood with his back pressed hard against the cell wall for twenty minutes, every muscle tensed, every sound an imagined threat of attack.

Nothing had happened.

His fifteen fellow prisoners had been to the toilet and showered and then gone to the kitchen for an early breakfast, but none of them had stopped outside his door, no one had tried to open it. He was still only Piet Hoffmann here, a member of Wojtek, arrested with three kilos of Polish Yellow in his trunk and convicted of possession, and a previous conviction for having beaten some bastard pig before firing two shots at him.

They had disappeared, one by one, some to the laundry and the workshop, most to the classrooms, a couple to the hospital. No one went on strike and stayed in their cell, which often happened: the striker laughed at the threat of punishment and continued to refuse to work as the extra couple of months on twelve years existed only on official papers.

"Hoffmann."

It was the principal prison officer who had welcomed him the day before, with blue eyes that pierced whoever was standing in front of him.

"Yes?"

"Time to get out of your cell."

"Is it?"

"Your work duties. Cleaning. The administration building and the workshops. But not today. Today you're going to come with me and try to learn how and where and when to use your brushes and detergents."

They walked side by side down the corridor through the unit and down the stairs to the underground passage.

When Paula arrives at Aspsås, his work duties will already be fixed. On his first afternoon, he'll start as the new cleaner in the administration block and workshop.

The shapeless fabric of the prison-issue clothes chafed against his thighs and shoulders as they approached the second floor of Block B.

Prison management usually only grants cleaning duties as a reward.

They stopped in front of the toilets outside the main door to the workshop.

Then reward him.

Piet Hoffmann nodded—he would start his cleaning round here, with the cracked basin and piss pot in a changing room that stank of mold. They continued into the big workshop with its faint smell of diesel.

"The toilet out there, the office behind the glass window, and then the entire workshop. You got it?"

He stayed standing in the doorway, looking around the room. Workbenches with something that looked like bits of shiny piping on them,

211

shelves with piles of packing tape, punch presses, pallet jacks, half-full pallets, and at every workstation, a prisoner who earned ten kronor an hour. Prison workshops often produced simple items that were then sold to commercial manufacturers; at Österåker, he had cut out square red wooden blocks for a toy manufacturer. Here it was lamppost components: decimeter-long rectangular covers for the access hatch to the cables and switches that is positioned at the base, the kind that you see ten meters apart along every road, which no one ever notices but has to be made somewhere. The principal prison officer walked into the workshop and pointed at the dust and overflowing bins, while Hoffmann nodded at prisoners he didn't recognize: the one in his twenties standing by a punching press bending over the edges of the rectangular cover; the one who spoke Finnish over by the drilling machine and made small holes for every screw; and the one farthest away by the window who had a big scar from his throat to his cheek and was leaning over the barrel of diesel as he cleaned his tools.

"Look at the floor. It's damned important that you're thorough about it. Scrub as hard as you damn well can, otherwise it smells."

Piet Hoffmann didn't hear what the principal prick was saying. He had stopped by the barrel of diesel and the window. It was the one he had aimed at. He had lain on the church tower balcony holding an imaginary gun and shot at the window he selected exactly fifteen hundred and three meters away. It was a beautiful church and you got a clear view of the tower from here, as free a view as you got of the window from the tower.

He turned around, back to the window, memorized the rectangular room that was divided by three thick, whitewashed concrete pillars, big enough for a person to stand behind and not be seen. He took a couple of steps forward toward the pillar that was nearest to the window and stood close by it. It was just as big as he thought—he could stand there and be completely hidden. He walked slowly back across the room, getting the feel of it, getting used to it, didn't stop until he got to the room behind the glass wall that was an office for the prison wardens.

"Good, Hoffmann, that room . . . it's got to shine."

A small desk, some shelves, a dirty rug. There was a pair of scissors in the pen holder, a telephone on the wall, two drawers that were unlocked and mostly empty.

It was a matter of time.

If everything went wrong, if Paula was exposed, the more time he had, the more chance he had of surviving.

The principal officer walked in front of him along the passage and under the prison yard to the administration building, four locked doors with four watchful cameras. They looked up into each one, nodded to the lens, then waited for central security to press one of their buttons and the click that told them that the door was open. It took them more than ten minutes to put a couple of hundred meters underground behind them.

The first floor of the administration block was a narrow corridor with a view of the prison reception area. Every prisoner who was escorted in fresh from the chain, through security to reception, could be studied from the six offices and the poky meeting room. The chief warden and his administrative staff had seen him as he was led in yesterday, a priority prisoner with handcuffs and leg irons in Kronoberg remand clothes, with streaky fair hair and a salt-and-pepper two-week beard.

"Are you following me, Hoffmann? You'll be coming here every day. And when you leave, there won't be a speck of dirt left behind. Will there? Loads of floors to be scrubbed, desks to be dusted, trash cans to be emptied and windows to be cleaned. Do you have a problem with that?"

The rooms had institution-gray walls and floors and ceilings, as if the gloominess and hopelessness of the corridor spilled over into the offices. There were a few pots with green plants and a few circles of ceramic tiles on one of the walls, otherwise it was all dead, furniture and colors that did not tempt you to dare dream of anywhere else.

"Perhaps we should introduce you. Get a move on."

The chief warden was in his fifties, a man who was as gray as his walls. It said OSCARSSON on his door.

"This is Hoffmann. He's the new cleaner here from tomorrow."

The chief held out a hand that was soft, but with a firm grip.

"Lennart Oscarsson. I want both cans emptied every day. The one under the table and the one over there by the visitors' chairs. And if there are any unwashed glasses, take them with you."

It was a big room with windows that faced the fence and prison yard, but the same feeling as in all the others: a joyless institution, no room for anything private here, not even a family photo in a silver frame or a diploma on the walls. With one exception. On the desk, two bunches of flowers in crystal vases.

"Tulips?"

The principal officer went over to the desk and the long green stems with equally green buds. He held the white greeting cards in his hand while he read the message on both of them out loud.

"With thanks for a successful partnership, Aspsås Business Association."

The warden arranged one of the bunches on his desk, twenty-five yellow tulips that hadn't yet bloomed.

"I think so, they certainly look like tulips. We get a lot of flowers nowadays. The whole of Aspsås works here. Or supplies us with something. And all the study visits. It wasn't long ago that everyone looked down on the prison service. Now it's bloody nonstop, and every arrangement or incident fills the news bulletins and front pages."

He looked with pride at the flowers that he had somehow just complained about.

"They'll open soon. It usually takes a couple of days."

Piet Hoffmann nodded and then left, the principal prison officer a few meters in front, as before.

Tomorrow.

They would bloom tomorrow.

Ewert Grens removed two empty plastic cups and a half-eaten almond slice from the small wooden table, then sat down and sank into the softness of the corduroy sofa while he waited for Sven and Hermansson to sit down on either side.

The handwritten, single sheet of paper from a notepad was stained brown in one corner where some coffee had spilled, and had grease marks in another from stray almond-slice crumbs.

A list of seven names.

People who were on the periphery of the preliminary investigation and who they had three days to investigate and who perhaps meant the difference between the case staying live or being scaled down—between a solved and an unsolved murder.

He divided them into three columns.

Drugs, thugs, Wojtek.

Sven was going to concentrate on the first column, on the known drug dealers who lived or operated in the vicinity of Västmannagatan 79: Jorge Hernandez on the second floor of the same building; Jorma Rantala in the block where a bloody shirt was found wrapped in a plastic bag in the garbage bin.

Hermansson chose the second column: Jan du Tobit and Nicholas Barlow, two international hit men who according to the Swedish Security

Service were in Stockholm or the surrounding area at the time of the murder.

Ewert Grens was going to look after the last three names: three men who had previously worked with Wojtek International AB. A certain Maciej Bosacki, Piet Hoffmann, and Karl Lager. Each one the owner of a Swedish security firm, which—entirely legally—had been contracted for bodyguard services by Wojtek's head office when Polish officials were on state visits, the official business that any well-functioning and untouchable mafia organization is dependent on, a visible shell that both hides and hints at their business. Grens was one of the people in the Stockholm police who knew most about organized crime from the other side of the Baltic, and in this room, the only one who knew how to investigate whether any of the three could be linked to the other Wojtek, the unofficial organization, the real one, the one that was capable of carrying out assassinations in Swedish flats.

No one questioned him anymore.

No bastard sat too close or stared at him while he ate his meat and two veg. By lunch on the second day he was already someone but they didn't have a clue that very soon he would also be the one who decided everything, thanks to the power of drugs, and in two days he would control all supplies and sales and surpass even murderers in the prison hierarchy. Anyone who had killed someone was the most highly appreciated inside, got the most respect, then the big-time drug dealers and bank robbers and, at the bottom of the pile, pedophiles and rapists. But even the murderers bowed to whoever controlled the drugs and supplied the syringes.

Piet Hoffmann had followed close behind the principal prison officer in order to learn his new cleaning duties and had then waited on his bunk in his cell until the other men in the unit had come back from the workshop and classrooms for food that tasted of nothing. He had had eye contact with both Stefan and Karol Tomasz several times—they were impatient and waiting for instructions so he mouthed *wieczorem* at them until they understood.

This evening.

This evening they would knock out the three main dealers.

He offered to clear the table and wash up while the others smoked roll-your-owns with no filter out in the gravel yard or played stud poker for thousand-kronor toothpicks. Alone in the kitchen, there was no one who saw him wiping down the sink and worktop and stuffing two spoons and a knife into the front pockets of his trousers at the same time.

He walked over to the aquarium, the guards' glass box, knocked on the pane and got an irritated flick of the wrist back. He knocked again, a bit harder and a bit longer, making it clear that he had no intention of leaving.

"What the hell d'you want? It's lunchtime. Wasn't it you who was going to clean the kitchen?"

"Does it look like there's anything left to do out there?"

"That's not the point."

Hoffmann shrugged, he wasn't going to pursue it.

"My books?"

"What about them?"

"I ordered them yesterday. Six of them."

"Don't know anything about it."

"Well, then it might make sense to have a look, eh?"

He was an older warden, not one of the ones who had dealt with him yesterday. He waved his arm around in irritation, but after a while went into the glass box and looked on the desk.

"These ones?"

Hardbacks, library covers. A label stuck on the front of each one: STORAGE in blue typed letters.

"That's them."

The older guard glanced quickly at the author presentations on the back sleeve, leafed through some pages here and there without really concentrating, and then handed them over.

"*Nineteenth Century Stockholm. The Marionettes.* What the hell is all that?"

"Poetry."

"A bit gay, eh?"

"Maybe you should try reading some."

"Listen here, you prick, I don't read faggot books."

Piet Hoffmann closed his cell door enough so that no one could see, but not so much that it would arouse suspicion. He put the six books on the small bedside table; titles that were seldom borrowed and which therefore had to be collected from the storeroom in the basement of Aspsås library when the request from the large prison came through that morning, and that were then handed over to the driver of the library bus by an out-of-breath, single female librarian in her fifties.

216

The knife he had stolen from the kitchen had felt sharp enough when he had run his fingertips across the blade.

He pressed it hard down the hinge between the front board and the first page of Lord Byron's *Don Juan*. It loosened thread by thread and soon the front and the spine were hanging just as freely as they had thirteen days earlier when he had opened it at a desk on Vasagatan. He thumbed to page 90, took hold of all the pages and pulled them off in one go. In the left-hand margin of page 91, a hole that was fifteen centimeters long and one centimeter wide, with thin walls constructed of Rizla papers, three hundred pages deep. The contents lay there untouched, just as he had left them.

Yellowish white, a little sticky, exactly fifteen grams.

Ten years earlier he had consumed most of what he smuggled in himself. Only occasionally when he had too much might he sell some on. On a couple of occasions he was so hard up that he used it as part payment for his most pressing debts. This time, it was going to be put to different use. Four books with a total of forty-two grams of thirty percent manufactured amphetamine was his weapon for squashing the competition and taking over himself.

Books, Blossom.

Small amounts, but he didn't need more right now. The tricks he had learned over the years were foolproof and wouldn't be discovered by prison routines.

Back then, he'd been sent to Österåker as soon as he'd come back from his first secure leave. Someone had tipped the guards off about drugs up his ass or in his belly, and he'd been put in the dry cell, with glass walls, a bunk to lie on and a toilet that was a closed system . . . that was it. He had stayed there for a week, naked twenty-four/seven, three guards watching him when he went for a dump, checking his shit, eyes staring at him through the glass as he slept, always without a blanket, an ass that couldn't be covered.

He had had no choice then, what with the debts and threats, he became just another dry celler. But now, he had a choice.

Every day in every prison, every waking hour was about drugs: how to get them in, and how to use them without it being discovered by the regular urine tests. A relative who came to visit was also a relative who could be forced to smuggle in some urine, their own, urine that was clean and would test negative. Once, in his first few weeks in Österåker, some mouthy Serb got his girlfriend to piss into a couple of mugs, the content of which was then sold for a great deal of money. None of them tested positive, despite the fact that more than half of them were under the influence, but the tests did show something else, and that was that every man in the unit was pregnant.

Don Juan, The Odyssey, My Life's Writings, French Landscape.

He emptied them one after the other, stopping every now and then when he heard steps passing his cell door or sounds that were unfamiliar—forty-two grams of amphetamine in four books that not many people chose to read.

Two books left. *Nineteenth Century Stockholm* and *The Marionettes.* He left them on the bed, untouched, texts that he hoped he would never need to read.

He looked at the yellowish-white substance that people killed for.

Every gram would cost more in here.

Here demand was greater than supply. Here the risk of being caught was greater in a locked cell than when you were free. Here the judgment inside would be harsher than outside; the same amount would always give you a longer sentence.

Piet Hoffmann divided up the forty-two grams of amphetamine into three plastic bags. He would keep one himself for the Greek in Cell 2 and put the other two out for collection, for Block H where the two other major suppliers were, on the top and bottom floor. Three plastic bags with fourteen grams that would knock out all the competition in one go.

The spoons from the kitchen were still in one of his trouser pockets.

He took them out and felt them, then pressed them hard against the edge of the steel bunk until they were both bent to nearly right angles like two hooks; he checked them, they would do. His blue jogging pants with the Prison and Probation Service logo were lying on his bed. With the knife he cut the waistband, pulled the elastic out and then cut it again into two lengths.

The cell door ajar, he waited—the corridor was empty.

The bathroom was fifteen fast steps away.

He closed the door behind him, went into the toilet cubicle furthest to the right and made sure that the door was properly locked.

Ewert Grens had gone to get another plastic cup of black coffee and bought yet another crumbly almond slice with sickly icing on top. The handwritten list of seven names had acquired several more brown stains, but it was still legible and it would stay where it was on the table by the sofa until they had all been investigated and struck off one by one.

They had three days.

One of those handwritten, coffee-stained names held the key to keeping open the investigation into an execution carried out during the day at a rented flat in the middle of Stockholm. Or else, in three days, it would be scaled down to one of the thirty-seven preliminary investigations in thin files on his desk and would probably never amount to much more than that. There was always a new murder case, or an assault that would gobble up all the resources for a week or two until it was solved or left on a forgotten pile.

He studied the names. Maciej Bosacki, Piet Hoffmann, Karl Lager. All owners of security firms, which, like all other security firms, installed alarm systems, sold flak jackets, gave courses in self-defense, offered bodyguard services. But these three had all been used by Wojtek Security International in connection with Polish state visits. Official jobs with official invoices. Nothing strange about that, really. But it piqued his curiosity. Sometimes what was official concealed what was unofficial and he was looking for things that couldn't be seen, if they existed at all—links to another Wojtek, the real organization, the one that bought and sold drugs, weapons, people.

Ewert Grens got up and went out into the corridor.

The feeling that the truth was laughing at him got stronger. He tried to catch it and it just slipped through his fingers.

He had spent two hours studying three personal ID numbers in the Police Authority's databases—page after page with lists of ARREST WARRANT INFORMATION, IDENTIFICATION INFORMATION, CRIMINAL RECORDS, INTELLIGENCE INFORMATION, PERSONAL HEALTH—and he had got a number of hits. All three had previous convictions, all three names were in the criminal intelligence database and suspects' register, they had all given fingerprints, two were in the DNA register and had been wanted at some point, and at least one of them was a previously confirmed gang member. Grens hadn't been entirely surprised, as more and more people moved in a gray zone where knowledge of crime was a prerequisite for knowing about security.

He walked a couple of doors down the corridor. He should perhaps have knocked, but seldom did.

"I need your help."

The room was considerably bigger than his and he didn't come here very often.

"How can I help you?"

It wasn't something they'd ever talked about. But in some way they had just agreed. In order to work together, they made sure they never met.

"Västmannagatan."

Chief Superintendent Göransson has no piles of paper on his desk, no empty paper cups, no crumbs from artificial cakes from the vending machine.

"Västmannagatan?"

So he can't understand where it's coming from; this feeling of discomfort, that there's no room.

"That says nothing to me."

"The killing. I'm investigating the last names and want to check them against the firearms register."

Göransson nodded, turned to his computer and logged on to the register which only a few authorized people had access to, for security reasons.

"You're standing too close, Ewert."

The discomfort.

"What do you mean?"

It came from inside.

"Can you move back a couple of steps?"

Whatever it was that demanded more space.

Göransson was looking at a person he didn't like and who didn't like him, so they seldom got in each other's way. That was all there was to it.

"Personal ID?"

"721018-0010. 660531-2559. 580219-3672."

Three personal ID numbers. Three names on the screen.

"What do you want to know?"

"Everything."

Västmannagatan.

Suddenly he understood.

"Göransson? Did you hear? I want everything."

That name.

"One of them has a license. For work, plus four hunting guns."

"Guns for work?"

"Pistols."

"Make?"

"Radom."

"Caliber?"

"Nine millimeter."

The name that was still blinking on the screen.

"Damn it, Göransson. Damn it!"

The detective superintendent had gotten up quickly and was already halfway out the door.

"But we already have access to them, Ewert."

Grens stopped mid-step.

"What do you mean?"

"There's a memorandum here. All the weapons have been seized. Krantz has them, no doubt."

"Why?"

"It doesn't say. You'll have to ask him."

The dull sound of a heavy body limping away down the corridor. Chief Superintendent Göransson didn't have the energy to fight the feeling that something was afoot, the dread that made him shrivel inside. He looked at the name on the screen for a long time.

Piet Hoffmann.

Ewert Grens would only have to press a few buttons and make a couple of phone calls to find the registered gun owner's current domicile and then go to the small town with a big prison to the north of the city and he would question him until he got the answer he mustn't get.

What wasn't meant to happen had just happened.

Piet Hoffmann waited behind the locked toilet door until he was absolutely sure he was alone.

Elastic, spoon, plastic bag.

This was exactly how he had hidden drugs and syringes in Österåker. Lorentz had told him that it still worked despite the fact that it was so damn simple. Maybe that was why. No guard in any prison would search the actual toilet U-bend.

The cistern, the drains, the waste pipe under the sink, hiding places that you might as well forget these days. But the U-bend, after all these years, they still had no idea.

He put the elastic, the bent spoon, and the plastic bag full of amphetamine down on the filthy toilet floor. He attached the plastic bag to one end of the elastic and the spoon to the other, then got down on his knees beside the toilet bowl, holding the plastic bag in his hand and pushing it as far down the pipe as he could, stretching the elastic. His arm and sleeve were wet up to his shoulder when he flushed and the pressure of the water pushed the plastic bag even farther down the pipe, the bent spoon catching on the edge of the pipe. He waited, flushed again. The elastic should stretch even more and the plastic bag would be suspended at the other end somewhere far down the pipe.

You couldn't see the spoon that was hooked over the edge of the pipe, holding the plastic bag in place.

But it would be easy to get hold of next time.

Down on his knees, hand in the wet, carefully haul it in.

Ewert Grens had left Göransson and the Homicide offices, and the truth that he couldn't quite grasp wasn't laughing so loud now. *Radom.* For the first time since the preliminary investigation started he had a lead, a name. *Nine millimeter.* Someone who might be the link to an execution.

Piet Hoffmann.

A name he had never heard before.

But who owned a security firm that got official bodyguard jobs from Wojtek International when there were state visits. And who had a license for Polish-manufactured guns, for work purposes, despite having served a five-year sentence for aggravated assault. Guns which, according to the register, were already in the hands of the police. Seized two weeks ago.

Ewert Grens got out of the elevator on his way to the forensics unit.

He had a name.

Soon he would have more.

Piet Hoffmann had sore knees when he got up off the toilet floor and listened to the silence. He had flushed twice more, listened again, but there were still no other sounds when he unlocked the door and went out into the corridor, making it look like he'd been sitting in there for a while, dicky tummy that took its time. He went over to the TV corner, shuffled a pack of cards, made it look like he was entertaining himself for a few minutes, while he sneaked a look over at the wardens' office and the kitchen in order to locate the guards that ran around in the unit.

Faces that were turned away, uniformed backs doing something. He held up his middle finger, that usually got them moving.

Nothing. No one reacted, no one saw.

The others still had an hour left of their afternoon stint in the classroom and workshop, the corridor was empty, the guards were someplace else.

Now.

He walked toward the row of cells. A quick look back at nothing. He opened the door to number 2.

The Greek's cell.

It looked the same, the same damn bed and the same damn wardrobe and chair and bedside table. It smelled different, stuffy, maybe sour, but it was just as fucking warm and the air he breathed was just as dusty. A photo of a child on the wall, a girl with long dark hair, another photo of a woman, his daughter's mother, Hoffmann was convinced.

If anyone opened the door.

If anyone saw what he was holding in his hand right now, what he was about to do.

He gave a start, just an instant—he mustn't start to feel.

Not many injections or snorts—thirteen or fourteen grams—but enough in here, enough for a new judgment and extended sentence and immediate removal to another prison.

Thirteen or fourteen grams that had to be put somewhere up high.

He tested the curtain rail, pulling it carefully; it came loose on the first attempt. A bit of tape around the plastic bag and it stayed in place against the wall. It was easy to lift the curtain rail back.

He opened the door and had a last look around the room—he stopped at the photo on the wall. The girl was about five, she was standing on a lawn, and in the background some happy children were waving. They were all on their way somewhere, a school trip, backpacks in their hands and yellow and red baseball caps on their heads.

Her father wouldn't be here when she came to visit next time.

Ewert Grens bent forward over the low workbench and the row of seven guns.

Three Polish-manufactured Radom pistols and four hunting rifles.

"In one gun cabinet?"

"In two gun cabinets. Both approved."

"He had a license for them?"

"The very ones issued by city police."

Grens was standing beside Nils Krantz in one of the forensic unit's many rooms that look like a small laboratory with fume cupboards and microscopes and tins of chemical preparations. He lifted up one of the pistols, held the plastic-covered weapon in his hand, weighed it in front of him in the air. He was absolutely certain—the dead man lying on the sitting room floor had been holding one like this in his hand.

"Two weeks ago?"

"Yes. An office in a flat on Vasagatan. Serious drug offense."

"And nothing?"

"We've test-fired them all. None of them have been used for any other crime."

"And Västmannagatan 79?"

"I know that you hoped you'd get another answer. But you're not going to. None of these weapons have anything to do with the shooting."

Ewert Grens hit his hand hard on the piece of furniture that was closest. A metal cupboard shuddered as the books and files fell to the floor.

"I don't get it."

He was about to hit the cupboard again when Krantz stood in his way to save it.

Grens chose the wall instead—it didn't shudder as much but made just as much noise.

"Nils, I don't bloody get it. This investigation . . . it's like I'm standing on the sideline the whole time, watching. So, you seized all his weapons? Twenty days ago? Damn it, Nils, there's something that's not right. Don't you understand, this bastard, he shouldn't have any guns at all, even less a license issued by us. Okay, it's ten years ago, but . . . given the conviction . . . I've never heard of such a serious criminal being given a permit."

Nils Krantz was still standing in front of the metal cupboard. It was never easy to know if his colleague was done with thumping inanimate objects.

"You'll have to talk to him, then."

"I'm going to. When I find out where he is."

"In Aspsås."

Ewert Grens looked at the forensic scientist who was one of the few people who had been in the building as long as he had.

"Aspsås?"

"That's where he's doing his time. And it's a long sentence, I believe."

He had sat in his new place in the TV corner this afternoon again and waited until his neighbors came back from the workshop and classroom one by one. They had played more stud poker and a couple of games of casino and talked about the bastard guards who had been on duty that morning and quite a bit about a bank job in Täby that had gone wrong and then got engrossed in a passionate discussion about how many times you could jerk off on a gram of injected amphetamine. They had laughed raucously at several graphic descriptions of a speed hard-on, and Stefan as well as Karol Tomasz and a couple of Finns had bragged about having a boner and fucking for days, as long as there was enough strong whizz. After a while, Piet had given the Greek a vague nod and offered him a chair without getting any response; the man who sold and controlled the supply here, who had the highest status wasn't prepared to talk to a fish.

A couple of hours more.

The plastic bag would be sitting there behind the curtain rail and the hard fuckwit wouldn't know what had hit him before it was over.

Ewert Grens stood behind his desk clutching the telephone receiver even though the conversation had finished some time ago now. He was holding a piece of paper that was stained with coffee and almond slice crumbs.

Nils Krantz had been right.

The name at the bottom of his short list *was* already in prison.

He had been caught with three kilos of amphetamine in his car trunk, had been held on remand and in record time had been convicted and taken to the prison at Aspsås.

Amphetamine that smelled of flowers.

A distinct scent of tulip.

He lay down on the hard bunk and smoked a cigarette. It was several years now since he'd rolled his own—not since the days when there were no children, as both he and Zofia had stopped the day they saw a centimeter-long life on a monitor; something that was barely visible but which was affected by every breath they took. He was restless, smoked too fast and soon lit another . . . it was hell just lying here waiting.

He got up, listened, his ear to the hard cell door.

Nothing.

He heard sounds that weren't there. Maybe the faint clunking that frequently came from the pipes in the ceiling. Maybe someone's TV. He'd chosen not to have one so that he didn't need to participate in the world outside.

If everything went according to plan, they would come any minute.

He lay down again, a third cigarette, it was good just to hold something in his hand. Quarter to eight. It was only quarter of an hour since lockup, and normally it took about half an hour—they usually waited until everyone had settled.

Everything was in place, just as he wanted it. He had had final confirmation in the bathroom that evening when the guards were waiting for everyone to go back to their cells. Both the plastic bags that until recently had been stowed some meters down one of the toilets' waste pipes at the end of a piece of elastic were now in Block H, hidden behind two curtain rails.

Now.

He was absolutely certain.

Dogs barking eagerly, black shoes slapping on the corridor floor.

You'll get my name and personal details. So that you can put me in the right prison, give me the right work and make sure that at lockup time exactly two days after I've arrived, there will be an extensive spot check of every cell in the prison.

Farther down the corridor, the first cell doors were flung open.

Loud voices clashed as one of the Finns started to shout and one of the guards screamed even louder.

It took twenty-five minutes and eight cells before they got to him and a hand threw open his door.

"Inspection."

"You can suck my cock, you fucking screw."

"Out of the cell, Hoffmann. Before you get what you want."

Piet Hoffmann spat as they dragged him out into the corridor. *Criminal.* He carried on spitting as they checked all the cavities. *You have to be a criminal to play a criminal.* He stood outside the door in white, badly fitting boxers while two guards went into his cell and searched everywhere for what might be hidden, but couldn't be found.

Two cells were inspected at the same time, always the two opposite each other, and there wasn't much room where the open doors met.

Two guards in each cell, two guards outside to watch the prisoners who were swearing, mouthing off, threatening.

He watched as the bedclothes were pulled off and shaken out, the wardrobe tipped forward and every shoe emptied, every sock turned inside out, the pile of six library books on the bedside table flicked through, several meters of floorboards taken up, pockets and seams on his trousers and jackets and tops pulled open at the stitching and the barking dogs let in and lifted up to the ceiling and the lamp and the curtain rail when there was chaos on the linoleum floor.

What the hell . . .

With dogs. That's important.

With dogs? And what happens when we find what you've planted? To the fellow prisoner who you've wasted your drugs on?

One more floorboard, under the sink.

And behind the bedside lamp, the small hole in the wall for the wall plug.

"Everything all right? You found anything? No? What a shame. You'll have to go jerk off in some other cell. Or d'you want me to help you?"

The guy opposite laughed. The guy beside him banged on his door and hissed *keep doing them up the ass, Hoffmann.*

They had heard.

Piet Hoffmann sat down on the edge of the bunk when they locked the door again and went on to the next cell. There was half a cigarette under a pair of boxer shorts in the mess under the bedside table; he lit up and lay down.

Ten minutes more.

He smoked and scoured the ceiling, then the dogs began to bark.

"What the fuck, fucking hell, it's not mine, for fuck's sake!"

The Greek in Cell 2 had a piercing voice, the kind that opened locked cell doors.

"What the fuck, that— you've planted that, you fucking bastard screws, I'm going to—"

One of the security guards had lifted up the black dog that was now frantically pawing above the window behind the curtain rail. The plastic bag had been taped to the wall and contained fourteen grams of high-quality amphetamine. The Greek was escorted down the corridor and out of the unit, shaking and swearing, and would be transported to Kumla or Hall the next day to serve the rest of a long sentence that just got longer. At roughly the same time, two more plastic bags with the same amount of amphetamine were found in two cells on the top and bottom floors of

Block H and three inmates in all would now be spending their last night in Aspsås.

Piet Hoffmann lay on the bed and could smile for the first time since he'd been inside the high walls.

Right now.

Right now, we've taken over.

wednesday

HE HAD SLEPT HEAVILY FOR NEARLY FOUR HOURS WHEN IT WAS DARKEST outside the barred windows and once the Finn two cells away had presumably calmed down. The jangling of keys had penetrated his brain and prevented him from sleeping every time the bastard rang the bell and demanded attention. The unit hadn't settled until a couple of the other prisoners had threatened a riot the next time a Finnish finger played with the bell.

Piet Hoffmann pressed his back against the wall. An anxious glance at the pillow under the covers and the chair in the threshold and the sock between the door and its frame. His protection, exactly the same as yesterday and as tomorrow, two and a half seconds if anyone knew and attacked at the only time of day when the guards couldn't see or hear.

One minute past seven. Nineteen minutes left. Then he would go out, have a shower, and eat breakfast with the others.

He had taken the first step. He had felled the three main dealers in Aspsås prison with forty-two grams of thirty percent manufactured amphetamine. Warsaw and the deputy CEO had already received the reports they needed and opened a bottle of Żubrówka, raised a glass to the next stage.

Eight minutes left.

His breathing was measured, every muscle tensed, death didn't come knocking.

Today he was going to take the next step. For Wojtek, the first grams to the first customers and the rumor that there was a new supplier in one of Sweden's hardest prisons. For the Swedish police, more information about supplies, delivery dates, and distribution channels until the operation had been built up enough for it to be destroyed—days or weeks waiting for the moment when the organization had full control but hadn't yet expanded to the next prison, when an informant's knowledge was sufficient to reach the very heart of the organization back in a black building on ul. Ludwika Idzikowskiego in Warsaw.

Hoffmann looked at the alarm clock that was ticking too loud. Twenty past seven. He moved the chair, made his bed, and after a while opened the door to a sleepy corridor. Stefan and Karol Tomasz smiled at him as he passed the kitchen and breakfast table. The prison bus usually came with any new prisoners around this time and it was obvious that someone who was called the Greek was now sitting on one of the evil-smelling seats with a couple of guys from Block H opposite him and presumably they weren't saying much to each other as they looked out of the windows and tried to understand what the fuck had actually happened.

He had a hot shower, washing away the tension of twenty minutes behind a cell door ready to fight and flee. He looked in the part of the mirror that wasn't steamed up yet at someone who was unshaven and whose hair was a bit too long—leave the razor in his pocket, the salt and pepper stubble would stay where it was today.

The cleaning cart was in a cupboard just outside the main door to the unit.

A metal frame with a black garbage bag, hard rolls of considerably smaller white trash bags, a small brush with a wobbly dustpan, a smelly plastic bucket, small bits of material that he assumed were used for washing the windows, and at the bottom some unperfumed detergent that he had never seen before.

"Hoffmann."

The principal prison officer with piercing eyes was sitting in the aquarium with the wardens when he passed the big glass panes.

"First day?"

"First day."

"You have to wait at every locked door. Look up at every camera. And if and when central security decides to let you through, you do it as fast as possible in the few seconds that it's open."

"Anything else?"

"I looked through your papers yesterday. You've got . . . now, what was it? . . . ten years. I don't know, Hoffmann, but with a bit of luck that should be enough time for you to learn how to clean properly."

The first locked door was at the start of the underground passage. He stopped the cart, looked up at the camera, waited for the clicking sound and then went on through. The air was damp and he felt chilled as he walked under the prison yard; he had been escorted through a similar passage several times in the year he was at Österåker: to the hospital unit, or the gym, or the kiosk where every kronor earned could be exchanged for shaving cream and soap. He stopped in front of each door, nodded at the watchful cameras, and then hurried through while the door was open—he wanted to attract as little attention as possible.

"Hey you!"

He had nodded at a group of prisoners from the other side of the prison on their way to their various workplaces when one of them turned around, looked at him.

"Yeah?"

A druggie. Skinny as hell, evasive eyes, feet that found it hard to stand still.

"I heard— I want to buy. Eight g."

Stefan and Karol Tomasz had done a good job.

A big prison is a small place when messages pass through walls.

"Two."

"Two?"

"You can get two. This afternoon. In the blind spot."

"Two? Fuck, I need at least—"

"That's all you'll get. This time round."

The skinny prick was waving his long arms when Hoffmann turned his back and carried on down the wide passage.

He would stand there. His body shaking, counting the minutes until he got that feeling that made this all bearable. He would buy his two g and he would inject them with a dirty syringe in the first available toilet.

Piet Hoffmann walked away slowly and tried not to laugh.

Only a few hours to go.

Then he would have taken over all drug dealing in Aspsås prison.

The lights in the Homicide corridor were strong and flickered every now and then. An irritating brightness that blinded you, combined with a jarring, whirring sound every time they flickered. The two strip lights by the vending machines were worst. Fredrik Göransson could still feel the dread of yesterday in his body; it had taken him all afternoon and evening, a night's sleep and some time after he had woken to realize that the visit from Grens had sparked a gnawing, consuming feeling that would not go away, no matter how hard he tried. Prioritizing infiltration inside prison walls over and above a murder investigation was not a good solution. He had sat at the table in Rosenbad and weighed it against control over the Polish mafia and had chosen to restrict criminal expansion.

"Göransson."

That bloody voice.

"I want to talk to you, Göransson."

He had never liked it.

"Morning, Ewert."

Ewert Grens limped more noticeably now—either that or the corridor walls just amplified the hard sound of a healthy leg meeting a concrete floor.

"The firearms register."

Whatever it is that takes up so much room.

Fredrik Göransson avoided the heavy hands that fumbled for plastic cups and the coffee machine buttons beside him.

There's no room here again.

"You're standing too close."

"I'm not going to move again."

"If you want an answer, you're going to have to."

Ewert Grens stayed where he was.

"721018-0010. Three Radom pistols and four hunting rifles."

The name that was still blinking on his screen.

"Yes, what about it?"

"I want to know how someone with his criminal record was granted a firearms license for work."

"I'm not sure what you're getting at."

"Assaulting a police officer. Attempted murder."

The plastic cup was full. Grens tasted the warm liquid, gave a satisfied nod and pressed the button for another.

"I don't get it, Göransson."

I get it, Grens.

He has a firearms license because he is not violent and is not a classified psychopath and does not need to be branded dangerous and has not been convicted of attempted murder.

Because the database entries that you've seen are a tool, fake.

"I'll look into it. If it's important."

Grens tested the second cup, looked just as happy and started to walk away, slowly.

"It *is* important. I want to know who issued that license. And why."
It was me.
"I'll do what I can."
"I need it today. He's in for questioning first thing tomorrow morning."
Chief Superintendent Göransson stood where he was under the flickering, whirring light as Grens walked away.
He shouted after the detective who had demanded answers.
"And the others?"
Grens stopped without turning around.
"Which others?"
"You had three names when you came to me yesterday."
"I'm dealing with those two today. This bastard is doing time already, so I know where I've got him, he'll be there tomorrow too."
Too close.
The ungainly body carrying a plastic cup in each hand limped off down the corridor and disappeared into an office.
Grens had been standing too close.

The toilet bowl was yellow from piss and the sink was full of wet tobacco and cigarette butts with no filter. The unscented detergent didn't even remove the top layer of dirt. He scrubbed for a long time with the brush and then with the scouring cloth, but they only slid over the worn porcelain surface. The toilet outside the door to the workshop was small and used by people who pissed outside the bowl in the short breaks they could get from the work they hated, a couple of minutes' respite from a punishment that was never clearer than when you were standing by a machine that drilled small holes for screws at the bottom of a lamppost hatch.

Piet Hoffmann went into the big room and greeted the same faces that he had the day before. He wiped over all the workbenches and shelves, washed the floor around the diesel barrel, emptied the bins, cleaned the large window that faced the church. Every now and then he'd glance over at the small office behind the glass wall and the two guards sitting there. He was waiting for them to get up and do their round of the workshop, which they had to do every half an hour.

"Is it you?"

He was big, hair in a long ponytail and a beard that made him look much older than his—Hoffmann guessed—twenty years.

"Yes."

He was working on the press, big hands holding metal that would be shaped into rectangular hatches—he could do a couple a minute if he didn't stop to look out the window.

"One g. For today. Every day."

"This afternoon."

"Block H."

"We've got a man there."

"Michal?"

"Yes. You get it off him and pay him."

Hoffmann took his time. He wiped and scrubbed for an hour or more—it was a good way of getting to know the room and working out the distance from the window to the pillars and noting the position of all the surveillance cameras, to know more than everyone else, to be able to control every situation, the difference between life and death. The guards got up from their chairs and left the office and he hurried in with his cart to wipe over an empty desk and an equally empty can, careful to stand with his back to the glass wall and workshop the whole time. He only needed a couple of seconds, the razorblade was in his pocket and he switched it to the top drawer of the desk in an empty space between the pens and paperclips. A new bag in the can, still with his back to the glass, then he went out, took the elevator down to the passage with four locked doors to the administration block.

His body felt itchy and his suit was too tight over the chest. He loosened his tie a touch and ran even faster down the corridor and through the door into the larger building that had swallowed the surrounding buildings and now constituted the greater part of a block dedicated to police operations.

Fredrik Göransson had sweat on his cheeks, neck, back.

Piet Hoffmann. Paula.

Ewert Grens was on his way there, to Aspsås prison, had already booked the time and room. He would only have to question Hoffmann for a couple of minutes, no more, before Hoffmann would lean over the table, ask Grens to switch off the recorder and then burst out laughing and explain that you can go home now, we're working for the same side, for Christ's sake, I'm here working for one of your colleagues and it was your bosses, in that room in the Government Offices, who chose to overlook an execution in a flat in the center so that I could carry on my infiltration here, on the inside.

Göransson stepped out from the elevator and into a room without knocking on the door and without any consideration to the hand that was holding a telephone receiver and the arm that waved that he should wait outside until the call was finished. He sank down into one of the sofas and tugged absent-mindedly at his increasingly red throat. The national police commissioner asked if he could call the person on the other end of the phone back and finished the conversation, looking at a person who was a stranger to him.

"Ewert Grens."

His forehead was moist and his eyes were darting around.

The national police commissioner got up from the desk and walked over to a cart filled with big glasses and small bottles of mineral water. He opened one and poured it over two ice cubes, hoping that it would be sufficiently cool to calm the man down.

"He's on his way there. He's going to question him. It's not good . . . it's . . . we have to burn him."

"Fredrik?"

"We have to—"

"Fredrik, look at me. Exactly what are you talking about?"

"Grens. He's going to question Hoffmann tomorrow. At the prison, in one of the visiting rooms."

"Here. Take the glass. Have some more to drink."

"Don't you understand? We have to burn him."

There were people at every desk in the administration block. He started with the narrow corridor outside, cleaned and scrubbed it until the gray linoleum almost sparkled. Then he waited until one at a time they signaled that he could come in and empty the can and dust the shelves and desk. The rooms were small and anonymous and all looked out over the prison yard. He saw groups of prisoners he didn't know out there, cigarettes in hand as they sat down in the sun to daydream, some with a football on their lap, a couple walking around the track alongside the inner wall. Only one door was shut and he passed it at regular intervals, hoping that it would be open enough for him to look in, and a couple of hours later, it was the only room that remained.

He knocked, waited.

"Yes?"

The chief warden didn't recognize him from yesterday.

"Hoffmann. I'm here to do the cleaning, I thought—"

"You'll have to wait. Until I'm ready. Clean the other rooms in the meantime."

"I have."

Lennart Oscarsson had already closed the door. But Piet Hoffmann had seen what he wanted to see over his shoulder. The desk and the vases of tulips. The buds that had started to open.

He sat down on a chair near the door, with one hand on the cart. He looked over at the door at shorter and shorter intervals. He was starting to get impatient, it was all in place, now all he needed to do was take the second step.

Knock out all existing players.

Take over.

"You there."

The door was open. Oscarsson was looking at him.

"It's fine to go in now."

Oscarsson was on his way to the neighboring office, a woman who according to the sign on her door was something to do with finance. Piet Hoffmann nodded and went in, positioned the cart by the desk and waited. One minute, two minutes. Oscarsson had still not come back, his voice intertwined with the woman's when they laughed at something.

He leaned forward toward the bouquets. The buds had opened enough, not completely open, but enough for fingers to pluck out the cut-down, knotted condoms that contained three grams of chemical amphetamine, made with flower fertilizer rather than acetone in a factory in Siedlce, hence the strong smell of tulips.

Piet Hoffmann emptied fifteen buds in one go, dropped the condoms into the black garbage bag on his cart, listened to the voices in the next room.

He smiled.

He would soon have completed Wojtek's first delivery to the closed market.

☙

Göransson had drunk two glasses of mineral water and had painstakingly chewed each ice cube, a crunching sound that was not nice to listen to.

"I don't understand, Fredrik. Burn who?"

"Hoffmann."

The national police commissioner found it difficult to sit still. He had felt it already when his colleague had walked straight into the room: something that he couldn't put his finger on had barged its way in.

"Would you like coffee?"

"Cigarette."

"But you only smoke in the evening."

"Not today, I don't."

The packet of cigarettes was unopened and lying at the back of the bottom drawer of his desk.

"It's been there for about two years. I don't know if you can smoke them anymore, but it was never my intention to offer them to anyone. They were just meant to be there after every cup of coffee, when there's a yawning hole in your stomach, just as proof that I hadn't started again."

He opened the window as the first puff of smoke drifted over the desk.

"I think it's better if we keep it closed."

The national police commissioner looked at the man who was drawing hard on the cigarette and was right, so he closed the window again and breathed in a smell that was so familiar.

"I don't think you understand—we haven't got much time. Grens will sit down opposite him and listen to the consequences of a meeting we should never have had. Grens will—"

"Fredrik?"

"Yes?"

"You're here. And I'm listening. Just calm yourself down now and give me the full picture."

Fredrik Göransson smoked until there was nothing left to smoke, stubbed out the cigarette, lit a new one and smoked it halfway down. He went back to the sinking feeling by the coffee machine and a detective superintendent who was following up a name that had popped up on the periphery of an investigation—someone who had worked for the official Wojtek and who, according to the authorities' records, had been convicted of aggravated assault and still been given a gun license, a name that was now serving a long sentence for drug offenses and tomorrow morning would be questioned in connection with a murder at Västmannagatan 79.

"Ewert Grens."

"Yes."

"Siw Malmkvist?"

"That's the one."

"The sort who doesn't give up."

The sort who never gives up.

"It'll be a disaster. Do you hear, Kristian, a disaster?"

"It won't be a disaster."

"Grens doesn't let go. Once he's questioned Hoffmann . . . it'll be us, the ones who legitimized all this, protected him."

The national police commissioner didn't say anything, didn't break out in a sweat, but he now understood the anxiety that had entered the room, the kind of anxiety that had to be chased off immediately so that it couldn't grow.

"Wait a moment."

He got up from the sofa and went to the phone, flipped to the back of a black diary and then after a while dialed the number he had been looking for.

The ringing tone when he got through was louder than normal and could even be heard from where Göransson was sitting on the sofa . . . three rings four rings five rings . . . until a deep man's voice answered and the national police commissioner pulled the mouthpiece in closer.

"Pål? It's Kristian. Are you alone?"

The deep voice was a bit too far away, just a faint murmur, but the national police commissioner looked satisfied, gave a brief nod.

"I need your help. We have a mutual problem."

Piet Hoffmann stood in front of the first locked security door in the passage between the administration block and Block G. The camera moved, central security changing the angle and zooming in on a bearded face of around thirty-five that was studied on the monitor, perhaps also compared with a photo in the prison files, a prisoner who had arrived a couple of days ago and was still just one of a whole host of criminals who had been given long sentences.

He had been careful when emptying the trash to make sure that the contents lay on top of the big trash bag on the cleaning cart, so that anyone passing who looked into it would see crumpled-up envelopes and empty plastic cups, not fifty condoms and one hundred fifty grams of amphetamine. He had used the forty-two grams that were in the four library books to knock out the three main dealers in the prison and would now use what had been hidden in the buds of fifty yellow tulips for the first sales from the prison's new dealer. In a few hours, all the prisoners in all the units would know that plenty of chemical drugs were now being sold and distributed by a new prisoner called Piet Hoffmann somewhere in Block G. He wasn't going to sell more than two grams to any of them the first time round, no matter how much they begged or threatened; Wojtek's maiden fix had to be divided among seventy-five imprisoned drug addicts—their first debt with a ruler who would definitely demand it back. He would sell more in a few days once he had taken over the two prison wardens in Block F who were paid by the Greek to regularly smuggle in large amounts.

The clicking sound, central security had finished checking him and opened the door for a few seconds. Hoffmann went through, turned right up the first side passage and stopped after a few long strides, about two and a half meters in. A five-meter blind spot between two cameras. He looked around, no one coming from Block H, no one leaving the administration block.

He rummaged around in the trash bag until he had fished out fifty condoms and emptied the contents into a black plastic bag on the hard floor. A small teaspoon from one of the cups in the chief warden's office held exactly two grams if the powder was level; he divided up the drug into seventy-five small piles.

He worked fast but meticulously, ripping the small white bags into strips and wrapping the two-gram piles in plastic; seventy-five portions at the bottom of the big trash can liner covered by the contents of the admin cans.

"We said eight g, didn't we?"

He had heard him coming, a druggie's steps, feet dragging on concrete. He knew that he would stand there and fawn.

"Eight, that's right isn't it? We said eight?"

Hoffmann shook his head in irritation.

"What's so bloody hard to understand? You'll get two."

Every customer would be able to get at least one hit—today once again journey to a world that was artificial and therefore so much easier to live in. But no one would get enough to begin with to be able to sell on, no other dealers, no competition, the drugs would be controlled from a cell in the left-hand corridor, G2.

"Fucking hell, I—"

"You'll fucking shut up if you want anything at all."

The skinny junkie was shaking even more than he had been in the morning, his feet moving constantly, his eyes everywhere except for the face they were talking to. He was silent, held his hand out until he was given a small white ball and started to walk off before he'd even put it in his pocket.

"I think you've forgotten something."

The skinny prick had a twitch by his eyes, the spasms increased and his cheeks rippled unrhythmically.

"I'll fix the money."

"Fifty kronor a gram."

The twitch stopped for a couple of seconds.

"Fifty?"

Hoffmann smiled at his confusion. He could ask anything from three hundred to four hundred fifty. Now when there were no other suppliers, maybe even six hundred. But he wanted the news to pass through all the walls, and then they could raise it, when all the customers were on one list, the one that belonged to the prison's sole supplier.

"Fifty."

"Fuck, fuck . . . then I want twenty g."

"Two."

"Or thirty, maybe even—"

"You're in debt now."

"I'll fix it."

"We keep an eye on our debts."

"Don't worry, man, I mean I've always—"

"Good. We'll find a solution then."

Faint steps thumping down the passage from Block H that quickly got louder. They could both hear them and the druggie had already started to walk away.

"Do you work?"

"Study."

"Where?"

The skinny guy was sweating and his cheeks were twitching and rippling.

"Fuck, does it—"

"Where?"

"Classroom F3."

"You can order from Stefan from now on. And collect from him."

Two locked doors and the elevator up to Block G. He pushed the cart into the cleaning cupboard that stank of damp cloths, stuffed eleven of the small plastic balls into his pockets and left the rest under the crumpled documents. In an hour they would be passed to other hands in the various prison buildings and in each unit there would be consumers who knew about the new supplier and the quality and the price, and he and Wojtek would have taken over, the lot.

They were waiting for him.

Some in the corridor, a couple in the TV corner, evasive eyes full of hunger.

He had eleven sales in his pockets for a unit that was like all the others: five were going to pay from cash that could be counted in millions, earnings from criminal activities that society seldom managed to stop; six didn't have enough money to pay for the socks on their feet and would end up working for Wojtek on the outside to pay off their debt—they were an investment, criminal labor, and he owned them.

Fredrik Göransson sat on one of the national police commissioner's sofas and listened to the voice on the other end of the telephone talk loudly, the initial low murmur had become clear words in short bursts.

"Mutual problem?"

"Yes."

"This early in the morning?"

The deep man's voice sighed and the national police commissioner continued.

"It's about Hoffmann."

"Well?"

"He's going to be called in for questioning this morning, in one of the visiting rooms. A detective superintendent from city police who's investigating Västmannagatan 79."

He waited for an answer, a reaction, anything. He got nothing.

"That interview, Pål, is not going to happen. Under no circumstances are you going to let Hoffmann meet a policeman as part of the preliminary investigation in connection with that address."

Silence again and when the voice responded, it was once more a low murmur that couldn't be heard from a few meters away.

"I can't say any more. Not here, not now. Apart from that you've got to fix it."

The national police commissioner was sitting on the edge of the desk and it was starting to be uncomfortable. He straightened his back and there was a crunching sound from somewhere in his hip.

"Pål, I just need a couple of days. A week maybe. I want you to do this for me."

He put the phone down and leaned forward, a few more crunches, sounded like his lower back.

"We've got ourselves a few days. Now we have to take action. In order to avoid the same situation happening again in seventy-two or ninety-six hours."

They shared what was left in the coffeepot. Göransson lit another cigarette.

The meeting a couple of weeks earlier in a beautiful room with a view of Stockholm had mutated into something new. Code Paula was no longer an operation that the Swedish police had worked on and waited for for several years; it now also involved a criminal counterpart who they did not know much about and who had knowledge that would have consequences far beyond that oblong meeting table if it were to be passed on.

"So, Erik Wilson is abroad?"

Göransson nodded.

"And Hoffmann's Wojtek contacts in the unit, do we know who they are?"

Chief Superintendent Göransson nodded again, leaned back a touch and for the first time since he sat down, the fabric felt almost comfortable.

The national police commissioner looked at his face, which seemed calmer.

"You're right."

He lifted up the empty coffeepot to see if there was anything left. He was thirsty: he'd never really understood all the fuss about water with bubbles, but poured himself a glass as it was there and, because the room was full of cigarette smoke, found it refreshing.

"If we let it out who Hoffmann is? If the members of an organization find out there's an informant among them—what the organization does then with that knowledge is not our problem. We will not and cannot be responsible for other people's actions."

One more glass, more bubbles.

"Like you said, we'll burn him."

thursday

HE HAD DREAMED ABOUT THE HOLE. FOR FOUR NIGHTS IN A ROW, THE straight edges in the dust on the shelf behind his desk had become a yawning, bottomless hole and no matter where he was or how much he tried to get away, he was drawn toward the black hole and then just as he started to fall, he woke up breathless on the floor behind the corduroy sofa, his back slippery with sweat.

It was half past four and already warm and bright in the courtyard of Kronoberg. Ewert Grens went out into the corridor and over to the small pantry, where a blue hand towel was hanging from the tap. He wet it and went back to the office and the hole that was much smaller in reality. So many hours, such a large part of his day for thirty-five years had revolved around a time that no longer existed. With the wet cloth he wiped over the long, hard edges that marked where the cassette recorder he had been given for his twenty-fifth birthday had stood, then the considerably shorter edges from the cassettes and the photo, even the squares that had been the two loudspeakers, which were kind of beautiful in their clarity.

And now there wasn't even dust.

He moved a cactus plant from the windowsill, the files from the floor—the majority of which contained long-since completed preliminary investigations that should have been filed somewhere—and filled every tiny space on the now empty shelves so that he wouldn't need to fall anymore; the hole had gone and if there wasn't a hole, there couldn't be a bottomless pit.

A cup of black coffee around which the air was still full of swirling dust particles looking for a new home didn't taste as good as usual, as if the dust had dissolved in the brown liquid; it even looked a shade lighter.

He left early—he wanted straight answers and prisoners who were still sleepy were often less mouthy, not so insolent and scornful; interviews were either a power struggle or an attempt to gain confidence and he didn't have time to build up trust. He drove out of the city too fast and along the first kilometers of the E4, then suddenly slowed when he passed Haga and the large cemetery on the left, hesitated before continuing straight on and accelerating again. He could turn off the road on the way back, drive slowly past the people with plants and flowers in one hand and a watering can in the other.

It was still thirty kilometers to the prison that he had visited at least twice a year for the past three decades. As a policeman in Stockholm he would regularly be involved in investigations that ended up there, questioning, prison transport, there was always someone who knew something and someone who had seen something, but the hatred of uniforms was greater there than anywhere else and their fear of the consequences justified, as a snitch never survived long in an enclosed space, so the most usual answer on the recorder was a sneering laugh or simply empty silence.

Yesterday, Ewert Grens had met and written off two of three names on the periphery of the investigation who owned security firms with official links to Wojtek International. He had drunk coffee with a certain Maciej Bosacki in Odensala outside Märsta, and more coffee with Karl Lager in Södertälje and after only a couple of minutes at each table had known that they didn't do executions in city center flats.

Far in the distance, the mighty wall.

He had on occasion walked under the huge prison yard through a network of passages and each time he had met people he avoided in reality, in life. He had taken days and years from them, and he understood why they spat at him, he even respected it, but it did not affect him. They had all pissed on other people and in Ewert Grens's world, anyone who felt they had the right to harm someone else should have the balls to stand up for it later.

The gray concrete grew longer, higher.

He had one name left on the brown-stained paper. Piet Hoffmann, previously convicted of aiming and firing at a policeman, and who had then been granted a gun license all the same. Something was amiss.

Ewert Grens parked the car and walked over to the prison entrance and the prisoner who would shortly be sitting in front of him.

It didn't feel right.

He didn't know why. Maybe it was too quiet. Maybe he was getting locked into his own head as well.

He had fought off any thoughts that carried Zofia with them, which had been worst around two in the morning, just before it started to get light.

He had gotten up, like before, chin-ups, jumping with his feet together until the sweat poured from his forehead and down his chest.

He should be relaxed. Wojtek had gotten their reports, three days in a row. He had stamped out and taken over. From this afternoon, he would be getting bigger deliveries and selling more.

"Morning, Hoffmann."

"Morning."

But he couldn't relax. Something was bothering him, something that demanded space and couldn't be reasoned away.

He was scared.

The doors had been unlocked, his neighbors were moving around out there, he couldn't see them but they were there, shouting and whispering. The sock between the door and the doorframe, the chair in front of the threshold, the pillow under the covers.

Two minutes past seven. Eighteen minutes to go.

He pressed himself against the wall.

The older man at central security studied his police ID, typed something on a computer, sighed.

"Questioning, you say?"

"Yes."

"Grens."

"Yes."

"Piet Hoffmann?"

"I've reserved a room. So it would be great if you could let me in. So I could get to it."

The older man was in no rush. He lifted the phone and punched in a number.

"You'll have to wait a moment. There's something I need to check."

It took fourteen minutes.

Then all hell broke loose.

The door was pulled open. *One second.* The chair was kicked over. *One second.* Stefan passed close to him on the right, a screwdriver in his fist.

There's a moment left, a beat, people always experience half a second in such different ways.

There were probably four of them.

He had seen this happen several times, even taken part himself twice.

Someone ran in with a screwdriver, a table leg, a cut piece of metal. And straight behind, more hands to punch or kill. Two out in the corridor, always at a distance to keep watch.

The pillow and sweatshirt under the covers, his two and half seconds were over, his protection, his escape.

One blow.

He wouldn't manage more.

One single blow, right elbow to the carotid receptors on the left side of the throat, a hard blow right there and Stefan's blood pressure would rocket, he would collapse, faint.

His heavy body fell to the floor, blocking the door for the next pair of balled fists, a sharp piece of metal from the workshop, Karol Tomasz hit out in the air with it in order to keep his balance. Piet Hoffmann squeezed out between the doorframe and a shoulder that still hadn't quite fathomed where the person who was going to die was hiding. He ran out into the corridor between the two who were standing guard and on toward the closed door of the security office.

They know.

He ran and looked around, they were standing there.

They know.

He opened the door and went into the guards' room and someone roared *stukatj* behind him and the principal prison officer shouted *get the hell out of here.* He probably didn't shout anything himself, he couldn't be certain but it didn't feel like it, he stayed where he was in front of the closed door and whispered *I want to be put in isolation*, and when they didn't react, he said a bit louder *I want a P18* and when none of the goddamn staring guards moved at all, in spite of everything, he did scream, *now, you fuckers*, presumably that's what he did, *I need to be in isolation now.*

Ewert Grens sat on a chair in the visiting room and looked at a roll of toilet paper on the floor by the bed and a mattress that was covered in plastic and stuck out over the end of the frame—fear and longing that for one hour every month was distilled down to two bodies holding each other tight. He moved over to the window, not much of a view: a couple of crude bars edged with barbed wire and farther back, the lower part of a thick gray concrete wall. He sat down again, the restlessness that was always in him and never let him relax. He played with the black cassette recorder that stood in the middle of the table every time he came here to question people who hadn't seen or heard anything; he remembered the faces as they came closer and lowered their voices, stared at the floor, full of hate, until he shut off. He wasn't sure that any of the interviews he'd done in this room had ever really helped him to solve an investigation.

There was a knock at the door and a man came in. According to the documents, Hoffmann was not yet middle-aged, so this was someone else, considerably older and in a blue prison staff uniform.

"Lennart Oscarsson. Chief Warden of Aspsås."

Grens took his outstretched hand and smiled.

"Well blow me down, the last time we met you were just a lowly principal officer. You've come up in the world. Have you managed to let anymore go?"

A few years in a couple of seconds.

They were there, back to the time when Principal Prison Officer Lennart Oscarsson had granted a convicted, relapsed pedophile an escorted hospital visit, a pervert who had done a runner while he was being transported and murdered a five-year-old girl.

"Last time we met, you were *just* a detective superintendent. And now . . . you still are?"

"Yes. You need to make major mistakes to be kicked up the ass."

Grens stood on the other side of the table and waited for more sarcasm, something just as funny, but it didn't come. He'd seen it as soon as Oscarsson entered the room—the chief warden seemed distant, unfocused, his mind elsewhere.

"You're here to talk to Hoffmann."

"Yes."

"I've just come from the hospital wing. You can't see him."

"I'm sorry, I notified you of my visit yesterday and he was fit as a fiddle then."

"They were hospitalized last night."

"They?"

"Three so far. Soaring temperatures. We don't know what it is. The prison doctor has decided that they should be in isolation. They are not permitted to see anyone at all until we know what it is."

Ewert Grens gave a loud sigh.

"How long?"

"Three, maybe four days. That's all I can say at the moment."

They looked at each other, there wasn't much more to say and they were just getting ready to go when a piercing noise ripped through the air. The black square of plastic on Oscarsson's hip flashed red, one flash for every loud bleep.

The warden grabbed the alarm that hung on his belt and read the display, his face aghast at first, then stressed and evasive.

"Sorry, I've got to go."

He was already on his way out.

"Something has obviously happened. Can you find your own way out?"

Lennart Oscarsson ran toward the stairs, down and along the passage toward the prison units. Checked the alarm display again.

G2.

Block G, first floor.

That was where he was.

The prisoner he had just lied about on the explicit order of the head of the Prison and Probation Service.

HE HAD SHOUTED AT THEM AND THEN SAT DOWN ON THE FLOOR.

They had reacted after a while—one of the guards had locked the door from the inside and stayed by the glass window to keep an eye on the men out in the corridor, and another had rung central security and asked for assistance from the prison riot squad to escort a prisoner to an isolation cell following a supposed threat.

He had moved to a chair and was now partially hidden from the people circling outside who whispered *stukatj* sufficiently loud for him to hear as they passed.

Stukatj.

Snitch.

The door to the national police commissioner's office was open.

Göransson knocked lightly on the doorframe. He was expected—a large silver thermos on the table between the sofas, open sandwiches in crumpled paper bags from the small breakfast café at the other end of Bergsgatan. He poured two cups of coffee and wolfed down a sandwich. He was hungry, the anxiety was draining him. He had walked down the corridor and slowly past Grens's office, the only one where the lights were often on early in the morning, drowning everything in banal music. It was as empty as Göransson felt. Ewert Grens, who normally slept there and was at his desk working as soon as it was light outside, wasn't there. He had already left for the prison in Aspsås, as early as he said he would yesterday. *Grens must not talk to Hoffmann.* A large piece of bread got stuck in his mouth and grew until he was forced to spit it out onto the paper plate. *Hoffmann must not talk to Grens.* He drank some more coffee, rinsing down what was still stuck.

"Fredrik?"

The national police commissioner had returned and sat down beside his colleague.

"Fredrik, what's wrong? Are you okay?"

Göransson tried to smile but couldn't, his mouth just wouldn't do it.

"No."

"We'll manage to sort this out."

He took a bite of a sandwich, lifted up the cheese—something green underneath, pepper or maybe a couple of slices of cucumber.

"I've just gotten off the phone. Grens is on his way back from Aspsås. And has been told he won't be able to see the prisoner called Piet Hoffmann for three, maybe even four days."

Göransson looked at the piece of bread. The cramps in his body receded somewhat, so he picked it up and tried to fill the void again.

"Troubled."

"Pardon?"

"You asked how I was. Troubled. That's what I am. Bloody troubled."

He left the cheese and bread on the plate, and later threw it in the trash. He couldn't do it. His mouth, his throat, he was so dry.

"Troubled in case Hoffmann talks. Troubled to find out what I'm prepared to do to stop him."

They had burned informants before. *We don't know who he is.* Dropped them when there were too many questions. *We don't work with criminals.* Looked the other way when the hunt began and the criminal organization that had been infiltrated found its own solutions.

But never in a prison, never locked up with no escape.

Life, death.

Suddenly it was all so clear.

"What troubles you most?"

The national police commissioner leaned toward him.

"You have to think about it, Fredrik. What troubles you the most? The consequences if Hoffmann talks? Or the consequences if we take action?"

Göransson was silent.

"Do you have any choice, Fredrik?"

"I don't know."

"Do I have any choice?"

"I don't know!"

The silver thermos fell to the floor when Göransson made an uncontrolled, sweeping gesture over the table. The national police commissioner waited, then picked it up when he decided that the man wasn't going to strike out again.

"Fredrik, listen to me."

He moved closer.

"What we are doing is not wrong. It's just the way things are. *We are doing no wrong.* The only thing *we* are doing and the only thing *we* have done is to talk to a lawyer who represents two Wojtek members who are doing time in Aspsås. If *he* then decides to give that information to his clients, if *he* decided to do that yesterday evening, then we can't be held responsible. And if his clients then choose to do something, which prisoners often do, we are not responsible for that either."

He didn't come much closer but did move forward a little more.

"*We* can't be responsible for anything other than *our own* actions."

It was possible to see Kronobergsparken from the window. There were some small children playing in the sandpit and a couple of dogs running around that refused to listen to their masters who each waited with leash in hand. It was a lovely little park right in the middle of Kungsholmen. Göransson looked at it for a long time, he didn't normally go there and he wondered why.

"The consequences if he talks."

"Sorry?"

Göransson stayed standing by the window, soothed by the air that came in through the small open rectangle at the top.

"Your question. What troubles me most. The consequences if Hoffmann talks."

He moved the chair slightly to the left. Now he could see the whole corridor through the glass, and the pool table where the four who had just attacked him were pretending to play while keeping an eye on him. It was obvious that they wanted him to know that he was a goddamn rat who had nowhere to go, a prison is a closed system with walls that shut you in and anyone who wants to run will soon meet something hard that they can't get past. Karol Tomasz was standing closest—he raised his arm, pointed at his mouth, formed the word *stukatj* over and over again.

Paula no longer existed.

Piet Hoffmann tried to find somewhere deep inside that wasn't roaring, he had to try to understand that he now had a new mission, to survive.

They knew.

They must have found out in the evening, during the night. Nothing had changed at lockup time, someone had communication channels that opened locked doors.

If you're about to be exposed, you can't escape very far in a prison, but you can demand to be put in isolation.

There were ten of them, helmets and riot shields to protect them, and armed with sedatives to keep control. The prison riot squad had run across the yard and up the stairs of Block G. Six of them would stay to prevent and discourage repeated violence, four of them would escort the vulnerable prisoner down the passage and deep into the bowels of the earth, to Block C and the voluntary isolation unit, two escorts behind, two in front.

You might be given a death sentence. But you're not going to die.

Sixteen cells here as well. Voluntary isolation was built to look like any other unit in any prison—the wardens' room, the TV corner, the showers, the kitchen, the Ping-Pong table—the people who asked to come here could move around freely without the risk of bumping into prisoners from other units in the prison. The faces he saw were the only ones he would meet.

A week.

He would wait, avoid confrontation; he could stay alive here, survive here. Outside the door he was dead—every part of the big prison was a potential screwdriver to the throat, a table leg against his forehead as many times as was needed to make it cave in. In one week, Erik and the city police would come and get him. He wouldn't die, not yet, not with Hugo and Rasmus, not with Zofia, he wouldn't

would not

would not

would

not

"Are you all right?"

He had fallen to the floor without using his hands, hitting his cheek and chin, and for a few seconds was somewhere else: the attack, the guards in the aquarium, the mouths forming *stukatj*, the riot guys in their black uniforms . . . He suddenly found it hard to breathe and had felt his legs swaying as he tried to stay upright.

He hadn't known until now that all the damned energy just drains from your body when the only thing that exists is a fear of death.

"I don't know. Toilet, I need to wash my face, I'm sweating."

The sink in the middle looked almost clean. He turned on the tap and let the water run until it was cold, stuck his head under it to cool his neck and back, then filled his hands and rubbed against the skin of his face, as if he was returning—he wasn't even particularly dizzy.

The kick caught him on the side.

The pain was intense, burning from somewhere on his hip.

Piet Hoffmann hadn't seen or heard the solid, long-haired guy in his twenties coming in, running toward him, but with guards from the riot squad outside he wasn't going to do much more, he just spat and whispered *stukatj* and closed the door when he left.

Death sentence. Already on his head.

He got up, coughed, and felt over his hip with one hand. The kick had caught him farther up than he first thought, broken a couple of his ribs. He had to get out of here. To the next level. Solitary confinement. Total isolation, only contact with the guards, never have any contact with other prisoners, twenty-four hours a day, locked in a cell with no way in and no way out.

Stukatj.

He had to get away again. He mustn't die.

Ewert Grens had stopped halfway back from Aspsås, at the OK gas station in Täby, and was sitting on one of the stools by the window with an orange juice and a cheese sandwich. *Soaring temperatures. Isolation. Three, maybe four days.* He had stood in the visiting room with its toilet rolls and plastic-covered mattress and wanted to thump the walls, but had refrained; it would be pointless to argue with a prison doctor about infections he'd never heard about. He bought another artificial sandwich, it was the final stretch back to Stockholm and he couldn't put it off any longer. He turned off the E4 at Haga South, drove past the hospital and stopped some way down Solna Kyrkväg. Entrance 1, as far as he had come the last time.

He was not alone.

Visitors, park attendants, and watering cans, all heading toward the grass and rows of headstones. He rolled down the window, it was muggy, air that stuck to your back.

"Do you work here?"

A person in blue overalls with two spades on the back of a moped. The park attendant, or church warden, stopped by the man who was still in his car, shielded by the door, not daring to get out.

"Have for seventeen years."

Grens fidgeted uneasily and moved the sandwich wrapper that rustled on the seat. His eyes followed an old lady leaning over a small gray stone that looked new, a plant in one hand and an empty pot in the other.

"So you know the place well?"

"You could say that."

She started to dig, then with great care put the plant in the soil, had just enough room in the thin strip between the headstone and the grass.

"I was wondering . . ."

"Yes?"

"I was wondering . . . if you want to find out about a particular grave, where someone is buried . . . what do you do?"

Lennart Oscarsson stood by the window at the far end of a room he had aspired to all his adult life. The chief warden's office at Aspsås prison. After twenty-one years as a prison warden, principal officer, and acting chief, he had finally been appointed as chief warden four months ago and had moved all his files into the shelves that were slightly longer and attached to the wall next to the sofas that were slightly softer. He had dreamed of having this office for so long that when he stood there with his dream in his hands, he didn't know what to do with it. What do you do when you no longer have dreams? Escape? He gave a faint sigh as he looked out of the window at prisoners on a break in the yard: large groups of people who had murdered, abused, stolen, and were sitting out there on the dry gravel, either reflecting or repressing their emotions in order to cope. He looked up over the wall to the small town with rows of white-and-red houses, stopped at the window that had for a long time been a family bedroom—now he lived there alone, he had made a choice, but he had made the wrong choice, and sometimes it is too late to right our wrongs.

He sighed again without realizing it. The evening and night had been filled with fury, the sort that crept up on you, started to ferment in your mind, then grew into frustration. It had started with a feeling of irritation just by his temples when he heard the voice that he recognized, but had never spoken to before. He had been sitting at the kitchen table eating his supper as he always did, even though it was now only set for one, and he had almost finished when the phone rang. The general director had been friendly but firm when he told him that the detective superintendent from city police who was coming to Aspsås in the morning to question a prisoner in G2, Piet Hoffmann, must not be allowed to do so. They must not meet under any circumstances, not today nor the next day nor the next. Lennart Oscarsson had not asked any questions and had not understood until later, when he was washing up one plate, one glass, one knife and fork, where the irritation that had turned into rage was coming from.

A lie.

A lie that had just been born.

He had asked Ewert Grens to leave and had been on his way out when the alarm sucked all the air from the small room. A prisoner had been threatened, an emergency escort from G2 to the voluntary isolation unit.

Piet Hoffmann.

The name he had been ordered to lie about.

Oscarsson bit his lower lip until it started to bleed. He chewed the wound with his teeth until it stung, as if to punish himself, maybe in order to forget for a moment the fury that made him want to open the window and jump out and run to the town and the people who knew nothing.

The attack and the phone call to say that a policeman must not be allowed to carry out an interview were linked. There was more—he had been given another order—he was to allow a lawyer to visit a client last evening. They did come knocking every now and then when an imminent trial or recently pronounced sentence required a lawyer in the cell, but never on order and seldom after lockup. This one had visited a Pole in G2 and was one of the lawyers paid to convey planted information, Oscarsson was sure of it.

A late visit by a lawyer in the same unit as a reported attack the next morning.

Lennart Oscarsson bit his lower lip again, his blood tasting of iron and something else. He didn't know what he'd expected. Perhaps he had been naive, all the days he had looked up at the room where he was now standing and thought about the uniform he was now wearing. Whatever it was, he had never imagined that it would mean this.

A cell with absolutely no personal belongings, just a bunk, a chair, a wardrobe, no colors and no soul. He had not left it since he got here and he wasn't going to be staying. His death sentence had gotten here before him. It had been standing in the bathroom, waiting, with a kick to the hip and a mouth that whispered *stukatj* with the promise of more. If he was going to survive a week, he could only do it in another sort of isolation, solitary confinement, where prisoners were separated not only from the rest of the prison but also from each other, locked into the cells every hour of the day.

He stood on his toes when he pissed—the sink was a bit too high on the wall, but he wasn't going to go out there, not to the toilets.

Then he pressed a button by the door and held it down.

"You want something?"

"I want to make a phone call."

"There's a phone in the corridor."

"I'm not going out there."

The guard stepped into the cell and bent over the sink.

"It stinks."

"I have the right to make a phone call."

"Fuck, you pissed in the sink."

"I have the right to call my lawyer, noncustodial services, the police and my five approved numbers. And I want to do that now."

"In this unit, which you asked to come to yourself, we use the toilets in the corridor. And I haven't got your damn list."

"The police. I want to call a number on the city police switchboard. You can't refuse me."

"There's a telephone in—"

"I want to call from here. I have the right to call the police in private."

Twelve rings.

Piet Hoffmann held the cordless phone in his hand. Erik Wilson wasn't there, he knew that he was away in the United States, at some course in the southeast, during the period that they were not going to have any contact. But that was where he called, his office, that was where he had to begin.

He was put through again.

When you've asked to be put in isolation, once you have that protection, contact us and wait for a week. That's the time we'll need to get the papers sorted for someone to come and get you out.

Fourteen rings.

Erik wasn't going to answer, no matter how long he waited.

"I want to call the switchboard."

I am alone.

The regular tone of a switchboard, muffled, feeble.

No one knows yet.

"Police Authority, Stockholm, can I help you?"

"Göransson."

"Which one?"

"The head of criminal operations."

The female voice put him through. Then that muffled, feeble ringing, again and again. *I am alone. No one knows yet.* He waited with the receiver pressed to his ear. The regular sound got louder, with each ring it got a little louder until it was piercing his brain and mixing with the voice from the bathroom that passed the closed cell and shouted *stukatj* once, twice, three times.

Ewert Grens lay on the corduroy sofa and looked at the shelf behind the desk and the hole that he had filled again early that morning, the row of files and a lonely cactus that concealed a whole life. *As if there hadn't been any dust.* He turned around and looked at the ceiling, spotted new cracks that were about to separate and then come together, only to separate again. He had stayed in the car. The park attendant had pointed toward the lawns and trees that were practically a forest, explained that the new graves were at the far end toward Haga. He had even offered to go with him, show the way to someone who had never been there before. Grens had thanked him and shaken his head, he would go there another day.

"The noise?"

Someone had stopped in his doorway.

"Do you want something?"

"The noise."

"What damned noise?"

"The noise. That . . . atonal one. Dissonance."

Lars Ågestam crossed the threshold.

"The noise that I normally hear. Siw Malmkvist. I was heading for it now. Until I realized that I'd walked past. That it was . . . silent."

The public prosecutor stepped into an office that looked different, as if it had taken on new dimensions and what had previously been at the center had disappeared.

"Have you rearranged the furniture?"

He looked at the shelf. The files, preliminary investigations, a dead potted plant. A bit of wall that had previously been something else, presumably the center.

"What have you done?"

Grens didn't answer. Lars Ågestam listened to the music that had always been there, that he detested and had been forced to listen to.

"Grens? Why . . . ?"

"That's got nothing to do with you."

"You've—"

"I don't want to talk about it."

The prosecutor swallowed—there might have been something to talk about that wasn't to do with law; he had tried and he regretted it as usual.

"Västmannagatan."

"What about it?"

"I gave you three days."

Not a sound. And that wasn't how it should be, in here.

"Three days. For the last names."

"We're not quite finished."

"If you still haven't got anything . . . Grens, I will scale down the case this time."

Ewert Grens had been lying down until now. He quickly got up, his body leaving a deep impression on the soft sofa.

"You damn well won't! We've done exactly what you suggested. Identified and contacted several names on the periphery of the investigation. We've questioned them, dismissed them. All except one. A certain Piet Hoffmann who is already doing time and right now is in the prison's hospital unit and out of bounds."

"Out of bounds?"

"Isolation. For three or four days."

"What do you think?"

"I think he's very interesting. There's something . . . he doesn't fit."

The young prosecutor looked at the files and the potted plant that disguised what once had been. He would never have believed it, that Grens would let go of something that he only needed to love at a distance.

"Four days. So that you can question this last guy. Either you manage to link him to the crime in that time, or I scale it down."

The detective superintendent nodded and Lars Ågestam started to walk out of the room he had never laughed in, not even smiled in. Every visit here had been fraught with conflict and an inhabitant that tried at once to repel and hurt. He moved quickly in order to get away from the staleness and so didn't hear the cough and didn't notice when a piece of paper was pulled from an inner pocket.

"Ågestam?"

The prosecutor stopped, wondered whether he'd heard correctly. It was Grens's voice and it sounded almost friendly, perhaps even apologetic.

"Do you know what this is?"

Ewert Grens unfolded the piece of paper and put it down on the table in front of the sofa.

A map.

"North Cemetery."

"Have you been there?"

"What do you mean?"

"Have you? Been there?"

Strange questions. The closest they had ever come to a conversation.

"Two of my relatives are buried there."

Ågestam had never seen this arrogant bastard so . . . small. Grens played with the map of one of Sweden's largest cemeteries and struggled for words.

"Then you'll know . . . I wondered . . . is it nice there?"

The door to the cell at the end of the corridor in the voluntary isolation unit was open. The prisoner from G2 had been escorted there through the underground tunnel by four members of the prison riot squad and after that he had demanded to phone the police, and then proceeded to make their lives hell. He had kept ringing the bell and demanding to be moved again, had shouted about solitary confinement and hit the walls, overturned the wardrobe, smashed the chair and pissed all over the floor until it ran out under the door into the corridor. He had been terrified but seemed to hold himself together, scared but in control. He knew what he was saying and why and he didn't go to pieces and collapse—the prisoner called Piet Hoffmann would only be quiet when he knew that someone was listening. Lennart Oscarsson had been standing in his office looking out over the prison yard and town hall in the distance when he had been informed of the disturbance involving a prisoner in the voluntary isolation unit in Block C and had decided to go there himself, to meet someone he didn't know but who had haunted him since a late phone call the night before.

"In there?"

He had seen him before. The cleaner in the administration block. He had seemed taller then, more straight-backed, eyes that were curious and alert. The person sitting on the bunk with his knees pulled up under his chin and his back pressed hard to the wall was someone else.

Only death, or fleeing from it, could change someone so quickly.

"Is there a problem, Hoffmann?"

The prisoner who couldn't be questioned tried to look more together than he actually was.

"I don't know. What d'you think? Or did you come here to get your trash emptied?"

"I think it would seem so. And that it's you that's causing it. The problem."

The order to grant a lawyer access to your unit.

"You asked for voluntary isolation. You refused to say why. And now you've got it, voluntary isolation."

The order that you must not be questioned.

"So . . . what's your problem?"

"I want to be put in the hole."

"You want what?"

"The hole. Solitary confinement."

I see you.

You're sitting there in the clothes we've issued.

But I don't understand who you are.

"Solitary confinement? Exactly . . . what exactly are you talking about, Hoffmann?"

"I don't want to have any contact with the other prisoners."

"Are you being threatened?"

"No contact. That's all I'm saying."

Piet Hoffmann looked out through the open door. Prisoners who moved around freely represented death just as much here as in any other unit. They had been moved away from others but not from each other.

"That's not the way it works. Hoffmann, solitary confinement is our decision. It's not something that individual prisoners can decide. You've been moved here on your request, in accordance with Paragraph eighteen. That's our duty. We are under obligation to do that if you request it. But the hole, solitary confinement, has a completely different set of regulations and conditions. Paragraph fifty is not something you can request, it's not voluntary, it is a decision that is enforced. By a principal officer in your unit. Or by me."

They were walking around out there, and they knew. He wouldn't survive the week here.

"Enforced?"

"Yes."

"And how the fuck is that decision made?"

"If you're a danger to someone else. Or to yourself."

With walls that locked you in there was nowhere to hide.

"A danger?"

"Yes."

"In what way?"

"Violence. Toward fellow prisoners. Or one of us, one of the staff."

They were waiting for him.

They whispered *stukatj*.

He moved closer to the chief warden and looked into a face that crumpled with pain—he had hit him hard.

HE SAT ON THE HARD CONCRETE FLOOR. HE'D HEARD TALK OF SOLITARY confinement cells that were called the hole or the cage, he'd heard tales of people who excelled in violence in the world outside but who had broken after a few days in solitary confinement and were taken to the hospital unit in a fetal position, or those who had quietly hanged themselves with a sheet. A person couldn't be further removed from life, from what was natural.

He was sitting on the floor as there wasn't a chair. A heavy metal bed and a cement toilet bowl that was solidly attached to the floor. That was it.

He had hit the chief warden in the middle of the face with his fist. The top of the cheek, eye, and nose. Oscarsson had fallen from the chair onto the floor, bleeding but conscious. The guards had rushed in, the chief warden held his hands in front of his face to protect himself against anything else, and Piet Hoffmann had voluntarily stretched his arms and legs for them to carry him out. The four guards each struggled with a part of his body while the prisoners lined the corridor and watched.

He had survived the attack. He had survived voluntary isolation. He had managed to get here, as much protection as you could get in a closed prison, but he shrank just as he had before, *I am alone, no one knows yet*, he curled up on the hard surface, freezing then sweating then freezing again. He was still lying there when one of the guards opened the square hatch in the door to ask if he wanted his hour out in the fresh air—an hour a day in a cake slice–shaped cage with blue sky high above the metal mesh—but he shook his head. He didn't want to leave the cell, didn't want to expose himself to anyone.

Lennart Oscarsson closed the door to the voluntary isolation unit and went slowly down the stairs, one at a time, to the ground floor of Block C. One hand to his cheek, his fingertips touching the swelling. It was tender and particularly swollen along the zygomatic bone, and there was a taste of blood on his tongue and in his throat. Give it about an hour, then the area around his eye would turn blue. The chief warden felt physical pain every second from a face that would take a long time to heal, but it meant nothing. It was the other pain, the one from the inside that he felt—all his working life he had lived with men who had no place in real society and he had been proud that he could read difficult people better than anyone, his professional knowledge, the only thing he felt was worth anything anymore.

This punch, he hadn't seen it coming.

He hadn't understood the desperation, hadn't anticipated the force of Hoffmann's fear.

The riot squad had carried him down to where the bastard belonged, and he would stay there for a long time in the shittiest of shitty cells. Lennart Oscarsson would file a report that afternoon, and a long sentence would become even longer. It didn't help. He felt his tender cheek with his fingers. It didn't change anything, didn't ease his frustration at having misread a prisoner.

The iron bed, the cement toilet. No matter how long he waited, the cell was never going to be more than that. The dirty walls that had once been white, the ceiling that had never been painted, the floor that was so cold. He rang the bell again, kept his finger on the button long enough to irritate them. One of the guards would break in the end and hurry over to tell the prisoner who had assaulted the chief warden to stop ringing the bell or to look forward to days in a straitjacket.

He was cold again.

They knew. He was a snitch, he had a death threat. They would manage to get in here too. It was just a matter of time, as not even a carefully locked cell door could protect him. Wojtek had money and anyone could be bought when death was involved.

The square hatch was some way up the door. It scraped and whined when it was opened.

Staring eyes.

"You want something?"

Who are you?

"I want to make a phone call."

Guard?

"And why should we let you phone?"

Or one of them?

"I want to call the police."

The eye came closer, laughed.

"You want to call the police? And do what? Report that you've just assaulted a prison warden? Those of us who work here don't have much time for that sort of thing."

"None of your fucking business why and you know that. You know that you can't refuse me a phone call to the police."

The eye was silent. The hatch was closed. Steps disappeared.

Piet Hoffmann got up from the cold floor and threw himself over the button on the wall, held it in, he guessed for about five minutes.

Suddenly the door was pulled open. Three blue uniforms. The staring eyes that he now was convinced belonged to a guard. Beside him, another one, the same kind. Behind them, a third, with enough stripes for him to be a principal officer, an older man, in his sixties.

He was the one who spoke.

"My name is Martin Jacobson. I'm the principal officer here. Boss in this unit. What's the problem?"

"I've asked to make a phone call. To the police. It's my damn right."

The principal officer studied him—a prisoner in oversize clothes who was sweating and found it difficult to stand still—then looked at the guard with the staring eyes.

"Roll in the phone."

"But—"

"I don't care why he's here. Let him phone."

He crouched on the edge of the iron bed with the telephone receiver in his hand.

He had asked for the city police every time he got through. More rings this time—he had counted twenty for both Erik Wilson and Göransson.

Neither of them had answered.

He sat locked in a cell that had nothing other than an iron bed and a cement toilet bowl. He had no contact with the world outside or the other prisoners. None of the guards outside his cell door had any idea that he was there on behalf of the Swedish police.

He was stuck. He couldn't get out. He was alone in a prison where he had been condemned to death by his fellow prisoners.

He undressed himself and stood there shivering. He waved his arms around and started to sweat. He held his breath until the pressure in his chest was more than pain.

He lay face down on the floor, wanting to feel something, anything, that wasn't fear.

Piet Hoffmann knew as soon as the door into the corridor opened and then shut again.

He didn't need to see, he just knew—they were there.

The heavy steps of someone moving slowly. He hurried over to the cell door, put his ear to the cold metal, listened. A new prisoner being escorted by several wardens.

Then he heard it, a voice he recognized.

"*Stukatj.*"

Stefan's voice. On his way to a cell farther down the corridor.

"What did you say?"

The guard with the eyes. Piet Hoffmann pressed his ear even harder to the inside of the cell door—he wanted to be certain that he heard every word.

"*Stukatj. It's Russian.*"

"We don't speak Russian down here."

"*There's someone who does.*"

"Into the cell with you now, just get in!"

They were here. Soon there would be more, every prisoner in solitary confinement from now on would know that there was a snitch here, stewing in one of the cells.

Stefan's voice, it had been pure hate.

He pressed the red button and he would continue to press it until the guards came.

They had let him know they were there. Now it was just a question of when, of time. Hours, days, weeks, the pursuers and the pursued knew that the moment would come when there was no more waiting.

The square hatch opened, but it was other eyes, the older principal officer.

"I want—"

"Your hands are shaking."

"For fuck's sake—"

"You're sweating heavily."

"Telephone, I want—"

"You've got a twitch in your eye."

He was still pressing on the button. A piercing pitch that echoed in the corridor.

"Finger off the button, Hoffmann. You've got to calm down. And before I do anything . . . I want to know what's up."

Piet Hoffmann lowered his hand. It was eerily quiet around them.

"I have to make another phone call."

"You just made one."

"The same number. Until I get an answer."

The cart with the phone and telephone directory on it was wheeled in and the gray-haired principal officer dialed the number he knew by heart. He watched the prisoner's face the whole time: the spasms in the muscles around his eyes, his forehead and hairline that were shiny and dripping, a person who was fighting his own fear as he waited for a phone that was not answered.

"You're not looking good."

"I have to make another call."

"You can do it later."

"I have to—"

"You didn't get an answer. You can call again later."

Piet Hoffmann didn't let go of the receiver. He held it in his hands that were shaking as he met the eyes of the warden.

"I want my books."

"Which books?"

"In my cell. In G2. I have the right to have five books down here. I want two of them. I can't just sit here staring at the walls. They're on my bedside table. *Nineteenth Century Stockholm* and *The Marionettes*. I want them here, now."

The prisoner didn't shake as much when he talked about his books. He calmed down.

"Poetry?"

"You got a problem with that?"

"Not often that it's read down here."

"I need it. It helps me to believe in the future."

The flush on the prisoner's face had started to recede.

"Then suddenly it hits me that the ceiling, my ceiling, is someone else's floor."

"What?"

"Ferlin. *Barefooted Child.* If you like poetry, I can—"

"Just get me my books."

The older warden said nothing, just pulled the cart out of the cell and locked the heavy door. It was quiet again. Piet Hoffmann stayed on the cold floor and wiped his wet brow. He had twitches and spasms, he was shaking, he was sweating. He hadn't realized that it was visible, his fear.

HE HAD MOVED FROM THE FLOOR TO THE BED AND LAIN DOWN ON THE thin mattress that didn't have any sheets or covers. He was freezing and had curled up in his stiff, oversize clothes and eventually fallen asleep, dreamed that Zofia was running in front of him and he couldn't get close to her no matter how much he tried, her hand disintegrated when he touched it, she shouted and he answered but she couldn't hear him, his voice dwindled to nothing and she got smaller and smaller, farther and farther away until she disappeared.

He was woken by noise outside in the corridor.

Someone was being escorted to the bathroom or the cage for some air, someone who had said something. He went over to the door, ear to the square hatch. It was another voice this time, Swedish, no accent, a voice that he hadn't heard before.

"Paula, where are you?"

He was sure that he'd heard it right.

"Paula, you're not hiding are you?"

The warden with the eyes told the voice to shut up.

It had shouted in no particular direction, but just outside his cell, selected a specific listener.

Piet Hoffmann sank down behind the door, sat there with his chest and chin against his knees, his legs weren't working.

Someone had exposed him as a *stukatj* last night, he had been given a death sentence. But . . . Paula . . . he hadn't understood it, not until now, that this someone had also known his code name. Paula. Christ . . . there were only four people who knew the code name Paula. Erik Wilson had made it up. Chief Inspector Göransson had approved it. Only those two, for many years, only those two. After the meeting in Rosenbad, two more. The national police commissioner. The state secretary. No one else.

Paula.

It was one of those four.

It was one of them, his protection, his escape—one of them had burned him.

"Paula, we want to meet you so much."

The same voice, farther away now toward the showers, then the same tired "shut up" from the wardens who didn't understand.

Piet Hoffmann held his legs even tighter, pressed them into his body.

He was already everyone's quarry. He was a snitch in a prison where informants were hated as much as sex offenders.

Someone banged on their door.

Someone screamed *stukatj* on the other side.

Soon it would be as it always was when the shared hate was focused on one locked cell door. First, two who banged, then three and four, then more, minute by minute, hatred channeled into the hands that hit harder and harder. He put his hands to his ears, but the banging penetrated his head until he couldn't stand it anymore, he pressed the button and held it down until the noise of the bell drowned out the monotone rhythm.

The square hatch opened. The principal officer's eye.

"Yes?"

"I want to make that phone call. And I want my books. I have to phone and I have to have my books."

The door opened. The older principal prison officer came in, ran his hand through his thick, gray hair and pointed out into the corridor.

"All that banging . . . has that got anything to do with you?"

"No."

"I've been working here for a long time. You're twitching, you're shaking, you're sweating. You're bloody frightened. And I think that's why you want to phone."

He closed the door and made sure that the prisoner made note.

"Am I right?"

Piet Hoffmann looked at the blue uniform in front of him. He seemed friendly. He sounded friendly.

Don't trust anyone.

"No. It's got nothing to do with that. I just want to make a phone call now."

The principal prison officer sighed. The telephone cart was standing at the other end of the corridor, so this time he got out his mobile phone, dialed the number of city police and handed it over to the prisoner who refused to admit that he was frightened and that the banging out there had anything to do with it.

The first number. Ringing tone and no answer.

Twitching, shaking, sweating, it all got worse.

"Hoffmann."

"One more. The other number."

"You're not in a good way. I want to call a doctor. You should go to the hosp—"

"Dial the fucking number. You're not moving me anywhere."

Ringing tone again. Three rings. Then a man's voice.

"Göransson."

He had answered.

His legs, he could feel them again.

He had answered.

He was just about to tell them, in a couple of moments they could start the administrative procedures that would mean freedom in a week.

"Jesus, finally, I've been trying . . . I need help. Now."

"Who am I talking to?"

"Paula?"

"Who?"

"Piet Hoffmann."

The silence didn't last that long, but it sounded like the phone had been put down, the electronic void that is empty, dead.

"Hello? For fuck's shake, hello, where—"

"I'm still here. What did you say your name was?"

"Hoffmann. Piet Hoffmann. We—"

"I'm very sorry, I have no idea who you are."

"What the fuck . . . you know . . . you know perfectly well who I am, we met, just recently in the state secretary's office . . . I—"

"No, we've never met. Now, if you'll excuse me, I've got a lot to do."

Every muscle was tensed, his stomach was burning and his chest and his throat and when everything is burning you have to scream or run or hide or . . .

"I'm going to call the hospital unit now."

The telephone in his hand. He refused to let go.

"I'm not going anywhere until I've got my two books."

"The phone."

"My books. I have the right to have five books in solitary confinement!"

He loosened his grip on the phone and let it slip out of his hand.

It cracked when it hit the floor, plastic bits bouncing in every direction. He lay down next to them, his arms around his stomach and chest and throat, it was still burning and when everything is burning, you have to run or hide.

"DID HE SOUND DESPERATE?"

"Yes."

"Stressed?"

"Yes."

"Frightened?"

"Very frightened."

They looked at each other. *If we let it out who Hoffmann is?* They had more coffee. *What the organization then does with that knowledge is not our problem.* They moved the piles of paper from one side of the table to the other. *We will not and cannot be responsible for other people's actions.*

It should have been over.

They had arranged a meeting for a lawyer with one of his clients that evening. They had burned him.

And yet, not long ago, he had called from a cell, from prison.

"Are you sure?"

"Yes."

"It can't have—"

"It was him."

The national police commissioner fetched the pack of cigarettes that was kept in a desk drawer and not to be smoked. He offered the open pack to his colleague, the matches were on the table and the room was immediately awash with white fug.

"Give me one too."

Göransson shook his head.

"If you haven't smoked for two years, I don't want to encourage you."

"I'm not going to smoke it. I'm just going to hold it."

He felt it between his fingers, sorely missed and familiar—now it offered calm when he most needed it.

"We've got plenty of time."

"Four days. And one's already gone. If Grens and Hoffmann meet . . . If Hoffmann talks . . . if—"

Göransson interrupted himself. He didn't need to say more. They could both visualize the limping detective inspector, aging and obstinate, the sort who never gives up, who pursues the truth as far as he can and then some more when he realizes that a handful of colleagues have known it from the start. He would carry on and he wouldn't stop until he found the ones who had protected it and then buried it.

"It's just a matter of time, Fredrik. An organization that gets hold of that kind of information and has the means will use them. It might take a bit more time when there's no contact with fellow prisoners, but the moment will come."

The national police commissioner fingered the cigarette that wasn't lit.

It was so familiar. He would soon smell his fingertips, hold on to the forbidden pleasure a bit longer.

"But, if you want, we can . . . I mean, being locked away like that, in solitary confinement, it's a terrible place. No human contact. He should be moved back to the unit he came from, to the men he's gotten to know—if he's suffering down there, he should . . . well, he should be with other prisoners. On . . . humanitarian grounds."

HE PAUSED AS HE NORMALLY DID IN FRONT OF THE WINDOW IN THE chief warden's office and looked out over his universe: the big prison and the small town. He had never been particularly curious about what might be elsewhere, what could be seen from here was all he had ever wished for. The reflection of the sun made the window a mirror and he gingerly touched his cheek, nose, forehead. He felt tender, it was hard to see properly in the darkened glass, but looked like the blue around his eye was already changing shade.

He had misread him, a desperation that he hadn't recognized.

"Hello?"

The telephone on the desk had interrupted the feeling of his skin tightening.

"Lennart?"

He recognized the director general's voice.

"It's me."

There was a faint crackling in the receiver, a mobile somewhere outdoors and a strong wind.

"It's about Hoffmann."

"Okay."

"He's to go back. To the unit he came from."

The crackling was now nearly inaudible.

"Lennart?"

"What the hell are you saying?"

"He's to go back. First thing tomorrow morning at the latest."

"There's a serious threat involved."

"On humanitarian grounds."

"He is not going back to that unit. He should not even be in the same prison. If he's going anywhere, it's away, express transport, to Kumla or Hall."

"You're not going to express him anywhere. *He's going to go back.*"

"A prisoner who has been threatened is *never* sent back to the same unit."

"It's an order."

The two bunches of tulips on his desk had started to open, the yellow petals like lit lamps in front of him.

"I was given an order to allow a late visit from a lawyer and I did it. I was given an order not to let a DS carry out an interview, and I did it. But this— I won't do it. If 0913 Hoffmann is sent back to the unit where he was threatened—"

"It's an order. Nonnegotiable."

Lennart Oscarsson bent down toward the yellow petals, wanted to smell something that was genuine. His cheek brushed against a flower and tightened again; it had been a powerful punch.

"I personally would have nothing against seeing him go to hell. I have my reasons. But as long as I'm head of this prison, it's not going to happen. That would only mean death and there have been enough murders in Swedish prisons in recent years, investigations that no one has seen and no one has heard of and bodies that are eventually hidden away as no one is actually that interested."

The crackling again, whether it was the wind or labored breathing into a sensitive microphone.

"Lennart?"

It was breathing.

"You'll do it. Or you'll lose your post. You've got two hours."

He was lying on the iron bed with his eyes shut. *I'm very sorry, I have no idea who you are.* The people who were supposed to open the door and lead him back to reality had declared that he didn't exist.

He was officially condemned to ten years' imprisonment.

If those in the know denied it, if the people who had arranged a fake trial and produced a criminal record, if they denied it, there was no one else who could explain.

He wouldn't get out. He would be pursued to the death and no matter how much he ran and how long he managed to stay hidden, there was no one there on the other side of the wall who would open the door and help him out.

It was windy out in the prison yard, warm air rebounding off the concrete wall and coming back with even less oxygen. The prison's chief warden walked briskly and wiped his damp forehead with his shirt sleeve. The main door to solitary confinement was locked and he rattled through his keys. It wasn't often he visited the dismal corridor that was the temporary home of those who couldn't conform even with the country's most serious criminals.

"Martin."

The wardens' room was just inside the door and he nodded to three of his employees, Martin Jacobson and two temporary wardens, youngsters whose names he hadn't learned yet.

"Martin, I'd like to talk to you for a moment."

The two temps nodded; they had heard what he hadn't said and went out into the corridor, closing the door behind them.

"Hoffmann."

"Cell 9. He's not looking good. He—"

"He's to go back. To G2. By tomorrow morning at the latest."

The principal officer looked out into the empty corridor, heard the big ugly clock on the wall ticking, the second hand filling the room.

"Lennart?"

"You heard right."

Martin Jacobson got up from the chair by the narrow desk that was largely used as a place to put cups, looked at his friend, colleague, boss.

"We've been working together here for . . . a good twenty years. We've been neighbors for almost as long. You are one of my only friends in here, and out there, one of the few people I ask over for a Sunday drink."

He tried to catch the eye of someone who wasn't there.

"Look at me, Lennart."

"No questions."

"Look at me!"

"I'm asking you, Martin, this time, no goddamn questions."

The gray-haired man swallowed, in surprise, in anger.

"What's this all about?"

"No bloody questions."

"He'll die."

"Martin—"

"This goes against everything we know, everything we say, everything we do."

"I'm going now. You've got an order. Do it."

Lennart Oscarsson opened the door; he was already on his way out.

"He punched you, Lennart . . . is this personal?"

It tightened. And when he moved, every step ached, a shooting pain from his cheekbone down.

"Is it? Is it personal?"

"Just do as I ask."

"No."

"In that case, Martin, do as you are ordered!"

"I won't do it. Because it's wrong. If he's going to be moved back . . . then you're going to have to do it yourself."

Lennart Oscarsson walked toward Cell 9 with two huge holes in his back. He could feel his perhaps best friend's eyes, staring, and he wanted to turn around and explain the order that he himself had so recently been appalled by. Martin was a wise friend, an experienced colleague, the sort who had the courage to speak up when someone who should know better was wrong.

An unconscious hand to the back of his jacket as he approached the locked cell, brushed over the fabric, by the holes, the eyes, trying to get rid of them. The temps with no names were close behind him and stopped by the door, keys jangling as they looked for the right one.

The prisoner was lying on the iron bed, naked except for a pair of white underpants. He was resting, trembling, his torso as white as his face.

"You're going back."

The pale body, he didn't look like much, but only a couple of hours ago he had punched him hard in the face.

"Tomorrow morning. Eight o'clock."

He didn't move.

"To the same unit and the same cell."

He didn't seem to hear, to see.

"Did you hear what I said?"

The chief warden waited, then nodded to his young colleagues and to the door.

"The books."

"Excuse me?"

"*I need the books.* It's my legal right."

"Which books?"

"I've asked for two of the five books that I have the right to have. *Nineteenth Century Stockholm. The Marionettes.* They're in my cell."

"You're going to read?"

"The nights are long here."

Lennart Oscarsson nodded to the wardens again—they should close and lock and leave the cell.

He sat up. *Back*. He was going to die. *Back*. He was dead the moment he went back into the same unit, hated, hunted, he had broken one of the first prison rules, he was a snitch, and you killed snitches.

He got down on his knees in front of the cement toilet bowl, two fingers down his throat, he held them there until he started to puke.

Fear had sucked everything out of him and he spat it out, he had to get rid of it. He stayed on his knees and emptied himself, emptied out everything that had been, everything that was inside him, he was on his own now, the people who could burn him had burned again.

He pressed the button.

He wasn't going to die, not yet.

He had kept it pressed in for fourteen minutes when the hatch in the door opened and the warden with the eyes shouted at him to goddamn take his finger off.

He didn't turn around, just pressed even harder.

"The books."

"You're going to get them."

"The books!"

"I've got them with me. Chief's orders. If you want me to come in, take your finger off the button."

Piet Hoffmann spotted them as soon as the door opened. His books. In the guard's hand. His chest, the pressure that had been there, making him shake, was released. He relaxed, wanted to collapse, wanted to cry, that was how it felt, released and he just wanted to cry.

"It smells of puke in here."

The guard peered into the cement hole, started retching, and moved back.

"It's your choice. You know that no one cleans in here. That smell, you'll just have to get used to it."

The warden gripped the books in his hands, shook them, flicked through, shook them again. Hoffmann stood in front of him but felt nothing, he knew that they would hold up.

He had sat on the iron bed for a long time holding the two books from Aspsås library close by. They were intact. He had just been down on his knees and emptied himself, now, now he was calm, his body felt soft, he could nearly bend over again and if he rested, if he slept for a while, he could refill it with energy, he wasn't going to die, not yet.

friday

HE HAD WOKEN GLEAMING WITH SWEAT, FALLEN ASLEEP AGAIN, DREAMED in fragments and without color, the sort of sleep that is shallow and black and white and far away. He had woken again and sat up on the iron bed and looked at the floor and the books that were lying there for a long time—he wouldn't lie down again, his body was screaming for rest, but as sleep took more energy than it gave he chose to stay sitting where he was and wait as the dawn turned into morning.

It was quiet, dark.

The solitary confinement corridor would sleep for a few more hours.

He had emptied himself yesterday of the fear that got in the way and had to be gotten rid of, the smell still stringent in the air around the cement hole. He had emptied himself and now there was only one thing left, the will to survive.

Piet Hoffmann lifted up the two books and put them down in front of him on the bed. *Nineteenth Century Stockholm. The Marionettes.* Bound in hard, monocolored library boards, marked with STORAGE in blue and ASPSÅS LIBRARY in red. He opened the first page, got a firm grip of the cover, and with a powerful tug pulled it loose. Another tug and the spine of the book collapsed, a third and the back came off. He looked over at the locked cell door. Still quiet. No one walking around out there, no one who had heard and hurried over to the hatch at the top of the door with meddlesome eyes. He changed position, back to the door—if anyone were to look in, all they would see was a fidgety long-termer who couldn't sleep.

He ran his hand carefully over the torn book. His fingers along the left-hand margin and a cut-out, rectangular hole.

It was there. In eleven pieces.

He turned the book over, coaxed out the metal that in a matter of minutes would be a five-centimeter-long mini-revolver. First the larger pieces, the frame with the barrel and cylinder pivot and trigger, a couple of gentle taps with the handle of the sewing machine screwdriver on the millimeter-long pins between them, then the barrel protector with the first screw, the butt sides with the second screw, and the butt stabiliser with the third.

He turned to the door, but the footsteps were only in his head, as before.

He spun the tiny revolver's cylinder, emptied it, took his time checking the six bullets as long as half a thumbnail that were lined up on the iron bed—ammunition that together weighed no more than a gram.

He had seen a person stop breathing in that godforsaken toilet far away in Świnoujście ferry terminal, the short barrel right up close to a petrified eye, the miniature revolver had killed with a single shot.

Piet Hoffmann held it, raised it, aimed it at the dirty wall. Left index finger light on the trigger—there was just enough room with the trigger guard sawn off—slowly pull back, he watched the hammer follow the movement of the finger, a final squeeze and it leaped forward, then the sound, the sharp click. It worked.

He ripped apart the second book in the same way, revealing a hole in the left-hand margin, a detonator the size of a nail and a receiver the size of a penny. He ran the sewing machine screwdriver along the bottom edges of the book's thick covers, front and back, cut open the glued hinge, and pulled out two nine-meter-long pieces of pentyl fuse and an equally thin plastic envelope containing twenty-four centiliters of nitroglycerine.

It was a few minutes past seven.

He heard the wardens changing shift out in the corridor behind the locked door—night shift to day shift. One more hour. Then he would be collected and taken back.

G2 left. *Back*. He was condemned to die there.

He pressed the button on the wall.

"Yes?"

"I need a shit."

"You've got a hole beside the bed."

"It's blocked. My puke from yesterday."

The single speaker crackled.

"How urgent?"

"As soon as possible."

"Five minutes."

Piet Hoffmann stood by the door, footsteps, several footsteps, two guards coming to get someone, *to the cell*, who unlocked the door and opened it, *toilet visit*, never two prisoners in the corridor at the same time, *get in your cell for Christ's sake*. The revolver was resting in the palm of his hand—he opened the cylinder, counted the six bullets, pushed it to the bottom of one of the deep front pockets on his trousers and the coarse fabric hid it, just as it hid the detonator and receiver in the other pocket and the pentyl fuse and plastic envelope with nitroglycerine stuffed down his underpants.

"Open for the prisoner in number nine."

The guard who had shouted was right outside his door. Hoffmann ran back to the bed, lay down, and watched the square hatch opening and the guard looking in long enough to confirm that the prisoner was lying down precisely where he should be.

The jangling of keys.

"You wanted to go to the toilet. Get up and do it then."

One warden by the cell door. Another one farther down the corridor. Two more out in the yard.

Hoffmann looked over at the wardens' room. The fifth one was sitting there. The older one, Jacobson, the principal officer, gray thinning hair and his back to the corridor.

They're too far apart from each other.

He walked slowly toward the shower room and toilets, three guards inside, *they're too far apart from each other.*

He sat down on the dirty plastic toilet seat, flushed, turned on the tap. He breathed deeply, each breath from somewhere deep in his stomach, the calm that was down there, he needed it, he wasn't going to die, not yet.

"I'm ready. You can open again."

The warden opened the door and Piet Hoffmann launched himself forward, showed the mini-revolver first and then held it hard to the bastard's eye that stared at him through a hatch in the cell door.

"Your colleague."

He whispered.

"Get your colleague to come here."

The warden didn't move. Maybe he didn't understand. Maybe he was petrified.

"*Now*. Get him to come here *now*."

Hoffmann kept his eye on the personal alarm hanging from the warden's belt and pressed the muzzle of the gun even harder against the closed eyelid.

"Erik?"

He had understood. His voice was feeble, a careful wave of the hand.

"Erik? Can you come here?"

Piet Hoffmann saw the second warden come closer, then stop suddenly, realizing that his colleague was standing stock-still with what looked like a piece of metal to his head.

"Come here."

The warden who was called Erik hesitated then started to walk, casting a glance up at the camera that maybe someone was watching right now up in central security.

"Once more and I'll kill him. Kill. *Kill him*."

With one hand he pressed even harder against the eyelid and with the other he tore loose two pieces of plastic that were their only way to raise an alarm.

They waited. They did precisely what he said. They knew that he had nothing to lose, it was obvious.

One more.

One more person who could move around freely in the corridor. Hoffmann looked over toward the wardens' office. The face was still turned away, the neck bent forward, as if he was reading.

"Get up."

The older, gray man turned around. There was about twenty meters between them, but he knew exactly what was going on. A prisoner holding something to someone's head. A colleague standing absolutely still beside them, waiting.

"No alarm. No locked doors."

Martin Jacobson swallowed.

He had always wondered how it would feel. Now he knew.

All these damn years waiting for an attack and all the damn anxiety that just this sort of situation might arise.

Calm.

That was how he felt.

"No alarm! No locked doors. *I'll shoot!*"

Principal Prison Officer Jacobson knew the security instructions for Aspsås prison by heart. *In the event of attack: lock yourself in. Raise the alarm.* He had many years ago helped to formulate the instructions that underpinned a prison culture with unarmed staff, and now for the first time was about to put them into action.

He should first lock the door to the wardens' office from the inside.

Then he should raise the alarm with central security.

But the voice, he had listened to it, and the body, he had watched it, he had heard and seen and knew Hoffmann's aggression and he knew that the prisoner who was shouting and holding a gun was both violent and capable. He had read the prison file and the reports on an inmate who was classified as psychopathic, but his colleagues' lives, human lives, were so much more important than security instructions. So he did not stay in the office and he did not lock the door. He did not press his personal alarm nor the one on the wall. Instead, he approached them slowly just as Hoffmann had indicated that he should, past the first cell door where someone started to bang on it from the inside, a heavy monotonous sound that echoed in the corridor walls. A prisoner reacting to something that was going on out there and doing what they always did when they were angry or wanted attention or were just happy about something, anything that was out of the ordinary. Every door he passed, someone else began to knock, others who had no idea what was actually going on out here but were keeping up with something that was better than nothing.

"Hoffmann, I—"

"Shut up."

"Maybe we—"

"Shut up! *I'll shoot.*"

Three guards. All sufficiently close now. It would take at least a few minutes more before the ones out in the yard would come in.

He shouted down the empty corridor.

"Stefan!"

Again.

"Stefan, Stefan!"

Cell 3.

"Fucking snitch."

The voice was vicious, ripping through words and walls.

Stefan.

A couple of meters away, a locked door, the only thing that separated them.

"You're going to die, you fucking snitch."

When he pressed the gun harder against the young warden's eyelid it slid on something.

Something wet, tears, he was crying.

"You're going to swap places. You go in there. Into Cell 3."

He didn't move. It was as if he hadn't heard.

"Open the door and go in! That's all you've got to do. Open the door, for fuck's sake!"

The warden moved mechanically, pulled out his keys, dropped them on the floor, tried again, turned the key with great precision, moved once the door had slowly swung open.

"Fucking snitch. With his new pals."

"You're going to swap places. Now!"

"Bastard snitch. What—what the fuck you got in your hand?"

Stefan was considerably taller and considerably heavier than Piet Hoffmann.

When he stood in the cell doorway, he filled it—a dark and despising shadow.

"Get out."

He didn't hesitate. Sneering, he moved too fast, too close.

"Stop!"

"And why should I do that? 'Cause some little snitch shit has a gun to a screw's head?"

"Stop!"

Stefan kept coming toward him, the open mouth, the dry lips, the warm breath. His face was too close, it was invasive, it was attacking.

"Go on, fucking shoot. Then there's one screw less in the world."

Piet Hoffmann's mind was blank as the heavyweight body approached him. He had wanted to swap hostages, threaten Wojtek rather than the Prison and Probation Service, but had underestimated the hatred. When Stefan broke into a run for the last few steps toward him, his brain wasn't working, only his fear gave him the drive to survive. He pushed the guard away and aimed the revolver at the hating eyes and fired, one single bullet through the pupil, the lens, the vitreous, to the soft mass of the brain, where it stopped somewhere.

Stefan took one more step, still sneering—he appeared to be unaffected, but a second later he fell heavily forward and Hoffmann had to move to avoid finding himself underneath him, then he bent down toward him, pressed the muzzle to his other eye, one more bullet.

A person lay dead on the floor.

The thumping banging that had drummed persistently and the echo of the shot . . . suddenly, suddenly everything was silent.

A strange, breathless silence.

"You can go in now."

He pointed to one of the younger men, but it was the older one, Jacobson, who answered.

"Hoffmann, now let's—"

"I'm not going to die yet."

He looked at the three guards that he needed, but were in the way. Two were younger, shaking, close to breakdown. The older one was fairly calm, the sort who would carry on trying to intercede, but also the sort who wouldn't break down.

"Go into the cell."

Metal on eyelids that were crying, darkness only a finger twitch away.

"Get in!"

The young warden went into the empty cell and sat down on the edge of the iron bed.

"Close! And lock!"

Hoffmann tossed the keys to Jacobson; not a word this time, no attempt to communicate, no false contact intended to confuse, generate trust, emotion.

"The body."

He kicked it, it was about maintaining power, keeping distance.

"I want it outside Cell 6. But not too close, so that the door can still be opened."

"He's too heavy."

"*Now.* Outside Cell 6. *Okay?*"

He moved the gun from his temple to his eye, to his temple from his eye.

"Where do you think it will be when I pull the trigger?"

Jacobson got hold of the soft arms that no longer had muscle reflex; the sinewy, elderly body pulled, dragged 250 pounds of death along the hard linoleum floor and Hoffmann nodded when it was positioned just so the cell door could be opened.

"Open it."

He didn't recognize him, they had never met, but it was the voice that had passed his cell yesterday and called him Paula several times, one of Wojtek's runners.

"*You fucking stukatj.*"

The same voice, shrill as he stormed out, when he stopped in his tracks.

"*Jesus . . .*"

He looked down at someone lying at his feet, stock-still, lungs that weren't breathing.

"*You fucking bastard . . .*"

"Down on your knees!"

Hoffmann pointed at him with the miniature gun.

"Get down!"

Hoffmann had expected threats, maybe contempt.

But the man in front of him said nothing as he collapsed beside the motionless body and for a second Hoffmann stood still—he had been prepared to kill again, and was now standing in front of someone who obeyed.

"What's your name?"

The young warden, when he felt the pressure of the muzzle, had closed his eyes and cried.

"Jan. Janne."

"Janne. Get in there."

Another person in a prison uniform sitting on the edge of yet another empty iron bed when Jacobson locked the door to Cell 6.

Hoffmann counted quickly. It felt like eternity, but he had only just begun. Eight, maybe nine minutes had passed since he opened the door to the toilet and raised the gun, no more. Two of the guards were locked up, the third was in front of him and the fourth and the fifth would stay out in the yard for a while longer. But central security could choose at any moment to look at the cameras in this unit on their monitors, or guards from other units might pass. He had to hurry. He knew where he was going. He had been on his way there since he realized he was on his own, with a death threat, burned by some of the few who knew his purpose and code name; on his way to the place he had chosen a long time ago in order not to die if what shouldn't happen happened.

They were standing close by. Just as close as they had to. Enough distance for him to be in full control but to avoid being overpowered, and the prisoner who still had no name was dangerous, he would kill if he could.

"I want you to get that lamp there."

He held his outstretched arm toward a simple standard lamp that was lit in one of the corners of the wardens' office and waited until Jacobson had put it on the floor in front of him.

"Tie him up. With the extension cord."

Hands behind the prisoner's back and Jacobson pulled the white cord until it pressed into the equally white skin. Hoffmann felt it, checked, then wound the cord around the warden's waist and they started to move up the stairs that seemed to be alive: closed unit doors held back loud exchanges between angry prisoners and the rattling clatter of plates being laid on the table and the voices of irritated card players and a lonely TV that had been left on full volume. One single scream, one single kick on a door and he would be caught. He moved the gun barrel between the prisoner's and the guard's eyes, they should know, they should know.

They got to the top of the building, to the narrow corridor just outside the workshop.

The door was open. All the lights in the large space were turned off.

The inmates who worked here were still eating breakfast with an hour to go before the morning shift.

"That's not enough."

He had waited to command the prisoner down onto his knees until they were in the middle of the workshop.

"Even lower. And bend forward."

"*Why?*"

"Bend forward!"

"*You can kill me. You can kill the fucking screw. But Paula, that's what your fucking pig friends call you, isn't it, you're still dead. In here. Sooner or later. Doesn't matter. We know. We won't let you go. You know that's the way it works.*"

Hoffmann brought his free fist down on the prisoner's neck with force. He didn't know why, it was just what happened when he couldn't answer. After all, it was true. Wojtek's runner was right.

"Take down some packing tape. Bind his wrists! And then pull off the cord!"

Jacobson stood on his toes as he lifted a roll of the hard gray plastic packing tape that is used for cardboard boxes down from the shelves over the press machine. He had to cut two half-meter lengths and tape them around the prisoner's arms, tight, until it cut into the skin and made it bleed, then he had to rip the clothes from the kneeling prisoner and undress himself, each piece of clothing on the floor in two piles, then he had to turn around, his naked back to Hoffmann, the hard plastic around his own wrists as well.

Piet Hoffmann had carefully remembered everything about the room that smelled of oil and diesel and dust. He had located the surveillance cameras over the drilling machine and the smaller pallet jacks, paced out the distance between the rectangular workbenches and the three large pillars that held up the ceiling; he knew exactly where the diesel barrel was and which tools were kept in what cupboard.

The prisoner with no name and the gray-haired guard were on their knees, naked, with their hands behind their backs. Hoffmann checked again that they were properly bound, then lifted up both piles of clothes and carried them over to a workbench near the wall with the big windows facing the church. The receiver was in one of his front pockets. He put it in his ear, listened, smiled, and looked out of the window toward the church tower—he heard the wind blowing gently across a transmitter; it worked.

Then the wind was drowned out.

A loud, repetitive sound took over.

The alarm.

He hurried toward the piles of clothes, grabbed the plastic thing that was flashing red from the belt in the waist of the blue uniform trousers and read the electronic message.

B1.

Solitary confinement. The unit they had just left. It was sooner than he had expected.

He looked out through the window.

Toward the church. Toward the church tower.

He still had another fifteen minutes before the first police reached the outer wall. And another couple of minutes before the correctly trained staff were in the correct position with the correct weapons.

The alarm had been raised by one of the principal officers who was on his way to the prison yard, but who on passing the closed door to the stairs had popped in to say *morning* and to check that everything was okay. The first guards now rushed down the dimly lit corridor, then all stopped at the same time, all looking at the same scene.

A dead man lying on the floor.

Persistent banging on locked cell doors from confused and aggressive prisoners.

A pale and sweating colleague was released from Cell 6.

The released colleague was agitated and pointed to Cell 3.

Another imprisoned colleague was let out, a young man who was crying—he looked down at the floor and said something, *he shot him*, and then repeated it much louder, as if to drown out the banging, or perhaps because he needed to say it again, *he shot him through the eye.*

He heard them storming up the stairs, and saw even more rushing over the prison yard. The two naked bodies on the floor twitched anxiously. He moved the gun from one face to the other, the eyes, reminding them: he needed some more time before they discovered him.

"What's this all about?"

The older warden, crouched over on his knees, his joints aching intensely, didn't say anything else but it was obvious that he was rocking back and forth to distribute the weight.

Piet Hoffmann heard him but didn't answer.

"Hoffmann. Look at me. What is this all about?"

"I've already answered that."

"I didn't understand the answer."

"Not dying yet."

The man leaned his head back, face up, and looked at the revolver with one eye and Hoffmann with the other.

"You won't get out of here alive."

He looked at him, demanding an answer.

"You've got a family."

If he spoke, became someone, changed from an object to a subject, a person who communicated with another person . . .

"You've got a wife and children."

"I know what you're doing."

Piet Hoffmann moved, walked behind the naked bodies, maybe to check that the plastic tape around their wrists was still in place, but probably to avoid the watching, demanding eyes.

"You see, I have too. A wife. Three children. All grown up now. It—"

"Jacobson? Is that what you're called? Shut up! I just said in a friendly way that I know exactly what you're fucking up to. I don't have a family. Not now."

He pulled at the plastic which cut in deeper, bled some more.

"And I'm not going to die, yet. If that means that you have to die instead, so fucking what. You're just my protection, Jacobson, a shield and you'll never be anything more than that. With or without your wife and children."

The principal officer from B2 had tried to make a connection with the colleague he had just released from Cell 3 a couple of minutes ago. A young man, not much older than his son, just covering for the summer. He hadn't even been there a month yet. That's the way it goes. Someone might spend their entire working life waiting for a morning like this. Others could experience it after only twenty-four days.

Only the one sentence.

He had repeated the same thing in answer to every question.

He shot him, through the eye.

The young warden was suffering from acute shock—he had seen a man die and had had a gun pressed to his eye, the circle on the soft skin still obvious. He had then sat and waited, locked inside a solitary confinement cell with death. There wouldn't be anymore words, not for a while. The principal officer instructed the guards who were nearest to look after him, and went on to the other colleague, the one who had been in Cell 6 and who was pale and sweaty, the one who whispered, but was perfectly audible.

"Where's Jacobson?"

The principal officer put a hand on his shoulder, which was thin and trembling.

"What do you mean?"

"There were three of us. Jacobson, he was here too."

The conversation had ended some time ago.

When the words dried up, he was irritated and hoped for more, something mitigating, calming, a continuation that assured him everything was fine now. But there wasn't any more to say. The principal officer from B2 had explained all there was to explain.

Two guards locked in. A dead prisoner.

And an assumed hostage taking.

The chief warden hit the receiver against the desk and a vase of yellow tulips fell to the floor. A third warden, Martin Jacobson, had been taken by an armed prisoner serving a long sentence who had been in solitary confinement, a certain 0913 Hoffmann.

He sat down on the floor, his fingers distracted by the yellow petals that floated in the spilled water.

Of course he had put up a protest. Just as Martin had later put up a protest.

I lied outright to a detective superintendent. I lied because you ordered me to. But this, I won't do this.

He tore the yellow petals to shreds, one at a time, small, porous strips that he dropped onto the wet floor. Then he reached over for the telephone receiver that was still hanging from the wire, dialed a number and didn't stop talking until he was absolutely certain that the director general had understood every word, every insinuation.

"I want an explanation."

A cough. That was all.

"Pål, an explanation!"

Another cough. And nothing more.

"You call me at home late at night and order me to move a prisoner back to the unit where he was threatened, and no questions. You tell me that it has to happen by this morning at the latest. Right now, Pål, that prisoner has a loaded gun aimed at one of my employees. Explain the connection between your order and the hostage taking. Or I'll be forced to ask someone else the same questions."

It was warm in the security office that was part of the entrance to Aspsås prison and was called central security, just as it is in every prison in Sweden. The warden in a creased blue uniform, who was called Bergh, was sweating despite the fan on the table right behind him that made any loose paper and his thin fringe flutter. So he turned around and looked for the towel that hung in the space between the red and green buttons on the control panel and the sixteen TV monitors.

Naked bodies.

The resolution of the black-and-white image wasn't great, and it flickered a bit, but he was sure.

The picture on the screen closest to the towel showed two naked bodies on a floor and a man wearing prison-issue clothes holding something to their heads.

He looked up at the beautiful blue sky. A few wispy clouds, a pleasant sun and a warm breeze. It was a lovely summer day. Apart from the sound of the sirens from the first police car, two uniformed officers in front, both from Aspsås police district.

"Oscarsson . . .?"

The chief warden of Aspsås prison was standing by the main gate in the asphalt garage, the concrete wall like an unpainted gray set behind him.

"What the hell—"

"He's already shot someone."

"Oscarsson?"

"And threatened to do it again."

They were in the front with the windows rolled down: a young policewoman whom Lennart Oscarsson had never seen before sitting beside a sergeant of about his own age, Rydén—they didn't know each other, but knew of each other, one of the few policemen who had served in Aspsås for as long as Oscarsson had worked at the prison.

They turned off the blue light and got out.

"Who?"

I've just come from the hospital unit. You can't see him.

"Piet Hoffmann. Thirty-six years old. Ten years for drug offenses. According to our records, extremely dangerous, classified psychopath, violent."

A sergeant from the Aspsås district who had been to the large prison enough times to know his way around.

"I don't understand. Block B. Solitary confinement. And armed?"

He's going back. To G2. By tomorrow morning at the latest.

"We don't understand it either."

"But the gun? For Christ's sake, Oscarsson . . . how? Where from—?"

"I don't know. I don't *know*."

Rydén looked at the concrete wall, over it and at what he knew was the second floor and roof of Block B.

"I need to know more. What kind of gun?"

Lennart Oscarsson sighed.

"According to the warden who was threatened—he was confused, in shock, but he described some kind of . . . miniature pistol."

"Pistol? Or revolver?"

"What's the difference?"

"With a magazine? Or a rotating cylinder?"

"I don't know."

Rydén's gaze lingered on the roof of Block B.

"A hostage taking. A violent, dangerous convict."

He shook his head.

"We need a completely different kind of weapon. Different knowledge. We need policemen who are specially trained for this."

He went over to the car, a hand in through the open window. He could just reach the radio microphone.

"I'll contact the inspector on duty at the CCC. I'll ask them to send the national task force."

The dirty floor was hard and cold against his bare lower leg.

Martin Jacobson moved carefully, tried to rock his body back, pain pressing on his joints. Crumpled, bent forward, hands behind their backs, they had been kneeling beside each other since they came into the main workshop. He shot a look at the prisoner who was so close he could feel his breath. He couldn't remember his name, it was seldom that those who were locked up in solitary confinement became individuals. Central European, he was sure of that, big, and his hate was tangible, there was bad blood between them, something old—when their eyes locked, he spat, sneered, and Hoffmann had gotten tired of him screaming in a language that Jacobson didn't understand, had kicked him in the cheek and wound the sharp plastic tape around his legs as well.

Martin Jacobson had gradually started to feel what he hadn't had the energy to feel when everything was chaos and he had to concentrate on trying to get the hostage taker to communicate.

A creeping, terrible, engulfing fear.

This was serious. Hoffmann was under pressure and resolute and another person who would never think, talk, or laugh again was already lying on another floor.

Jacobson rocked gently again, took a deep breath—it was more than fear, perhaps. He had never felt like this before, absolute terror.

"Keep still."

Piet Hoffmann kicked him in the shoulders, not hard but enough for his bare skin to shine red. He then started to walk through the workshop, along the rectangular workbenches, and reached up and turned the first camera to the wall, and then the second and the third, but he held the fourth in both hands for a while, his face right up to the lens, he stared into it, moved even closer until his face filled the entire screen, then he screamed; he screamed and then turned that one to the wall as well.

Bergh was still sweating. But he wasn't aware of it. He had moved the chair in the glass box that was central security and was now leaning forward in front of the monitors, four of them with pictures from the Block B workshop. A couple of minutes ago, someone had joined him. The chief warden was standing right behind him and they were watching the same black-and-white sequences with shared concentration, almost silence. Suddenly something changed. One of the monitors that was connected to the camera nearest the window went black. But not an electronic black, it was still working—it was more like it was obstructed by something or someone. Then the next one. The cameras had been turned quickly, maybe to the wall—the darkness could be a film of gray concrete only centimeters away. The third one, they were prepared. They spotted the hand just before it was turned, a person who forced the camera around on its fixture.

One left. They stared at the monitor, waiting, then both jumped.

A face.

Close up, as close as you could get, a nose and a mouth, that was all. A mouth that screamed something before it disappeared.

Hoffmann.

He had said something.

He was cold.

It wasn't a chill from the cold floor, it came from fear, from losing the will to fight thoughts of his own death.

The prisoner beside him had made a threat again—more hate, more scorn—until Hoffmann got a rag from one of the workbenches and stuffed it in his mouth and his words were swallowed.

They both lay still, even when he left them every now and then, purposeful steps over to the far glass wall, a window into the office. When he turned his head, Martin Jacobson could see him go into the small room, bend down over the desk and lift something that from a distance looked like a telephone receiver.

The mouth moved slowly. Narrow, tight lips that looked chapped, almost split.

He is.

They looked at each other, nodded.

They had both recognized the movements of the mouth that formed the words.

"Next."

Oscarsson was sitting beside Bergh in the cramped security office and eager fingers pressed the play button, one frame at a time. The mouth filled the whole screen, the next word, the lips wide and stretched.

"Did you see?"

"Yes."

"One more time."

It was so clear.

The words, the message from the lips, said with such aggression that they were an attack.

He is a dead man.

His hand was shaking—it happened so suddenly he had been forced to let go of the telephone receiver.

What if he got an answer?

What if he didn't get an answer?

A quick look out through the internal window into the workshop and the naked men; they were still lying there, without moving. A porcelain cup in the middle of the desk, half full of day-old coffee, which he downed, cold and bitter but the caffeine would stay in his body for a while.

He dialed the number again. The first ring, the second, he waited. Was she still there, did she still have the same number, he didn't know, he hoped, maybe she—

Her voice.

"You?"

It had been so long.

"I want you to do exactly what we agreed."

"Piet, I—"

"*Exactly* what we agreed. *Now.*"

He hung up. He missed her. He missed her so much.

And now he wondered if she was still there, for him.

The blue, flashing light got stronger, clearer, and would soon push its way through the woods that separated the country road from the drive up to Aspsås prison. Lennart Oscarsson was standing next to Sergeant Rydén in the parking place by the main gate when two heavy, square, black cars approached. The national task force duty troops had left their headquarters at Sörentorp and Solna twenty-four minutes earlier and dropped off—while the heavy vehicles were still moving—nine identically clad men in black boots, navy blue overalls, balaclavas, protective visors, helmets, fireproof gloves, and flak jackets. Rydén rushed forward and greeted the tall thin man who got out of the passenger seat of the first car. Head of the task force, John Edvardson.

"There. The black roof. Top floor."

Four windows in the building nearest the outer wall. Edvardson nodded; he was already heading over there and Oscarsson and Rydén had almost to run to keep up. They looked around and saw the eight others following, submachine guns in hand, two of them with long-distance sniper guns.

They passed central security and the administration block, continued through an open gate in the next wall which was slightly lower and divided the prison up into different sectors, identical squares with identical three-story L-shaped buildings.

"G Block and H Block."

Lennart Oscarsson kept close to the inner wall where they had an overview but were still protected.

"E Block and F Block."

He pointed at the buildings one by one, the home of long-term prisoners.

"C Block and D Block."

Sixty-four cells and sixty-four prisoners in each complex.

"Normal prisoners. The special sex offenders' unit is in a separate part of the prison, as we had a few problems some years ago when several prisoners crossed paths."

They continued sprinting along meter after meter of thick concrete, getting closer to the last L-shaped building. Oscarsson was flagging a bit, but he kept up.

"Blocks A and B. One in each arm. Block B faces the other way. He's been spotted a few times in the big window, the one that looks out over the fields, toward the church over there, Aspsås church. I've had sightings from two separate wardens and they're absolutely certain."

A gray concrete bunker, a Lego brick, an ugly and hard and silent building.

"At the bottom, the isolation unit. Solitary confinement. B1. That's where he took the hostages. That's where he escaped from."

They stopped for the first time since the armed task force had arrived in their vehicles a couple of minutes earlier.

"One floor up, B2 left and B2 right. Sixteen cells on each side. Normal prisoners, thirty-two of them."

Lennart Oscarsson waited for a few seconds, still speaking in short bursts—he hadn't caught his breath yet.

He lowered his voice a bit.

"There, at the top. B3. The workshops. One of the prisoners' workplaces. You see that window? The one that faces the yard?"

He stopped talking. The big window, it felt so strange—it was beautiful outside, the sun and the green fields and the blue sky, and inside, behind the glass, death.

"Armed?"

While he waited for Rydén's answer, Edvardson ordered six of the national task force men to position themselves at the three entrances to Block B and the two snipers to check out the roofs of the nearby buildings.

"I've asked the guards who saw his weapon twice. They're still confused, in shock, but I'm fairly certain that what they're describing is a kind of miniature revolver that can take six bullets. I've only ever seen one in real life, a SwissMiniGun, made in Switzerland and marketed as the world's smallest gun."

"Six bullets?"

"According to the guards he's fired at least two."

John Edvardson looked at the chief warden.

"Oscarsson . . . how the hell did a prisoner who's locked up manage to get hold of a deadly weapon in the hole, in one of Sweden's high-security prisons?"

Lennart Oscarsson couldn't bear to answer, not right now. He just shook his head in despair. The national task force chief turned toward Rydén.

"A miniature revolver. I don't know anything about it. But you reckon it's powerful enough to kill?"

"He's already done it once."

John Edvardson looked up at the window that faced the beautiful church; the hostage taker had been spotted there, a prisoner serving a long sentence who obviously had contacts who could get him a loaded gun in a high-security prison.

"Classified psychopath?"

"Yes."

Reinforced glass in the window.

Two hostages lying naked on the floor.

"And a documented history of violence?"

"Yes."

The man in there had known what he was doing the whole time. According to the wardens he was calm and determined, he had chosen the workshop, and that wasn't by chance, either.

"Then we've got a problem."

Edvardson looked at the front of the building where they wanted to get in. They didn't have much time, the hostage taker had just threatened to kill for a second time.

"He's been seen in the window, but the snipers can't access it from inside the prison. And given your description of this Hoffmann and his record . . . we can't force our way in either. Break down the door or smash in one of the skylights on the roof, it would be simple enough, but with such a dangerous and sick prisoner . . . if we were to do that, if we stormed him, he wouldn't turn on us, he'd stand his ground, he'd point the gun at the hostages, no matter how threatened he was himself, and he'd do what he's promised to do. He'd kill."

John Edvardson started to walk back toward the gate and the wall.

"We're going to get him. But not from here. I will position the snipers. *Outside* the prison."

He moved away from the window.

They were lying naked at his feet.

They hadn't moved, hadn't tried to communicate.

He checked their arms, legs, pulled a bit at the sharp plastic band, which already was cutting in deeper than was necessary, but it was all about power. He had to be sure that word of his potency got out to those who were just turning theirs in toward him.

He had heard sirens for the second time. The first, about half an hour ago, were police from the local station, the only ones who could get here that fast. These ones had a different sound, more persistent, louder, and had lasted for as long as it took for them to get from the national task force headquarters in Sörentorp to the prison.

He walked across the room, counted his steps, studied the door, studied the second window, looked up at the ceiling and the layer of loose fiberglass tiles, used to absorb and dampen sound in the noisy workshop. He picked up a long, narrow metal pipe from one of the workbenches and started to force the fiberglass tiles loose until they fell to the floor, one after the other, and revealed the actual ceiling.

The heavy black car left the parking place outside the main gate into Aspsås prison and stopped about a minute and a kilometer later outside another, considerably smaller gate—one that opened onto a gravel path that led up to a proud white church. John Edvardson walked along the newly raked gravel, Rydén beside him and the two marksmen right behind. Some visitors to the sunny, well-maintained graveyard looked uneasily at the armed, uniformed men with black faces—they didn't fit together somehow, violence and peace. The church door was open and they looked into an empty but impressive nave, and then chose the door to the right and the steep stairs up to the next door which, given the fresh evidence on the door frame, looked like it had recently been forced open, and then finally the aluminum steps that led to a hatch in the roof and to the church tower. They bent down to pass under the cast-iron bell and didn't straighten up until they were out on the narrow balcony, where the wind was stronger and they got a clear view of the gray, square blocks of the prison. They kept a firm hold on the low railing as they studied the building nearest the wall and the window on the second floor where the hostage taker had been seen and was assumed to be hiding.

Piet Hoffmann had knocked down half of the fiberglass tiles from the ceiling when he suddenly stopped his angry movements. He had heard something. A noise in his ear. He'd heard it clearly. What until now had just been a light wind in the receiver became a bang, then steps, and then scraping. Someone was walking around, more than one, there were several pairs of feet. He ran to the window. He could see them, they were standing up on the church tower, four of them, standing there, looking at him.

A shadow at the very edge of the window, just briefly, then gone.

He had been standing there, he had seen them and then disappeared.

"This is a good place. The best place to access him. We'll operate from here."

John Edvardson gripped the iron balcony railings even harder. It was blowing more than he'd realized up here and it was a long way down.

"I need your help, Rydén. From now on, I'll be working from here but I also need someone closer to the prison, with an overview, someone like you, eyes that know the surroundings."

Rydén watched some of the visitors to the graveyard; they had looked up anxiously at the tower several times and were now leaving; the peace they had sought and shared with others was gone and wouldn't be recaptured here today.

He nodded slowly. He had been listening and understood, but had another solution.

"I'd be happy to do that, but there's a policeman, a commanding officer, who knows the prison even better, who worked in this district while it was being built and who has come here regularly ever since, to hand over prisoners for questioning. A proper detective."

"And who's that?

"A DS at city police. His name's Ewert Grens."

EVERY WORD WAS TRANSMITTED WITH PERFECT CLARITY, THE SILVER receiver worked just as well as he knew it would.

"And who's that?"

He adjusted it slightly, a gentle push on the thin metal disc with his index finger to push the earpiece harder against his inner ear.

"A DS at city police. His name's Ewert Grens."

Their voices were clear, as if they were holding the transmitter to their mouths and trying to talk straight into it.

Piet Hoffmann waited by the window.

They were standing by the low iron railing, perhaps even leaning ever so slightly forward.

Then something happened.

Clear scraping noises, first a metal gun meeting a wooden floor, then a heavy body lying down.

"Fifteen hundred and three meters."

"Fifteen hundred and three meters. Is that right?"

"Yes."

"Too far. We don't have any equipment for that distance. We can see him, but we can't reach him."

THE CAR WAS BARELY MOVING.

The morning traffic was bumper to bumper, tired and tetchy as it crept along in both lanes of the Klarastrand road.

An angry passenger got off a bus in front and started to walk along the edge of the busy main artery, and looked happier as he passed the warm vehicles and reached the slip road to the E4 long before his fellow passengers. Ewert Grens thought about tooting at the man who was walking where he shouldn't, or maybe even getting out his police sign, but he didn't; he understood him and if a furious walk in polluted air alongside cars that had fused together prevented people from thumping the dashboard and frightening their fellow commuters, then that was exactly what they should be allowed to do.

He fingered the crumpled map that was lying in the passenger seat.

He had decided. He was on his way to her.

In a couple of kilometers he would stop in front of one of the gates to North Cemetery that were always open and he would get out of the car and he would find her grave and he would say something to her that resembled a farewell.

His mobile phone was under the map.

He let it stay there for the first three rings, then looked at it for the next three, then picked it up when he realized that it wasn't going to stop.

The duty officer.

"Ewert?"

"Yes."

"Where are you?"

The familiar tone. Grens had already started to look for ways out of the frozen queue—a duty officer who sounded like that wanted help quickly.

"The Klarastrand road, northbound."

"You've got an order."

"For when?"

"It's damned urgent, Ewert."

Ewert didn't like changing plans that had been decided.

He liked routine and he liked closure and therefore found it difficult to change directions when in his heart he was already on his way.

And so he should have sighed, perhaps protested a bit, but what he felt was relief.

He didn't need to go. Not yet.

"Wait."

Grens signaled, nudged the nose of the car out into the opposite lane to make a U-turn over the continuous white line, accompanied by hysterical honking from vehicles that had to brake suddenly. Until he'd had enough, rolled down the window, and put the blue flashing light on the roof.

All cars went silent. All the drivers ducked their heads.

"Ewert?"

"I'm here."

"An incident at Aspsås prison. You know the prison better than any other officer in the county. I need you there, now, as gold command."

"Okay."

"We've got a critical situation."

John Edvardson was standing in the middle of the beautiful churchyard at Aspsås. Twenty minutes earlier he had come down from the church tower, leaving the marksmen who had seen Hoffmann and the hostages on two occasions now. They could force their way in whenever they wanted—a few seconds was all they needed to break down the door or come through a skylight and overpower the hostage taker, but as long as the hostages were alive, as long as they were unharmed, they wouldn't risk it.

He looked around.

The churchyard was being guarded by a patrol from Uppsala Police, who had cordoned off the area. No visitors were allowed inside the blue-and-white plastic tape, no priests, no church wardens. Two patrol cars had come from Arlanda and another two from Stockholm and he had positioned one at each corner of the concrete wall that surrounded the prison. He now had four police officers from Aspsås district, and as many again each from Uppsala, Arlanda, and Stockholm, and when the twelve remaining members of the national task force arrived shortly, a total of thirty-seven police officers would be in place to watch, protect, attack.

John Edvardson was tense. He stood in the churchyard looking at the gray wall and felt the unease that had been there from the start, gnawing at him, irritating him, yet he couldn't put a finger on it, there was something . . . something that wasn't right.

Hoffmann.

The man over there who had threatened to kill again, it didn't fit.

In the past decade, Edvardson guessed there had been two, maybe three hostage takings a year in Swedish prisons. And each time the national task force was called in, with the same predictable scenario. An inmate had somehow managed to get hold of moonshine somewhere in the prison and had got steaming drunk, and then come to the conclusion that he had been wronged and treated unfairly, by the female prison staff in particular and, with the grandiosity that so often accompanies intoxication, had acted on impulse, become potent, dangerous, and had taken hostage some poor twenty-nine-year-old female warden who was only working there for the summer, rusty screwdriver to her throat. The alarm had been raised and two dozen specially trained police marksmen had been called out and then it was just a matter of time—the amount of time it took for the alcohol to leave his system and for it to gradually dawn on the hungover prisoner where the balance of power actually lay—before he gave himself up with hands above his head, and as a result was given a further six years and more stringent terms for parole.

But Hoffmann didn't fit that pattern.

According to the wardens he had locked up in two separate cells, he was not under the influence, his actions were planned, each step seemed to have been analyzed, he was not acting on impulse, but with purpose.

John Edvardson turned up the volume on his radio when he gave out instructions for the twelve members of the task force who had just arrived: four outside the door into the workshop in Block B to set up microphones, five to scale the walls of the building to get up onto the roof with more listening equipment, and three to reinforce those already out in the stairwell.

He was closing in on the workshop and he had sealed off the churchyard.

He had done everything that he could and should for the moment.

The next step was up to the hostage taker.

The heavy steel door into the third floor of the police headquarters was open. Ewert Grens ran his card through the card reader, punched in a four-digit code, and waited while the wrought-iron gate slid open. He went into the small space and over to the box with a number on it, opening it with his key and taking out the gun that he seldom used. The magazine was full and he pushed it into place: ammunition with a slightly pitted jacket, which was compensated for with something that looked like transparent glass, the kind of bullet that tore things to shreds. He then hurried back to Homicide, slowed down as he passed Sven Sundkvist's office, *we've got a job, Sven, and I want to see you and Hermansson in the garage in fifteen minutes and I want to know what we've got in our database for 721018-0010*, then rushed on. Sven may have answered something, but in that case he didn't hear.

There was something up on the roof.

Scraping noises, shuffling noises.

Piet Hoffmann was standing by the pile of fiberglass tiles. He had made the right decision. If they had still been up there under the ceiling, they would have swallowed and muffled the small movements that were now happening above his head.

More scraping sounds.

This time outside the door.

They were up the church tower, on the roof, by the door. They were reducing his field of action. There were enough of them now to guard the prison and still prepare for an assault on several fronts.

He picked up the square fiberglass tiles and threw them, one after the other, at the door. They would hear it. They would be standing out there with their listening equipment and they would know that it was now more difficult to get in; that there was something in the way that would take another second to pass, the extra time a person holding a gun needs to shoot his hostages.

Mariana Hermansson was driving far too fast, sirens wailing and blue lights flashing. They were now some distance north of Stockholm and were strangely silent, perhaps remembering previous hostage takings, or earlier visits to the prison as part of their day-to-day investigations. Sven rummaged around in the glove compartment and after a while managed to find what he was looking for, as he usually did: two cassettes of Siwan's sixties hits. He put one into the player, as they had always listened to Grens's past in order to avoid talking and gloss over the realization that they didn't have much to say to each other.

"Take that out!"

Ewert had raised his voice and Sven wasn't sure that he understood why.

"I thought—"

"Take it out, Sven! Show some respect for my grief."

"You mean—"

"Respect. Grief."

Sven ejected the cassette and put it back in the glove compartment, careful to close it in a way that Ewert would see and hear. He rarely understood his boss and he had learned not to ask questions, that sometimes it was easier just to let people's peculiarities be just that. He himself was one of the boring ones, someone who didn't seek out conflict, who didn't demand answers in order to position himself in the hierarchy. He had long since decided that those who were anxious and lacked confidence could do that.

"The hostage taker?"

"What about him?"

"Have you got the background then?"

"Hold on a sec."

Sven Sundkvist pulled a document out of an envelope and then put on his glasses. The first page, from the criminal intelligence database, had the special code that was only used for a handful of criminals. He passed it to Grens.

KNOWN DANGEROUS ARMED

"One of *those*."

Ewert Grens sighed. One of the ones who always meant reinforcement or special units with specially trained policemen whenever an arrest was planned. One of the ones who had no limits.

"More?"

"Criminal record. Ten years for possession of amphetamines. But it's the earlier conviction that's interesting for us."

"Right."

"Five years. Attempted murder. Aggravated assault of a police officer."

Sven Sundkvist looked at the next document.

"I've also got the grounds for judgment. When he was arrested in Söderhamn, the hostage taker first hit a policeman in the face several times with the butt of a gun, then fired two shots at him, one in the thigh and one in the left upper arm."

Ewert Grens put his hand up.

His face had turned a shade of red. He leaned back, and drew his other hand through his thinning hair.

"Piet Hoffmann."

Sven Sundkvist was taken aback.

"How do you know that?"

"That's what his name is."

"I hadn't even read his name yet, but, yes, he is named that. Ewert . . . how did you know?"

The red in Ewert's face deepened, his breathing was perhaps more labored.

"I read the judgment, *Sven, precisely that goddamn judgment* less than twenty-four hours ago. It was Piet Hoffmann I was going to see when I went to Aspsås in connection with the murder at Västmannagatan 79."

"I don't understand."

Ewert Grens shook his head slowly.

"He's one of the three names I was going to question and eliminate from the Västmannagatan investigation. *Piet Hoffmann.* I don't know why or how, but he was one of them, Sven."

The churchyard should have been beautiful. The sun was shining through the high, green leaves, the gravel paths had recently been raked, and the grass was in neat squares in front of the gravestones that stood silently waiting for the next visitors. But the beauty was an illusion, a facade that when they got closer was replaced with danger, anxiety, and tension, and the visitors had replaced their watering cans and flowers with semi-automatics and black visors. John Edvardson met them at the gate and they hurried toward the white church with the high steps up to a closed wooden door. Edvardson handed the binoculars to Ewert Grens, waiting in silence while the detective superintendent looked and found the right window.

"That part of the workshop."

Ewert Grens handed the binoculars to Hermansson.

"There's only one entrance and exit to that part of the workshop. If you want to take hostages . . . that's completely the wrong place to go."

"We've heard them talking."

"Both of them?"

"Yes. They're alive. So we can't go in."

The room that was to the right just inside the church door wasn't particularly big, but it was big enough to be made into a control post. A room where the immediate family would gather before a funeral, or the bride and groom would wait before a wedding. Sven and Hermansson moved the chairs back to the wall while Edvardson went over to the small wooden altar and unfolded a plan of the whole prison and then a detailed plan of the workshop.

"And visible . . . all the time?"

"I could order the marksmen to shoot at any time. But it's too far. Fifteen hundred and three meters. I can only guarantee that our weapons will hit at max six hundred meters."

Ewert Grens pointed a finger at the drawing and the window that, for the moment, was their only contact with a person who had committed murder a few hours ago.

"He knows that we can't shoot him from here, and behind bars, behind reinforced glass . . . he feels safe."

"He *thinks* that he's safe."

Grens looked at Edvardson.

"Thinks?"

"*We* can't shoot him. Not with *our* equipment. But it is possible."

There was a drawing lying on the large conference table in one of the corner rooms in the Government Offices. It was bright and the light from the ceiling blended with light from the high window with a view over the water at Norrström and Riddarfjärden. Fredrik Göransson smoothed the folds in the stiff paper with his hand and moved it so that it would be easier for the national police commissioner and the state secretary to see.

"Here, this building nearest the wall, is Block B. And here, on the second floor, is the workshop."

The three faces leaned over the table and, with the help of a piece of paper, studied a place they had never visited.

"So Hoffmann is standing here. Close to him, on the floor, are the hostages. A prisoner and a warden. Completely naked."

It was hard to comprehend, from the straight lines on the architect's drawing, that there was someone standing there, threatening to kill.

"According to Edvardson, he has been totally exposed in the window since the national task force arrived."

Göransson moved the files and a thick folder with the Prison and Probation Service documents from the table onto one of the chairs in order to make more space, and when that wasn't sufficient he moved the thermos and three mugs. He then unrolled a map of Aspsås district and with a felt pen drew a straight line from the squares that were the various prison buildings across the green area and open space to one of the other rectangles on the map, the one marked with a cross.

"The church. Exactly fifteen hundred and three meters away. The only place with a view that is clear enough for the snipers. And Hoffmann knows that, Edvardson is sure of it. He knows that the police don't have the equipment to reach him and that's what he's telling us by standing there."

There was a little coffee left in the thermos and the state secretary poured herself half a cup. Then she got up and moved away, looked at her visitors and spoke in a quiet voice.

"You should have informed me yesterday."

She didn't expect an answer.

"You've maneuvered us into a corner."

She was shaking with rage. She looked at them one at a time, then lowered her voice even more.

"You have forced him to action. And now I don't have any choice, I have to act as well."

She continued to look at them as she walked toward the door.

"I'll be back in fifteen minutes."

Each step had been painful, and when Ewert Grens spied the aluminum ladder that led up to a hatch in the church tower, his stiff leg protested with a series of small sharp twinges that obliterated any other thoughts. He said nothing when he slipped on the first rung, nor when his chest seemed to push up into his throat a few rungs up. His forehead shone with sweat and his arms were numb when he hauled himself through the wooden hatch and banged his head on the edge of the heavy cast-iron bell, cutting himself. He lay down and managed to creep the final stretch to the door that led out onto the balcony and the cooling breeze.

They now had forty-six police officers positioned outside the prison, inside the prison, outside the church, and two up here, in the church tower—marksmen who were keeping an eye through binoculars on a window on the second floor of Block B.

"There are two possibilities. The railway bridge over there is probably a couple of hundred meters closer, but the angle is harder and the target area is too small. Whereas from here the target area is perfect. We have full view of him. But we have a problem. Our marksmen use a gun which is called a PSG 90 and is designed for firing distances of around six hundred meters. That's what our men are trained for. And the distance from here is far greater, Ewert."

Ewert Grens had gotten up and was now standing at the far end of the narrow balcony, gripping the railing with his hands. He saw the shadow again, Hoffmann's shadow.

"And what does that mean?"

"The distance is impossible. For us."

"Impossible?"

"The greatest known distance that a sniper has covered successfully is two thousand, one hundred and seventy-five meters. A Canadian marksman."

"So?"

"So what?"

"So it's not impossible."

"Impossible. For us."

"But it's nearly nine hundred meters less! So what's the bloody problem?"

"The problem is that we have no officers who can shoot at that distance. *We* don't have the training. *We* don't have the equipment."

Grens turned toward Edvardson and the balcony shook—he was heavy and he had pulled hard at the railing.

"Who?"

"Who what?"

"Who does? Have the training? The equipment?"

"The army. They train our marksmen. They have the training. And they have the equipment."

"Then get one of them here. *Now.*"

The balcony shook again. Ewert Grens was agitated and his ponderous body swayed as he tossed his head and stamped his foot. John Edvardson waited until he was done; he normally didn't care that much when the detective superintendent tried to look menacing.

"It doesn't work quite like that. The armed forces can't be used for police matters."

"We're talking about someone's life!"

"Statute SFS 2002:375. *Ordinance on support for civil activities by the Swedish Armed Forces.* I can read it for you, if you like. Paragraph seven."

"I don't give a damn about that."

"It's Swedish law, Ewert."

He had listened to them moving around on the roof, small movements, they were there the whole time, they were ready and waiting.

Then there was a crackling in his earpiece.

"The army. They train our marksmen. They have the training. And they have the equipment."

Piet Hoffmann smiled.

"Then get one of them here. Now."

He smiled again, but only inside. He was careful to stand in profile, his shoulder at a right angle to the window.

The equipment, the training, the know-how.

A sniper. A *military* sniper.

The map of Aspsås district was still lying on the conference table when the state secretary returned to the room and made a point of closing the door behind her.

"So, let's continue."

She had been tense and flushed when she left the room fifteen minutes ago, and whatever it was she had done, whoever it was she had spoken to, had done the trick—she looked calmer, and she was resolute and concentrated as she drank the rest of her coffee.

"The log book?"

She nodded at one of the files that had been moved from the table.

"Yes?"

"Give it to me."

Göransson handed her the thick black file and she noticed as she leafed through that the pages were handwritten alternately in black and blue ballpoint pen.

"Are all the meetings between your handler and this Hoffmann recorded here?"

"Yes."

"And this is the only copy?"

"It's the copy that I keep as CHIS controller. The only one."

"Destroy it."

She put the file down on the table and pushed it over toward Göransson.

"Are there any other formal links between the police authority and Hoffmann?"

Göransson shook his head.

"No. Not for him. Not for any other informant. That's not how we work."

He seemed to relax a bit.

"Hoffmann has been paid by us for nine years. But only from the account that we call reward money. An account that can't be linked to personal data and therefore doesn't need to be reported to the tax authorities. He's not on any payrolls. Formally, he doesn't exist for us."

The file with the Prison and Probation Service documents was still lying on one of the chairs.

"And that one? Is that his?"

"That's only about him."

She opened it, looked through the printouts and reports about his mental health.

"And this is all?"

"That is our picture of him."

"Our picture?"

"The image we've created."

"And the overall image . . . if I can put it like this . . . does it give a sufficient basis for the gold commander to make a clear decision about Hoffmann . . . well, the consequences of the hostage taking?"

The room brightened as the sun flooded in and the white sheets of paper intensified and reflected the light.

"It was a sufficiently strong image for him to be accepted by the mafia branch that he penetrated. We've since developed it to make him totally credible in relation to the work inside Aspsås."

The state secretary put the file down to one side, looked at Göransson, who as commanding officer could easily have been in charge of the hostage-taking operation.

"Would you . . . with this information and in the current situation at Aspsås where the hostages' lives are in danger . . . would you make a decision based on the fact that Hoffmann is dangerous, capable?"

Chief Superintendent Göransson nodded.

"Without a doubt."

"Would all the police officers who might be assigned as gold commander make the same decision based on that information?"

"Given our information about Hoffmann, no police officer at the scene would question the fact that he is prepared to kill a prison warden."

The sun wearied of fighting the light clouds outside the window of the Government Offices and the bright light subsided, making it more comfortable to look around the room.

"So . . . if the gold commander at Aspsås is convinced that Hoffmann is prepared to kill the hostages . . . and has to make a decision . . . what would he do?"

"If the gold commander considers the hostages to be in acute danger, and that Piet Hoffmann will kill them, he would then order the men to storm the premises in order to safeguard the hostages' lives."

Göransson moved closer to the table and the map, and drew his finger over the paper from the rectangle that represented Block B to a rectangle one and a half kilometers away that represented a church.

"But it's not possible from here."

He drew a circle in the air over the building that was marked with a cross and kept his hand there, a slow movement, around and around, a circle that stopped when he did.

"So the gold commander will, if he must, order the national task force marksmen to take out the hostage taker."

"Take out?"

"Shoot."

"Shoot?"

"Put out of action."

"Put out of action?"

"Kill."

THE ROOM WITH THE SMALL WOODEN ALTAR HAD ALREADY BEEN transformed into the control post. There were drawings of Aspsås prison lying on every surface intended for the priest to prepare his services. Paper cups of vending machine coffee from the local gas station stood empty or half finished on the floor, the small window, which had been opened wide to let in some oxygen to replace that which had long since been breathed out by stressed and raised voices, creaked gently on the breeze. Ewert Grens moved restlessly between Edvardson, Sundkvist, and Hermansson, loud but not aggressive or even angry; he had just taken over as gold commander and was resolute and solution-oriented. He would have to make the final decision in a while. It was he, and he alone, who was directly responsible for several people's lives. He left the room with no air, wandered through the empty churchyard, between the headstones and newly planted flowers and saw in his mind's eye another cemetery that he had not yet dared to visit, but that he would now, later, when this was all over. He stopped between a gray, rather beautiful headstone and a tree that looked like it might be a maple, lifted the binoculars from his chest and studied the building behind the Aspsås prison wall. The man who could be seen behind the window, the one who was called Piet Hoffmann, whom Grens should have questioned the day before . . . there was something odd going on, something wasn't right—people who suddenly got ill rarely had the strength and focus to shoot someone else through the eye.

"Hermansson?"

He had gone over to the open window and shouted through.

"I want you to contact the prison doctor. I want to know how a prisoner who was put in isolation in the hospital unit yesterday morning is now, at lunchtime today, standing over there pointing a gun at hostages."

Ewert Grens stayed outside the open window for a while and looked over at the prison. The inner strength he had, the one that was always there and forced him to keep at it, keep at it, keep at it until he had an answer, he knew exactly where it was coming from this time. The older warden. If the

322

two people who had been taken hostage were both fellow prisoners, he wouldn't have been so motivated, he wouldn't have felt the same driving edge. That's just how it was. He didn't care much about one of the naked bodies on the workshop floor, he felt nothing for the prisoner who in theory could be in cahoots with the hostage taker. It wasn't something that he was proud of, but that was how he felt. The warden, on the other hand, who wore a uniform and worked there, *an ordinary representative of a workplace that the general public hated*, an older man who had given his life to this crap, shouldn't have to deal with such deep humiliation, a person who believed they had the right to take his life, a gun to his head.

Grens swallowed.

It was the warden, that's what this was all about.

He lowered the binoculars and fished out his mobile phone. He tried to remember if he had ever before asked his line manager for help two days in a row. After all, they had had an unspoken understanding for a long time to stay out of each other's way in order to avoid conflicts. But he had no choice. He dialed the number of the office only a couple of doors down from his own. No reply. He dialed again, the switchboard this time, asked them to put him through to his mobile phone. Chief Superintendent Göransson answered after the first ring, his voice hushed, as if he was in a meeting and leaning forward to speak.

"Ewert . . . I don't have time right now. I'm trying to find a solution to a critical problem."

"This is critical too."

"We—"

"I'm exactly fifteen hundred and three meters away from the prison in Aspsås. I'm responsible for an ongoing hostage situation. There's a risk that one of the prison wardens might die if I make the wrong decision and I'm going to do everything I can to make sure that that doesn't happen. But I need some bureaucratic assistance. You know, the sort of thing you do."

Chief Superintendent Göransson ran his hand over his face and through his hair.

"You're at Aspsås, you say?"

"Yes."

"And you're the gold commander?"

"I just took over from Edvardson. He's focusing on the task force."

Göransson held the telephone high up over his head and pointed at it with big gestures, catching the attention of the national police commissioner and state secretary and nodding vehemently at them until they understood.

"I'm listening."

"I need a competent marksman."

"The national task force are there, aren't they?"

"Yes."

"Then I don't understand."

"I need someone who is trained and equipped to shoot over a distance of fifteen hundred meters. Apparently the police aren't. So I need a *military* marksman."

They were listening, the national police commissioner and the state secretary, they were sitting next to him and had started to get the picture.

"You know as well as I do that the armed forces can't be used against civilians."

"You're the bureaucrat, Göransson. If you're good at anything, then it's that. Being a pencil pusher. I want you to come up with a solution."

"Ewert—"

"*Before* the hostage dies."

Göransson held the phone in his hand.

Dread.

It was there again.

"That was Ewert Grens. The DS who's investigating Västmannagatan 79. And right now he's standing right here."

He pointed at the map, at the thin lines that symbolized something that actually existed. Ewert Grens was actually standing there. It was Ewert Grens who would shortly make a decision based on the doctored information that was accessible in the databases and records, an image that was developed by his own colleagues and that for any police officer would provide powerful grounds to shoot.

Shoot.

"Here . . . he's standing precisely here, as the assigned gold commander. He's the one who is leading the whole operation, who is responsible for it, who will make the decision on *how* to resolve it."

Göransson's hand was shaking. He pressed it hard against the paper of the map, but it continued to shake—it didn't normally do that, shake.

"He is fifteen hundred and three meters from the window where

Hoffmann has been sighted regularly, but the snipers, the police marksmen, don't have the right training and equipment. So he's asking for a military marksman. A more powerful weapon, heavier ammunition, someone trained to shoot at extreme distances."

Shoot to kill.

"There's always a solution. Always a reasonable solution if you really want to find it. And clearly it is in all our interests to find it, to help to resolve this."

The state secretary's voice was calm, clear.

"It is our responsibility to save the hostages' lives."

Ewert Grens had asked for a suitably trained and equipped marksman.

With the information that was now common knowledge in the prison corridors, Hoffmann would not give up his hostages.

If Grens got his military marksman, he would also use him.

"What are you actually saying?"

Göransson straightened his back. He looked at the slight woman sitting in front of him.

They wouldn't have their finger on the trigger.

It would be the gold commander who ordered the sniper to fire. It would be the marksman who fired.

They wouldn't make the decision.

They were giving others the opportunity to make the decision.

"But . . . Jesus Christ—"

Göransson's finger was still on the map when he suddenly pulled the paper toward him and scrunched it into a ball with both hands.

"—what the hell are we doing?"

He got up abruptly, his face stiff and flushed.

"We're making Ewert Grens into a murderer!"

"Calm down, please."

"We're legitimizing murder!"

He threw the ball of paper so that it hit the window and fell with a thud onto the state secretary's desk.

"If we give the gold commander the solution that he's asking for . . . if he then makes a decision based on the information he has about Hoffmann . . . Ewert Grens could be forced to order a shot to be fired at a person who has actually never committed a violent crime, but who is believed to be violent, merciless, and capable!"

The state secretary leaned forward and picked up the paper ball, held it in her lap, for a long time looked at the face that was about to explode.

"If that is the case, if the gold commander has the military marksman and then later decides to shoot . . . then it will be to save the hostages' lives."

Her voice was controlled, and was quiet enough to be heard but not loud enough for those listening not to hold their breath.

"Hoffmann is the only one who has killed anyone. And it is only Hoffmann who is threatening to do so again."

The square yard at Aspsås prison was covered in coarse, dry gravel that was dusty, no people, no noise; all the prisoners had been locked in their cells for the past few hours, behind doors that would not be opened until the hostage siege was over. Grens was walking with Edvardson beside him, two members of the national task force in front of him and Hermansson a couple of steps behind. She had been waiting for him just inside the prison gate and had briefly told him about her meeting with the prison doctor who had heard nothing about an epidemic and had never asked for anyone to be isolated in all his time at Aspsås. As they approached the outside door to Block B, Grens stopped and waited for her.

"It's all a goddamn lie, all of it, all this is connected. I want you to carry on, Hermansson, find the prison chief warden and get an answer out of him."

She nodded and turned around and he watched her rather slim back and shoulders through the light cloud of dust. They hadn't spoken much together recently, not at all in the past year—he hadn't really spoken to anyone. Once he had been to the grave he would seek her out again. He who was never going to talk to a policewoman again had learned to appreciate her more and more each year. He was still not sure when she was laughing at him or was annoyed with him, but she was good at her job and intelligent and she looked at him in a way that was at once demanding and uncompromising, in a way that very few dared. He would talk to her again, maybe even ask her to leave the offices with him for a while, ask her for a coffee and a cake in the café on Bergsgatan. It felt good to be having these thoughts, to look forward to something, to having a coffee with the daughter they never had.

Ewert Grens opened the door to the solitary confinement unit and the corridor where everything had kicked off a few hours ago. The body that had fallen forward with blood pouring from the head had already

been removed—strapped onto a stretcher and taken for an autopsy—
and the two prison wardens who had been threatened with a gun and
each locked away in a cell were now with a crisis management team in
one of the visiting rooms, talking to a prison psychologist and prison
chaplain.

His first thought was actually about the banging.

In each cell on the ground floor, the prisoners in solitary confinement
were banging on their closed, locked doors. A regular thumping sound that
made your heart beat out of rhythm. He knew that that was what they did
and had decided to ignore it, but it forced its way into his mind and he was
relieved to go up the stairs behind Edvardson and past the armed police on
the first landing.

They stopped when they got to the second floor and nodded silently to
the eight members of the national task force standing outside the workshop
ready for an order to break down the door, throw in a shock grenade and
take full control of the situation within ten seconds.

"That's too long."

Ewert Grens was talking quietly and John Edvardson leaned in closer in
order to reply in an equally quiet voice.

"Eight seconds. With this team, Ewert, I can get it down to eight
seconds."

"It's still too long. Hoffmann, to aim and then move the muzzle from
one head to the next and shoot, he doesn't need more than one and a half
seconds. And in his frame of mind . . . I can't risk a dead hostage."

John Edvardson nodded at the ceiling and the dull shuffling of bodies
changing position every now and then.

Grens shook his head.

"That's not going to work either. From the door, from the roof, the
number of seconds you're talking about . . . the hostages could die several
times over."

The banging, he couldn't stand it much longer, his concentration
couldn't stretch to encompass both the madmen downstairs and the
madman in there. He was on his way back down the stairs to the
thundering noise, but turned when Edvardson put a hand on his shoulder.

"Ewert . . ."

"Thank you."

They stood in silence, with the waiting police breathing behind their backs.

"In that case, Ewert, unless Hoffmann suddenly gives himself up, if and when we deem his threat to be more than just a threat . . . then there's only one solution. The military marksman. With a weapon that is powerful enough to kill."

The dread hounded him, translating into jerky movements and a nervous cough. Fredrik Göransson had been walking for ten minutes now in endless circles, between the window and the desk in one of the rooms of the Government Offices, and he hadn't gotten anywhere.

"*We* made sure that the prisoners got the information about a snitch."

The crumpled map was in the wastepaper basket—he picked it up and unfolded it.

"*We* forced him to act."

"He had a job to do."

The national police commissioner had let the state secretary answer thus far. Now he looked at his colleague.

"That didn't involve threatening another person's life."

"We burned him."

"You've burned other informants before."

"I have always denied that we even work with infiltrators. I've stood by and watched without giving any protection when an organization has dealt with that person. But this . . . this isn't the same. This isn't burning him. This is murder."

"You still haven't understood. We are not the ones who will make the decision. We are only providing a solution for the police officer who *will* make that decision."

The agitated man with the jerky movements couldn't bear to stand still any longer, and with the dread chasing right behind him, he made a dash past the table to the closed door.

"I want no part in this."

He wasn't cold anymore. The floor that smelled of diesel was just as hard and just as cold, but he didn't feel the cold, nor the pain in his knees, he didn't even think about the fact that he was naked and bound, and would shortly get another kick in the side from someone who intermittently whispered that he was going to die. Martin Jacobson didn't have the strength to speak, to think—he lay down and didn't move. He wasn't even sure if he was seeing the things he saw now, if Hoffmann really did walk over to the largest workbench and pull a plastic pocket from the waist of his trouser that had some kind of fluid in it; if he then cut it into twenty-four equally sized pieces and with a roll of tape from the shelf, attach them to the nameless prisoner's head, arms, back, stomach, chest, thighs, lower legs, and feet; and if he took from the same place something that looked like a thin piece of pentyl fuse that was several meters long and wrapped it around and around the prisoner's body. If that was the case, if what he saw was what was really happening, he couldn't face anymore. He turned his eyes slowly the other way so he didn't need to see—there was no room left for things he didn't understand.

One of the three chairs that had been pulled out from the conference table was empty, and the person whose office it was, a state secretary from the Ministry of Justice, ran her hand back and forth over a crumpled map as if subconsciously trying to smooth out the bumps that shouldn't be there.

"Can we do this?"

The man opposite her, a national police commissioner, heard her question but knew that it didn't mean just that she was asking if they were capable of something, no one would contend that, it wasn't Göransson alone who was going to solve this, the possibility didn't vanish along with him. What she was really asking was *do we trust each other*, or perhaps *do we trust each other enough to first solve this and then to stick to what we've decided, especially the consequences?*

He nodded.

"Yes, we can do this."

The state secretary had moved over to the bookshelf behind the desk and taken a pile of black spines from a file. She leafed through them and found the statute she was looking for: SFS 2002:375.

Then she turned on her computer and logged on, opened the complete version and printed out two copies.

"Here. Take one."

SFS 2002:375.

Ordinance on support for civil activities by the Swedish Armed Forces.

She pointed at the seventh paragraph.

"This is what it's about. This is what we have to find our way around.

> When support is given pursuant to this Ordinance, members of the Armed Forces
> cannot be used in situations where there is a risk that they may be required to use force
> or violence against a private individual.

They both knew exactly what that meant. It would not be possible to use the armed forces for police activities. For nearly eighty years, this country of theirs had sought not to resolve problems by allowing the military to shoot at civilians.

But that was precisely what they had to do.

"Are you of the same opinion? Do you agree with the DS who is in situ? That the only way to resolve this, for a shot to be fired from here that will reach . . . here, to this building . . . is to use a military marksman?"

The state secretary had smoothed out the map enough for it to be possible to follow her finger.

"Yes. I'm of the same opinion. More powerful guns, heavier ammunition, better training. I've been asking for that for several years now."

She smiled wearily, got up and walked slowly around the room.

"So, the police are not allowed to use the snipers who are employed by the armed forces."

She stopped.

"The police can, however, use the marksmen who are employed by the police. Is that not the case?"

She looked at him and he gave a hesitant nod and threw his hands up in the air—she was aiming at something, but he had no idea what. She went over to the computer again, looked at the screen for a while, then printed out another document in duplicate.

"SFS 1999:740."

She waited until he had found the right page.

"Ordinance on police training. Paragraph nine."

"What about it?"

"We'll start there and work our way forward."

She read out loud:

> The National Police Board can, under special circumstances, grant exemptions
> from the training set out in this Ordinance.

The national police commissioner shrugged.

"I'm familiar with that paragraph. But I still don't understand what you're getting at."

"We'll employ a military marksman. For police service as a police sniper."

"He would still be military staff and not have formal police training."

The state secretary smiled again.

"You are, like me, a lawyer, is that not so?"

"Yes."

"You are the national police commissioner. You have police authority, don't you?"

"Yes."

"Despite the fact that you do not have formal police training?"

"Yes."

"So let's use that as our starting point, and work toward a solution."

He was none the wiser as to where she was heading.

"We'll find a trained, equipped military marksman. With the cooperation of his superiors, we'll discharge him from service in the armed forces and then make the newly discharged military marksman an offer of a . . . say . . . six-hour temporary contract with the police. As a superintendent or another rank. You choose what rank and title you want him to have."

He wasn't smiling, not yet.

"So, he will be employed by the police for exactly six hours. He will complete his contract. And he will then, six hours later, apply for the vacant position that the armed forces haven't yet had time to advertise, and be reinstated."

Now he was starting to understand what she was getting at.

"And what's more, the police never give out the names of their marksmen, during or after an operation."

Exactly what she was getting at.

"And so no one will know who fired the shot."

AN EMPTY, CLEAN BUILDING.

A floor that no feet had stamped on, windows that no eyes had stared through.

There were no lights on in the building, no sound, even the unused door handles shone. Lennart Oscarsson had envisaged the inauguration of the newly built Block K, with even more cells, greater capacity, more prisoners, as a manifestation of a newly appointed chief warden's ambition and drive. That would never happen now. He walked down the empty corridor, past the wide-open cell doors. He was about to turn on the strong lights and activate the new alarm system and soon the smell of paint and newly upholstered pine furniture would blend more and more with fear and badly brushed teeth. The uninhabited cells would instead be inaugurated in a few minutes' time by hastily evacuated prisoners from Block B who were under serious threat with the national task force prepped at every door and window, guns at the ready, and a hostage situation on the second floor of the building that no one really knew anything about, why the man had done it, his aims and demands.

Another day from hell.

He had lied to an investigating officer and chewed his lower lip to shreds. He had forced a prisoner to go back to the unit where he was threatened and when the prisoner had taken hostages, had ripped the yellow petals of the tulips into tiny, porous pieces and dropped them on the wet floor. When his mobile phone rang, the ringtone echoing in the empty surroundings, he went into one of the empty cells and lay down exhausted on one of the bunks with no mattress.

"Oscarsson?"

He recognized the director general's voice immediately, stretched out his body on the hard bunk.

"Yes?"

"His demands?"

"I—"

"What are his demands?"

"Nothing."

"Three hours and fifty-four minutes. And not a single demand?"

"No communication at all."

He had just seen a mouth fill a TV monitor, tight lips that slowly formed words about death. He couldn't bear to talk about it.

"If there are demands, *when* he makes demands, Lennart, he's not allowed to leave the prison."

"I don't understand."

"If he asks for the gate to be opened, you mustn't allow it. Under any circumstances."

The hard bunk. He couldn't feel it.

"Am I understanding you correctly? You want me to . . . to ignore the policy that you yourself have written? And that all of us who hold senior positions have signed? That if anyone's life is in danger, if we believe a hostage taker is prepared to carry out any threats he has made, if he demands to be released, we *should* open the gates to save lives. And that is the agreement that you now want me to ignore?"

"I know what policies and regulations I've formulated. But . . . Lennart, if you still like your job, then you'll do as I ask you."

He couldn't move. It was impossible.

"As *you* ask *me*?"

Everyone has their limits, an exact point beyond which they can't go. This was his.

"Or as *someone* has asked *you*?"

"Get up."

Piet Hoffmann was standing between the two naked bodies. He had bent down toward one of them and spoken close to the tired, old eyes until they had finally understood and started to get up. The prison warden who was called Jacobson grimaced with pain as he straightened his knees and back and started to walk in the direction pointed out by the hostage taker—past the three solid concrete pillars and in behind a wall near the door, a separate part that seemed to be some kind of storeroom: unopened cardboard boxes stacked up one on the other with sticky labels from tool and machine part suppliers. He was to sit down—Hoffmann pushed him to the floor in irritation when he didn't move fast enough—he was to lean back and stretch out his legs, so that it would be easier to tie his feet together. The older man tried to reach out to him in desperation several times, asking why and how and when, but got no answer, then watched Piet Hoffmann's silent back until it disappeared somewhere behind a drill and a workbench.

That bloody banging. Ewert Grens shook his head. It seemed to follow a pattern. The nutters banged on their cell doors for two minutes, then waited for one, then banged for two more. So he walked over to the security office, with Edvardson directly behind him, and made sure he closed the door properly. The two small monitors side by side on a desk showed the same picture, all black, a camera turned to the workshop wall. He reached over for the coffeepot, which was cold and had a brown, heavy fluid at the bottom. He turned it almost upside down and waited while brown fluid trickled slowly into one of the already used mugs, offered it to John Edvardson, but had it all to himself. He drank and swallowed—it wasn't particularly nice, but strong enough.

"Hello."

He had just about emptied the white plastic mug when the telephone in front of him started to ring.

"Detective Superintendent Grens?"

He looked around. All these damn cameras. Central security had seen him go into the security office and connected the call.

"Yes."

"Can you hear who it is?"

Grens recognized the voice. The bureaucrat who sat a couple of floors up from him in the police headquarters at Kronoberg.

"I know who you are."

"Can you talk? There's something making an almighty din there."

"I can talk."

He heard the national police commissioner clear his throat.

"Has the situation changed at all?"

"No. We want to act. We should be able to. But right now we haven't got the right people. And time is running out."

"You asked for a military marksman."

"Yes."

"That's why I'm calling. Your request is now on my desk."

"Just a moment."

Grens waved at Edvardson, he wanted him to check the door, make sure that it was closed properly.

"Hello?"

"I think I have a solution."

The national police commissioner was quiet, waiting for a reaction from Grens, but then carried on when the void was filled with the noise from the corridor.

"I've just signed a contract. I have employed an instructor and military marksman, who was recently discharged, as an assistant commissioner for six hours. He's been serving with the Svea Life Guards at Kungsängen. The position will initially entail supporting Aspsås police district. He has just left Kungsängen in a helicopter and will land at Aspsås church in ten, max fifteen minutes. When his contract ends, in exactly five hours and fifty-six minutes, he will be collected and taken back to Kungsängen in the same helicopter and will then apply for the newly vacant position for an instructor and military marksman which has not yet been advertised."

He heard it when it was no more than a small spot in the cloudless sky. He ran over to the window and watched it grow as the noise got louder and then land, blue and white, on the tall grass in the field between the prison wall and the churchyard. Piet Hoffmann looked at the two people waiting high up on the church tower balcony, then at the helicopter and the police officers running toward it. He listened to the people moving around on the roof above his head and the ones just outside the door and he nodded to no one in particular. Now, now everything was in place. He checked that the nameless prisoner's hands and legs were tied well enough and then hurried over to the wall that separated the storeroom from the rest of the workshop, managed to get the old warden up, forced him to walk in front of him across the floor to one of the cameras that was pointing to the wall—he turned it and made sure that the whole of his mouth and the warden's was clear when he spoke.

He leaned forward as he walked, dressed in a white-and-gray camouflage uniform. He was in his forties and had introduced himself as Sterner.

"I can't do this."

As they walked over to the church and then went up the stairs and the aluminum ladder, Ewert Grens had described a hostage drama that was out of control and might culminate in a shot from the church tower.

"Can't? What the hell do you mean?"

The military marksman who, for another five hours and thirty-eight minutes, would legally serve as a policeman, had emerged onto the narrow balcony and switched places with one of the two men already lying there.

"This is not a normal sniper rifle. It's an M107. It's a heavier, more powerful, anti-materiel rifle. For targeting buses. Or boats. Exploding mines."

He had greeted the colleague who was still there and would function as an observer.

"Long distance. That was the information I was given. That was what I should be prepared for. But this— I can't shoot at a soft target."

Holding the binoculars, he had observed Piet Hoffmann in one corner of the window and realized what this was all about.

Now he looked at Grens.

"I'm sorry, so he—that man there—is a *soft target*?"

"Yes."

"And . . . what exactly does that mean?"

"It means that the ammunition that I have with me is fire and explosive ammo, and can't be used for a person."

Grens laughed—at least that was what it sounded like: a short, irritated laugh.

"So . . . what the hell are you doing here?"

"The firing distance is fifteen hundred and three meters. That was the job I was given."

"*The job you were given* was to prevent someone from taking the lives of two other people. Or, if you prefer it—one soft target taking the life of another soft target."

Sterner focused the binoculars on the hostage taker, he was still standing in the same place by the window, exposing himself, and it was hard to understand why.

"I'm just complying with international law."

"A law . . . *for Christ's sake, Sterner* . . . they're made up by people who hide behind desks! But this . . . this is reality. And if the guy who is standing there, *the soft target*, the one who is our reality right now, if he's not stopped, other people will die. And both of them and their nearest and dearest will presumably be extremely pleased to know that you are complying with . . . what was it now . . . *international law.*"

The binoculars' zoom was powerful and despite the fact that his hands were moving in the wind, it was easy to follow the man who had long fair hair and sometimes turned and looked down at something—the hostages, Sterner was sure of it—that was lying on the floor close to him; that was where they were.

"If I do what you want me to, if I fire at this man, with the ammo I've got here, he'll lose his arms and legs. They'll be blown clear off the body. There will be nothing left."

He lowered the binoculars and looked up at Grens.

"You'll find the soft target, the person—you'll find body parts everywhere."

THE FACE, THE MOUTH, IT WAS THERE AGAIN.

The man in the blue crumpled guard uniform got up. The same monitor as the last time, the same camera that had been turned away from the concrete wall. Bergh was still warm but had switched off and moved the desk fan so that it was now by the wall in the small central security room—he needed more space in order to see properly when he linked up and transmitted the picture on all sixteen screens.

The mouth was saying something, and then the other one, another person, Jacobson, naked and bound. The hostage taker was holding him and suddenly took a step back: he wanted to make sure that they could see that he had a miniature revolver to Jacobson's head. And then he said the words again.

Bergh didn't need to rewind this time.

He recognized the first words.

He is a dead man.

And the three last words were incredibly easy to interpret from the clear lip movements.

In twenty minutes.

Sven Sundkvist ran up the church stairs with the mobile phone in his hand. His conversation with a distressed voice from central security had been clear: they had been given a countdown and every minute, every second meant less time to make a decision. He straightened the ladder, opened the hatch and crawled out onto the balcony. Ewert was there with the new marksman and his observer. Sven told them all loudly that there wasn't time anymore to discuss things that had already been discussed.

Ewert looked at him, his eyes alert, the vein on his temple pulsing.

"How long ago?"

"One minute and twenty seconds."

Ewert Grens had been expecting it, but he thought that it might take longer, that he would have more time. He sighed; so that's how it was, that's how it always was, there was never enough time. He held on to the railing and looked out over the small town, over the prison. Two worlds only meters apart, but two separate, unique worlds with their own rules and expectations, that had absolutely fuck-all to do with each other.

"Sven?"

"Yes?"

"Who is he?"

"Who?"

"The prison warden?"

The man in the window over there, behind the reinforced glass, he knew, Hoffmann knew exactly how it fucking worked and he had decided that it would start now, that we will act because of an elderly guard. And he's right. It's the gray-haired prison warden we care about. If . . . if it had only been a drug dealer with a long sentence, well, it wasn't easy to say, to imagine, we might not have made such an effort.

"Sven?"

"Just a moment."

Sven Sundkvist looked through his notebook, tightly written pages in foutain pen ink, not used by many these days.

"Martin Jacobson. Sixty-four. Has worked at Aspsås since he was twenty-four. Married. Grown-up children. Lives in the town. Liked, respected, no threat."

Grens gave a distracted nod.

"Do you need more?"

"Not right now."

The anger. His inner engine, the driving force, without which he would be nothing. Now it took hold of him, shook him hard. No way, no goddamn way was that naked, bound man with a miniature gun to his eye, who had worked for forty years for peanuts with people who hated him, going to die on a foul-smelling workshop floor one year before retiring, no bloody way.

"Sterner?"

The military marksman was lying by the railing a bit farther along the balcony, holding up the binoculars.

"You're a police officer now. *You are a police officer now.* For five and a half hours more. And I have been assigned as gold commander here. So I am your boss. And that means that from now on you must do exactly as I order you to do. And I am, *now listen carefully*, not particularly interested in arguments about soft targets and international law. Do you understand?"

They looked at each other—he didn't get an answer, but he hadn't expected one either.

The big window.

A naked, sixty-four-year-old man.

He remembered another person, another hostage, nearly twenty years ago now, but he could still feel the choking rage. Some children in care, lethal and criminal, had planned to escape, so they decided they needed a hostage and had assaulted a retired woman who was doing some extra work in the kitchen. Cheap screwdriver to her throat, they chose the weakest member of staff and she had later died, not while she was being held hostage but as a result of it—they had somehow stolen her life from her and she didn't know how to take it back.

This was just as bloody cowardly, just as premeditated, the oldest member of the staff, the weakest in the group.

"I want to take him out of action."

"What do you mean."

"Injure him."

"I can't."

"Can't? I just explained—"

"I can't, as I would have to shoot at his torso. And from here . . . the target's too small. If I was to shoot at one of his arms, say, first of all there is a risk that I would miss, and second, if I did hit one arm, other parts of his body would also be shot to bits."

Sterner handed the gun to Grens.

The black, almost skinny weapon was heavier than he had imagined, he guessed about fifteen kilos, the hard edges pressing against his palm.

"That sniper gun . . . the force of impact would destroy a human body."

"And if you hit him?"

"He'll die."

The earpiece had almost fallen out a couple of times so he kept his finger on it, like before, every word was crucial.

"Injure him."

Something crackled, a disturbance. He changed ears—the reception

340

wasn't any better. He concentrated, listened, he had to—*had to*—understand every word.

"And if you hit him?"

"He'll die."

That was enough.

Piet Hoffmann crossed the room to the small office with a desk at the back. He pulled open the top drawer and picked up the razor that was lying in an otherwise empty compartment between the pens and paperclips, then a pair of scissors from the pencil case. He continued on to the storeroom, to the warden called Jacobson who was still sitting against the wall. Hoffmann checked the plastic packing tape around his wrists and ankles, then with one tug he pulled down the curtain from the window and, picking up the rug from the floor, he went back into the workshop and the other hostage.

The little plastic pockets of nitroglycerine were still attached to his skin. The pentyl fuse was tightly wound around his body. Hoffmann met his pleading eyes as he threw the rug over him and secured it with the curtain.

He pushed the barrel of diesel by the workbench over and positioned it by the hostage's legs.

He groped under the rug, found the detonator, and taped it to one end of the pentyl fuse.

Then he went back to the window, looked up at the church tower, and at the gun that was pointing at him.

THEY WERE STANDING BY ONE OF THE TALL WINDOWS ON THE SECOND floor of the Government Offices. They had just opened the thin glass window wide and were drinking in the fresh, cool air. They were ready. Forty-five minutes earlier they had informed the gold commander on site at Aspsås church that he would shortly have the military marksman he had requested. He was already on his way.

What was irresolvable was now resolvable.

Everything was in place for a decision to be made based on the available documentation.

A decision that was Ewert Grens's alone, that he would shortly make on his own and for which he would be solely responsible.

HE HAD NEVER BEEN IN A CHURCH TOWER BEFORE. NOT AS FAR AS HE COULD remember. Maybe as a child, on some school trip traipsing behind an ambitious class teacher. Strange, really—all these years of training and he had never fired from such an obvious place: a church that was the highest point here as in many other places. He leaned back against the wall and looked at the heavy cast-iron bell. He was sitting in there alone, resting as he should do, as a marksman always does before firing, a moment of peace in his own world while the observer stayed with the gun.

He had arrived at the church an hour earlier. In five hours' time he would be back in Kungsängen, he would have left his temporary post with the police and have been re-employed by the army. On his way here he had assumed it was a matter of shooting at an inanimate target. But that was not the case. In a few minutes he was going to do something he had never done before. Aim and fire a loaded gun at a person.

A real person.

The kind that breathes and thinks and will be missed by someone.

"Object in view."

He wasn't afraid of firing the shot, of his ability to hit the target.

But he was afraid of the consequences, the internal ones, which you can never prepare for, like what death does to the person who kills.

"I repeat. Object in view."

The observer's voice was urgent. Sterner went out into the light wind, lay down, held the weapon steady in his hands, waited. The shadow in the window. He looked at the observer—he felt the same thing, had made the same observation: neither of them were convinced that the man standing down there in profile didn't realize that it *was* in fact possible to hit him at this distance.

"Preparing to fire."

The heavy detective superintendent with the aggressive manner and a stiff leg that looked like it hurt more than he wanted to show was standing directly behind him.

"If Hoffmann doesn't withdraw his threat, I'm going to order you to shoot. His time runs out in thirteen minutes. Are you ready?"

"Yes."

"And the ammo?"

Sterner didn't turn around, he stayed lying on his stomach the whole time, facing the prison, his eye focused on the telescopic sight and a window on the top of Block B.

"*With the correct information*, I would have loaded and used the undercalibrated ammunition that is leaving Kungsängen in a helicopter this very moment and that won't get here in time. With this . . . if I'm going to penetrate reinforced glass to hit the target . . . it'll work. But I repeat . . . it isn't possible just to injure him. Once it's fired, the shot will be lethal."

THE DOOR WAS SHUT.

Brown, maybe oak, several scratches around the lock, a set of keys that scraped the door a little each time a key was turned twice in the stiff barrel.

Mariana Hermansson knocked lightly on the door.

No footsteps, no voice—if anyone was in there they didn't move, or say anything, it was someone who didn't want to make contact.

On Ewert's order she had gone to look for the prison doctor on the other side of the large prison, inside the same walls, but several hundred meters away from the workshop and Hoffmann and the risk of more death. In Block C, through one of the hospital unit's small windows, she had watched a prisoner coughing in bed while a man in a white coat explained to her that 0913 Hoffmann had never been in any of the beds, that the symptoms of an epidemic had never been identified, and that isolation had therefore never been ordered.

Ewert Grens had come up against a lie. The chief warden had prevented him from questioning an inmate. And right now that prisoner was holding a gun to a principal officer's head.

She knocked again, harder.

She pressed the handle down.

The door was unlocked.

Lennart Oscarsson was sitting in a dark leather armchair, his elbows on the wide desk in front, his head in his hands. His breathing was labored, deep and irregular, and she could see his forehead and cheeks shining in the harsh ceiling light; it could be sweat, it could be tears. He hadn't even noticed her coming into his office, that she was now standing only a few meters from him.

"Mariana Hermansson, City Police."

He jumped.

"I'd like to ask a few questions, about Hoffmann."

He looked at her.

"He is a dead man."

She chose to stay where she was.

"He said that."

His eyes were evasive—she tried to catch them, but couldn't, they were always somewhere else.

"He is a dead man. He said that!"

She didn't know what she had expected. But it wasn't this. Someone who was on the verge.

"His name is Martin. Did you know that? One of my best friends. No, more than that, my *closest* friend. The oldest employee at Aspsås. Forty years. He's been here forty years! And now . . . now he's going to die."

She pursued the darting eyes.

"Yesterday, Ewert Grens, a detective superintendent who is in fact leading the operation right now from the church tower, was here. He came to question one of the prisoners. Piet Hoffmann."

The square monitor.

"If Martin dies . . ."

The mouth that moved so slowly.

"If he dies . . ."

He is a dead man.

"I don't know if—"

"You said that it wasn't possible. That Hoffmann was ill. That he was in isolation in the hospital unit."

"—I don't know that I could bear that."

Lennart Oscarsson hadn't heard her.

"I have just been to Block C. I spoke to Nycander. Hoffmann was never there."

The mouth.

"You lied."

Moving.

"You lied. Why?"

When it moves slowly on that monitor, it looks like it's talking about death.

"Oscarsson! Listen to me! A person is lying dead on the floor in one of the corridors in Block B. Two other people have exactly nine minutes left to live. We need to make a decision. We need your answer!"

"Would you like a cup of coffee?"

"Why did you lie? What is this all about?"

"Or tea?"

"Who is Hoffmann?"

"I've got green and red and normal tea in bags. The sort that you dunk."

Large drops of sweat fell from the chief warden's face onto the shiny desktop when he got up and walked over to a glass and gold-frame cart stacked with porcelain cups and saucers in the corner of the room.

"We need an answer. Why? Why did you lie?"

"It's important not to leave it in too long."

He didn't look at her, didn't turn around despite the fact that she had raised her voice for the first time. He held one of the cups under the thermos and filled it with steaming water, then carefully dropped a bag with a picture of a red rosehip attached into the middle.

"About two minutes. No more."

She was losing him.

"Would you like milk?"

They needed him.

"Sugar? Both perhaps?"

Hermansson put her hand under her jacket, angled her gun so that it slipped out of its holster, stretched out her arm in front of the chief warden's face, recoil operation: the shot hit the middle of the rectangular cupboard door.

The bullet went straight through, hitting the back wall, and they heard it falling to the floor among the black and brown shoes.

Lennart Oscarsson didn't move. The warm cup of tea still in one hand.

She pointed to the wall clock behind the desk with the muzzle of her gun.

"Eight more minutes. Do you hear? I want to know why you lied. And I want to know who Hoffmann is, why he's standing in the workshop window with a revolver to the hostage's head."

He looked at the gun, at the cupboard, at Hermansson.

"I was just lying on a . . . an unused bunk in Block K, searching the nice, newly painted white ceiling. Because . . . because I don't know who Hoffmann is. Because I don't know why he's standing there, claiming that he's going to shoot my best friend."

His voice—she wasn't quite sure whether he was going to cry, or whether it was just the fragility of having given up.

"What I do know is . . . is that it's about something else . . . that there's other people involved."

He swallowed, swallowed again.

"I was ordered to allow a lawyer to visit a client the evening before Grens was here. A prisoner in the same unit as Hoffmann. Stefan Lygás. He was one of the people who attacked him. And he was the one who . . . who was shot this morning. Lawyers, you might know, are often used as messengers when someone wants information to be spread inside . . . that's often the way it's done."

"Ordered? By whom?"

Lennart Oscarsson gave a fleeting smile.

"I was ordered to prevent Grens—or any other police officer for that matter—from getting near Hoffmann. I stood there in reception, tried to look him in the eye, explain that the prisoner he wanted to see was in the hospital unit, that he would be there for three, maybe four days more."

"By whom?"

Same smile, impotent.

"I was ordered to move Hoffmann. Back to the unit he'd come from. Even though a prisoner who's been threatened should never be moved back."

Hermansson was shouting now.

"*By whom?*"

The smile.

"And I was given orders, just now, that if Hoffmann demands that the gates are opened for him and the hostages . . . *that I mustn't let him out.*"

"Oscarsson, I have to know who—"

"I want Martin to live."

She looked at the face that wouldn't manage to hold on for much longer, then at the clock that was hanging on the wall.

Seven minutes left.

She turned around and ran out of the office, his voice following her down the corridor.

"*Hermansson!*"

She didn't stop.

"*Hermansson!*"

Words that ricocheted off the cold walls.

"*Someone wants Hoffmann to die.*"

HIS LEGS TIED. HIS HANDS TIED. HIS MOUTH GAGGED. HIS HEAD COVERED.

Nitroglycerine against his skin. Pentyl fuse around his chest, torso, legs.

"Setting thirty-two."

He dragged the heavy body over to the window, hit it, forced it to stand there.

"TPR three."

"Repeat."

"Transport right three."

They were close to firing. The dialogue between the marksman and the observer would carry on until they fired.

He needed more time.

Hoffmann ran across the workshop to the storeroom and the other hostage, the prison warden with the pale face.

"I want you to shout."

"The packing tape, it's cutting—"

"Shout!"

The older man was tired. He panted, his head hung to one side, as if he didn't have the strength to hold it upright.

"I don't understand."

"Shout, for fuck's sake!"

"What . . . ?"

"What the fuck you like. There's five minutes left. Scream that."

The frightened eyes looked at him.

"Shout it!"

"Five minutes left."

"Louder!"

"Five minutes left!"

"Louder!"

"Five minutes left!"

Piet Hoffmann sat still and listened: careful sounds outside the door.

They had understood.

They had understood that the hostages were still alive; they wouldn't break in, not yet.

He carried on to the office and the telephone, the ringing tone, once, twice, three times, four, five, six, seven. He was holding the empty porcelain cup and threw it against the wall, shards all over the desk, the pencil holder, the same wall, she hadn't answered, she wasn't there, she . . .

"Object out of sight for one minute, thirty seconds."

He hadn't been visible enough.

"Repeat."

"Object out of sight for one minute, thirty seconds. Can't locate either object or hostages."

"Prepare for entry in two minutes."

Hoffmann ran out of the office and they were moving on the roof again, getting ready, finding their positions. He stopped by the window and pulled the rug toward him—the hostage had to be close and he heard him wince as the plastic cut deeper into the wounds around his ankles.

"Object in view again."

He stood still, waiting, now, *abort now for Christ's sake.*

"Abort. Abort preparations for entry."

He let out a slow sigh and waited, then he ran back to the office and the telephone, try again. He dialed the number, the ring tone, he couldn't bear to count them, that bloody ringing, the bloody fucking ringing, that bloody—

It stopped.

Someone had answered but didn't say anything.

The sound of a car, a car driving, the person who answered was in a car driving somewhere, and maybe, very faint, as if they were sitting farther away, it had to be, the sound of two children.

"Have you done what we agreed?"

It was difficult to hear, but he was sure, it was her.

"Yes."

He put the phone down.

Yes.

He wanted to laugh, to jump up and down, but just dialed another number.

"Central security."

"Transfer me to the gold commander."

"Gold commander?"

"Now!"

"And who the hell are you?"

"The person in one of your monitors. But, I guess for this room it's completely black."

A clicking sound, a few seconds' silence, then a voice, one that he had heard before, the one that made the decisions—he had been transferred to the church tower.

"HE IS A DEAD MAN IN THREE MINUTES."

"What do you want?"

"He is a dead man in three minutes."

"I repeat . . . what do you want."

"Dead."

THREE MINUTES.

Two minutes and fifty seconds.

Two minutes and forty seconds.

Ewert Grens was standing in a church tower and felt totally alone. He was about to make a decision about whether another person should live or die. It was his responsibility. And he wasn't sure anymore if he had enough courage to do it and then live with it afterward.

The wind wasn't blowing anymore. He certainly felt nothing on his forehead and cheeks.

"Sven?"

"Yes?"

"I want to hear it again. Who he is. What he's capable of."

"There isn't anything else."

"Read it!"

Sven Sundkvist was holding the documents in his hand. There was only time for a few lines.

"Extremely antisocial personality disorder. No ability to empathize. Extensive reports, significant characteristics include impulsiveness, aggression, lack of respect for own and others' safety, lack of conscience."

Sven looked at his boss but got no answer, no contact.

"Shooting incident involving a police officer in Söderhamn, at a public space on the edge of town, he hit—"

"That's enough."

He bent down toward the prostrate marksman.

"Two minutes. Prepare to fire."

He pointed to the door into the tower and the aluminum ladder peeping over the top of the hatch. They would go down into the room with the wooden altar—the marksman was to be disturbed as little as possible. He was about halfway down when he turned on the radio and held it to his mouth.

"From now on, I only want traffic between myself and the marksman. Turn

off your mobile phones. Only the marksman and I will communicate until the shot has been fired."

The wooden stairs creaked with every step—they were approaching the control post and he would only leave again once it was over.

Mariana Hermansson knocked on the dirty window and looked at the camera that was focused on her. It was the fourth locked door in the long passage under the prison and when it was opened, she ran toward central security and the exit.

Martin Jacobson didn't understand what was happening. But he felt that it was nearing the end. In the last few minutes, Hoffmann had run back and forth several times, he was out of breath and he had shouted loudly about time and death. Jacobson tried to move his legs, his hands, he wanted to get away. He was so frightened, he didn't want to sit here anymore, he wanted to get up and go home and eat supper and watch TV and have a drink of Canadian whisky, the kind that tasted so soft.

He was crying.

He was still crying when Hoffmann came into the cramped storeroom, when he pushed him up against the wall and whispered that soon there would be an almighty explosion, that he should stay exactly where he was, that if he did that he would be protected and wouldn't die.

He was lying with both elbows positioned on the wooden floor of the balcony and enough room for his legs; his position was comfortable and he could concentrate on the telescopic sight and the window.

It was close.

Never before on Swedish soil had a marksman taken another life in peacetime, not even shot to kill. But the hostage taker had threatened his hostages, refused to communicate, made another threat. He had gradually forced the situation to this choice between one life and another.

One shot, one hit.

He was capable; even at this distance he felt confident: one shot, one hit.

But he would never see the consequences, a person blown to bits. He remembered one morning during training, the remains of live pigs that had been used as target practice—he couldn't bear to see a person like that.

He edged fractionally farther out on the balcony so that he could see the window even better.

She ran through the open prison gates and out into the nearly full parking lot, she rang Ewert's number for the second time and for the second time was cut off, she was nearly at the car and tried Sven and tried Edvardson without getting through, she got into the car, started it and drove over the grass and plants, looking up at the church tower as much as at the road as there was someone lying there, waiting.

Ewert Grens removed his earpiece, he wanted to get rid of the voices that were there because he had ordered them to be, that were his responsibility now and that had one single task.

To kill.

"Target?"

"Single man. Blue jacket."

"Distance?"

"Fifteen hundred and three meters."

He didn't have much time left.

Hermansson turned out of the prison drive and drove toward the small town of Aspsås on the wrong side of the road.

"Wind?"

"Seven meters per second right."

She accelerated fast as she turned up the volume on the radio to max.

"Outside temperature?"

"Eighteen degrees."

Oscarsson, what he had just said, Ewert . . . before anything was fired, before . . . he had to know.

I have never shot at a person.

I have never ordered anyone else to shoot at a person.

Thirty-five years in the police. In one minute . . . less than one minute.

"Grens, over."

Sterner.

"Grens here, over."

"The hostage . . . he's covered . . . as if there's some sort of blanket wrapped around him."

"Right?"

Ewert Grens waited.

"I think . . . the blanket . . . Grens, it looks pretty weird . . ."

Grens was shaking.

It wasn't the people outside the walls who were going to decide, it was the hostage taker, he was the one who moved the boundaries, challenged them, forced them.

"Continue!"

". . . I think he's preparing for a . . . an execution."

You've worked there your whole life.

You're the oldest one there. You're the weakest. You're the chosen one.

You are not going to die.

"Fire."

He had been watching the tower and the people up there the whole time. He had been careful to stand in profile, with the hostage close by, the diesel barrel close by, he had listened to their voices which had been crystal clear, it had been easy to understand the order.

"Fire."

Fifteen hundred three meters.

Three seconds.

He heard the click.

He hesitated.

He moved.

The shot.

Death.

They waited.

"Abort. Object out of sight."

Hoffmann had stood there, his head cocked, in profile, he had been easy to see and easy to hit. Suddenly he moved. One single step was enough.

Ewert Grens was breathing heavily, he hadn't noticed before. He put a hand to his cheek, it was hot.

"Object in sight again. Ready to fire. Awaiting second order."

Hoffmann was back, he was standing there again.

One more time.

A new decision.

He didn't want to do it, couldn't face it.

"Fire."

He had heard a click. When the gun was cocked. And he had moved. This time he stayed where he was. In the middle of the window.

The first click in his ear and he stayed where he was.

Next.

The second click.

A finger on a trigger.

Fifteen hundred and three meters. Three seconds.

He moved.

One single moment.

It stretched out. It was empty and it was silent and prolonged.

Ewert Grens knew everything about moments like this, how they tormented you, ate you up and never, never let go.

"Abort. Object out of sight."

He had moved again.

Ewert Grens swallowed.

Hoffmann was about to die and it was as if he knew—one single moment, he used it and moved again.

"Object in sight again. Ready to fire. Awaiting third order."

He was back.

Grens grabbed hold of the earpiece that was resting on his shoulders, put it back in.

He turned toward Sven, looking for a face that was turned away.

"I repeat. Ready to fire. Awaiting third order. Over."

It was his decision. And his alone.

A deep breath.

He fumbled for the transmission button, felt it with his fingertips, pressed it, hard.

"Fire."

Piet Hoffmann had heard the order for the third time.

He had stood still when the gun was cocked.

He had stood still when the finger pressed on the trigger.

It was a strange feeling, knowing that a bullet was on its way, that he had three seconds left.

The explosion blocked out all sound, light, her breath . . . somewhere behind her something detonated that sounded like a bomb.

She braked abruptly and the car lurched, pulling her over toward the edge of the road and the ditch. She hung on, braked again, and regained control. She stopped the car and got out, still so shaken that she hadn't had time to be scared.

Mariana Hermansson had only had a couple of hundred meters left before she would reach Aspsås church.

She turned around, toward the prison.

A sharp, intense fire.

Then thick, black smoke that forced its way out of a gaping hole that until moments ago had been a window in the front of a prison workshop building.

PART FOUR

saturday

IT WAS PROBABLY AS DARK AS IT COULD GET AT NIGHT TOWARD THE END of May.

The houses and trees and fields were waiting all around with dissolving corners, to reappear when the light crept back.

Ewert Grens was driving along the empty road, almost halfway, about twenty kilometers north of Stockholm. His body was tense, every joint and every muscle still ached with adrenaline, even though it was more than twelve hours now since the shot had been fired, the explosion and death. He hadn't even tried to sleep, though he had lain down for a while on the sofa in his office and listened to the silent police headquarters, without closing his eyes—he just couldn't turn off the roaring inside. He had tried to lose himself in thoughts of Anni and the cemetery, imagined what her resting place looked like. He still hadn't been there, but he would go soon. It was one of those nights when, eighteen months ago, he would have talked to her, nights that he had managed to survive with her help; he would have called the nursing home, even though he wasn't supposed to, nagged one of the staff until they woke her and handed over the receiver, and gradually calmed down as he told her everything, her presence in his ear. After she was gone, he had stopped calling and instead took the car and drove out toward Gärdet and Lidingö bridge and the nursing home that was so well situated on the wealthy island. He would sit in the parking place by her window, look up at it, and after a while get out of the car and walk around the house.

Ewert, you can't regulate your grief. Ewert, what you're frightened of has already happened. Ewert, I never want to see you here again.

Now he didn't even have that.

After a few hours he had gotten up, walked down the corridor and to the car on Bergsgatan and started to drive toward Solna and North Cemetery. He wanted to talk to her again. He had stood by one of the gates and searched the shadows and then carried on north, through the smudged landscape to a wall around a prison and a church with a beautiful tower.

"Grens."

The dark, the quiet—if it had not been for the searing smell of fire and soot and diesel, it could all have been a dream, a head in a window, a mouth forming the word *death*, and in a while there would perhaps be nothing more than the birds singing their hearts out to the dawn and a town waking up without having heard anything about a hostage drama and a person lying motionless on the floor.

"Yes?"

He had pressed the button beside the gate and was talking into the intercom.

"I'm the detective investigating all this mess. Can you let me in?"

"It's three in the morning."

"Yes."

"There's no one here who—"

"Can you let me in?"

He slipped through the gate and central security, then crossed one of the prison's dry inner yards.

He had never fired death at a person before.

It had been his decision.

His responsibility.

Ewert Grens approached the building called Block B, paused a while outside the front door, and looked up at the second floor.

The acrid smell of fire had almost intensified.

First an explosion and a projectile that penetrated and shattered a window and a person's head. Then another, more powerful one, the godawful black smoke that never seemed to stop, that concealed what they were trying to see; an explosion that could not be explained.

His decision.

He started to walk up the stairs, past all the closed doors, toward the smell of smoke.

His responsibility.

Ewert Grens had in fact never had any relationship to death. He worked with it, frequently came face-to-face with it, and any thoughts of his own death were irrelevant. They had stopped thirty years ago the moment that he, as the driver of a police van, had driven over a head that had then ceased to function. Anni's head. He had no desire to die, it wasn't that, nor did he desire to live. In his meeting with guilt and grief he had developed the ability to encapsulate it, and had continued to do so, and now he didn't even know where to start.

The door was open and the inside was black with soot.

Grens looked into the burned-out workshop, pulled some transparent plastic bags over his shoes, and stepped over the blue-and-white cordon.

There was always something lonely about places that have been destroyed by fire, the all-engulfing flames that eventually turned and subsided. He was walking on the remains of shelves that had fallen, between machines that were black and had been chewed and stopped.

It was there. On the ceiling, on the walls. What he had come for.

He had seen the white ones before, the forensic team's markers for body parts. More than in Västmannagatan. But the red ones, he had never been to a crime scene with red flags.

Two bodies, hundreds . . . maybe thousands of pieces.

He wondered whether Errfors, the forensic pathologist, would ever be able to piece enough together for an identification. People who had been alive until recently, who no longer existed, other than in bits marked by small flags. He started to count them without knowing why, just a few square meters of wall, but tired of it when he reached three hundred seventy-four. He crossed over the window that was no longer there, a light breeze through the hole in the wall. He stood in the place where Hoffmann had stood, the church and the church tower silhouetted against the sky. The sniper had lain up there, he had aimed and fired a bullet on Ewert Grens's command.

Aspsås shrank in the rearview mirror.

He had stayed for a couple of hours in the stench of burned oil and heavy smoke. The feeling had continued to torment him, no matter how many red and white flags marking body parts he counted, he still couldn't understand it, and the unease kept him awake, a reminder of the adrenaline and irritation. He didn't like it, tried to lose it in the mess on the floor and the tools that would never be used again, but it clung to him, whispering something he couldn't understand. He was approaching Stockholm through the northern satellite towns and suburbs when his mobile phone sang out from the backseat. He slowed down, leaned back for his jacket.

"Ewert?"

"Are you awake?"

"Where are you?"

"This early, Sven? Shouldn't it be me who's calling you?"

Sven Sundkvist smiled. It was a long time since he and Anita had been bothered by the phone ringing in the bedroom between midnight and dawn. Ewert always called the minute he had something that needed an immediate answer, and that tended to be at night when everyone else was asleep. But he hadn't been able to sleep himself last night. He had lain close to Anita and listened to the ticking of the alarm clock until, after a couple of hours, he crept out of bed and went down to the kitchen on the ground floor of their terraced house, and sat there doing crosswords, as he sometimes did when the nights were long. But the unease refused to leave his house. The same unease that Ewert had talked about earlier that evening, thoughts that had nowhere to go.

"I'm on my way into the city, Ewert. I'm just by Gullmarsplan and then heading west. To Kungsängen. Sterner just called."

"Sterner?"

"The sniper."

Grens accelerated—the early morning commuters were still in their garages, so it was easy to drive.

"Then we've got about the same distance. I'm just passing Haga Park. What's it about?"

"Tell you when we get there."

Another locked gate in another uniformed world.

Grens and Sundkvist arrived at the Svea Life Guards in Kungsängen only a few minutes apart. Sterner was waiting for them by the regiment guardhouse. He looked rested, but was wearing the same clothes as the day before, white-and-gray camouflage, creased after a night on top of the bedclothes. Standing in front of the closed gate and with the barracks behind him, he looked the cliché of a model American marine, cropped hair and broad shouldered, square face, the kind that on films always stand too near and shout too loud.

"Same clothes as yesterday?"

"Yup. When the helicopter dropped me off . . . I went and lay down."

"And you slept?"

"Like a baby."

Grens and Sundkvist exchanged looks. The guy who had fired had slept. But the one who had made the decision to fire, and his closest colleague, had not.

Sterner signed them in and showed the way to a deserted barracks square, with solid buildings that stared down at all visitors. Sterner walked fast and Grens had difficulty keeping up when they went through the first door and carried on up the stairs, down long corridors with stone floors, conscripts still in underpants ahead of a day in uniform.

"Life Guards. First company. The ones who are going to be officers and stay longest."

He stopped in a room with simple, institutional furniture, white walls that needed painting, and plastic flooring on hard concrete.

Four work stations, one in each corner.

"My colleagues won't be coming in today. A two-day exercise in north Uppland, around Tierp. We won't be disturbed here."

He closed the door.

"I called as soon as I woke up. The thought that I had as I fell asleep came back to me and refused to leave the bed."

He leaned forward.

"I observed. With the binoculars. I watched him for a long time. I followed his movements, his face for nearly half an hour."

"And?"

"He was standing in the window, fully exposed. You mentioned it too, I heard you. Like he knew he could be seen, that he wanted to demonstrate his power over the hostages, the whole situation, maybe even you. You said that he was doing it because he was sure he was out of range."

"Right."

"That's what *you* said. What *you* believed."

He looked at the door, as if he wanted to reassure himself that it really was shut.

"*I* didn't think that. Not then. And not now."

"I think you'll need to explain that."

Grens felt uneasy, the same feeling that had kept him awake, that was in some way connected to the feeling he got in the burned-out workshop.

There was something that wasn't right.

"When I was watching him through the binoculars. *Object in clear sight. Awaiting order.* I don't know, it was like he knew. *I repeat. Awaiting order.* As if he knew that he was in range."

"I don't understand."

"I aborted. *Abort. Object out of sight.* I aborted twice."

"Yes, and?"

Well, both times . . . it was like he knew when I was going to shoot. He moved so . . . precisely."

"He moved several times."

Sterner got up, he was restless, went over to the door, checked it, then over to the window with a view of the square.

"He did. But both times . . . *precisely* as I was about to fire."

"And the third time?"

"He stood still. Then . . . it was like . . . like he'd decided. He stood still and waited."

"And?"

"One bullet, one hit. The motto of sniper training. I only shoot if I know I'm going to hit the target."

Grens went over to the same window.

"Where?"

"Where . . . ?"

"Where did you hit him?"

"The head. I shouldn't have done it. But I had no choice."

"What do you mean?"

"I mean that from a distance, we always aim at the chest. The largest target area. I should have aimed there. But he was standing in profile the whole time and so . . . to get as big a target area as possible . . . I shot at his head."

"And the explosion?"

"I don't know."

"Don't know?"

"*I don't know.*"

"But you—"

"It wasn't connected to the shot."

A group of about twenty teenagers in uniform marched across the gravel in two rows.

They tried to lift their legs and swing their arms at the same time, while someone who was a bit older walked beside them screeching something.

They weren't succeeding.

"And one more thing."

"Yes?"

"Who was he?"

"Why?"

"I killed him."

The two rows were now standing at ease.

The older uniform demonstrated how their guns should lie on their shoulders while they marched.

It was important that they all held them the same way.

"I killed him. I want to know his name. I feel I have the right."

Grens hesitated, looked at Sven, and then back at Sterner.

"Piet Hoffmann."

Sterner's face showed nothing. If it was a name he recognized he hid it well.

"Hoffmann. Do you have his personal details?"

"Yes."

"I want to go over to administration. And I'd like you to come with me. There's something I want to check."

Ewert and Sven followed Sterner's back across the barracks square to a building that was smaller than the others and housed the regimental commander's quarters, administration, and a slightly better officers' mess. On the second floor, Sterner rapped on the doorframe of an open door, and an older man sitting in front of a computer gave them a friendly nod.

"I need his personal ID number."

Sven had already gotten out a notebook from his inner pocket, which he flicked through until he found what he was looking for.

"721018-0010."

The older man in front of the computer typed in the ten-digit number, waited for a few seconds, and then shook his head.

"Born in the early 1970s? Then he won't be here. Ten years back, that's what the law stipulates. Any documents older than that are stored in the military archives."

He smiled, looked pleased.

"But . . . I always make my own copies of anything we have before sending it off. Svea Life Guards' own archive. Every young man who has done his military service here in the past thirty years can be found on the shelves next door."

A room crowded with shelves on every wall, from floor to ceiling. He got down on his knees and ran his finger along the backs of the files before picking out a black one.

"Born 1972. Now, if he was here . . . ninety-one, ninety-two, ninety-three, maybe even ninety-four. Life Company, you said. Sniper training?"

"Yes."

He leafed through the papers, put the file back, then took out the one beside it.

"Not ninety-one. So we'll try ninety-two."

He had got about halfway when he stopped and looked up.

"Hoffmann?"

"Piet Hoffmann."

"Then we've got a match."

Ewert and Sven stepped forward simultaneously to get a better look at the papers that the archivist was holding up. Hoffmann's full name, Hoffmann's personal ID number, then a long row of combined numbers and letters, some sort of record.

"What does that mean?"

"It means that someone called Piet Hoffmann, someone with the personal ID number that you just gave me, completed his military service here in 1993. He followed an eleven-month training program, as a sniper."

Ewert Grens scanned the piece of paper once more.

It was him.

The person they had seen die sixteen hours earlier.

"Special training in weapons and shooting, all positions—prone, kneeling, standing, short range, long range . . . I think you get the gist?"

Sterner opened the file, took out the piece of paper and copied it on a machine that was as big as the room.

"That feeling that I had . . . that he knew exactly where I was, what I was doing. If he was trained here . . . he would have enough skills to know that Aspsås church tower was the only place that we could get him from. He knew that it *was* possible to kill him."

Sterner held the copy crushed in his hand and then gave it to Grens.

"He'd chosen that place with great care. It's no coincidence that he went to the workshop and that window, in particular. He provoked us to fire. He knew that a good, well-trained marksman could shoot him if he had to."

He shook his head.

"He wanted to die."

The corridor of the intensive care unit at Danderyd hospital had yellow walls and a light blue floor. The nurses sent them friendly smiles and Ewert Grens and Sven Sundkvist gave equally friendly smiles back. It was a quiet morning—they had both been there for work on many occasions before, often in the evening or weekend, injured people waiting on beds in the harsh light of the corridor, which was empty now, as it normally was when alcohol, football matches, and snowy roads were not the order of the day.

They had driven there straight from Kungsängen and the Svea Life Guards, via Norrviken and Edsberg, through small and pleasant suburbs with big detached houses, which made Sven phone home to Anita and Jonas. They had had breakfast together and were about to go to their separate schools. He missed them.

The doctor was a young man, tall and thin, on the verge of skinny, with reserved eyes. He greeted them and showed them into a dark room with drawn curtains.

"He's got a severe concussion. I'll have to ask you to keep the room dark."

One single bed in the room.

A man in his sixties, graying hair, tired eyes, scratches and wounds on both his cheeks, a cut on his forehead that looked deep, his right arm in a sling.

He was found lying under a wall.

"My name is Johan Ferm. We met last night when you came in. I've got two policemen with me who would like to ask you some questions."

The fire and rescue service had searched the burned-out workshop for a long time before they heard faint sounds from underneath one of the piles of rubble. A naked and bruised prison officer with a broken collarbone, but a person who was still breathing.

"I've given them five minutes. Then I'll ask them to leave."

The gray-haired man pulled himself up, grimaced with pain, and threw up in a bowl by the side of the bed.

"He is *not* allowed to move. Severe concussion. Your five minutes have already started."

Ewert Grens turned toward the young doctor.

"We'd prefer it if we could be left alone."

"I'm staying here. For medical reasons."

Grens stood by the window while Sven Sundkvist moved a stool from the sink to the bedside, making sure that his face was at about the same height as the injured prison warden's.

"You know Grens?"

Martin Jacobson nodded. He knew who Ewert Grens was, they had met several times; the detective superintendent regularly visited the place where he had chosen to work all his life.

"This is not an interview, Jacobson. We'll do that later, when you're well enough and we have more time. But we do need some information now."

"Sorry?"

"This is not—"

"You'll have to speak louder. My eardrums burst in the explosion."

Sven leaned forward and raised his voice.

"We've got a fairly good picture of what happened when you were taken hostage. Your colleagues have given us a detailed description of the shooting of a prisoner in solitary confinement."

The doctor tapped on Sven's shoulder.

"Ask short questions. That's all he can manage. Short answers. Otherwise you'll just be wasting your five minutes."

Sven considered turning around and telling the man in the white coat to shut up. But he didn't. He never snapped at people as it seldom helped the situation.

"First of all . . . can you remember any of what happened yesterday?"

Jacobson was breathing heavily, he was in a lot of pain and struggled to find the words that disappeared in his seriously concussed brain.

"I remember everything. Until I lost consciousness. If I've understood correctly, a wall fell on me?"

"It fell down as a result of an explosion. But I want to know . . . what happened just before?"

"I don't know. I wasn't there."

"You weren't . . . there?"

"I was in another room, Hoffmann put me there, hands tied behind my back, somewhere at the back of the workshop, near the main door. He moved me there after we'd stripped. And after that I think we only had contact once. *You're not going to die.* That's what he said. Just before the explosion."

Sven looked at Ewert—they had both registered what the elderly guard had just said.

"Jacobson . . . do you think that Hoffmann moved you in order to . . . protect you?"

Martin Jacobson answered straightaway.

"I'm sure that's why he did it. Despite everything that happened . . . I didn't feel threatened anymore."

Sven leaned even farther forward, it was important that Jacobson could hear.

"The explosion. I want to ask more about that. If you think back, can you remember anything that might explain it? And the incredible force of it?"

"No."

"Nothing at all?"

"I've thought about it. And of course, it was a workshop and there was diesel. That explains the smoke. But the actual explosion . . . nothing."

The color of Jacobson's face had changed from white to ashen gray and large drops of sweat were running from his hairline.

The doctor moved over to the bed.

"He can't deal with much more. Just one more question. Then I'll have to ask you to leave."

Sven nodded. The final question.

"Throughout the entire hostage drama, Hoffmann is silent. No communication. Except for right at the end. *He's a dead man.* We don't understand why. I want to know if you saw him communicating at any point? Or anything that might resemble communication? We don't understand his silence."

The warden who was lying in a hospital bed with a wounded ashen-gray face took a while to answer. Sven got the feeling that he was drifting off, and the doctor had indicated that he should stop when Jacobson raised an arm, he wanted to continue, he wanted to answer.

"He used the phone."

Jacobson looked at Sven, at Ewert.

"He used the phone. In the office at the back of the workshop. Twice."

Ewert Grens was driving to Aspsås and the large prison for the second time that morning.

They had paid for a cup of bitter tea and a white bread sandwich with meatballs and something purplish that Sven claimed was beetroot salad. They had sat in the café by the hospital entrance and eaten in silence, with Jacobson's answers to keep them company. According to the injured warden, Hoffmann had left the hostages on two occasions and gone into the workshop office. He kept them in full view through the glass partition wall while he lifted the receiver of the phone that sat on the desk and talked for about fifteen seconds each time. Once right at the start, Hoffmann had warned them not to move and had walked backward toward the office with the gun pointing at them, the other time just before the explosion. From his position behind the partition wall, the naked and bound guard had clearly seen him phoning again and saw that he was now very nervous, only a few seconds, but Jacobson was sure of it; a few moments of doubt and fear, maybe the only ones throughout the whole drama.

There were no empty spaces in the parking lot that had been peaceful only a few hours ago. Morning had woken one of Sweden's maximum-security prisons. Ewert Grens parked on some grass near the wall and, while he waited for Sven Sundkvist, made a phone call to Hermansson, who for the third day was working on a report of the murder at Västmannagatan 79, which was to be delivered to the prosecutor that afternoon. He would then decide whether to downgrade the investigation.

"I want you to put it to one side for the moment."

"Ågestam was here yesterday. He wants it this afternoon."

"Hermansson?"

"Yes?"

"Ågestam will get the report when you've finished it. *Put it to one side.* I want you to make a list of all outgoing calls from Aspsås prison between eight forty-five and nine forty-five in the morning and one-thirty and two-thirty in the afternoon. Then I want you to check them. I want to know which ones we can forget and which ones might have been made from the workshop office."

He had expected her to protest.

She didn't.

"Hoffmann?"

"Hoffmann."

The prison yard was full of inmates—it was the morning break with spring sun and they sat in groups and looked up at the sky with cheeks that turned rosy. Grens had no wish to listen to sarcastic remarks from anyone he had previously investigated and questioned and so chose to go underground, via a concrete passageway that reminded him of another investigation. Neither Ewert Grens nor Sven Sundkvist said anything, but they were thinking about the same case, how they had walked side by side five years ago, a father who had killed his daughter's murderer and then been given a long sentence himself, a case that often returned and niggled, with images that they had tried to forget for a long time. Some investigations did that.

They came out of the passage and were struck by the silence, even in the stairwell of Block B. The annoying banging had stopped. They passed solitary confinement in B1 and the normal units in B2, which were all empty as the prisoners had been evacuated to Block K and would remain there as long as the building that still echoed from the explosion was a cordoned-off crime scene and part of an investigation.

Four forensic technicians were creeping around in different parts of the charred workshop and soot-licked walls that had once been white. The smell of diesel oil stuck to everything, a thick and sharp smell that reminded those there of how poisonous each breath had been only a day earlier. Nils Krantz left the remains of death, concentrated and determined. Neither Ewert nor Sven had ever seen him laugh; he was simply someone who functioned far better with a microscope than a cocktail glass.

"Follow me."

Krantz walked over to the part of the workshop that looked out over the prison yard, hunkered down in front of a wall with a hole about the size of a grapefruit, then turned and pointed straight across the room.

"So, the bullet penetrated the window there. The window that you could see from the church tower, where Hoffmann chose to stand, fully exposed, for the whole drama. We're talking about fire and explosive ammunition and an initial velocity of eight hundred and thirty meters per second. That means three seconds from the shot being fired to hitting its target."

Nils Krantz had never witnessed a crime happening, he had never been in a place when it became a crime scene. But that was precisely what his work entailed, being there, getting others to be there later, at the exact time that it happened.

"The projectile penetrated a window and a skull with massive impact. Then it flattened and the velocity slowed until it reached here, see the big hole, and met the next wall."

He closed his hand around a long metal pole in the middle of the hole that showed the angle of the trajectory—the shot had been fired from somewhere higher up.

"The bullet when loaded is nearly ten centimeters long. But the part that is fired, the bit that remains if you discount the jacket, is three, maybe even three and a half centimeters, and this then hit and ripped through parts of the wall and continued out into the prison yard. And a projectile that slices through glass, human bone, and a thick concrete wall in that order will totally flatten out and look more or less like an old eighteenth-century coin."

Grens and Sundkvist looked at the crater in the wall. They had both listened to Jacobson talking about a sound like a whiplash, the force had been unimaginable.

"It's out there somewhere. We haven't found it yet, but we will soon. I've got several police officers from Aspsås district on their hands and knees in the gravel looking."

Krantz walked over to the window where Hoffmann had stood. Red and white flags on the wall, the floor, the ceiling. More than Grens could remember from his visit during the night.

"I've had to make a kind of system. Red for bloodstains, white for remains. I've never worked with bodies that have been so totally blown apart."

Sven studied the small flags, tried to understand what they actually signified, moved closer—he who normally avoided unmistakeable death.

"We're talking about an explosion and fragments of dead people. But there's something I don't understand."

This time, Sven moved even closer. He wasn't frightened, didn't feel any discomfort. This wasn't death, he couldn't see it like that.

"Human tissue. Thousands of bits. This type of projectile rips bodies apart. Into big bits. It doesn't explode."

People broken down into particles that were only centimeters away from Sven, they stopped being people then.

"So we're looking for something else. Something that exploded. Something that blows things into smithereens, not big bits."

"Such as?"

"An explosive. I can't think of any other explanation."

Ewert Grens saw the red and white flags, shards of glass, soot that blanketed everything.

"Explosive. What kind?"

Krantz made an irritation gesture with his arms.

"TNT. Nitroglycerine. C4. Semtex. Pentyl. Octogen. Dynamex. Or something else. *I don't know, Grens.* We're still looking. But what I do know . . . it was definitely close to the bodies, maybe even directly on the skin."

He nodded at the flags.

"Well . . . you understand."

Red for bloodstains, white for remains.

"We also know that it was an explosive that generates extreme heat."

"I see . . ."

"Enough heat to ignite the diesel in the barrel."

"I can smell it."

The forensic scientist gave a gentle kick to the barrel standing below the hole that had been a window the day before.

"It was the diesel that had been mixed with gas that caused all that godawful smoke. You find barrels and cans of diesel oil in every workshop in every prison, fuel for the machines and any forklift trucks, and for cleaning the tools. But this barrel . . . it was standing very close to Hoffmann. And it had been moved there."

Nils Krantz shook his head.

"Explosives. Poisonous smoke. It was no accident that the barrel was there, Ewert. Piet Hoffmann wanted to be certain."

"Certain?"

"That he and one of the hostages would die."

Grens turned off the engine and got out of the car. He waved at Sven to drive on ahead and started to walk over the fields in what was to be a fifteen-hundred-and-three-meter stroll from Aspsås prison to Aspsås church. The open areas of grass cleansed him of the lack of sleep and the stench of diesel oil, but not the feeling that had gripped him, which he didn't like and knew would stay with him until he understood what it was he couldn't see.

He should have worn other shoes.

The green that looked so soft from a distance was full of dips and clay and he had stumbled a couple of times, fallen heavily to the ground, his trousers stained green by the grass and brown by the earth by the time he finally stopped outside a side gate into the churchyard.

He turned around. The morning mist had evaporated and the gray walls were clear in the sunlight. He had stood here exactly twenty-four hours ago; he still hadn't made the decision about another person's death.

A handful of visitors were moving around between the headstones, flowers in their hands, spouses or children or friends who cared. Grens avoided their eyes but watched their hands as they dug in between the green bushes and wreaths, as if he was testing himself, but being by a grave that meant nothing didn't feel like anything either.

A plastic cordon was wound between the trees and some arbitrary poles. He pushed it down and stepped over it, raising his stiff leg high in the air. Four people were waiting at the heavy church door. Sven Sundkvist, two uniformed policemen from Aspsås district, and an older man with a dog collar.

He held out his hand, took another hand.

"Gustaf Lindbeck. I'm the parish priest."

The sort who pronounced Gustaf with a very clear f. Grens felt his mouth twitch. *I* should perhaps say Ewert with a very clear w.

"Grens, detective superintendent with city police."

"Are you the one who's responsible for this?"

The parish priest tugged at the cordon.

"I'm leading the investigation, if that's what you mean."

Ewert Grens pulled at the same tape.

"Is this a problem for you?"

"I've already had to cancel a christening and a marriage. I have a funeral in an hour. I just wanted to know whether it would be possible to go ahead."

Grens looked at the church, at Sven, at the visitors on their knees in front of gravestones, watering plants in narrow beds.

"This is what we'll do."

He tugged lightly at the tape until one of the temporary poles fell down.

"I need to look over parts of the ground floor again. That'll take about half an hour. In the meantime, you—and only you—can be there and prepare what you have to prepare. When we're done, we'll remove the cordon and the funeral party can come in. But, for investigation purposes, I'll keep the church tower cordoned off for another day. Does that sound like a reasonable solution?"

The priest nodded.

"I'm very grateful. But . . . one more thing. The passing bell should be rung in about an hour. Can we use the church bell?"

Ewert looked up at the tower and the heavy cast-iron bell that hung in the middle.

"Yes, you can. The bell itself isn't cordoned off."

They walked toward the now open door. *The church bell.* The churchyard was watching him. *The passing bell.* A year and a half had passed and he hadn't even chosen her gravestone.

The priest carried on straight ahead, into the cool and quiet church, whereas Grens and Sundkvist went right just inside the door. The chairs were still stacked up against the wall, the map folded out over the wooden altar near the only window in the vestibule.

"*Sven?*" "*Yes?*" "*I want to hear it again. Who he is. What he's capable of.*"

Ewert held the drawing of a prison.

"*Extremely antisocial personality disorder. No ability to empathize.*"

Slowly he folded it up.

"*Significant characteristics include impulsiveness, aggression, lack of respect for own and others' safety, lack of conscience.*"

Map in his inner pocket, they wouldn't need it anymore.

"Ewert, give me a hand."

Sven had picked up and emptied six plastic cups emblazoned with the red and yellow Shell logo—a couple of hours of decisions about life and death based on the energy from bad coffee from the nearest gas station. He picked up one of the chairs and waited pointedly until Ewert took the next one. They left the room that would soon be a private gathering place for the bereaved and opened the door to the stairs up into the tower, a swift glance into the nave and the priest who was pushing a cart of Bibles between two rows of pews. He saw them and raised his hand.

"Are you going up?"

"Yes."

"The passing bell . . . there's only twenty minutes to go."

"We'll be done by then."

They went up the stairs and the aluminum ladder and somehow it felt farther and higher than the day before. The door to the church tower balcony was open and creaked gently in the wind that played over the gravestones and grass. Grens was about to close it when he noticed the mark on the doorframe. The wood was newly splintered on a level with the door handle. It was obvious and he remembered that the first sniper had remarked that the door had been forced open. He poked the splintered wood with a pen—it hadn't even darkened yet, it couldn't have been that long ago.

The morning mist was clearing and the sky would soon be as blue as the day before. Aspsås prison was waiting under them like great lumps of gray, silent cement, walls and buildings that kept out dreams and laughter.

Ewert Grens went out onto the flimsy wooden structure.

"Sven, carry on reading."
A sniper had lain here twenty-four hours ago.
"There isn't anything else."
A gun aimed at a person's head.
"Read!"
"Shooting incident involving a police officer in Söderhamn, at a public space on the edge of the town, he hit—"
"That's enough."
He had made his decision.
His order was death.

The wind picked up. It felt good on his face, and for a while there was only the sun that warmed his pale cheeks and the birds flying way above his head, chasing what couldn't be seen. He held on to the low railing, a moment of dizziness, one single step would pitch him headlong. He looked at his feet and at a couple of dark round stains on the last wooden board, the one that stopped a few centimeters out from the railing. He touched them with his fingertips, smelled them. Gun grease, must have escaped from the gun barrel and would now forever discolor the floor of the balcony.

Ewert Grens knelt down, then lay so that his whole body was where the marksman had been. His elbows on the wooden floor, an imaginary gun in his hands, he aimed at the window that was no longer there, a hole surrounded by soot right up to the roof of the building called Block B.

"This was where he was lying. When he was waiting for my order."

Ewert looked up at Sven.

"When he was waiting for me to ask him to kill."

He waved impatiently at his colleague.

"You lie down too. I want you to know what it feels like."

"I don't like heights. You know that."

"Sven, just lie down. The railing, it's enough, it'll protect you."

Sven Sundkvist crept gingerly out, going a bit farther so he didn't need to lie near Grens's heavy body. He hated heights, too much to lose if you fell, a fear that got stronger every year. He crept and wriggled and stretched out his hand when he was sufficiently close, and clung to the railing.

It was high. Ewert was breathing heavily. The wind was blowing.

Sven wrapped his fingers tighter around a cold iron railing and felt something coming loose; he was holding something in his hand. He pulled it back, even more came off, something black and rectangular, three or four centimeters long, a wire at one end.

"Ewert."

An outstretched hand.

"This was on the railing."

They both realized what it was.

A solar cell.

Painted black, the same color as the railing, the hand that had put it there did not want it to be seen.

Sven pulled carefully at the equally black wire. It came loose and he pulled harder, hauling in a round piece of metal, smaller than the first, barely a centimeter in diameter.

An electronic transmitter.

When I was watching him through the binoculars. I don't know, it was like he knew.

"A transmitter, a wire, a solar cell. Ewert . . . Sterner was right."

As if he knew that he was in range.

Sven held the wire, swinging it back and forth, forgot for a moment to be frightened of what was far below.

"Hoffmann heard every word that was said between you and the sniper."

EWERT GRENS HAD BEEN CAREFUL TO CLOSE THE DOOR TO HIS ROOM.

Two cups of coffee and a cheese-and-ham roll from the vending machine in the corridor.

He could still feel the force of the explosion and the smell of smoke and imagined breathing that vanished as he watched.

He hadn't had a choice.

According to all the documentation, Piet Hoffmann was one of the few criminals who had the potential to actually do what he threatened. Ewert Grens went through the Prison and Probation Service documents, including psychopathic tests and sentences, read through his criminal record on the computer screen, five years, attempted murder and assault of a police officer, observations in the criminal intelligence database of a criminal who was KNOWN DANGEROUS ARMED.

He had not had any choice.

He was about to turn off the computer and go back out into the corridor for another cheese-and-ham roll when he noticed something at the bottom of the screen, the first entry in Piet Hoffmann's criminal record.

Date last modified.

Grens worked it out. Eighteen days ago.

A sentence that was served ten years ago.

He stayed in the room, pounding from wall to wall, from window to door, that feeling again that something was wrong, something didn't fit.

He dialed a number that he had long since learned by heart, data support, he had spent many a night swearing over the keys and symbols that seemed to have a mind of their own.

A young male voice answered. They were always young and they were always male.

"This is Grens. I need a bit of help."

"Detective superintendent? Just one moment."

Ewert Grens had on a couple of occasions walked through the whole building in order to see what they were explaining, which was why he knew that what he heard while he waited, metal against metal, was the young male voice, just like all the others, disposing of an empty Coke can on one of the piles around his computer.

"I want to know who's changed an entry in someone's criminal record. Can you access that?"

"I'm sure I can. But that comes under the national court administration. You'll need to talk to their support team."

"But if I was to ask you? Now?"

The young voice opened a new can.

"Give me five minutes."

Four minutes and forty-five seconds later, Grens smiled at the receiver.

"What have you got?"

"Nothing out of the ordinary. It was changed on one of the national court administration computers."

"By who?"

"Someone who's authorized. An Ulrika Danielsson. Do you want her number?"

He tramped around the room again, drank some cold coffee that was trying to stick to the bottom of the cup.

He remained standing up for the next phone call.

"Ulrika Danielsson."

"Grens, City Police in Stockholm."

"How can I help you?"

"It's about an investigation. 721018-0010. A judgment that's nearly ten years old."

"Right?"

"And according to the register it was modified recently. Exactly eighteen days ago."

"I see."

"By you."

He could hear her silence.

"I wanted to know why."

She was nervous. He was sure of it. Long pauses, deep breaths.

"I'm afraid I can't comment on that."

"You can't comment?"

"Confidentiality clause."

"Which damn confidentiality clause?"

"I'm afraid I can't say any more."

Grens didn't raise his voice, he lowered it—sometimes it worked even better.

"I want to know *why* you changed it. And *what* you changed."

"I said that I can't comment."

"Ulrika . . . can I call you that, by the way?"

He didn't wait for the answer.

"Ulrika, I am a detective superintendent. I'm investigating a murder. And you work for the national court administration. You can claim the confidentiality clause as much as you like for hacks. But not for me."

"I—"

"Now, you're going to answer me. Or I'll just get back to you, Ulrika, in a couple of days. That's as long as it takes to get a court order."

Deep breaths. She couldn't contain them any longer.

"Wilson."

"Wilson?"

"Your colleague. You'll have to ask him."

It was no longer just a feeling.

Something wasn't right.

HE LAY DOWN ON THE BROWN CORDUROY SOFA. HALF AN HOUR HAD PASSED and he had really tried, he had closed his eyes and relaxed and was even less likely to fall asleep than when he started.

I don't understand.

A prisoner in a workshop window kept getting in the way.

Why did you want to die?

A face in profile.

If you could hear, which Sterner is sure of, if what we found in the church tower and what is now lying on my desk is a working transmitter, why the hell did you dodge your own death twice and then choose to face it the third time?

A person who had made sure he was visible the whole time.

Had you decided but didn't dare?

Where then did you get the courage to stand still and die?

And why did you make sure that after the shot you would be blown into a thousand pieces?

"Are you sleeping?"

Someone had knocked on the door and Hermansson popped her head around.

"Not really."

He sat up, happy to see her; he often was. She sat down beside him on the sofa, a file on her lap.

"I've finished the report about Västmannagatan 79. I'm pretty sure that he'll still recommend that it's scaled down. We don't seem to be getting any further."

Grens sighed. "It feels . . . it feels very odd. If we close this . . . my third unsolved murder here."

"Third?"

"One at the start of the eighties, a body that was cut up into small pieces and found in the water near Kastellholmen by some fishermen pulling in a net. And then one a couple of winters ago, the woman in the hospital service passage, the one who was dragged from the tunnel system, her face covered in big holes from rat bites."

He tapped the file. "Is it me who's getting worse, Hermansson? Or is it reality that's getting more complicated?"

Hermansson looked at her boss and smiled.

"Ewert?"

"Yes?"

"And exactly how long have you worked here?"

"You know that."

"How long?"

"Since . . . before you were born. Thirty-five years."

"And how many murders have you investigated?"

"The exact number, I assume?"

"Yes."

"Two hundred and thirteen."

"Two hundred and thirteen."

"Including this one."

She smiled again.

"Thirty-five years. Two hundred and thirteen murders. Of which three are unsolved."

He didn't answer. It wasn't a question.

"One every twelve years, Ewert. I don't know how you measure things like that. But I'd say that's not too bad."

He glanced at her. Thought what he had often thought about. He knew already. If he had had a son, a daughter.

Kind of like her.

"There was something else?"

She opened the file and took out a plastic sleeve that was at the back.

"Two more things."

She pulled out two pieces of paper from the awkward plastic.

"You asked me to get a record of all outgoing phone calls from Aspsås prison between eight forty-five and nine forty-five in the morning and one thirty and two thirty in the afternoon."

Neat columns of numbers to the left and first name and last name to the right.

"Thirty-two calls. Even though restrictions had been placed on outgoing calls from the prison."

Hermansson ran down the long column of numbers with her finger.

"I've cleared thirty of them. Eleven calls from staff to their family who were worried or to say that they would be home late. Eight calls to us, the police, to Aspsås district or City. Three calls to the Prison and Probation Service in Norrköping. Four calls to inmates' families who were due to visit, to arrange new times. And . . ."

She looked at the detective superintendent.

". . . four calls to the major newspapers' hotlines."

Grens shook his head.

"About the same frequency as usual. The hotline calls, I guess that was our colleagues?"

Hermansson laughed briefly.

"According to the chancellor of justice that question qualifies as investigation of sources. And that, I believe, Ewert, is a crime that carries a prison sentence."

"Colleagues, in other words."

She continued.

"I've crossed them all out. So I have thirty qualified explanations."

She moved her finger to the numbers at the bottom.

"That leaves two phone calls. One in the morning, at nine twenty-three, and one in the afternoon at twelve minutes past two. Calls from Aspsås prison to a contract phone registered at the Ericsson offices in Västberga."

The next plastic sleeve, handwritten notes from a notepad.

"I followed the number up. According to Ericsson's HR department, the phone is used by one of their employees called Zofia Hoffmann."

Grens spluttered.

"Hoffmann."

"Married to a Piet Hoffmann."

She turned over the piece of paper. More handwriting.

"I checked the personal details I was given. Zofia Hoffmann is registered as living in Stockrosvägen in Enskede. According to her employer, the company's correct name is evidently Ericsson Enterprise AB. She disappeared from the workplace yesterday just before lunch."

"While the hostage drama was ongoing."

"Yes."

"Between phone calls."

"Yes."

Ewert Grens got up out of the soft sofa and stretched his aching back while Hermansson took out another piece of paper.

"According to the tax authorities, Zofia and Piet Hoffmann have two children together. The two boys have attended a nursery school at an address in Enskededalen every weekday for the past three years and are collected by either their mother or father at around five o'clock. But yesterday, a couple of hours before her husband was shot to death by us, and exactly twenty minutes after she left work, Zofia Hoffmann picked up the boys considerably earlier than normal without notifying any of the staff. She seemed tense—two of the nursery school teachers described her as that, she didn't meet their eye, didn't seem to hear their questions."

Mariana Hermansson studied the older man who bent down to touch the floor, then up and leaned back; his large body and an exercise that he had no doubt learned in a strict gym half a century ago.

"I sent a patrol car around to their house, a detached house built in the fifties, a few minutes' drive south of the city. We looked in through two closed windows, rang the doorbell, saw that the doors were locked, looked through the letter box and could see today's newspaper and yesterday's mail. Nothing. Nothing, Ewert, to indicate that anyone in the family had been there since yesterday morning."

Twice more. He bent forward and then leaned back.

"Issue an arrest warrant."

"An arrest warrant *was* issued for Zofia Hoffmann thirty minutes ago."

Ewert Grens nodded briefly; it might have been praise.

"He phoned her. He warned her. He protected her from the consequences of his own death."

She had stepped out into the corridor and closed the door when she stopped, turned around, and opened it again.

"There was one more thing."

Grens was still standing in the middle of the floor.

"Yes?"

"Can I come in?"

"You've never asked for permission before."

It felt ominous.

She had been on her way to tell him all morning and had still managed to leave his office without having spoken about why she really came.

"I know something that may hold the key. And that you should have known yesterday, but I didn't get to you in time."

She wasn't used to being out of control, of not being sure that she was doing the right thing.

"I was on my way to tell you. I ran through the prison corridors and drove as fast as I could toward the church."

It was a feeling she didn't like. Not anytime, and certainly not here, with Ewert.

"I tried to call but your phone was switched off. I knew that every minute, second counted. I could hear you and the sniper talking on the car radio. Your order. The sound of the gun being fired."

"Hermansson?"

"Yes?"

"Get to the point."

She looked at him. She was nervous. It was a long time since she had felt like this in here.

"You asked me to talk to Oscarsson. I did. The circumstances surrounding Hoffmann, Ewert—someone was giving Oscarsson orders, someone was telling him what to do."

She had learned to read his face.

She knew what it meant when the color started to rise in his cheeks and the vein on his temple started to throb.

"The night before you went there, Oscarsson was ordered to let a lawyer visit one of the prisoners in the same unit as Hoffmann, and then to prevent you or anyone else from questioning him or meeting him. He was ordered to move him back to the unit where he came from, despite the fact that prisoners who have been threatened are never moved back, and, in contravention of the prison service's own regulations, that the gates should be kept shut, even if Hoffmann demanded that they be opened."

"Hermansson, what the hell—"

"Ewert, let me finish. I had the information but I didn't get to you in time. And after . . . the explosion, it didn't seem relevant to talk about it just then."

He put his hand on her shoulder. Something he had never done before.

"Hermansson. I'm furious, but not at you. You did the right thing. But I do want to know who."

"Who?"

"Who gave the orders?"

"I don't know."

"Don't know!"

"He wouldn't tell me."

Ewert Grens almost ran across the room to the desk and the shelves behind. A hole with edges of dust. It wasn't there. The music that had given him comfort and strength for all these years. It was at times like this he had needed it most, when anger tipped over into rage, starting somewhere in his belly, burning its way to every part of his body, and it would stay there until he knew who had made him into a useful idiot, who had let him shoot.

"With that information, I wouldn't have ordered the sniper to fire."

He looked at his young colleague.

"If I had known what I know now . . . Hoffmann would never have died."

The brown plastic cup would soon be full of strong, black, bitter coffee. The machine rattled as it normally did, mostly toward the end, reluctant to give up the last drops. Chief Superintendent Göransson drank the coffee while he was out in the corridor. He saw Mariana Hermansson coming out of Grens's office, a file under her arm. He knew what their meeting had been about, they were doing exactly what they should, filing the reports required following a lethal shooting at Aspsås.

I did not participate.

He crushed the cup, the hot liquid running down the back of his hand.

I jumped ship.

Göransson drank some more of the bitterness, emptied the cup. He greeted Sven Sundkvist, who was passing. He also had a couple of files under his arm, on his way to the office that Hermansson had just left, to Ewert Grens.

He noticed the flushed cheeks, the pulsing vein by his temple.

Sven knew Ewert Grens better than anyone else in the building, he had had to face his boss's anger and learn to deal with it, so now when the shouting and the kicking of trash cans took over he no longer saw or heard it, it had nothing to do with him. Only Ewert could chase his own demons.

"You don't look happy."

"Drop by Hermansson when you're done here. She'll explain. I can't face it right now."

Sven looked at the man in the middle of the floor. They had met earlier that morning. This boiling rage hadn't been there then.

Something had happened.

"What do you know about Wilson?"

"Erik?"

"Are there any other Wilsons on the goddamn corridor?"

Another kind of anger. Clear, tangible. Ewert could be angry about most things, a difficult, irritated anger that was such a frequent caller that it never got through. But this anger was serious, it demanded space and he tried not to downplay it.

I must go to Hermansson afterwards.

"I don't know him. Even though we've been here almost the same length of time. It just turned out that way. But . . . he seems like a nice enough guy. Why?"

"I just heard his name today in the wrong circumstances."

"What do you mean?"

"We'll talk about that later too."

Sven didn't ask any more questions. He knew he wouldn't get any answers yet.

"I've got the first report on Hoffmann Security AB. You interested?"

"You know I am."

He put two pieces of paper down on Ewert's desk.

"I want you to have a look. Come over here."

Ewert stood beside Sven.

"A close company with annual reports and normal articles of association. I can look into that more, if you want, take a really good look at the figures."

He pointed at the second piece of paper.

"But this, I want you to have a look at this, right now."

A drawing of four squares stacked on top of each other.

"The ownership structure, Ewert. This is interesting. A board that consists of three people. Piet Hoffmann, Zofia Hoffmann, and a Polish citizen, Stanislaw Rosloniec."

A Polish citizen.

"I've run a check on Rosloniec. He lives in Warsaw, is not registered in any international criminal intelligence databases and—now it gets really interesting—is employed by a Polish company called Wojtek Security International."

Wojtek.

Ewert Grens searched Sven's pattern of squares but saw an airport in Denmark and a detective superintendent called Jacob Andersen.

Eighteen days ago.

They had sat in a meeting room at Kastrup police station and eaten greasy pastries and Andersen had spoken about a Danish informant who was supposed to buy amphetamines. In an flat in Stockholm. With two Poles and their Swedish contact.

Swedish contact.

"Damn it . . . hang on a minute, Sven!"

Grens pulled open one of his desk drawers and took out a CD player and the CD of the voice that Krantz had burned for him. Headphones on and three sentences he knew by heart.

A dead man. Västmannagatan 79. Fourth floor.

He removed the headphones and put them on Sven's head.

"Listen."

Sven Sundkvist had analyzed the recording from Emergency Services on the ninth of May at 12:37:50 as many times as Ewert.

"And now listen to this."

The voice had been stored in one of the computer's sound files. They had both encountered it when they were waiting in a churchyard twenty-four hours ago.

"He's a dead man in three minutes."

The one whispered *dead* and the other screamed *dead*, but when Ewert Grens and Sven Sundkvist listened carefully and compared the pronunciation of the *d* and the *e* and the *a*, it was obvious.

It was the same voice.

"It's him."

"It sure as hell is him, Sven! It was Hoffmann who was in the flat! It was Hoffmann who raised the alarm!"

Grens was already on his way out of the room.

Wojtek is the Polish mafia.

Hoffmann Security AB is linked to Wojtek.

The car was parked on Bergsgatan and he hurried down the stairs, even though the elevator was empty.

So why did you raise the alarm?

So why did you shoot another member in solitary confinement and blow a third member up?

He turned out of Bergsgatan and drove down Hantverkargatan toward the city. He was going to visit the person whose death he was responsible for.

He stopped the car in a bus lane outside the door to Vasagatan 42.

A couple of minutes, then Nils Krantz knocked on the window.

"Anything in particular?"

"I don't know yet. It just feels right. An hour maybe, I have to think."

"Here, keep them for the moment. I'll let you know if I need them."

Krantz gave him a set of keys and Ewert Grens put it in the inner pocket of his jacket.

"By the way, Ewert . . ."

The forensic scientist had stopped a bit farther down the pavement.

"I've identified the two explosives. Pentyl and nitroglycerine. It was the pentyl that caused the actual explosion, the wave that forced out the window and the heat that ignited the diesel. And the nitroglycerine had been applied directly onto someone's skin—I don't know whose yet, though."

Grens went up the stairs of one of the many buildings in central Stockholm from the turn of the century, the first few years of the 1900s when the cityscape changed dramatically.

He stopped in front of a door on the first floor.

Hoffmann Security AB. Same old trick. A security firm as a front for the Eastern European mafia.

He opened the door with the keys that he'd got from Krantz.

A beautiful flat, shining parquet floor, high ceilings, white walls.

He looked out of the window with a view of Kungsbron and the Vasa theater, an elderly couple on their way in to the evening performance, as he had often thought of doing himself, but never gotten around to.

You were sent up for a drug crime. But you weren't an amphetamine dealer.

He walked down the hall and went into what must once have been the drawing room, but was now an office with two gun cabinets by an open fireplace.

You had links with Wojtek. But you were not a member of the mafia.

He sat down in the chair by the desk that he guessed Hoffmann must have sat in.

You were someone else.

He got up again and wandered around the apartment, looked in the two empty gun cabinets, touched the deactivated alarm, rinsed out some dirty glasses.

Who?

When he left Hoffmann Security AB, Grens had gone to look at the storage spaces that belonged to the flat. He had opened a storeroom in the cellar with a strong smell of damp, and he had walked around in the loft with a fan heater whirring above his head while he looked for a storeroom that was more or less empty, except for a hammer and chisel that were lying on top of a pile of old tires.

It was late, and he should perhaps have driven the kilometer from the door on Vasagatan to his own flat on Sveavägen, but the anger and restlessness pushed back the tiredness—he wouldn't sleep tonight either.

The corridor of the homicide unit was waiting, abandoned. His colleagues would rather spend the first summer evenings with a glass of wine at one of the outside cafés on Kungsholmen followed by a slow walk home, than with twenty-four parallel investigations and unpaid overtime in a characterless office. He didn't feel left out, didn't miss it. He had chosen long ago not to take part and your own choice can never become ugly loneliness. This evening it would be a report on a shooting in a prison and tomorrow evening it would be a report on another shooting. There was always an investigation that was a trauma for the person who was shot, but for the investigator generated a vicarious sense of belonging. Grens was almost at the coffee machine and two plastic cups of blackness when he stopped by his pigeonhole and saw a large padded envelope in the pile of unopened letters; too many damn reference lists and soulless mass mailings. He pulled it out and weighed it in his hand—not particularly heavy—turned it over without seeing any sender. His name and address were easy to read, a man's handwriting, he was sure of that, something square, unrhythmical, almost sharp about it, possibly in felt pen.

Ewert Grens put the envelope down in the middle of the desk and stared at it while he emptied the first cup. Sometimes you just get a feeling, impossible to explain. He opened a drawer and a bag with unused rubber gloves, put on a pair and opened the end of the envelope with his index finger. He peeped cautiously in. No letter, no accompanying text or paper.

He counted five things, took them out one at a time and placed them in a row in front of him, between the files of ongoing investigations.

Half a plastic cup of coffee more.

He started from the left. Three passports. Red with gold letters. EUROPEAN UNION, SWEDEN, PASSPORT. All Swedish, genuine, issued by the police authority in Stockholm.

The photographs had been taken in a normal photo booth.

A few centimeters in size, black and white, slightly blurred, small reflections in the shining eyes.

The same face three times. Different names, different ID numbers.

The face of a dead person.

Piet Hoffmann.

Grens leaned back in his chair and looked over at the window and the light outside, dim streetlights that guarded the straight, empty asphalt paths of the inner courtyard at Kronoberg.

If this is you.

He picked up the envelope, turned it around.

If this has come from you.

He held it closer, fingertips brushed lightly over the front. There were no stamps. But there was something that looked like a postmark in the top right-hand corner. He studied it for a long time. Difficult to read, half the letters had disappeared. FRANKFURT. He was more or less certain. And six numbers. 234212. Then a kind of symbol, maybe a bird, or a plane.

The rest was mainly streaks that had seen too much water.

Grens scoured his desk drawer and the telephone list that he found there in a plastic sleeve. Horst Bauer, Bundeskriminalamt, Wiesbaden. He liked the German detective superintendent with whom he had worked a few years ago on an investigation in connection with a busload of abandoned Romanian children. Bauer was at home and having dinner, but was friendly and helpful and while Ewert waited and his food got cold, made three phone calls to confirm that the envelope that had recently arrived in a pigeonhole at the City Police in Stockholm had probably been sent by a courier company with offices at Frankfurt am Main International Airport.

Grens thanked him and hung up.

One of the world's largest airports.

He gave a deep sigh.

If it's you. If this comes from you. You instructed someone to send it for you. After your death.

Two more objects on the desk. The first wasn't even a centimeter big. He held it in his clumsy rubber fingers. A receiver, a silver earpiece, electronic devices for listening to conversations that were caught by transmitters of the same size.

Dear God.

It wasn't even twelve hours since Sven had held such a transmitter in his hand, attached to a black wire and a solar cell painted in the same color.

The church tower's fragile railing.

Fifteen hundred and three meters from the now blown-out workshop window.

Ewert Grens stretched up to the shelf behind the desk and the plastic bag that had not yet been recorded in any chain of custody list or delivered to forensics. He emptied the contents out of the bag, called one of the few numbers he knew by heart, and put the receiver down on the desk so that the talking clock voice was close to the transmitter. He then left the room and closed the door while he held the silver receiver to his ear and listened to the clock striking at ten-second intervals.

It worked.

The receiver that he had just been sent in an envelope was set at exactly the same frequency as the transmitter they had found on the tower railing.

One thing left. A CD.

Grens balanced the shiny disk on his hand. No text on either side, nothing to give away the content.

He pushed it into the narrow opening in the short end of his computer tower.

"Government Offices, Tuesday, tenth of May."

It was the same voice.

He had listened to it together with Sven only a couple of hours ago.

The voice that had raised the alarm. The voice that had threatened.

Hoffmann.

Grens swallowed the last drops in the plastic cup. A third?

Later. He read the numbers on the sound file. Seventy-eight minutes and thirty-four seconds.

When I've listened to this.

THE THIRD CUP OF COFFEE FROM THE MACHINE WAS ON THE DESK.

Ewert Grens had gone to get it but didn't need it. The racing in his chest that was making him dizzy had nothing to do with caffeine.

A *legal police operation* had just become *legitimized murder*.

He listened again.

First of all, scraping sounds, someone walking, fabric rubbing against a microphone with every step. After eleven minutes and forty-seven seconds—he checked on the sound file timer—a couple of voices, muffled. The microphone had been low, leg height, and it was obvious that Hoffmann moved every now and then to get closer to the sound source, had slowly stretched out a leg toward the person talking, suddenly got up and stood right next to them.

"The document . . . I've read it. I assumed . . . I assumed that it concerned a . . . woman?"

The only voice he hadn't heard before.

A woman, forty, maybe fifty years old. A soft voice with harsh sentences, he was sure he would recognize it if he heard it again.

"Paula. That's my name, in here."

The clearest voice.

The person with the microphone.

Hoffmann. But he called himself Paula. A code name.

"We have to make him more dangerous . . . He will have committed some serious crimes. He'll be given a long sentence."

The third voice.

Quite a high voice, the sort that doesn't fit the face, a colleague from the same corridor, only a few doors down and someone who had just happened to be passing on one of the first days of the investigation and had wanted to know how it was going and to give some ideas that pointed in the wrong direction.

Ewert Grens slammed his hand down on the desk, hard.

Erik Wilson.

He hit the desk again, with both hands this time, swore loudly at the cold office walls that just stood there.

Two more voices.

The two he knew best, part of a hierarchical chain of command, links between a criminal and a government office.

"Paula doesn't have time for Västmannagatan."

A sharp, nasal voice, a bit too loud.

The national police commissioner.

"You've dealt with similar cases before."

A deep, resonant voice, that didn't swallow its words, but held them, vowels that were prolonged.

Göransson.

Ewert Grens stopped the recording and in one gulp drank the coffee that was still too hot and burned its way down from his throat to his stomach. He didn't feel it—warm, cold, he was shaking as he had been since he listened to it the first time and was about to go back out into the corridor and pour more of the heat into himself until he managed to feel something other than the throttling rage.

A meeting at Rosenbad.

He took a felt pen from the pen holder and drew a rectangle and five circles straight onto the blotter.

A meeting table with five heads.

One who was probably a state secretary from the Ministry of Justice. One who called himself Paula. One who functioned as Paula's handler. One who was the most senior police officer in the country. And one, he looked at the circle that represented Göransson, who was Ewert Grens's immediate line manager and Erik Wilson's line manager and responsible for both their workloads and had therefore known all along why there were no answers in the Västmannagatan 79 case.

"I am a useful idiot."

Ewert Grens picked up the vandalized blotter and threw it to the floor.

"I am a bloody useful idiot."

He pressed play again, sentences that he had already heard.

"Paula. That's my name, in here."

You weren't the mafia. You were one of us. You were employed by us to pretend you were the mafia.

And I murdered you.

sunday

THE BIG CLOCK ON KUNGSHOLMS CHURCH STRUCK HALF PAST MIDNIGHT when Ewert Grens left his office and the police headquarters and drove the short distance to Rosenbad. It was a lovely, warm night, but he didn't notice. He knew what had happened at Västmannagatan 79. He knew why Piet Hoffmann had done time at Aspsås prison. And he suspected why the exact same people who had arranged for Hoffmann's prison sentence had suddenly been there, searching for a bureaucratic reason for killing him.

Piet Hoffmann was dangerous.

Piet Hoffmann knew the truth about a murder that was less important than continued infiltration.

When Grens identified Hoffmann's name on the periphery of the investigation and wanted to question him, he became even more dangerous.

They had burned him.

But he had survived an attack, taken hostages, and positioned himself where he was visible in a workshop window.

You recorded the meeting. You sent it to me. The man who had to decide on your death.

Ewert Grens parked on Fredsgatan close to the dark building from where Sweden was governed. He would soon make his way in there. He had just listened to a meeting that had been recorded in one of its many senior offices twenty-one days ago.

He got out his mobile phone and dialed Sven Sundkvist's number. Three rings. Someone coughed and struggled to find strength.

"Hello?"

"Sven, it's me. I want—"

"Ewert, I'm asleep. I've been asleep since eight. We missed out on last night, remember?"

"You're not going to get much more sleep tonight either. You're going to go to the USA, to south Georgia. Your plane leaves Arlanda in two and half hours. You'll arrive—"

"Ewert."

Sven had pulled himself up, his voice was stronger—it was probably easier to talk when your chest and airways were free of pillows and duvets.

"What are you talking about?"

"I want you to get up and get dressed, Sven. You're going to meet Erik Wilson and you're going to get him to confirm that a meeting I've now listened to actually took place. I'll call you in a couple of hours. By that time, you'll be sitting in a taxi and you'll have listened to the sound file that I've forwarded to your computer. You'll understand exactly what this is all about."

Grens cut the engine and got out of the car.

The doors to power were made of glass and had opened automatically whenever he had been there during the day. Now they remained closed and he had to press a bell to wake the security guard one floor up.

"Yes?"

"Detective Superintendent Grens, City Police. I'm here to look at some of your surveillance camera footage."

"Now?"

"Do you have anything else to do?"

Some rustling papers near the microphone made the speaker crackle.

"Did you say Grens?"

"You can see me in the camera. And now you can see the ID that I'm holding up."

"No one said you were coming. I want to see it again properly when you're in here with me. *Then* I'll decide whether you can stay or whether I'd rather you came back tomorrow."

Ewert Grens accelerated, the E18 north of Roslagstull was almost empty and right now he didn't give a damn about signs that limited the speed to seventy kilometers an hour.

He had first checked the security company's sign-in book.

The state secretary of the Ministry of Justice had had a total of four visitors on the tenth of May. They had arrived separately within twenty-five minutes of each other. First the national police commissioner, then Göransson, a bit later Erik Wilson, and finally, in handwriting that was difficult to read, Grens and the security man were eventually convinced that the visitor who had signed in at 15:36 was Piet Hoffmann.

He passed Danderyd, Täby, Vallentuna . . . for the third time in twenty-four hours he was approaching the small town of Aspsås, but he wasn't going to the prison or the church, he was going to a terraced house and a man he would not leave until he had answered the one question that Grens had come to ask.

With the sign-in book in his hand, Ewert Grens had demanded to see footage from two of the cameras that watched over the Government Offices and every person passing in or out. He had identified them one by one. First when they signed in, the camera was above the security desk in the entrance to Rosenbad and they stood there, all four of them, without looking up. Then a camera at face level in a corridor on the second floor opposite the door to the state secretary's office. He had seen the national police commissioner and Göransson knock on the door and go in, within a couple of minutes of each other. Wilson had arrived twenty minutes later and Hoffmann had sauntered down the corridor about seven minutes after that. He had known exactly where the camera was and twigged it early, looked into it for a bit too long, looked into the lens aware that his presence had been documented.

Piet Hoffmann had knocked on the door just like all the others but had not been let in immediately like them. He was instructed to stay in the corridor, to hold out his arms while Göransson frisked him. Grens found it hard to stand still when he realized that the loud noise he had heard about nine minutes into the recording was the chief superintendent's hand knocking the microphone.

He was speeding and slammed his foot on the brake when the turn to Aspsås emerged from the dark.

A couple more kilometers; he wasn't laughing yet, but he was smiling.

Sunday was only a few hours old. He didn't have much time but he would manage, still more than twenty-four hours left until Monday morning, when the security company's report of the weekend's surveillance tapes was passed on to the Government Offices' security department.

He had heard the voices, and now he had seen pictures as well.

He would shortly confirm the connection between three of the meeting participants and the orders that a chief warden had been given before and during a hostage drama that ended in death.

ତ

403

A terraced house on a terraced house road in a terraced house area.

Ewert Grens parked the car in front of a mailbox with the number fifteen on it and then sat there and looked at the silence. He had never liked places like this. People who lived too close to each other and tried to look alike. In his big flat in Sveagatan, he had someone walking on his ceiling and someone else standing under his floor and others who drank glasses of water on the other side of the kitchen wall, but he didn't see them, didn't know them; he heard them sometimes but he didn't know what they were wearing, what kind of car they had, didn't have to meet them in their bathrobe with the newspaper under their arm and didn't need to think about whether their plum tree was hanging a little too low over the fence.

He could hardly stand himself.

So how the hell was he going to stand the smell of barbecued meat and the sound of footballs on wooden doors?

He would ask Sven later, when this was all over, how you do it, how you talk to people you're not interested in.

He opened the door and got out into an almost balmy spring night. A couple of hundred meters away stood the high wall, a sharp line against the sky that refused to go dark and would continue to do so until yet another summer had turned into early autumn.

Square slabs in a well-trimmed lawn. He walked up to the door and looked at the windows that were lit both downstairs and up: probably the kitchen, probably the bedroom. Lennart Oscarsson lived the other side of his life only a few minutes' walk from his workplace. Grens was sure that being able to cope with living in a terraced house was somehow connected to not needing to separate one reality from the other.

His intention was to surprise. He hadn't phoned to say he was coming, had hoped to meet someone who had just been asleep and therefore didn't have the energy to protest.

It wasn't like that.

"You?"

He remembered Hermansson's description of a person on the edge.

"What do you want?"

Oscarsson was wearing the prison uniform.

"So you're still working?"

"Sorry?"

"Your clothes."

Oscarsson sighed.

"In that case I'm not alone. Unless you've come here in the middle of the night to have some tea and help me with the crossword?"

"Will you let me in? Or do you want to stand out here and talk?"

Pine floors, pine stairs, plain walls. He guessed that the chief warden had done up the hall by himself. The kitchen felt older: cupboards and counters from the eighties, pastel colors that you couldn't buy anymore.

"Do you live here on your own?"

"These days."

Ewert Grens knew only too well how a home sometimes refuses to be changed and a person who has moved out somehow seems to stay in the colors and furniture.

"Thirsty?"

"No."

"Then I'll have a drink myself."

Lennart Oscarsson opened the fridge, neat and well stocked, vegetables at the bottom, the beer bottle that he was now holding in his hand from the top shelf.

"You nearly lost a good friend yesterday."

The warden sat down and took a swig without answering.

"I went to see him this morning. Danderyd hospital. He's shaken."

"I know. I've spoken to him as well. Twice."

"How does it feel?"

"Feel?"

"To know that you're to blame."

The guilt. Grens knew everything about that too.

"It's half past one in the morning. I'm still in my uniform in my own kitchen. And you wonder how it feels?"

"Because that's right, isn't it? You're to blame?"

Oscarsson threw up his hands.

"Grens, I know what you're after."

Ewert Grens looked at another man who wasn't going to get to bed tonight either.

"You spoke to one of my colleagues about thirty-six hours ago. You admitted that you had made at least four decisions that had forced Hoffmann to act as he did."

Lennart Oscarsson was red in the face.

"I know what you're after!"

"Who?"

The chief warden jumped up, poured out what was left in the bottle, then threw it against the wall and waited until the last shard of glass was still. He unbuttoned his uniform jacket, put it on the now empty kitchen table, fetched big scissors from the cutlery drawer. With great care he straightened out one of the sleeves, stroked the material with the back of his hand until he was sure it was flat and then started to cut, quite a large piece, five, maybe six centimeters wide.

"Who gave you the orders?"

He held the first piece of material in his hand, felt the frayed edge. He smiled, Grens was convinced of it, an almost shy smile.

"Oscarsson, *who?*"

He cut as he had done before, straight, considerate lines, the rectangular pieces neatly on top of the first.

"Stefan Lygás. A prisoner you were responsible for. A prisoner who is now dead."

"It wasn't my fault."

"Pawel Murawski. Piet Hoffmann. Two other prisoners you were responsible for. Two other prisoners who are now dead."

"It wasn't my fault."

"Martin Jacobson. A—"

"All right, that's enough."

"Martin Jacobson, a prison warden who—"

"For Christ's sake, Grens, that's enough!"

The first arm was ready. Pieces of material stacked in a small pile.

Oscarsson pulled out the next one, shook it lightly, a crease more or less in the middle, hand backward and forward across it until it disappeared.

"Pål Larsen."

He cut again, faster now.

"Director General Pål Larsen ordered me."

Grens remembered, about half an hour into the recording, a trouser leg scraping against the microphone as it stretched, and the sound of a teaspoon against porcelain when someone had taken a sip from a coffee cup.

"*I appointed you. And that means that you decide what happens in the Prison and Probation Service.*"

A short pause while the state secretary left the room to get the head of the Prison and Probation Service, who had been sitting waiting outside in the corridor.

"You decide what you and I agree that you should decide."

The director general had been given an order. The director general had passed that order on. From the real sender.

Ewert Grens looked at a bare-torsoed man who was cutting to pieces the uniform that he had longed for all his adult life, and he hurried out of the kitchen that would never change color and the home that was even lonelier than his own.

"Do you know what I'm going to do with these?"

Lennart Oscarsson stood in the open doorway as Grens got into his car. The recently shredded pieces in his raised hands, he dropped a couple and they fell slowly to the ground.

"Wash the car, Grens. You know, you always need clean bits when you're polishing, and this, this is damn expensive material."

He dialed the number as the car rolled out of the silent rows of terraced houses. He looked at the church and the square church tower, at the prison and the workshop that could be seen behind the high wall.

Not even thirty-six hours had passed. It would haunt him for the rest of his life.

"Hello?"

Göransson had been awake.

"Difficulties sleeping?"

"What do you want, Ewert?"

"You and me to have a meeting. In about half an hour."

"I don't think so."

"A meeting. In your office. In your capacity as CHIS controller."

"Tomorrow."

Grens looked at the sign in his rearview mirror; it was hard to read in the dark but he knew what the town he had just left was called.

He hoped it would be a while before he had to return.

"Paula."

"Excuse me?"

"That's what we're going to talk about."

He waited; there was a long silence.

"Paula who?"

He didn't answer. The forest transformed slowly into high-rise blocks—he was getting close to Stockholm.

"Grens, answer me. Paula who?"

Ewert Grens just held his handset for a while, then hung up.

The corridor was empty. The coffee machine hummed, hidden by the dark. He settled on one of the chairs outside Göransson's office.

His boss would soon be there. Grens was convinced of it.

He drank the vending machine coffee.

Wilson was Hoffmann's handler. A handler records the informant's work in a logbook. The logbook is kept in a safe by the CHIS controller.

Göransson.

"Grens."

The chief superintendent opened the door to his office. Ewert Grens looked at the clock and smiled. Exactly half an hour since their conversation.

He was shown into an office that was considerably larger than his own and sat down in a leather armchair, wriggled a bit.

Göransson was nervous.

He was trying hard to pretend the opposite, but Grens recognized the breathing, the pitch, the slightly exaggerated movements.

"The logbook, Göransson. I want to see it."

"I don't understand."

Grens was furious but hadn't thought of showing it.

He didn't shout, he didn't threaten.

Not yet.

"Give me the logbook. The whole file."

Göransson was sitting on the edge of the desk. He waved at two walls of shelves, files on every shelf.

"Which goddamn file?"

"The file of the person I murdered."

"I have no idea what you're talking about."

"The snitch file."

"What do you want it for?"

I am going to nail you, you bastard. I've got a day to do it.

"You know."

"What I know, Ewert, is that there is only one copy of it, and it's in my safe, which only I have the code to, and there's a reason for that."

Göransson gave a light kick to the safe, which was green and stood against the wall behind his desk.

"As *no* unauthorized persons can see it."

Grens breathed slowly. He had been about to strike out, balled fist that was halfway to Göransson's face when he caught it, the desire was so strong.

He released his cramping fingers, held them out, an exaggerated gesture perhaps.

"The file, Göransson. And I'll need a pen."

Göransson looked at the hand in front of him, the gnarled fingers.

An Ewert Grens who shouts, who threatens, I can deal with that.

"Can I have it?"

"What?"

"The pen."

But the loud whispering.

"And a piece of paper."

"Ewert?"

"A piece of paper."

The gnarled fingers pointing at him.

He gave them a notebook and a pen, a red felt-tip.

"You got a name from me half an hour ago. I know that that name is in the informant file. I want to see it."

He knows.

Ewert Grens held the notebook against the armrest of the leather chair and wrote something. Handwriting that was normally difficult to read. But not now. Five carefully written letters in red felt-tip.

Grens knows.

Göransson went over to the safe, maybe his hands were shaking, maybe that was why it took so long to set the six digits, to open the heavy door, to take out a black, rectangular file.

"Are all the meetings between your handler and this Hoffmann recorded here?"

"Yes."

"And this is the only copy?"

"It's the copy that I keep as CHIS controller. The only one."

"Destroy it."

He put the black folder down in front of him on the desk and looked through the code names of criminals who were recruited to work as informants for the Swedish police. He had gotten halfway when he stopped.

I knew it was wrong and I said so.

"Grens?"

"Yes?"

I left her room.

"It's here. The name you're looking for."

Ewert Grens had already gotten up and was standing behind his boss, reading over his shoulder, tightly written pages.

First the code name. Then the date. Then a summary of that day's short meeting in a flat that could be entered from two different addresses.

Page after page, meeting after meeting.

"You know what I want."

I got out.

"You can't have it."

"Give me the envelope, Göransson. Give it to me."

With every logbook came an envelope with the informant's real name, sealed by the handler on the first day of the operation, a wax seal, red and shiny.

"Open it."

I can walk out of this with my head held high.

"I can't do that."

"Now, Göransson."

Grens clutched the envelope in his hand, read the name that he had heard spoken for the first time only days ago, on a recording of a meeting in an office in the Government Offices.

Five letters.

The same name that he had just written on a notepad.

P-a-u-l-a.

He reached over for Göransson's letter opener, broke the seal, and opened the brown envelope.

He knew it already.

But still the damned thumping in his chest.

Ewert Grens pulled out the piece of paper and read the name that he knew would be there. Confirmation that the person he had ordered to be shot really had worked for the city police.

Piet Hoffmann.

Piet.

Paula.

The Swedish code name system, first letter of a man's name became the first letter of a woman's name. The informant file was full of snitches called Maria, Lena, Birgitta.

"And now I want the secret intelligence report. About what actually happened at Västmannagatan 79."

THE WHISPERING AGAIN.

Göransson looked at the colleague he had never liked.

He knows.

"You can't have it."

"Where do you keep the secret intelligence report? What actually happened at Västmannagatan 79? That those of us investigating were not to know?"

"It's not here."

"Where?"

"There's only one copy."

"Jesus, Göransson, where?"

He knows.

"The county police commissioner has it. Our most senior officer."

He limped badly, it wasn't the pain—it was years since he'd bothered about that—this was just how he walked, left foot light on the floor, right foot heavy on the floor, left leg light on the floor. But with anger as his motor, he thumped his right leg down harder on the surface and the monotonous sound was quickly carried by the walls in the unlit corridor. The elevator down four floors, right toward the escalator, through the canteen, elevator five floors up. Then that sound again, someone limping down the last stretch of corridor who stopped outside the door of the county police commissioner's office.

He stood still, listened.

He pressed down the handle.

It was locked.

Ewert Grens had stopped in his travels three times: first at the data support office and one of the Coke-drinking young men to collect a CD with a surprisingly simple and accessible program that could open all code words on all computers in two minutes; then at the small kitchen opposite

412

the vending machine for a towel; and finally the maintenance office opposite the stores for a hammer and a screwdriver.

He wound the towel around the hammer several times, positioned the screwdriver in the gap between the upper door hinge and the pin, looked around in the dark one more time and came down hard on the screwdriver with the hammer until the pin was loose. He moved the screwdriver down to the lower hinge and the next pin, until the hammer blows released it. From there it was easy to separate the two hinges, to carefully rock the screwdriver back and forth between the door and the doorframe, to push the door back until the lock barrel slid out of its fixture.

He lifted the door and put it to one side.

It was lighter than he had imagined.

He had forced other doors during raids—a heart attack on the other side, scared children on their own—in order to avoid waiting for a locksmith who might never come.

But he had never broken into a senior police officer's room before.

The laptop was on the desk, just like his own. He started it, waited while the CD program identified and replaced the code words, and then searched the documents as he had learned to do.

A couple of minutes was all he needed.

Ewert Grens re-hung the door on its hinges, coaxed the pins back in, checked that there were no scratches or splinters on the doorframe, and then walked away with the computer in a briefcase.

THE ALARM CLOCK BEHIND THE TELEPHONE DIDN'T WORK. IT HAD STOPPED at a quarter to four. Grens focused on the white clock while he phoned the talking clock for the second time that night.

Three forty-five and thirty seconds. Precisely. It was working.

The night was receding without him having noticed.

He was sweaty. He unwound the towel from the hammer and wiped his forehead and neck. Walking through the building, forcing open a door, more exercise than he was used to.

He sat down at the computer that had until recently been on another desk, searched for the file he had started to read earlier.

Västmannagatan 79.

The secret intelligence report. The actual events.

He reached over for a thin file at the back of the desk, leafed through it. The same incident. But not the truth. The incomplete information that he and Sven and Hermansson and Ågestam had had access to, which therefore had resulted in the investigation being downgraded.

He continued to search the documents on the computer. He went back exactly one year. Three hundred two secret intelligence reports recounting how an informant's work to uncover one crime had given rise to another. He recognized several of them. Other investigations that had collapsed despite the fact that the knowledge was already in-house.

He hadn't slept the night before, he wouldn't sleep tonight; the anger that could not be released filled him instead, forcing out tiredness. There was no room.

I was a useful idiot.

I carried out legitimate murder.

I have carried the guilt all my adult life and I deserved it, but no bastard is going to force me to carry it for anyone else.

I don't know Hoffmann. I'm not interested in him.

But this, this godawful guilt that I have no intention of taking on, I know that.

He pulled the telephone over, remembered the number that he often dialed at this time of night. The voice was weak, as always when someone has just woken up.

"Hello?"

"Anita?"

"Who . . ."

"It's Ewert."

An exasperated sigh from a dark bedroom upstairs in a terraced house somewhere in Gustavsberg.

"Sven's not here. He's spending the night on an airplane, on the way to the USA. Because you sent him there a couple of hours ago."

"I know."

"So don't call here again tonight."

"I know."

"Good night, Ewert."

"I always phone Sven. So you'll have to take it. You see . . . I'm so damn angry."

Her slow breathing, he could hear it.

"Ewert?"

"Yes?"

"Phone someone else. Someone who gets paid for it. I have to sleep."

She hung up. He stared at the unfamiliar laptop sitting on his desk that stared back at him, at his concealed rage.

Sven was on an airplane somewhere over the Atlantic.

Hermansson. It didn't feel right to call her, a young woman and an old man in the middle of the night.

Grens lifted the plastic pocket on the blotter, ran his finger down the long list. He found what he was looking for and punched in the number of the one person he had absolutely no desire to talk to.

Eight rings.

He put the phone down, waited for exactly one minute, then called again.

Someone answered immediately. Someone snatched the phone from its cradle.

"Is that you, Grens?"

"So you were awake?"

"I am now. What the hell do you want?"

Ewert Grens loathed him. Inflexible, hierarchical. Qualities he despised, but actually ones he needed now.

"Ågestam?"

"Yes?"

"I need your help."

Lars Ågestam yawned, stretched, collapsed in a heap.

"Go to bed, Grens."

"Your help. Now."

"Simple answer. The same one you get every time you wake me and my family up at this time. Call the duty officer."

He hung up. Ewert Grens didn't wait this time, rang back straightaway.

"Grens! Don't you . . . bloody dare, you—"

"Hundreds of cases. In the last year alone. Witnesses and evidence and interviews that . . . that disappeared."

Lars Ågestam cleared his throat.

"What are you talking about?"

"We have to meet."

Someone said something in the background. Sounded like Ågestam's wife. Grens tried to remember what she looked like. They had met, he remembered that but not her face, one of the kind that lack definition.

"Grens, are you drunk?"

"Hundreds. You've been involved in several yourself."

"Of course. We can meet. Tomorrow."

"Now, Ågestam! I don't have much time. Monday morning. By then . . . then it's too late. And what I need to tell you . . . it's as much for your sake . . . don't you understand how bizarre it feels to say that? To you?"

The female voice in the background again. Grens could hear it, but not what it said. Ågestam whispered when he spoke again.

"I'm listening."

"It's not something I can say over the phone."

"But I'm listening!"

"We have to meet. You'll understand why."

The public prosecutor sighed.

"Come here then."

"To you?"

"To my house."

He had passed Åkeshov metro station and drove into an area of detached houses from the forties, the educated middle class. It was going to be a beautiful day, you could tell from the sun growing in the distance. He stopped the car in front of a garden with large apple trees at the end of a sleeping street. He had been here once before, about five years ago. The newly appointed prosecutor had received a number of threats during the trial of a young father accused of murder and Grens had not taken it very seriously until the yellow house had black paint, *you're dead, you bastard*, sprayed from the kitchen to the sitting room.

Two big cups on the table.

A pot of freshly brewed tea between them.

"Black, isn't it?"

"Black."

Grens drank the whole cup and Ågestam filled it again.

"Nearly as good as the stuff from the machine in the corridor."

"It's quarter past four in the morning. What do you want?"

The briefcase was already on the table. Grens opened it and pulled out three files.

"Do you recognize these?"

Lars Ågestam nodded.

"Yes."

"Three investigations that we've worked on together over the past year."

Ewert Grens pointed to them, one at a time.

"Serious drug offense, parking lot in Regeringsgatan. *Tried and acquitted.* Firearms offense, pathway under Liljeholm bridge. *Tried and acquitted.* Attempted kidnapping, Magnus Ladulåsgatan. *Tried and acquitted.*"

"Can you keep your voice down? My wife. My children. They're asleep."

Ågestam waved his hand at the ceiling, the floor above.

"Have you got children? You didn't the last time."

"Well, I do now."

Grens lowered his voice.

"Do you remember them?"

"Yes."

"Why?"

"You know why. I didn't get approval. Lack of evidence."

Grens put the files to one side, replaced them with a laptop that had until recently been on a high-ranking officer's desk behind a locked door. He searched through the documents, as before, turned the screen toward the prosecutor.

"I want you to read."

Lars Ågestam picked up the teacup, lifted it to his mouth and there it remained. He couldn't get it any farther, his fingers frozen.

"What is this?"

He looked at Ewert Grens.

"Grens? *What* is this?"

"What is it? The same addresses. The same times. But a different truth."

"I don't understand."

"This one? Serious drug offense, parking lot, Regeringsgatan. But what *actually* happened. Described in a secret intelligence report written by a policeman who wasn't part of the investigation."

Ewert Grens looked on the computer again.

"Two more. Read."

His neck was red. Hand through his hair.

"And this one?"

"This one? Firearms offense, pathway under Liljeholm bridge. And this one? Attempted kidnapping, Magnus Ladulåsgatan. Also what *actually* happened. Also described in a secret intelligence report written by police who weren't part of the investigation."

The prosecutor stood up.

"Grens, I—"

"And this is just three of three hundred and two cases from last year. They're all there. The truth we were never told. Crimes that were swept under the carpet so that other crimes could be solved. An official investigation, the sort that you and I deal with. And another that exists only here, in secret intelligence reports for police management."

Ewert Grens looked at the man in a robe in front of him.

"Lars, you were involved in twenty-three of them. Cases where you prosecuted and were unsuccessful. You closed them because you didn't have all the information that was included in the *real* report, the *secret* one, the one that would have nailed the snitch."

Lars Ågestam didn't stir.

He said Lars.

It feels . . . weird, uninvited. It's only my name. But when Grens says it . . . it's almost uncomfortable.

He has never used my first name before.

I don't want him to do it ever again.

"The snitch?"

"The snitch. The informant. The covert human intelligence source. A criminal who commits crimes that we then overlook because he's helping us to deal with other crimes."

Ågestam had been holding the cup in front of his mouth throughout the whole conversation. He put it down now.

"Whose laptop?"

"You don't want to know."

"*Whose?*"

"The county police commissioner."

Lars Ågestam got up from the table, disappeared out of the kitchen and up the stairs with hurried steps.

Ewert Grens watched him.

I've got more.

Västmannagatan 79.

You'll get that as well. When we wrap all this up. In the next twenty-four hours.

Hurried steps down again. The prosecutor had a printer in his arms, linked it up to the laptop—they listened to three hundred two paper copies forming a pile, one at a time.

"You'll give it back?"

"Yes."

"Do you need help?"

"No."

"Sure?"

"The door's unlocked."

The sun had taken over the kitchen, the light which had a short while ago been aided by bright bulbs was now strong enough to stand alone and he didn't notice when Ågestam switched off the lights.

It was half past four, but the day had dawned.

"Lars."

She was young and her hair was tangled. She had on a white robe and white slippers and she was very tired.

"I'm sorry. Did we wake you?"

"Why aren't you asleep?"

"This is Ewert Grens and—"

"I know who it is."

"I'll be up in a while. We just need to finish up here."

She sighed, she didn't weigh much, but her steps were heavier than even Grens's as she went back upstairs to the bedroom.

"Sorry, Ågestam."

"She'll go back to sleep."

"She's still upset, isn't she?"

"She believes you made an error of judgment. I do too."

"I apologized. Christ alive, it was five years ago now!"

"Grens?"

"Yes?"

"You're shouting again. Don't wake the children."

Lars Ågestam emptied both cups into the sink, the stuff that was viscous and bitter and stuck to the bottom of the cup.

"I don't need anymore tea."

He picked up the pile of three hundred two newly printed pages.

"Doesn't matter what time it is. This . . . I'm not tired anymore, Grens, I'm . . . angry. If I need anything it's to calm down."

He opened one of the cupboards. On the top shelf, a bottle of Seagram's and suitably sized glasses.

"What do you think, Grens?"

Ågestam filled two glasses to the halfway mark.

"It's half past four in the morning."

"That's the way it goes, sometimes."

Another person.

Ewert Grens gave a weak smile as Ågestam downed half of it.

If he had had to guess, he would have guessed teetotaller ten out of ten times.

Grens had a sip himself after a while. It was milder in taste than he had imagined, perfect for a kitchen, with pajamas and a robe.

"The truth we were never told, Ågestam."

He put a hand on the pile of papers.

"I'm not sitting here because I enjoy watching you wake up. And not for your tea, either, not even the whisky. I came here because I'm certain that we can resolve this together."

Lars Ågestam flicked through the secret intelligence reports that he had not known existed until now.

His neck was still red.

He still kept running his hands back and forth through his hair.

"Three hundred and two."

He paused every now and then, read something, then continued leafing through, arbitrarily choosing which document to read next.

"Two versions. One official. And one for police management."

He waved at the pile in front of him and poured another glass of whisky.

"Do you realize, Grens? I could prosecute them all. I could prosecute every single police officer who has anything to do with this. For forging documents. For fake certificates. For provoking crimes. There's enough here to merit a separate police unit at Aspsås."

He downed the glass and laughed.

"And all these trials? What do you think, Grens? All these pleadings and interviews and judgments without the knowledge that the heads of the police authority were already party to!"

He threw the pile down on the table. Some pages fell on the floor; he stood up and stamped on them.

"You've just woken the children."

They hadn't heard her coming—she stood in the doorway, in the white robe but without the slippers.

"Lars, you've got to calm down."

"I can't."

"You're frightening them."

Ågestam kissed her on both cheeks. He was already on his way to the children's room.

"Grens?"

He turned on the bottom step of the stairs.

"I'm going to spend the whole day on this."

"Monday morning. Or two tapes will be missing."

"I'll get back to you by this evening at the latest."

"Monday morning. Then the wrong people will be finding out how damn close I am."

"By tonight at the latest. That's the best I can do. Is that okay?"

"That's okay."

The prosecutor paused, laughed again.

"Grens, imagine! A separate police unit. A separate police unit at Aspsås!"

THE COFFEE TASTED DIFFERENT.

He had poured out the first cup after a couple of mouthfuls. A fresh one from the machine in the corridor had tasted the same. He was holding the third in his hand when he realized why.

It was like a film on his palate.

He had started the day with two whiskies in Ågestam's kitchen. He didn't normally do that. He didn't generally drink much spirits, it was years since he'd stopped drinking on his own.

Ewert Grens sat at his desk and felt strangely empty.

The first early birds had already come and passed his open door, but hadn't annoyed him, not even those who had tried to stop and say good morning.

He had released his anger.

He had driven from Ågestam, a few newspaper delivery boys, the odd cyclist, that was all—a city that was at its weariest just before five.

There had been plenty of room for guilt. The guilt that others had tried to lay on him. He had raged against it, tried to silence it when it sat beside him, chased it into the backseat. It had continued to nag him, forcing him to drive faster. He had been on his way to Göransson to offload it, then managed to control himself—he would confront them, but not yet, soon. He would meet the people who were truly responsible very soon. He had parked in Bergsgatan by the entrance to the police headquarters but had not gone directly to his office, he had taken the elevator up to Kronoberg remand and then gone on up to the roof and eight long, narrow cages. One hour of fresh air every day and twenty meters to move in, then jail. He had ordered the wardens on duty to call in two prisoners who, in ill-fitting prison clothes and separate cages, were standing looking out over the city and freedom, and then to leave their posts and go down two floors for an early morning coffee. Grens had waited until he was completely alone and then gone out into one of the small yards. He had looked at the sky through the crisscross of bars and he had screamed, high above the sleeping

422

buildings in the Stockholm dawn. For fifteen minutes he had held the stolen laptop with another reality in his hands and screamed louder than ever before, he had released his fury and it raced over the rooftops and evaporated somewhere above Vasastan, leaving him extremely hoarse, tired, almost spent.

The coffee still tasted odd. He put it to one side and sat down on the corduroy sofa, lay down after a while, closed his eyes while he searched for a face in the window of a prison workshop.

I don't get it.

Someone who chooses a life where each day is a potential death sentence.

For the excitement? For some kind of romantic spy nonsense? For personal morals?

I'm not convinced. That sort of thing just sounds good.

For the money?

Ten thousand crappy kronor a month paid from reward money in order to avoid formal payrolls and to protect your identity?

Hardly.

Grens straightened the fabric on the arm of the sofa that was slightly too high; it was chafing his neck and made it difficult to relax.

I just don't get it.

You could commit whatever goddamn crime you wanted, you were outside the law, but only for as long as you were useful, until you became someone who could be spared.

You were an outlaw.

You knew it. You knew that's how it worked.

You had everything that I don't have, you had a wife, children, a home, you had something to lose.

And still you chose it.

I don't get it.

HIS NECK WAS STIFF. THE SLIGHTLY TOO-HIGH SOFA ARM.

He had fallen asleep.

The face in the window of a prison workshop had disappeared, sleep had taken over; the kind that came after rage that was soft and had rocked him gently for nearly seven hours. He might have woken up once, he wasn't sure, but it felt like that, like the telephone had rung, like Sven had said that he was sitting in an airport outside New York waiting for the next flight to Jacksonville, that the sound file was interesting and that he had prepared himself on the plane for a meeting with Wilson.

It was a long time since Ewert Grens had slept so well.

Despite the bright sunlight in the room, despite all the damnable noise.

He stretched. His back was as sore as it usually was after sleeping on the narrow sofa, his stiff leg ached when it reached the floor. He was slowly falling to bits, one day at a time. Fifty-nine-year-old men who exercised too little and ate too much generally did.

A cold shower in the changing room that he seldom used, two cinnamon buns and a bottle of banana-flavored drinking yogurt from the vending machine.

"Ewert?"

"Yes?"

"Is that your lunch?"

Hermansson had come out of her office farther down the corridor. She had heard him, the limping, it was just Grens lumbering around.

"Breakfast, lunch, I don't know. Did you want something?"

She shook her head, they walked slowly, side by side.

"This morning, early . . . Ewert, was it *your* voice?"

"You live here in Kungsholmen?"

"Yes."

"Nearby?"

"I don't have far to go."

Grens nodded.

"Then it was probably me you heard."

"Where?"

"Up in the remand yards on the roof. You get a good view from up there."

"I heard. And so did the rest of Stockholm."

Ewert Grens looked at her, smiled, something he didn't do often.

"It was a choice between that and firing a bullet through a wardrobe door. I understand that some prefer the latter."

They had come to his door. He stopped. It felt like she was going to come in.

"Did you want something, Hermansson?"

"Zofia Hoffmann."

"Yes?"

"I'm not getting anywhere. She's disappeared."

The banana-flavored yogurt was finished. He should have bought one more.

"I've checked with her work again. She hasn't been in touch since the hostage drama. The children's nursery, same story."

Mariana Hermansson tried to peer into his office. Grens closed the door a bit more. He didn't know why, she had come there several times a day since he employed her three years ago. But he had just been asleep there, nearly seven hours on the sofa—it was as if he didn't want her to know that.

"I've located her closest family. Not many of them. Her parents, an aunt, two uncles. All in the Stockholm area. She isn't there. The kids aren't there."

She looked at him.

"I've spoken to the three women who are described as her best friends. With neighbors, with a gardener who works for the family for a couple of hours every now and then, with several members of a choir where she sings a couple of times a week, with the oldest son's football coach and the youngest son's gymnastics teacher."

She shrugged.

"No one has seen them."

Hermansson waited for a response. She didn't get one.

"I've checked the hospitals, hotels, hostels. They aren't anywhere, Ewert. Zofia and the two boys, they can't be found anywhere."

Ewert Grens nodded.

"Wait here. I want to show you something."

He opened the door, closed it behind him, careful that she shouldn't see in or follow him.

You came to Aspsås prison as Wojtek's contact man in Sweden.

You were there to knock out the competition for them and then establish Wojtek and expand.

One single moment and you were someone else.

One single meeting with a lawyer, a messenger, and they knew who you really were.

You called her. You warned her.

Grens lifted up a padded envelope that was lying on his desk and was now emptied of three passports, a receiver, and a CD with a secret recording. He went back out to the corridor and Hermansson with it under his arm.

"She received two short phone calls from Hoffmann. We don't know what they were about and we haven't found anything to indicate that she was involved in any way. We have no reasonable grounds to suspect her of anything whatsoever."

Grens held up the envelope so that Hermansson could see it.

"We can't issue a warrant for her arrest abroad. Even though that is where she is."

He pointed at the postmark.

"I'm convinced that it was Zofia Hoffmann who sent this. Frankfurt am Main International Airport. Two hundred and sixty-five destinations, fourteen hundred flights, one hundred and fifty thousand passengers. Every day."

He started to head for the vending machine—he needed another yogurt, another cinnamon bun.

"She's well gone, Hermansson. And she knows. She knows that we have no grounds to get her or even look for her."

THE SUN WAS HIGH.

It had been warm since early morning. He had fought with the damp sheets and a pillow drowned in sweat from his hairline, the temperature rising a couple of degrees every hour until now, just before lunch. The heat and the sharp light forced him to stop abruptly in front of the great gate until what was double had disappeared.

Erik Wilson sat quietly in the front seat of the rented car.

He had been here for five days, back in Glynco, Georgia, at a military base called FLETC, to continue the work that had been interrupted when Paula rang about a buyer in Västmannagatan who had paid with a Polish bullet to the head.

He started the car again, rolled slowly through the gate and past the guard who saluted. Three more weeks. Cooperation between the Swedish and European police and American police organizations was essential for the further development of their CHIS work, and this was where they had the strongest tradition and knowledge, and as Paula was out of contact while he worked behind the walls of Aspsås, it was the perfect time to finish the course he had started in advanced infiltration.

The heat was incredible.

He still hadn't gotten used to it—normally it was easier, less invasive. At least that's what he remembered from previous visits.

Maybe it was the climate that had changed. Maybe it was he who had gotten older.

He liked driving along the wide, straight roads in this great country that was built around traffic. He accelerated when he reached the I-95, sixty kilometers to Jacksonville and the other side of the state boundary, half an hour on a day like today.

He had been woken by the phone call.

It was still dawn, sharp sunlight and the birds with their piercing song had come alive outside his window.

Sven Sundkvist had been sitting in a bar eating breakfast at Newark Liberty International Airport.

He had explained that he would continue his journey in a few hours.

He said that he was on his way south because he needed immediate assistance with an investigation.

Erik Wilson had asked what it was about—they seldom talked to each other when they met in the corridors of the police headquarters in Kungsholmen, why should they do so here, seven thousand kilometers away? Sundkvist hadn't answered, and instead had repeatedly asked when and where until Wilson had suggested the only lunch restaurant that he knew, somewhere where you could sit without being seen, without being heard.

It was a pleasant place on the corner of San Marco Boulevard and Philips Street, quiet in spite of every table being taken and dark in spite of the sun blasting on the roofs, walls, and windows. Sven Sundkvist looked around. Men dressed in suits and ties who glanced at each other on the sly as they gave their best arguments accompanied by grilled fish; negotiations that involved European wine and mobile phones on the white tablecloth. Waiters who were invisible, but were by the table the moment a plate was empty or a napkin fell to the floor. The smell of food blended with candles and the scent of red and yellow roses.

He had been traveling for seventeen hours. Ewert had phoned just as Anita had turned off the light and snuggled up to him, her soft shoulder and breasts against his back, the first deep breaths on his neck as thoughts slowly evaporated and could not be caught no matter how hard he tried. Anita had avoided saying anything when he packed his bag and avoided looking at him when he tried to catch her eye. He understood her. Ewert Grens had for so long been part of their bedroom, someone who lived in his own time bubble and therefore didn't realize that others had their own too. Sven didn't have the strength to talk to him about it, to put down limits, but understood that Anita had to do just that sometimes in order to cope.

The taxi from the airport was one of the ones without air-conditioning and the heat had been as unexpected as it was forceful. He had traveled in clothes made for the Swedish spring and landed in a place near Florida's beaches with full summer heat. He walked toward the entrance of the restaurant and drank some mineral water that tasted of chemical additives. They had had offices on the same corridor for ten years and had worked together on several investigations, but all the same, he didn't know him. Erik Wilson was not someone you went out and had a beer with or maybe it was Sven you didn't do that with, or maybe they were just too different. Sven, who loved his life in a terraced house with Anita and Jonas, Wilson who scorned it. Now they were going to meet, tolerate each other, one asking for information and one with no intention of giving it.

He was tall, considerably taller than Sven, and even taller when he stood on his toes to scan all the guests in the restaurant. He seemed satisfied and sat down at the table at the back of the exclusive premises.

"I'm a bit late."

"I'm glad you're here."

The waiter appeared from nowhere, a glass of mineral water for each of them, two slices of lemon.

I've got one minute.

When he realizes why I'm here, one minute more to convince him he should stay.

Sven moved the white candle and silver candlestick and put a laptop down between them. He opened a program that contained several sound files, pressed a symbol that looked like a long dash, a couple of sentences, exactly seven seconds.

"We have to make him more dangerous. He will have committed some serious crimes. He'll be given a long sentence."

Erik Wilson's face.

It showed nothing.

Sven tried to catch his eye. If he was surprised to hear his own voice, if he felt uncomfortable, it didn't show, not even in his eyes.

Another snippet, a single sentence, five seconds.

"He'll only be able to operate freely from his cell if he gets respect."

"Do you want to hear more? You see . . . it's quite a long, interesting meeting. And I . . . I've got all of it here."

Wilson's voice was still controlled when he rose, as were his eyes, emotions that must not be shown.

"Nice to meet you."

Now.

This was the minute.

He was already on his way out.

Sven opened the third sound file.

"Before I leave, I'd like you to summarize exactly what you are guaranteeing me."

"You perhaps think that you know what you are hearing?"

Erik Wilson was already walking away, he was halfway to the door, that was why Sven almost shouted what he said next.

"I don't think you do. That's the voice of a dead man."

The guests in glossy suits hadn't understood what he said. But they had all stopped talking, put down their cutlery, looked at the person who had blemished their discretion.

"The voice of a man who two days ago stood in the window of a prison workshop window with a gun to a prison warden's head."

Wilson had reached the bar that was to the right of the door when he stopped.

"The voice of a man who was shot on the order of our colleague, Ewert Grens."

He turned around.

"What the hell are you talking about?"

"I'm talking about Paula."

He looked at Sven, hesitated.

"Because that's what you call him, isn't it?"

A step forward.

A step away from the door.

"Sundkvist, why the hell—"

Sven lowered his voice, Wilson listened, he wasn't going anywhere.

"I'm saying that he was eliminated. That you and Grens were both involved. That you are an accessory to legitimate murder."

Ewert Grens got up, an empty plastic cup in the trash, a half-eaten cinnamon bun from the shelf behind his desk gone in two bites.

He was restless, time was running out. He prowled between the ugly sofa and the window with a view over the Kronoberg courtyard.

Sven should have started his meeting with Wilson by now. He should have started the interview, to demand answers.

Grens sighed.

Erik Wilson was crucial.

One of the voices was dead. Grens would wait for three of them, they would listen, but only when he wanted them to.

Wilson was the fifth voice.

The one that could confirm that the meeting really did take place, that the recording was genuine.

"Have you got a minute?"

A blond fringe, swept to one side, and a pair of round glasses leaned around the door.

Lars Ågestam had exchanged his pajamas and robe for a gray suit and gray tie.

"Well, have you?"

Grens nodded and Ågestam followed the large body that limped over the linoleum to the sofa and sat down where the fabric was worn and shiny. It had been a long night. Grens, whisky and the county commissioner's computer in his kitchen. They had for the first time spoken to each other without mutual loathing. Ewert Grens had even used his first name. Lars. Lars, he had said. They had just then, just there, been almost close and Grens had tried to show it.

Lars Ågestam leaned back in the sofa, folded.

He wasn't tense.

He hadn't prepared himself to meet someone threatening and insulting.

All previous visits to this room had felt like an attack, difficult and full of animosity, but with the music gone and the feeling from last night still lingering, he giggled suddenly because it struck him it had almost felt good to come in.

He had two files on the table in front of them and opened the first one that was on top.

"Secret intelligence reports. Three hundred and two in total. The copies I printed out last night."

He then lifted up the second file.

"Summaries of the preliminary investigations into the same cases. What you knew, what you could investigate. I've managed to go through a hundred of them. One hundred of the cases that were closed or where prosecution did not result in a conviction. I've used every minute I've had since we met at my place to find, analyze, and compare them with what actually happened. In other words, the information that some of your colleagues already had, that's reported here, in the secret intelligence reports."

Ågestam was talking about copies that were taken from a laptop that had been on the desk of one of the top-ranking officers. Grens hoped that the door was still working as it should.

"Twenty-five of the cases ended in *nolle prosequi*—the prosecutor realized that there wasn't sufficient evidence to secure a verdict and the cases were dropped. In thirty-five cases, the accused was acquitted—the court disallowed the prosecutor to proceed."

Lars Ågestam's neck was turning flaming red as it normally did when he got agitated. Ewert Grens had witnessed it every time they faced each other with contempt. Only this time the anger was targeted at someone else and it was almost unsettling; disdain had been their only means of communication, where they felt secure—if they couldn't hide behind it, it felt awkward. Where did you start?

"If, and I'm quite sure about this, if the prosecution had had access to the facts that the police, *your colleagues, Grens,* already had and that were kept from us, if all the information in this damn file of secret intelligence reports hadn't been hidden on a computer in a commissioner's office, then all these cases, *all of them, Grens,* would have ended with a conviction."

Sven Sundkvist ordered some more mineral water, more lemon slices. He wasn't hot anymore, the exclusive restaurant was cool and the air was easy to breathe, but he was tense.

He had only had one minute.

He had gotten Wilson to stop, turn back, sit down again.

Now he had to get him to participate.

He looked at his colleague. His face was still expressionless. But not his eyes. There was an uneasiness in their depths. They didn't waver, Wilson was far too professional for that, but the voices in the recording had surprised him, disturbed him, demanded answers.

"This recording was in an envelope in Ewert Grens's pigeonhole."

Sven nodded at the symbol on the screen that meant sound file.

"No sender. The day after Hoffmann's death. The pigeonholes, about as far from your office as mine, wouldn't you say?"

Wilson didn't sigh, didn't shake his head, didn't tense his jaw. But his eyes, the uneasiness was there again.

"The envelope contained a CD of the recording. But there was more. Three passports issued under different names, all with the same photograph, a rather grainy black-and-white picture of Hoffmann. And at the bottom of the envelope, an electronic receiver, the small silver metal kind that you put in your ear. We've been able to link it to a transmitter that was attached to a church tower in Aspsås. The spot chosen by the sniper who Grens eventually ordered to fire, as he was guaranteed to hit the target from there."

Erik Wilson should have grabbed the edge of the white tablecloth and pulled it from the table, turning the floor to broken glass and petals. He should have spat, cried, snapped.

He didn't. He sat as still as he could, hoping that nothing would show.

Sundkvist had said they were accomplices to legitimate murder.

He had said that Paula was dead.

If it had been someone else he would have continued walking. If someone else had presented him with that goddamn recording he would have dismissed it as nonsense. But Sundkvist never bullshitted. He himself did. Grens did, most policemen did, most people he knew did. But not Sundkvist.

"Before I leave, I'd like you to summarize exactly what you are guaranteeing me."

No one except Paula could have recorded that meeting or had the motive to do so. He had chosen to let Grens and Sundkvist in on it. He had a reason.

They burned you.

"I want to show you some pictures as well."

Sven turned the screen toward Wilson, opened a new file.

A still, a frozen moment from one of Aspsås prison's many security cameras, a fuzzy frame around a fuzzy barred window.

"Aspsås workshop. Block B. The person you can see standing there, in profile, has eight and a half minutes left to live."

Wilson pulled the laptop over, angled the screen—he wanted to see that person, roughly in the middle of the window, part of a shoulder, part of a face.

He had met a man ten years younger. He himself had been ten years younger. If it had been today would he have recruited Hoffmann? Would Hoffmann have wanted to be recruited? Piet had done time in Österåker. A prison some way north of Stockholm with a whole host of small-time crooks. Piet had been one of them. His first sentence. The kind who would serve his twelve months, run around for a while, then be sentenced to twelve more.

But his roots, mother tongue, and personality could be used for more than just confirming statistics on reoffenders.

"This one? Five minutes left to live."

Sundkvist had changed the picture. Another security camera. It was closer, no frame, just the window, the face was clearer.

They had added a few pistols to the property seized in connection with the already registered judgment, probably some kind of Kalashnikov. They normally did. It had later been easy to ask for a new potential danger classification and tighter restrictions, no leave, no contact with the outside world. Piet had been desperate, he had listened; after months with no human contact, touch or talk, he could have been recruited for anything.

"Three minutes. I think you can see in this picture. He's shouting. A camera inside the workshop."

A face that filled the picture.

It's him.

"*He's a dead man.* We've analyzed it. That's what he's shouting."

Erik Wilson looked at the absurd picture. The distorted face. The open, desperate mouth.

He had built up Paula methodically.

A petty thief had been developed into one of the country's most dangerous criminals, document by document. Criminal record, the national court administration databases, the police criminal intelligence database. The myth of his potency enhanced by patrol after patrol who unknowingly responded on the basis of the available information. And when he was about to take that last step, right into Wojtek's nerve center, when the mission required even more respect, he had also provided it. Erik Wilson had copied a DSM-IV-TR statement, a psychopathic test that was carried out on one of Sweden's criminals with the highest security classification.

A document that had then been planted in the Prison and Probation Service records.

Piet Hoffmann suddenly had a chronic lack of conscience, was extremely aggressive and very dangerous in terms of other people's safety.

"My last picture."

Thick, black smoke, in the distance what might be a building, at the top, what might be blue sky.

"Two twenty-six p.m. When he died."

The square screen, he heard Sundkvist talking but continued to search in the dense blackness, tried to see the person who had just been standing there.

"There were five of you at that meeting, Erik. I need to know whether the recording that was left in an envelope in Grens's pigeonhole is genuine. If what can be heard here is exactly what was said. If three people who have never touched a trigger were accomplices to legitimate murder."

His neck was now red all the way up. His fringe had flopped and for a while stood out in every direction. He paced, frustrated, up and down in front of Grens's desk.

Lars Ågestam was almost hissing.

"This damned system, Grens. Criminals working for the police. Criminals' own crimes being covered up and downplayed. One crime is legitimized so that another one can be investigated. Policemen who lie and withhold the truth from other policemen. Damn it, Grens, in a democratic society."

During the night he had printed out three hundred two secret intelligence reports from the county police commissioner's laptop. So far he had managed to go through one hundred of them, comparing the truth with the city police investigations. Twenty-five had resulted in *nolle prosequi*, thirty-five in an acquittal.

"Judgments were given in the remaining forty cases, but I can tell you that the judgments were wrong due to the lack of underlying information. The people who were tried were given sentences, but for the wrong crime. *Grens, are you listening?* In all cases!"

Ewert Grens looked at the prosecutor, suit and tie, a file in one hand, glasses in the other.

A bloody rotten system.

And there's more, Ågestam.

Soon we'll talk about the intelligence report you haven't seen yet, the one that is so hot off the press that it's in a separate file.

Västmannagatan 79.

An investigation that we closed when other policemen with offices on the same corridor had the answer we lacked, which meant that a person had to be burned and they needed a useful idiot to carry the can.

"Thank you. You've done a good job."

He held out his hand to the prosecutor he would never learn to like.

Lars Ågestam took it, shook for a bit too long perhaps, but it felt good, personal, on the same side for the first time, the long hours at night, each with a glass of whisky and Grens who had called him Lars on one occasion.

He smiled.

Conscious spite and attempted insult, he didn't need to worry this time.

He let go of his hand and had just started to head for the door with a strange joy in his heart when he suddenly turned around.

"Grens?"

"Yes?"

"That map you showed me when I was here last."

"Yes?"

"You asked about Haga. North Cemetery. If it was nice there."

It was lying on the desk. He had seen it as soon as he came in. A map of a resting place that had been used for more than two hundred years and was one of the largest in the country.

Grens kept it at hand. He was going to go there.

"Did you find what you were looking for?"

Ewert Grens was breathing heavily, rocking his great bulk.

"Well, did you?"

Grens turned round pointedly. He said nothing, just the labored breathing as he faced the pile of files on the desk.

"Hm, Ågestam?"

"Yes?"

He didn't look at the visitor who was about to leave, his voice was different, it was a bit too high and the young prosecutor had long since learned that that often meant discomfort.

"You seem to have misinterpreted something."

"Right?"

"You see, Ågestam, this is just work. I am not your damn buddy."

They had gotten their food, fish that wasn't salmon, the waiter's suggestion. *I need to know whether the recording that was left in an envelope in Grens's pigeonhole is genuine.* They had eaten without speaking, without even looking at each other. *If what can be heard here is exactly what was said.* The questions were there on the table beside the candlestick and pepper grinder, waiting for them. *If three people who have never touched a trigger were accomplices to a legitimate murder.*

"Sundkvist?"

Erik Wilson put his cutlery down on the empty plate, emptied his third glass of mineral water, lifted the napkin from his knee.

"Yes."

"You've come a long way for nothing."

He had decided.

"You see, in some way . . . it's like we're all in the same business."

"You went to see Grens the next day. You knew, Erik, but you said nothing."

"In the same bloody business. The criminals. The people investigating the crime. And the informants make up the gray zone."

He wasn't going to say anything.

"And Sundkvist, this is the future. More informants. More covert human intelligence. It's a growth area. That's why I'm here."

"If you had talked to us then, Erik, we wouldn't have been sitting opposite each other today. On either side of a dead man."

"And that is why my European colleagues are here. We're here to learn. As it will continue to expand."

They had worked on the same corridor for so damn long.

Wilson had never before seen Sven Sundkvist lose control.

"I want you to listen bloody closely now, Erik!"

Sven grabbed the laptop, a plate on the white marble floor, a glass on the white tablecloth.

"I can fast-forward or rewind to wherever you want. Here? See that? The exact moment that the bullet penetrates the reinforced glass."

A mouth shouting in a monitor.

"Or here? The exact moment the workshop explodes."

A face in profile in a window.

"Or here, maybe? I haven't shown you this one yet. The remnants. The flags on the wall. All that remains."

A person stopped breathing.

"You're responding the way you're supposed to respond, the way you've always responded: You protect your informant. But for Christ's sake, Erik, he's dead! There's nothing to protect anymore! Because you and your colleagues failed to do exactly that. That's why he's standing there in the window. That's why he dies exactly . . . there."

Erik Wilson reached out to the computer screen that was turned toward him, closed it with a snap, and pulled out the plug.

"*I* have worked as a handler as long as you have sat a few doors down. *I* have been responsible for informants all my working life. *I* have never not succeeded."

Sven Sundkvist opened the laptop and turned it back again.

"You can keep the cord. The battery's got plenty of juice."

He pointed to the screen.

"I don't understand, Erik. You've worked together for nine years. But when I show you that picture there . . . the exact moment he . . . there, do you see, exactly *there* he dies . . . you don't react."

Erik Wilson snorted.

"He wasn't my friend."

You trusted me.

"But I was his friend."

I trusted you.

"That's the way it works, Sundkvist. A handler pretends to be the informant's best friend. A handler has to play the role of the informant's best friend so goddamn well that the informant is willing to risk his life every day to get more information for his handler."

I miss you.

"So the guy you saw on the screen? You were right. I didn't react."

Erik Wilson dropped his linen napkin on the table.

"Are you paying, Sundkvist?"

He started to leave. The tasteful restaurant around him, the lady on her own at the table to the left with a glass of red wine, two men to the right at a table full of papers and dessert plates.

"Västmannagatan 79."

Sven Sundkvist caught up with him, beside him.

"You knew everything, Erik. But you chose to say nothing. And contributed to the disappearance of someone associated with a murder. You manipulated police authority records and the national courts administration database. You placed—"

"Are you threatening me?"

Erik Wilson had stopped, red face, shoulders up.

He was showing something that was more than just nothing.

"Are you, Sundkvist? Threatening me?"

"What do you think?"

"What do I think? You've tried to convince me by showing me evidence and tried to get me to feel something by showing me pictures of death. And now you're trying to threaten me with some kind of goddamn investigation? Sundkvist, you've used all the chapters in the interview book. What do I think? You're insulting me."

He continued on down the small step, past the table with four older men who were looking for their glasses and studying the menu and the empty serving carts and the two green climbers on a white wall.

One last look.

He stopped.

"But . . . the truth is that I don't like people who burn my best informant when I'm not there."

He looked at Sven Sundkvist.

"So . . . yes, that recording. The meeting you're talking about. It did happen. What you heard is genuine. Every single word."

EWERT GRENS SHOULD PERHAPS HAVE LAUGHED. AT LEAST FELT WHATEVER it was that sometimes bubbles up in your belly, a delight that can't be heard.

The recording was genuine.

The meeting had taken place.

Sven had called from a restaurant in the center of Jacksonville as he watched Wilson walk to his car and start the journey back to south Georgia, after he had confirmed it all.

Grens didn't laugh. He had emptied himself that morning in a cage on a roof. He had screamed until the rage was released and let him sleep on a sofa. So now there was a space to be filled.

But not with more anger, that was no longer enough.

Not with satisfaction, even though he knew he was so close.

But hate.

Hoffmann had been burned. But survived. And taken hostages in order to continue surviving.

I carried out a legitimate murder.

Ewert Grens phoned a person he loathed for the second time.

"I need your help again."

"Okay."

"Can you come to my flat tonight?"

"Your flat?"

"Corner of Odengatan and Sveavägen."

"Why?"

"As I said. I need your help."

Lars Ågestam scoffed.

"You want me to meet you? After work? Why should I want to do that? After all . . . I'm not . . . now how did you put it . . . your *buddy*."

The secret intelligence report that was also on the laptop, but so fresh that it was in another file.

The one I didn't show you last night.

The one that I'm going to show you because I have no intention of carrying someone else's guilt.

"It's not social, it's work. Västmannagatan 79. The preliminary investigation you just scaled down."

"You're welcome to come to the Regional Public Prosecution Office tomorrow during the day."

"You can open it again. As I know what *actually* happened. But I need your help one more time, Ågestam. Tomorrow morning is too late. That is when the head of the Government Offices security realizes that something is missing and passes on that information. When the wrong people then have time to adapt their versions, manipulate the evidence, change reality yet again."

Grens coughed extensively close to the mouthpiece, as if he was uncertain as to how to continue.

"And I apologize. For that. I was perhaps . . . well, you know."

"No, what?"

"Damn it, Ågestam!"

"What?"

"I was perhaps . . . I may have been a bit . . . churlish, a bit . . . well, unnecessarily harsh."

Lars Ågestam walked down the seven flights of stairs in the offices at Kungsbron. A pleasant evening, warm, he longed for heat, as he always did after eight months of bitter wind and unpredictable snow. He turned around, looked at the windows of the Regional Public Prosecution Office, all dark. Two late phone calls had been longer than he expected: one phone call home—he had explained that he had to stay late and several times promised that he would wash the glasses from last night which still smelled of alcohol before he went to bed—then one call with Sven Sundkvist. He had gotten hold of him somewhere that sounded like an airport. He had wanted more information about the part of the investigation that involved Poland and their trip there to a now defunct amphetamine factory.

"His flat?"

"Yes."

"You're going to Ewert Grens's flat?"

Sven Sundkvist hadn't said anything but didn't want to hang up—their conversation was already finished and Ågestam was impatient, wanted to get on his way.

"Yes. I'm going to Ewert Grens's flat."

"I'm sorry, Ågestam, but there's something I don't quite understand. I've known Ewert, I've been his closest colleague for nearly fourteen years. But I have never, *never ever, Ågestam*, been invited to his flat. It's . . . I don't know . . . so private, a strange kind of . . . protection. Once, five years ago, one time only, Ågestam, the day after the hostage drama in the morgue at Söder hospital, I forced my way into his home, against his will. But now you're saying that he *asked* you there? And you're quite sure about that?"

Lars Ågestam wandered slowly through the city, lots of people on the street despite the fact it was a Sunday and past nine o'clock—after winter's drought of warmth and company it was always harder to go home when life had just returned.

He hadn't realized that it might be more than just an investigation, more than just a question of working late. It really felt like something had changed last night in the kitchen at Åkeshov; the whisky and three hundred two copies of secret intelligence reports resembled a kind of closeness. But Ewert Grens had soon killed that feeling, happy to hurt in the way that only he knew how. So if it was as extraordinary to be invited to his flat as Sven made out, maybe there *had* been a change, they were perhaps closer to tolerating each other.

He looked at the people around him again, those drinking beer in their coats and scarves in outside cafés, laughing, chatting, as people who get on well together do.

He sighed.

There had been no change, there never would be.

Grens had other reasons, Ågestam was sure of it, his own reasons, ones that he would never dream of sharing with a young public prosecutor he had decided to despise.

"Grens."

Still a lot of traffic on Sveavägen. He had to concentrate to hear the voice on the intercom.

"It's Ågestam, will you—"

"I'll open. Four flights up."

A thick reddish carpet on the floor, walls that were possibly marble, lights that were bright without being offensive. If he had lived in town, in a flat, he would have looked for an entrance like this.

He avoided the elevator, broad staircase all the way up, E AND A GRENS on the mailbox in a dark door.

"Come in."

The large detective superintendent with the thinning hair opened the door, same clothes as that afternoon and the night before, a gray jacket and even grayer trousers.

Ågestam looked around in wonder—the hall seemed endless.

"It's big."

"I haven't spent much time here in the last few years. But still manage to find my way around."

Ewert Grens smiled. It looked unnatural. He had never experienced it before. His coarse face was normally tense, harassing the people it was facing; the smile, a different face that made Ågestam uncertain.

He walked down the long hall with rooms opening off it, counted at least six empty rooms that looked untouched, asleep. That was how Sven had described them, rooms that didn't want to wake up.

The kitchen was as spacious, as untouched.

He followed Grens through the first section and into the next, a small eating area, a gateleg table and six chairs.

"Do you live here on your own?"

"Sit yourself down."

A pile of blue files and a large notepad in the middle, two glasses that were still wet with a bottle of Seagram's between them.

He was prepared.

"A dram? Or are you driving?"

He had made an effort. Even the same kind of whisky.

"Here? With you in the vicinity? I wouldn't dare. You might have some dusty parking fine papers in your glove compartment."

Ewert Grens remembered a cold winter's night one and a half years ago. He had crawled around on his hands and knees, his creased suit trousers in the wet new snow and measured the distance between a car and Vasagatan.

Ågestam's car.

He smiled again, a smile that was almost unnerving.

"As I remember it, the parking fine was dismissed. By the prosecutor himself."

In a fury, he had fined Lars Ågestam for his eight-centimeter error in parking, weary of a public prosecutor who made things difficult when the search for a sixteen-year-old girl who had disappeared forced them down into the tunnels under Stockholm.

"You can pour me half a glass."

They both took a drink while Grens produced a document from one of the files and put it down in front of Ågestam.

"You got three hundred and two secret intelligence reports. About what *actually* happened, things the rest of us didn't know and so couldn't present in our official investigations."

Lars Ågestam nodded.

"That unit at Aspsås. For only police officers. When I charge them all."

"They were reports from last year. But this copy, this is still warm."

```
M pulls a gun
(Polish 9mm Radom)
from shoulder holster.
M cocks the gun and holds it to
the buyer's head.
```

"Submitted to the county police commissioner, like all the others."

```
P orders M to calm down.
M lowers the gun, takes a step
back, his weapon half-cocked.
```

Lars Ågestam was about to speak when Grens interrupted.

"I've spent . . . I'd guess . . . half my time working on Västmannagatan since the alarm was raised. Sven Sundkvist and Mariana Hermansson as well. Nils Krantz estimates that he and three other colleagues spent a week searching the place with magnifying glasses and fingerprint-lifting tape, Errfors says that he used as much time to analyze the body of a Danish citizen. A number of constables and detectives have guarded the crime scene, questioned neighbors and looked for bloody shirts in garbage cans for—if I'm conservative—twenty days."

He looked at the prosecutor.

"And you? How many hours have you put into this case?"

Ågestam shrugged.

"Hard to say . . . a week."

```
Suddenly the buyer shouts
"I'm the police."
M again aims the gun
at the buyer's head.
```

Ewert Grens snatched the intelligence report out of Ågestam's hands and waved it in front of him.

"Thirteen and a half working weeks. Five hundred and forty man-hours. When my colleagues and bosses who sit in the same corridor already had the answer. He even phoned, Ågestam, it says here, Hoffmann damn well called himself and raised the alarm!"

Lars Ågestam reached out for the report.

"Can I have it back?"

He left the table, went into the other part of the kitchen and opened one of the wall cupboards, looking for something, opened another one.

"What's the purpose of all this?"

"I want to solve a murder."

"Do you not understand what I'm asking, Grens? What's the *purpose* of all this?"

He found what he was looking for, a glass, filled it with water.

"I have no intention of carrying the guilt."

"Guilt?"

"You've got nothing to do with it, Ågestam. But that's the truth. I'm not going to carry the guilt anymore. That's why I'm going to make sure that the people responsible are going to carry it for me."

The public prosecutor looked at the report.

"And you can use the report to do that?"

"Yes. If I manage to finish this. Before tomorrow morning."

Lars Ågestam stood in the middle of the large kitchen. He could hear the traffic through the open window—it had slowed, fewer cars that drove faster, it was starting to get late.

"Can I wander around a bit? Here in the flat?"

"Feel free."

The hall seemed even longer than before, thick rugs on a parquet floor that was dark but not worn, brown wallpaper with a seventies design. He turned off and into the first and best door, into something that resembled a library, sat down in the leather armchair that seemed to protest while the sunken seat waited for its owner. The only room in the flat that didn't scream loneliness. He followed the shelves and rows of same-size books, turned on the standard lamp that was beautifully angled and that gave off a light that colored the printed pages yellow. He leaned back as he imagined the detective superintendent did, once more read the secret intelligence report that had been written by a policeman the day after the murder at Västmannagatan 79, whereas the investigation for which he and Grens were responsible had slowly led to nothing and closure.

> M holds the gun harder to
> the buyer's head and pulls the trigger.
> The buyer falls to the floor, at a right angle to
> the chair.

Lars Ågestam reached for the lampshade and pulled it closer, he wanted to see properly, be sure, now that he had decided.

He wouldn't be going home tonight.

He would, in a while, go directly from here to the Regional Public Prosecution Office and reopen the preliminary investigation.

He stood up and was about to leave the room when he noticed two black-and-white photographs on the wall between two bookshelves: a woman and a man. They were young and full of anticipation, they were wearing police uniforms and their eyes were alive.

He had always wondered what he looked like, back then, when he was someone else.

"Have you decided?"

Grens was sitting where he had left him, among the blue files and empty glasses at an elegant kitchen table.

"Yes."

"If you prosecute, Ågestam, we're not just talking about normal policemen. I'll give you a commanding officer. And an even higher-ranking officer. And a state secretary."

Lars Ågestam looked at the three pieces of letter-size paper in his hand.

"And you maintain that there's enough? I assume that I haven't seen everything."

A security camera in Rosenbad with five people on their way into one of the offices. A recording of five voices in a closed meeting.

You haven't seen everything.

"There's enough."

Ewert Grens smiled for the third time.

Lars Ågestam thought that it looked almost natural, he smiled fleetingly back.

"Haul them in. I'll have the arrest warrants sorted within three days."

HE WENT DOWN THE STAIRS IN THE SILENT BUILDING.

It was years ago now, his painful leg on the stone stairs, but tonight he had walked past the elevator, his hand gripping the handrail. Two doors had greeted him with scurrying footsteps to doormats and peepholes as he passed, curious eyes that wanted to see him up on the fourth floor, he who never used the stairs suddenly doing so. At the bottom and the door nearest the entrance, a wall clock that chimed, he counted, twelve times.

Sveavägen was almost empty and it was still warm, maybe they'd get a damned summer this year as well. He breathed in, one deep breath, slowly released the air.

Ewert Grens had invited another person into his home.

Ewert Grens hadn't immediately experienced a pain in his chest and asked him to leave.

He had never done that before, not since the accident—it had been her place and their shared home. He shrugged off the gentle breeze and started to walk west along Odengatan, just as empty, just as warm. He took off his jacket and undid the top buttons on his shirt.

Of all people, the well-groomed prosecutor whom he hated, whom he had met a few years ago and loathed.

He had even almost enjoyed it.

He slowed down by the kiosk on Odenplan, stood in the queue with the mobile kids sending text messages to other mobile kids, bought a hamburger and a drink that tasted of orange but had lost its bubbles. He had said no to the prosecutor's suggestion of finishing the evening with a beer in the lawyers' haunt at Frescati, only to regret it and wander restlessly from room to room until he was compelled to go out, just somewhere else, at least for a while.

Two rats at his feet, from a hole under the kiosk into the park with sleeping men on wooden benches. Four young women over there, short skirts and high-heeled shoes, running toward one of the buses that had just closed its doors and was pulling out.

He ate his hamburger outside Gustav Vasa church, then turned right into a street he had visited several times in the past few weeks, blocks of flats that were on their way to bed. He looked at himself in the glass panes of the large front door, punched in the code which he now knew by heart, and took the elevator that creaked as it reached the fourth floor.

A new sign on the mailbox. The Polish name had been replaced. The brown wooden door was even older than his own. He looked at it, remembered the pool of blood under a head, small flags on the wall, the kitchen floor where Krantz had found traces of drugs.

It had started here.

The death that would force him to make a decision about more death.

Vanadisvägen, Gävlegatan, Solnabron, he carried on through the mild night, as if someone else was walking beside him and he was just following, he thought nothing, felt nothing, not until he stopped on Solna Kyrkväg in front of an opening in the fence that was called Gate 1 and was one of ten entrances to North Cemetery.

The expected edges in the inner pocket of his jacket.

He had let it lie at arm's length on his desk for months; then yesterday, without knowing why, he had taken it home with him. Now he was here, holding the map in his hand.

He wasn't even cold.

Despite the fact that he knew it was always cold in graveyards.

Ewert Grens followed the asphalt road that cut across large areas of green grass edged by birches, conifers, and trees he didn't know the names of. A hundred and fifty acres, thirty thousand graves. He had avoided looking at them—rather the branches on the trees than the gray stones that marked loss—but was now looking at some older graves, those who were buried as titles, not people: a postal inspector, a stationmaster, a widow. He went on past large engraved stones that housed entire families who wanted always to be close, past other large stones that rose up stern and proud from the ground—slightly more important than the rest, even in death—to stare at him.

Twenty-nine years.

He had several times a day for most of his adult life lived through a few tainted moments—*she falls out of the police van, he doesn't manage to stop in time, the back wheels roll over her head*—and sometimes, if he had forgotten to think about it, if he realized that several hours had passed since the last time, he had been forced to think about it a bit longer and a bit more, mostly about the red that had been blood that poured from the head on his lap.

He couldn't do it anymore.

He looked at the trees and the graves and even the memorial garden over there, but it didn't help, no matter how much he reprimanded himself, he could not focus on the flickering in her eyes or the spasms in her legs.

What you're frightened of has already happened.

He looked around, suddenly in a rush.

He cut across the graves in an area that according to the signs was called Section 15B: beautiful, understated gravestones, people who had died with dignity and didn't need to make such a bloody fuss afterward.

Section 16A. He lengthened his stride. Section 19E. He was out of breath, sweating.

A green watering can on a stand: he filled it with water from the tap close by, carried it with him as he hurried on and the asphalt changed to gravel.

Section 19B.

He attempted to stand still again.

He had never been here. He had tried, he had, but never managed.

It had taken him one and a half years to walk a couple of kilometers.

The failing light made it hard to see more than two headstones in front. He leaned forward so he could read more easily, each new sign marking a burial place.

Grave 601.

Grave 602.

He was shaking, finding it difficult to breathe. For a moment he was about to turn around.

Grave 603.

Some overturned earth, a temporary flowerbed with something green, a small white wooden cross, nothing more.

He lifted the watering can and watered the bush without flowers.

SHE'S LYING THERE.

The girl who holds his hand and forces him to walk close to her as they wander through the Stockholm dawn, the girl who struggles beside him on badly waxed skis through the snow-covered chestnut trees in Vasaparken, the girl who moves in with a young man to the flat on Sveavägen.

She is the one who is lying there.

Not the woman who sits in a wheelchair in a nursing home, the one who doesn't recognize me.

He didn't cry, he had already done that. He smiled.

I didn't kill him.

I didn't kill you.

What I am frightened of has already happened.

PART FIVE

a day later

HE LIKED THE BROWN BREAD, THICK SLICES WITH SEEDS ALL AROUND THE crust, it filled him and crunched a little when he chewed. Black coffee and orange juice that had been pressed as he watched. A couple of minutes from the flat, on the corner of Odengatan and Döbelnsgatan—Ewert Grens had eaten breakfast there a couple of times a week for as long as he could remember.

He had slept for nearly four hours, in his own bed, in the big flat, and without dreaming about running and someone in pursuit. He had known it would be a good night as soon as he had shut the door, sat down in the large kitchen and looked out of the window, gathered up all the files and papers that were still lying on the table, stood singing in the warm shower for a bit too long, listened to the voices of night radio.

Grens paid for his breakfast and four cinnamon buns, asked if they could be put in a bag, then a quick walk alongside the cars that stood waiting for each other in the dense morning traffic, Sveavägen to Sergels Torg, Drottninggatan to Rosenbad and the Government Offices.

The security guard, who was young and probably new, studied his ID and compared his name for a second and third time with the one given in the meeting book.

"The Ministry of Justice?"

"Yes."

"Do you know where her office is?"

"I was here a couple of nights ago, but we've never met."

The camera was in the middle of the corridor at face height. Ewert Grens looked into it, just as a police informant had done a few weeks ago, smiled at the lens, at roughly the same time that one of the security staff opened the door to a control room several floors down in the huge government building and discovered that the metal shelf with numbered security tapes was empty in two places.

They were waiting for him by the large table at the far end of the room.

A half-empty porcelain cup in front of each of them.

It was eight in the morning and they had already been there a while; they had taken him seriously.

He looked at them, still not a word.

"You asked for a meeting. Well, you've got a meeting. We presume it won't take long. We've all got other *planned* meetings to go to."

Ewert Grens looked at the three faces, one at a time, long enough for it to be just too long. The two first faces, if they were calm, if they were pretending to be. Göransson, on the other hand, had a shiny forehead, his eyes kept blinking, his lips creased as he pressed them together hard.

"I've brought some cinnamon buns."

He put the white paper bag on the table.

"For Christ's sake, Grens!"

Hoffmann had had a family.

Two children who would grow up without a father.

"Does anyone want one? I bought one for each of us."

What if they looked him up in years to come? What if they asked questions, what would he answer?

It was my job?

It was my damned duty?

Your father's life was not as valuable to me and society as that of the prison warden he was threatening?

"No? Well, I think I'll take one. Göransson, can you pass me a cup?"

He drank the coffee, ate a cinnamon bun, and one more.

"Two cinnamon buns left. If anyone changes their mind."

He looked at them again, one at a time as before. The state secretary met his gaze—she was calm, even a faint smile. The national police commissioner sat completely still, his eyes turned to the window, the Royal Palace roof and Storkyrkan tower. Göransson stared at the table. It was difficult to tell, but it looked like his shiny forehead was covered in droplets.

Ewert Grens opened the briefcase and produced a laptop.

"Good machine this. Sven took a similar one with him to the USA. He was there yesterday."

With fumbling fingers, he slipped in the CD, opened the file and a black square filled the screen.

"A lot of keys. But I'm quite good at it now. And by the way, it was Erik Wilson that Sven went to meet. With his laptop."

The security cameras were situated in two places. One about a meter above the glass security desk, the other in the corridor on the second floor. The footage he had seized late in the evening a couple of days ago was jumpy and slightly blurred, but they could all see what it was.

Five people entering one of the rooms in the Government Offices within a short space of time.

"Do you recognize them?"

Grens pointed at the picture.

"You might even recognize which room they're going into?"

He stopped the film, a still frame on the screen, someone standing with his back to the camera, arms outstretched, someone else behind him, hands on his back.

"The last thing that happens. The person in front here, with his arms out, is a man with a criminal record who, when this was recorded, worked as an informant for the city police. The man searching him, with his hands on the informant's back, is a chief superintendent."

Grens looked at Göransson, slumped at the table.

He paused, no eye contact.

"The laptop belongs to the police. But this is mine."

He had his hand in the outside pocket of the briefcase and was now holding a CD player.

"I was given it by Ågestam nearly five years ago after we'd had a slight altercation. It's a modern one, the kind that young people have. Don't tell him, but I haven't actually used it much. Until a couple of weeks ago, that is. When I started listening to some interesting recordings."

The bag of cinnamon buns was in the way, so he moved it.

"But these I've borrowed from the property store. From a burglary in a flat in Stora Nygatan. The preliminary investigation was closed. The seized property released. No one claimed it."

He positioned two small speakers on the table and took his time wiring them up.

"If they're good . . . who knows, I might just keep them."

Ewert Grens pressed one of the buttons.

Chairs scraping, noise of people moving.

"A meeting."

He looked around the room.

"In this room. At this table. Tenth of May at fifteen forty-nine. I'll fast-forward a bit, twenty-eight minutes and twenty-four seconds."

He turned to his line manager.

Göransson had taken off his jacket, revealing dark stains near the armholes of his light blue shirt.

"The person speaking. I think you'll recognize the voice."

"You've dealt with similar cases before."

"You let me, Sven, Hermansson, Krantz, Errfors and . . ."

"Ewert—"

". . . a whole bloody bunch of policemen work for weeks on an investigation that you already had the answer to."

Göransson looked at him for the first time. He had started to speak but Grens shook his head.

"I'll be done soon."

Fingers on the machine's sensitive buttons, got the right one after a while.

"I'll fast-forward some more. Twenty-two minutes and seventeen seconds. The same meeting. Another voice."

"I don't want that to happen. You don't want that to happen. Paula doesn't have time for Västmannagatan."

Ewert Grens looked at the national police commissioner.

Maybe the well-polished veneer was starting to crack, it certainly felt like that: too many twitches around the eyes, hands rubbing slowly together.

"Lie to your colleagues. Burn your employees. Give some crimes immunity so that others can be solved. If that is the future of policing . . . then I'm glad it's only six years until I retire."

He didn't expect a response, adjusted the speakers so they stood face on when he turned them toward the state secretary.

"He was sitting directly opposite you. Doesn't it feel strange?"

"I guarantee that you won't be charged for anything that happened at Västmannagatan 79. I guarantee that we will do our best to help you complete your operation in prison."

"A microphone, at about knee height, on a person who was sitting in the same place that I am now."

"And . . . that we will look after you when the work is done. I know that you will then have a death threat and be branded throughout the criminal world. We will give you a new life, a new identity, and money to start over again abroad."

Grens lifted the small speakers, moved them even closer toward the state secretary.

"I want to be sure that you hear what comes next."

Her voice again, exactly where he'd interrupted her.

"I guarantee you this in my capacity as a state secretary of the Ministry of Justice."

He reached for the white paper bag, first one more cinnamon bun, then what was left of the coffee at the bottom of his cup.

"Crime: failure to report a crime. Crime: protection of a criminal. Crime: conspiring to commit crime."

He was anticipating that they might ask him to leave, threaten to call security, ask him what the hell he thought he was doing.

"Crime: perjury. Crime: gross misuse of public office. Crime: forgery of documents."

They sat still. They said nothing.

"Perhaps you know of others?"

Some seagulls had been circling outside the window since the meeting began.

Their loud screeches were now the only thing to be heard.

That, and the regular breathing of four people around a table.

Ewert Grens stood up after a while, walked slowly across the room, first to the window and the birds, then back to the people who were no longer in a rush to get anywhere.

"I won't carry the guilt. Not anymore. Not again."

Three days earlier he had dared to make a decision he had dreaded throughout his working life—to fire a lethal shot at another person.

"I was not responsible for his death."

Last night he had dared to spend several hours in a cemetery—a modest grave that he had been more frightened of than anything else he could remember.

"I was not responsible for her death."

His voice, it was remarkably calm again.

"It was not me who committed murder."

He pointed at them, one at a time.

"It was you. It was you. It was you."

**another
day later**

A COUPLE OF CENTIMETERS ABOVE THE TAILBONE, THE THIRD OR FOURTH vertebra, the pain was unbearable at times. He moved with care, he pedaled with his feet in the air, one at a time, then nothing could be heard and the intense pain was dulled for a while.

He didn't notice the smell, the stench of urine and feces; in the first few hours perhaps, but that was a long time ago, not now, not anymore.

He had kept his eyes open the first evening and night and morning, looking for what couldn't be seen, shouting voices and running feet. But he had his eyes closed all the time now, the heavy darkness. He couldn't see anything in any case.

He was lying on square pieces of aluminum that had been welded to form a long, round pipe—he guessed about sixty centimeters in diameter, just enough room for his shoulders and if he stretched his arms up he could press his palms against the top of the pipe.

There was still pressure on his stomach and he let go of the drops that trickled down his thighs—it felt better, eased the discomfort. He hadn't had anything to drink since the morning before he took the hostages, only the urine he managed to catch and lift to his mouth, a couple of handfuls over a hundred hours.

He knew that a person could survive a week without water, but thirst was like hosting madness and his lips and palate and throat shriveled in the presence of dryness. He held out, just as he held out against the hunger and pain in his joints from lying so still, and against the dark that he had relaxed into once the shouting and running feet fell silent. It was the heat that had made him think about giving up a couple of times. All electricity had been turned off in connection with the smoke and fire and when the ventilation system no longer supplied fresh air, the temperature in the sealed pipe had risen and felt like a fever. In the last few hours he had just aimed at a couple of minutes at a time, but that didn't work anymore, he couldn't stand much more.

He should have left the pipe yesterday.

That was what he had planned: three days for the adrenaline and full alert to die down.

But yesterday afternoon someone had opened the door, come in, and walked around in the substation. He had lain petrified and listened to the footsteps and breathing of a guard or electrician or plumber only half a meter below him. The control room for the prison's water and electricity was only checked a few times a week, he knew that, but still he waited for another twenty-four hours to be on the safe side.

He pulled his left arm up toward his face, looked at the watch that had belonged to the elderly warden.

Quarter to seven. Another hour to lockup.

Then an hour and a quarter for the staff to change shifts, when the day guards became the night guards.

It was time.

He checked that the scissors were still in his trouser pocket, the ones that had been in a pen holder on the desk in the workshop office and that he had cut his long hair with on the first day, his arm and hand movements restricted by the inside of the pipe, but he had plenty of time to do it and it had been a good way to forget the sound of people looking for body parts. He teased them out of his pocket again and, arm back, hit the inside of the pipe hard with the point until his fingertips felt a hole and he could slash the soft metal with the blades. He braced his body directly above the cut and pushed back, feet against the base, both hands against the sharp edges of the metal. He was bleeding heavily when the pipe finally gave way and he sank through the aluminum and fell onto the stone floor of the substation.

He counted fifty-seven small red and yellow and green lights on panels that controlled the water and electricity; counted them one more time.

No steps, no voices.

He was certain that no one had heard a body landing on the floor in one of the rooms with a door straight out into the passage that linked Block G and central security. He grabbed hold of a washbasin with his hands and hauled himself up. He was dizzy but the sensation crawling around his body disappeared after a while and he trusted it again.

He searched around in the unnerving darkness.

There was a flashlight on a hook on the wall under a fuse box. He chose that rather than the ceiling light—he could turn on the flashlight and let his eyes slowly adjust to the light. It hurt more than he'd imagined when the dark became light and it's possible he cried out when it was thrown back at him by the mirror above the washbasin.

He closed his eyes and waited.

The mirror didn't attack him anymore.

He saw a head with hair of varying lengths, big tangles that hung loose. He picked the scissors up from the floor and straightened it, cut it as short as he could, only a few millimeters left. The razorblade had also been in one of the desk drawers and later in the same trouser pocket. He leaned down and gulped some water from the tap and then wet his face and bit by bit peeled off the beard he had started to cultivate on his way out of the meeting in Rosenbad, following the decision to infiltrate inside Aspsås's high prison walls.

He looked in the mirror again.

Four days earlier, he had had long, fair hair and a three-week beard.

Now he was cropped and clean-shaven.

Another face.

He let the water run, got undressed, and rubbed the piece of dirty soap that was lying on the washbasin. He washed his body and waited until it had dried in the warm room. He went back to the pipe and the sharp metal edges and with his hands felt around and caught the pile of clothes that a few days earlier had been worn by a principal prison officer called Jacobson, before becoming a makeshift pillow to save his neck and prevent the clothes from being soiled by body fluids.

They were about the same height and the uniform fit almost perfectly. The trousers were perhaps a bit too short, the shoes perhaps a bit too tight, but it didn't matter, it didn't show.

He stood by the door and waited.

He should be frightened, stressed, anxious. He felt nothing. He had been forced to adopt this life state when the ability not to feel meant the same as survival: no thoughts and no longings, no Zofia and Hugo and Rasmus, everything he had to remind him of life.

He had stepped into it as he passed through the prison gate.

Only dropped it for two seconds.

When the shot was about to be fired.

He had stood by the window and adjusted the earpiece and for the last time looked over at the church tower. He had glanced at the rug that concealed a body covered with explosives and the barrel of diesel and gasoline close to their feet and the fuse that was resting in his hand. He had checked his position, he had to stand in profile, he had to force them to aim at his head so no forensic scientist would later question the absence of a skull bone.

Two seconds of pure fear.

He had heard the order to fire on the receiver. He had to stand there and wait. But his legs had somehow moved too early, they had moved without him intending to do so.

Twice he had not managed.

But the third time, the state of control had returned, no thoughts and no feelings and no longings, he was protected again.

The shot was fired.

He stood firm.

He had exactly three seconds.

The time it would take for the ammunition, in a wind strength of seven meters per second and a temperature of eighteen degrees Celsius, to leave the church tower and at a distance of fifteen hundred three meters hit a head in a workshop window.

I mustn't move too soon, I know the sniper's observer is watching me with binoculars.

I count.

One thousand and one.

I hold the lighter in my hand with the flame naked and ready.

One thousand and two.

I take a swift step forward just as the bullet hits the window and I hold the flame to the fuse that is attached to the body under the rug.

The shot had been fired and it was no longer possible to see the object through a window that had been seriously damaged.

He now had two seconds left.

The time it would take for the fuse to burn down to the detonator, pentyl, and nitroglycerine.

I run to the pillar that I chose earlier, just a couple of meters away, one of the square concrete blocks that carry the ceiling.

I stand behind it when the last centimeters of fuse disappear and the stuff that is wound and taped around a person's body explodes.

My eardrums burst.

Two walls—the one behind the principal prison officer and the one into the office—collapse.

The shattered window is blown out and falls down into the prison yard.

The pressure wave finds me but is dampened by the concrete pillar and the rug over the hostage's body.

I am unconscious, but only for a few seconds.

I am alive.

He had been lying on the floor with the howling pain in his ears when the heat from the explosion reached the diesel barrel and black smoke assaulted the room.

He had waited until it had found its way out through the hole that had until recently been a window, creating a grayish-black wall that blanketed and hid much of the workshop building.

He had taken the pile of uniform clothes that belonged to the older guard and thrown it out through the window, then jumped out himself, onto a roof that was only a few meters below.

I sit without moving and wait.

I am holding the clothes in my arms, I see nothing through the thick smoke and with no eardrums I struggle to hear, but I feel the vibrations of people moving around on the roof close by, policemen who are there to put an end to a hostage drama; one of them even runs into me without realizing who I am.

I don't breathe, I haven't since I jumped through the window, I know that breathing in this toxic smoke is the same as death.

He had moved close to those who heard the steps without realizing that they belonged to the man they had just seen die, over the roof toward the shiny sheets of metal that looked like a chimney. He had climbed down into the hole, his arms and legs pressed hard against the walls until the pipe narrowed and it had been difficult to keep his grip, then he had let go, fallen the last bit down to the bottom of the ventilation shaft.

I crouch down and crawl into the pipe that is sixty centimeters in diameter and leads back into the building.

With my hands against the metal, I pull myself forward bit by bit, until I am above a room that is a substation and has a door straight out into the lower prison passage.

I lie down on my back, the pile of clothes under my head like a pillow. I am going to stay in the ventilation shaft for at least three days. I will piss and shit and wait but I will not dream, I will not feel, there is nothing, not yet.

He put his ear to the door.

It was difficult to make out, but there might be someone moving about out there—wardens walking past down the passage, not prisoners at this time of day, it was after lockup and they would all be in their cells.

He ran his hand over his face and head—no beard, no hair—down his thighs and calves—no dried urine.

The new clothes smelled of another person, some deodorant or aftershave that the old warden must have used.

Movements out there again, more people passing.

He looked at the watch. Five to eight.

He would wait a little longer; it was the guards coming off duty and on their way home, he had to avoid them, they had seen his face. He stood waiting for fifteen minutes more, the dark substation and fifty-seven yellow and red and green lights around him.

Now.

Several of them, and at this time of day, it could only be the night shift.

The ones that clocked in after lockup, who never met the prisoners and therefore didn't know what they looked like.

His hearing was dramatically impaired but he was certain that they had passed. He unlocked the door, opened it, went out and closed it again.

Three wardens with their backs to him about twenty meters down the passage that linked Block G with central security. One was roughly his age, the others much younger and presumably newly qualified, on their way to one of their first workplaces. At the end of May, Aspsås prison was always affected by the large influx of summer temps who, after a mere one-hour introduction and a two-day course, put on their uniforms and started to work.

They had stopped in front of one of the locked security doors that divided the passage up into smaller sections and he hurried to catch up. The older one was holding a set of keys and had just unlocked the door when he came up behind them.

"Can you wait for me, please?"

They turned around, looked at him, up and down.

"I'm a bit behind."

"On your way home?"

"Yes."

The guard didn't sound like he suspected anything when he spoke; it had been a friendly question, between colleagues.

"You new?"

"So new that I haven't got my own keys yet."

"Less than two days then?"

"Started yesterday."

"Just like these two. Third day for you all tomorrow. Your first key day."

He followed behind them.

They had seen him. They had spoken to him.

Now he was just one of four wardens walking together down a prison passage toward central security and the big gate there.

They parted at the stairs that went up to Block A and an eleven-hour shift. He wished them a good night and they looked with envy at their colleague who was about to go home for an evening off.

He stood in the middle of the reception area. There were three doors to choose from.

The first was diagonally opposite him—a visiting room for a woman or a friend or a policeman or a lawyer. It was there that Stefan Lygás had sat when he was told that there was an informant, a snitch in the organization, someone had whispered so someone must die.

The second one was directly behind him, the door that opened onto the corridor that ended in Block G. He almost laughed—he could walk back to his own cell dressed in uniform.

He looked at the third door.

The way past central security and the ever-watchful TV monitors and numbered switches that meant that all the locked doors in the prison could be opened from the large glass box.

There were two people sitting in there. At the front a fairly plump guard with a dark unkempt beard and a tie thrown over his shoulder. Behind him another, considerably slimmer, man with his back to the exit—he couldn't see his face but guessed he was around fifty and probably had some kind of senior position. He took a deep breath, stretched and tried to walk straight: the explosion that had taken both eardrums had also played havoc with his balance.

"Going home in your uniform? Already?"

"Sorry?"

The guard with the round face and sparse beard looked at him.

"You're one of the new ones, aren't you?"

"Yes."

"And you're going home in your uniform already?"

"Just the way it worked."

The guard smiled—he was in no rush, some more empty words and the evening would be shorter.

"It's warm out. Darn nice evening."

"I'm sure it is."

"Going straight home?"

The guard leaned to one side and moved a small fan that was standing on the desk, fresh air in the stuffy room. It was easier to see the other man, the one who was thin and sitting on a chair at the back.

He recognized him.

"I think so."

"Someone waiting for you?"

Lennart Oscarsson.

The chief warden he had assaulted a few days ago in a cell in the voluntary isolation unit, a fist in the middle of his face.

"Not at home. But we're meeting again tomorrow. It's been a while."

Oscarsson snapped shut the file and turned around.

He looked over at him.

He looked but didn't react.

"Not at home? I had one once, a family that is, but well, I don't know, it just, you know—"

"You'll have to excuse me."

"What?"

"I haven't got time."

His tie was still flung over his shoulder, there were bits of food on it, or maybe it was just wet and lying there to dry.

"Haven't got time? Who does have time?"

The guard pulled his beard, flared his nostrils, his eyes hurt.

"But by all means. Go. I'll open for you."

Two steps up to the metal detector.

Then two steps to the door that was opened from inside the glass box.

Piet Hoffmann turned around, nodded to the guard who was waving his hands around in irritation.

Lennart Oscarsson was still there, right behind him.

Their eyes met again.

He expected someone to start shouting, to come running.

But not a word, not a movement.

The man who was clean-shaven with cropped hair and wearing a warden's uniform when he disappeared out through the gate in the prison wall may have seemed familiar but he didn't have a name—the summer temps seldom did—this one smiled when his face was brushed by the warm wind. It was going to be a lovely evening.

yet another day later

EWERT GRENS WAS SITTING AT HIS DESK IN FRONT OF A BOOKSHELF WITH A hole that could not be filled, no matter how hard he tried, and the dust lay in straight lines no matter how often he wiped it away. He had been sitting there for nearly three hours. And he would continue to sit there until he had worked out whether what he had just seen was something he should be concerned about or whether it was just one of those moments that seemed to be important but that lost all significance if it wasn't shared with someone else.

The day had started with a beautiful morning.

He had slept on the brown corduroy sofa with the window to the courtyard open and had been woken by the first trucks on Bergsgatan. He had stood for a while looking up at the blue sky and gentle wind and then, with a coffee cup in each hand, had gone to the elevators and the remand jail a couple of floors up.

He couldn't resist it.

If you were there early enough and it was clear enough, at this time of day, for a few hours, you could walk along the obvious line cast by the sun in the corridor of the remand jail. This morning he had walked where the floor shone most, making sure to pass the cells where he knew they were in custody for the third day with full restrictions. Ågestam had been careful to ensure that they would wait for most of the statutory seventy-two hours and later that day Grens would attend the court proceedings for the issue of arrest warrants for a chief superintendent, a national police commissioner, and a state secretary from the Ministry of Justice.

The hole on the bookshelf. It was as if it was growing.

It would continue to do so until he had made up his mind.

He had spent two days fast-forwarding and rewinding tapes from the security cameras at Aspsås prison, frame by frame through locked doors and long passages and gray walls and barbed-wire barriers back to those seconds that exploded with thick smoke and dead people. He had studied

Krantz's forensic reports and Errfors' autopsy report and all Sven's and Hermansson's interviews.

He had spent considerable time on two things in particular.

A transcript of the dialogue between the sniper and the observer just before the shot was fired.

Where they talked about a rug that Hoffmann had put over the hostage and tied with something that later in the investigation proved to be a pentyl fuse.

A rug that encapsulates and directs the blast pressure downward, protecting anyone standing nearby.

An interview with a principal prison officer called Jacobson.

Where Jacobson described how Hoffmann covered the hostage's skin with small plastic bags filled with some sort of fluid, which later in the investigation proved to be nitroglycerine.

Nitroglycerine in such large amounts that every part of the body is shattered and can never be identified.

Ewert Grens had laughed out loud in the office.

He had stood in the middle of the floor and looked at the video recorder and the transcripts on the desk and had continued to laugh as he left the police headquarters and drove out to Aspsås and the wall that dominated the small town. He had gone to central security and requested to see all footage from the prison security cameras from twenty-six minutes past two in the afternoon of the twenty-seventh of May and thereafter. He had driven back, got himself some fresh coffee from the machine and sat down to watch every moment that had passed since a lethal shot was fired from a church tower.

Grens had already known what he was looking for.

He had selected the camera that was called number fourteen and was installed about a meter above the glass front of central security. He had then fast-forwarded and stopped to study every person who went out. Wardens, visitors, prisoners, suppliers, one head at a time as they passed, their hairline close to the lens; some showed their ID, some signed the register, most were waved through by a guard who recognized them.

He got as far as a tape that was recorded four days after the shot was fired.

Ewert Grens had known instantly that he'd found it.

A man with cropped hair in a Prison and Probation Service uniform had looked up at the camera as he left at six minutes past eight in the evening, looked up for just too long, and then gone on.

Grens had felt the pressure in his stomach and chest that was normally anger, but this time was something else.

He had stopped the tape and rewound, studied the man who chatted with the guard for a while and then looked up at the camera in the same way that he had done three weeks earlier with another guard in another glass-fronted security office, the one in the Government Offices. Grens had followed the uniformed person through the metal detector and the gate and the wall via cameras number fifteen and sixteen and had observed that the person had problems with his balance: it had been an almighty blast, the sort that could burst your eardrums.

You're alive.

That was why he had been sitting at his desk for three hours looking at a hole growing on the bookshelf.

I didn't make a decision about death.

That was why he had to determine if what he had just seen was something he should be concerned about or whether it was of no significance if no one else knew.

Hoffmann is alive. You didn't make a decision about death either.

He laughed again while he took a document out of the desk drawer—summons to the court proceedings for the issue of arrest warrants that he was about to attend and that would lead all the way to a conviction and long sentences for three high-ranking officers who had abused their power.

He laughed even louder, danced across the floor of the silent office, after a while quietly humming something that anyone passing just then might have recognized as a melody that perhaps sounded like a song from the sixties, like "Somebody's Fool" and Siw Malmkvist.

**and yet
another
day later**

IT WAS AS IF THE SKY WERE SLOWLY CLOSING IN.

Erik Wilson stood in the asphalt yard, his thin clothes itching as nervous flies searched among the pearls of sweat. Ninety-nine degrees Fahrenheit, just above body temperature and it would be even hotter in a couple of hours, in the early afternoon—the heat seemed to settle around that time of day.

He wiped his forehead with an already moist handkerchief and wasn't sure whether his skin or the material benefited most. It had been hard to concentrate in the lecture hall, the air-conditioning in the building had broken down in the morning and the discussion about the follow-up course *advanced infiltration* had petered out. Even the heads of police from the western United States who normally liked to listen to their own voices were listless.

He watched, as he usually did, through the fence and barbed wire that overlooked the large practice ground—six black figures trying to protect a seventh, shots fired from two low buildings and two of them threw themselves over the protected object and the car raced forward and then off. Erik Wilson smiled. He knew how it would end: this president would also survive and the baddies who fired from the buildings would be unsuccessful. The Secret Service won every time, the same exercise as three weeks ago, different police officers, but the same exercise.

He turned his face up to the cloudless sky, as if to torment himself; the sun would wake him up.

At first he had blamed the heat. But it wasn't that.

He just wasn't there.

He hadn't been present at all in the last few days—he had taken part in the discussions and exercises, but he wasn't in the room, his thoughts and energy drained from his body.

Four days had passed since Sven Sundkvist had asked him to drive seventy kilometers to the state line and Jacksonville for lunch in a restaurant that had room for laptops with security camera images on its white tablecloths. He had seen Paula's face in a prison window and then an explosion and black smoke when the shot fired by a sniper had ripped apart a human being.

They had worked together for nearly nine years.

Paula had been his responsibility. And his friend.

He was nearly at the hotel, fleeing the heat on his cheeks and forehead. The spacious lobby was cool, jostling with people who were delaying going out. He headed for the elevator and the eleventh floor, the same room as before.

He got undressed and had a cold shower and lay down on top of the bed in his robe.

They burned you.

They whispered and then looked the other way.

He got up, the restlessness had returned, the lack of focus. He flicked through the day's edition of *USA Today*, yesterday's *New York Times*, drowned himself in TV ads for detergent and local lawyers. He wasn't there, no matter how hard he tried. He wandered around the room, stopping after a while in front of the mobile telephones he had already checked in the morning, his link to all the informants: five handsets side by side on the desk since the evening he arrived. It was usually enough to check once a day, but the restlessness and the feeling of being absent . . . he checked again.

Lifted them up, studied them, one by one.

Until he held the fifth phone in his hand. He sat down on the edge of the bed, shaking.

One missed call.

On a mobile phone that he should have disposed of as the informant was dead.

You don't exist anymore.

But someone is using your phone.

He was sweating again, but it wasn't the heat; this came from inside, a feeling that burned and cut, like nothing he had known before.

Someone has control of your phone. Someone has found it and has dialed the only number that is stored there.

Who?

Someone investigating? Someone in pursuit?

The room was cool, he was freezing so he pulled back the bedclothes and crept down under the duvet that smelled of scented conditioner and lay still until he started to sweat again.

Someone who doesn't know who has this phone. Someone who is calling a number that isn't registered anywhere.

He was shivering again, more than before; the thick duvet was chafing his head.

He could phone. He could listen to the voice with no risk of being identified.

He dialed the number.

A sound wave looking for a harbor in the weightless air, a few seconds stretched to hours and years, then the ringing tone, a long shrill peep.

He listened to the tone that rasped in his ear three times.

And a voice he could recognize.

"*Mission completed.*"

Careful breathing on the other end, at least that's what it sounded like— perhaps it was just the signal that was weak and atmospheric interference was trying to muscle in.

"*Wojtek eliminated in Aspsås.*"

He lay on the bed, didn't move, scared that the person talking to him would vanish from his hand.

"*See you in an hour at number three.*"

Erik Wilson smiled to the voice that blended with another, a repeated call over the loudspeakers, probably in an airport.

He had perhaps known, somewhere deep, deep down, or at least hoped.

Now he knew.

He answered.

"Or another time, another place."

From the Authors

Three Seconds is a novel about today's criminals and the two authorities—the police and the Prison and Probation Service—who meet and are responsible for them.

And a novel allows the authors liberties.

Fact and fiction.

Together.

The Swedish Police Service

FACT The Police Service has for many years used criminals as covert human intelligence sources. A cooperation that is denied and concealed. In order to investigate serious crime, other crimes have been marginalized and a number of preliminary investigations and trials have therefore been carried out without the correct information.

FICTION Ewert Grens does not exist.

FACT Only criminals can play criminals and have, if so required, been recruited when on remand or later. The police criminal intelligence database and reports have been used as tools to develop suitable and credible personal backgrounds. Extensive doctoring of information has become standard working practice in a society based on the rule of law.

FICTION Sven Sundkvist does not exist.

FACT Criminal informants are, in our time, outlaws. When a criminal informant is exposed, the authorities deny having used their services, and look the other way while the organization that has been infiltrated tries to resolve the problem. The police supervisory authority is convinced that conventional intelligence methods are not sufficient to combat organized crime and will continue to develop their work with covert human intelligence in the future.

FICTION Mariana Hermansson does not exist.

The Swedish Prison and Probation Service

FACT Most prison inmates are drug users. Anyone serving a prison sentence can continue to use drugs inside. A drug user who is released from prison having served their sentence often returns to crime in order to continue to feed their habit and to pay back drug-related debts incurred in prison.

FICTION Aspsås prison does not exist.

FACT Anyone who works with criminals knows that drug abuse is a major contributor to reoffending. Despite this, it is still possible to distribute drugs in high-security prisons by hiding amphetamines in bunches of yellow tulips that are sent to wardens, in the left-hand margin of hardback books from library stores, and in plastic bags stuffed down toilets using elastic bands and spoons. The Prison and Probation Service could—*for goodness sake, a prison is a closed system*—stop all drug supplies, but refrains from doing so.

FICTION Lennart Oscarsson does not exist.

FACT Drugs are effective in reducing anxiety levels and an amphetamine user who has had his fix will borrow a pile of porn magazines and disappear into his cell to masturbate. A prison system without drugs would therefore entail chaos and heightened anxiety and would thus put new demands on its staff. If prisoners were not high on chemical substances, the Prison and Probation Service would be forced to improve skills and competence at a cost that we, society, would not be prepared to pay.

FICTION Martin Jacobson does not exist.

With enormous gratitude to:

Billy, Kenta, C, R, and T, who have served or are serving long sentences, who have lived longer inside than outside, who in this book, as in all our previous books, have provided us with the necessary knowledge, authenticity, and credibility to write about crime, whether it is about why forty degrees is not as good as fifty degrees when preparing tulips to be filled with amphetamine, or the necessary consistency for rubber to protect the stomach, or what a toilet outside a workshop in a maximum security prison looks like. Your trust strengthens our resolve to differentiate between bad people and bad actions.

The wise and courageous police officers who have guided us through the extraordinary gray zone that unites police and criminals. Without you we would not have had the knowledge or legitimacy to describe in a novel how the work with covert human intelligence unravels the legal security that others take for granted in a democracy.

Prison personnel—security, wardens, principal officers, and chief wardens— who, when you have met us, have always helped, but who are caught between the ambition to try to do a good job and a system that forces you to reach for the scissors and cut your uniform into rags for cleaning the car.

Reine Adolfsson for your expertise on explosives, *Janne Hedström* for your knowledge of forensic science, *Henrik Hjulström* for your expertise on snipers, *Henrik Lewenhagen* and *Lasse Lageren* for your medical knowledge, *Dorota Ziemiańska* because you speak better Polish than we do.

Fia Roslund because you are there for us and the text throughout the writing process.

Niclas Breimar, Ewa Eiman, Mikael Nyman, Daniel Mattisson, and *Emil Eiman-Roslund* for your extraordinarily wise opinions.

Niclas Salomonsson, Tor Jonasson, Catherine Mörk, Szilvia Molnar, and *Leyla Belle Drake* at Salomonsson Agency for your energy, competence, and presence here and abroad.